THE TAINTED THRONE

Also by Alex Rutherford

Raiders from the North
A Kingdom Divided
Ruler of the World

THE TAINTED THRONE

Empire of the Moghul

Alex Rutherford

Thomas Dunne Books
St. Martin's Press
New York

THOMAS DUNNE BOOKS.
An imprint of St. Martin's Press.

www.thomasdunnebooks.com
www.stmartins.com

ISBN 978-0-312-59703-0 (hardcover)
ISBN 978-1-250-03445-8 (e-book)

First published in Great Britain by HEADLINE REVIEW, an imprint of HEADLINE PUBLISHING GROUP, an Hachette UK Company

First U.S. Edition: May 2013

10 9 8 7 6 5 4 3 2 1

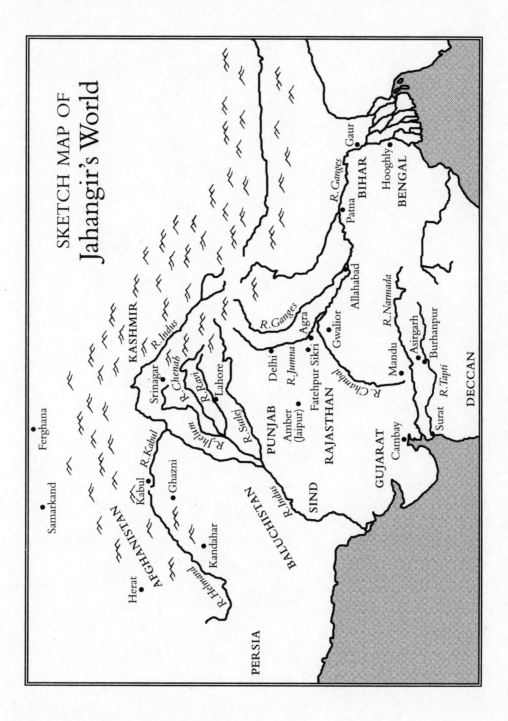

SKETCH MAP OF
Jahangir's World

Main Characters

Jahangir's family

Akbar, Jahangir's father and the third Moghul emperor

Humayun, Jahangir's grandfather and the second Moghul emperor

Hamida, Jahangir's grandmother

Kamran, Jahangir's great-uncle

Askari, Jahangir's great-uncle

Hindal, Jahangir's great-uncle

Murad, Jahangir's brother

Daniyal, Jahangir's brother

Khusrau, Jahangir's eldest son

Parvez, Jahangir's second son

Khurram (later the Emperor Shah Jahan), Jahangir's third son

Shahriyar, Jahangir's youngest son

Man Bai, Jahangir's wife and mother of Khusrau

Jodh Bai, Jahangir's wife and mother of Khurram

Sahib Jamal, Jahangir's wife and mother of Parvez

Mehrunissa (also known as Nur Mahal and Nur Jahan), Jahangir's last wife

Mehrunissa's family

Ladli, Mehrunissa's daughter by Sher Afghan

Ghiyas Beg, Imperial Treasurer and Mehrunissa's father

Asmat, mother of Mehrunissa and her brothers

Asaf Khan, commander of the Agra garrison and Mehrunissa's elder brother

Mir Khan, Mehrunissa's younger brother

Arjumand Banu, Mehrunissa's niece, Asaf Khan's daughter and wife of Khurram (Shah Jahan)

Sher Afghan, commander of the garrison at Gaur in Bengal, Mehrunissa's first husband

Jahangir's commanders, governors and courtiers

Suleiman Beg, Jahangir's milk-brother

Ali Khan, Governor of Mandu

Iqbal Beg, a senior commander in the Deccan

Mahabat Khan, a Persian and one of Jahangir's leading generals

Majid Khan, Jahangir's vizier and chronicler

Yar Muhammad, Governor of Gwalior

Dara Shukoh, Khurram's (Shah Jahan's) eldest son

Shah Shujah, Khurram's (Shah Jahan's) second son

Aurangzeb, Khurram's (Shah Jahan's) third son

Murad Bakhsh, Khurram's (Shah Jahan's) youngest son

Jahanara, Khurram's (Shah Jahan's) elder daughter

Roshanara, Khurram's (Shah Jahan's) younger daughter

In the imperial haram
Mala, *khawajasara*, superintendent, of the imperial *haram*
Fatima Begam, a widow of the Emperor Akbar
Nadya, Fatima Begam's maid
Salla, Mehrunissa's Armenian lady-in-waiting

Khurram's circle
Azam Bahksh, one of Akbar's aged former commanders
Kamran Iqbal, one of Khurram's commanders
Walid Beg, one of Khurram's gunnery commanders

Others
Aziz Koka, adherent of Khusrau
Hassan Jamal, adherent of Khusrau
Malik Ambar, former Abyssinian slave and now commander of
   the armies of the Deccan sultanates against the Moghuls
Shaikh Salim Chishti, a Sufi mystic, and his son, also a Sufi.

Foreigners in the Moghul empire
Bartholomew Hawkins, English soldier and adventurer
Father Ronaldo, a Portuguese priest
Sir Thomas Roe, English ambassador to the Moghul court
Nicholas Ballantyne, squire to Sir Thomas Roe

Part I

Sun Among Women

Chapter 1

Blood in the Sand

Northwest Hindustan, spring 1606

Jahangir ducked out from beneath the awning of his scarlet command tent and in the half-light peered towards the ridge where the forces of his eldest son Khusrau were encamped. Beneath the clear skies the early morning in the semi-desert was chill. Even at this distance Jahangir could see figures moving around, some carrying flaring torches. Here and there cooking fires had been lit. Banners were silhouetted against the rising dawn in front of a large tent on the very crest of the ridge, presumably Khusrau's personal quarters. As he watched, a sudden sadness as chill as the morning air ran through Jahangir. How had matters come to this? Why would he face his son in battle today?

Only five months ago, following the death of his father Akbar, everything he had wanted for so long had finally become his. He had been proclaimed Moghul emperor – the fourth of the dynasty. Jahangir, the name he had chosen to reign under, meant 'Seizer of the World'. What a feeling it was to be master of an empire stretching from the mountains of Baluchistan in the west to the swamps of Bengal in the east and from the saffron fields of Kashmir in the north to the parched red plateau of the Deccan in the south. The lives of one hundred million people were subject to him and he subject to none.

As he had stepped out on to the *jharoka* balcony of the Agra fort to show himself to his people for the first time as emperor, and heard the roars of acclamation rising from the crowds cramming the banks of the Jumna river below, it had seemed incredible that his father was dead. Akbar had brushed aside difficulties and dangers to create a rich and magnificent empire. Just as Jahangir felt he had never fully won Akbar's love nor lived up to his expectations during his life, suddenly he had doubted whether he could do so after his death. But, closing his eyes, he had made a silent promise. *You have bequeathed me wealth and power. I will prove worthy of you. I will protect and build on what you and our forefathers created.* The very act of making the vow had renewed his confidence.

But then only weeks later had come the blow, struck not by a stranger but by his own eighteen-year-old son. Treason – and the climate of distrust it created – was always ugly, but how much worse when the instigator was his offspring. The Moghuls had often been their own greatest enemy, fighting one another when they should have been united. He could not, would not, allow the pattern to repeat itself and now, at the start of his reign, he would demonstrate how seriously he took familial disloyalty and how swiftly and utterly he would crush it.

In the past few weeks nothing had mattered except closing the gap between his own forces and those of his son. Late the previous evening he and his army had caught up with Khusrau and encircled the ridge on which he was encamped. The more he thought of his son's treachery, the more a visceral anger surged through him, and he ground his heel into the sandy earth. Suddenly he was aware of his milk-brother Suleiman Beg at his side. 'Where have you been?' he demanded, his tone harsh with pent-up emotion.

'Hearing the latest reports from our scouts who got close to Khusrau's camp during the night.'

'What do they say, then? Has my son realised he can't outrun us and must face the consequences of his rebellion?'

'Yes. He's readying his army for battle.'

'How are he and his officers deploying their men?'

'There are a few small sandstone Hindu cenotaphs on the ridge. They've overturned their baggage wagons around them and are throwing up earth barricades to shield their cannon and protect their musketmen and archers.'

'So they're preparing to withstand an attack rather than deliver one?'

'Yes. They know it's their best chance of success. Neither Khusrau nor his chief commander Aziz Koka is a fool.'

'Except in defying my authority,' Jahangir broke in.

'Should I order our men to form up for an immediate assault?'

'Before I decide, do we know if there is a spring or any water on the ridge?'

'I questioned the single herdsman we came across last evening. He said no but he was so terrified he might have just been saying what he thought I wanted to hear. However, the ridge is mostly red dust and rocks with only a few dead-looking trees and scarcely a blade of grass.'

'The herdsman's probably right, then. In that case, rather than attack immediately let's leave them to eke out what water they have a little longer while they ponder their fate in the fighting. Like Khusrau, most are young and inexperienced in war. Their imaginings will exceed even the worst horrors of battle.'

'Perhaps, but not so many as I expected have taken up our offer to surrender.'

Jahangir grimaced. The previous evening he had agreed to Suleiman Beg's suggestion that arrows should be fired into Khusrau's camp carrying the message that any junior officer or soldier who left Khusrau's camp during the night and surrendered would save his life. There would be no second chance. None could count on any mercy after the battle.

'How many gave themselves up?'

'Fewer than a thousand, mostly poorly armed and clothed foot soldiers. Many are little more than boys who joined Khusrau's ranks as they passed in the hope of booty and excitement. A deserter told how one young soldier captured trying to escape was thrown alive into a blazing campfire on Khusrau's orders and held in the flames by spear points until his screams ceased. His charred body was then paraded around the camp to deter others from following his example.'

'How many men does that leave Khusrau with?'

'The deserters say twelve thousand. I think that's an under-statement but there's certainly no more than fifteen thousand.'

'We still outnumber them by three or four thousand men. That should be enough to compensate for our troops, as the attackers, being more exposed than Khusrau's men crouching behind their defences.'

As he paced his command tent waiting for his *qorchi*, his squire, to ready him for battle, questions raced through Jahangir's mind. Had he done all he could to ensure success? Over-confidence could be as big a threat to a commander as the lack of it. Was the plan he and Suleiman Beg had devised, talking late into the evening, robust enough to give him victory in this, his first battle as emperor? Why hadn't he been prepared for Khusrau's treachery? During Akbar's lifetime Khusrau had tried to ingratiate himself with his grandfather, hoping to be named his heir. When Akbar had instead chosen Jahangir, Khusrau had seemed to accept it but had only been waiting his moment. On the pretext of inspecting progress in the construction of his grandfather's great tomb at Sikandra, five miles from Agra, he had ridden out of the Agra fort with his entourage. Instead of making for Sikandra, he had wheeled north towards Delhi, raising recruits as he went.

The sun had risen high in the sky when Jahangir gathered his senior commanders for their final orders. 'You, Abdul Rahman, will lead our war elephants, together with a battalion of mounted musketeers and archers, round to the west where the ridge drops gently to the plain. Once there, you will advance up the spine of the ridge, making Khusrau believe that this will be, as conventional strategy might suggest, the route of our main attack.

'But it won't be. It'll be a diversion to tie down as many of Khusrau's forces as possible. Once I see you are fully engaged, Suleiman Beg and I will lead out another battalion of horsemen. First, we will feign a move west to support you, but then we will wheel and charge up the ridge directly in front of us towards Khusrau's tent on the crest. Ismail Amal, you will remain here to command the reserve and protect our camp against any attempt at plunder. Do you all understand the parts you are to play?'

'Yes, Majesty,' came the immediate response.

'Then God go with us. Our cause is just.'

• ◆ •

Half an hour later, Jahangir was fully dressed for war, sweating beneath his steel helmet and the engraved steel breast- and backplates protecting his torso. Seated on his white horse, which was pawing the ground as if it scented the action to come, he watched Abdul Rahman's force advance at a steady pace, trumpets blaring, side drums beating with an ever increasing rhythm and green banners fluttering in the gentle breeze. As they were approaching the bottom of the spine of the ridge, puffs of white smoke rose from the nearest of Khusrau's positions as his artillerymen fired some of his larger cannon towards the attackers.

However, the gunners were clearly nervous and unable to restrain themselves from firing too soon, because their first shots fell short, raising showers of dust in front of Abdul Rahman's advance. But then to Jahangir's dismay he saw one of his leading war elephants collapse despite its steel plate armour, spilling its howdah as it fell. Another elephant slumped to the ground. To Jahangir the attack seemed to falter but then, urged on by the *mahouts* sitting behind their ears, the remaining elephants surged past their fallen

8

companions, advancing quickly for all their size up the ridge. Occasional spurts of smoke showed that the *gajnals*, small cannon, in their howdahs were being brought into action. At the same time, Jahangir could see his cavalry charging up the spine, green banners held aloft and lances extended as they leapt the makeshift red earth barricades and clashed with Khusrau's horsemen. Men from both sides fell and riderless horses galloped from the battle, some impeding the attackers. More and more drifting white smoke obscured Jahangir's view but not before he saw a squadron of horsemen, breastplates glistening in the midday sun, move quickly out from their positions in front of Khusrau's tents and turn to the west to reinforce their comrades against Abdul Rahman's onslaught. The crisis of the battle was upon him.

'Now it's time for us to go,' Jahangir shouted to Suleiman Beg as he pulled his ancestors' eagle-headed sword Alamgir from its scabbard and, rising in his stirrups, waved it to indicate to his trumpeters to sound the advance. Soon his white horse was moving smoothly into the gallop, raising dust as it pounded the ground in the planned feint to support Abdul Rahman.

Jahangir's pulses were racing at the prospect of action. Despite his thirty-six years he had experienced far fewer battles than had his forebears at his age, partly because his father had refused to grant him military commands, partly because Akbar's successes had diminished the number of conflicts the Moghuls had engaged in. Now command was his, as the empire was his, and he would crush all challengers.

He kicked his mount out in front of the rest of his men and then signalled them to wheel to make the frontal attack up the ridge. As they did so, twisting in the saddle Jahangir saw one rider and his chestnut horse crash to the ground, clearly having tried to turn too tightly. Another horse stumbled over the fallen chestnut, whose legs were thrashing the air as it tried to rise. Within moments both fallen mounts and their riders were submerged beneath the charge as it continued to gather pace despite the rising slope of the ridge.

Crouched low over his white horse's neck, with his sword Alamgir extended before him, Jahangir concentrated on avoiding the many rocks littering the slope. Then he heard a crackle and a hiss as a musket ball passed his ear. He was almost upon the first of the earth barricades. Slackening the reins, he urged his horse to jump the obstacle, which was barely three feet high. The horse stretched willingly and leapt. As he rose over the barricade, Jahangir slashed at a tall musketeer sheltering behind it who was desperately trying to reload, ramming a fresh ball down into the long barrel of his musket. He never completed his task. Jahangir's heavy stroke caught him on the nape of his neck, crunching through bone and removing his head from his shoulders.

Breathing hard, Jahangir was galloping on towards the crest of the ridge and what he assumed was Khusrau's command tent, still about half a mile away, when suddenly his horse's pace slackened. Glancing down, he saw two arrows protruding from its left flank. Crimson blood was already welling from the wounds to stain its white coat. Jahangir scarcely had time to think how lucky he had been – one of the arrows was embedded only an inch or two from his left knee – before the horse began to crumple and he had to throw himself from the saddle to avoid being crushed beneath it as it collapsed. Losing his helmet and his sword as he fell, he hit the stony ground with a thump which knocked most of the wind out of him.

Rolling over and over, Jahangir attempted to curl himself into a ball and to protect his head with his gauntleted hands as he tried to avoid the hooves of the men who had followed him into the attack. Nevertheless, a flying hoof caught him a blow on his steel backplate before he came painfully to rest some distance down the slope against one of a group of jumbled rocks away from the charge of the horses and the main action. Dazed and with his ears ringing and his vision blurred, he was scrambling to his feet when he saw a man rise from the shelter of another group of dark rocks nearby and rush towards him brandishing a sword, clearly having recognised him and intent on the profit and glory his killing or capture would bring.

Jahangir reached instinctively to his belt where his dagger had been in its jewelled scabbard. It was still there and he drew it quickly just as the man – a burly, rough-looking fellow wearing a black turban above a bushy beard – was upon him. Jahangir dodged his first attack but as he did so slipped and collapsed back to the ground. Gripping his heavy double-edged sword in both hands his assailant tried to bring it down into Jahangir's neck with all the force he was capable of, but he was too hasty and his clumsy stroke caught Jahangir's breastplate and skidded off, throwing the man off balance himself. Jahangir lashed out hard with his booted foot and felt a satisfying yielding of soft tissue as he caught his opponent full in the groin. The man dropped his weapon and doubled up, clutching at his battered, burning testicles.

Seizing his advantage, Jahangir stuck his dagger twice into the hard muscle of his attacker's bare calf, causing him to stagger sideways and fall. Scrambling across the dusty ground, Jahangir flung himself on him and buried the long dagger deep in his exposed throat just by his Adam's apple. Blood spurted wildly for a moment and then the man lay motionless.

Relieved but still on all fours and gasping for breath, Jahangir looked about him. Although it felt longer it was probably less than five minutes since he had fallen from his horse. Most of the fighting seemed to be going on further up the ridge. But then though his vision was still blurred he made out a mounted figure a little way off but fast approaching and, as far as he could discern, leading another horse. Jahangir rose unsteadily to his feet and tried to brace himself, ready for any new onslaught, but then he heard a familiar voice. 'Jahangir, are you all right?' It was Suleiman Beg.

'Yes, I think so . . . Do you have any water?'

Suleiman Beg held out a leather bottle towards him. Jahangir seized it in both hands, upended it and drank greedily.

'You should not have been so reckless in the charge. You outdistanced me and your bodyguard. The emperor should not expose himself in such a way.'

'It is my fight. My son has rebelled against my throne and it is my duty to crush him,' Jahangir snapped, then added, 'How is the battle going? Give me that spare horse. I must return to lead the attack once more.'

'I brought it for you – and I retrieved your sword,' said Suleiman Beg, extending both reins and weapon to Jahangir. 'But are you really sure you're all right?'

'Yes,' Jahangir said with more certainty than he felt. With Suleiman Beg's help he clambered into the saddle of his new mount, a rangy chestnut. To his relief his head was clearing all the time, and followed by Suleiman Beg and several of his bodyguard who had regrouped around him he pushed forward again back up the ridge towards the fighting around the tents. Khusrau's men were putting up stiff resistance. He could see horses rearing as their riders clashed with each other. Some of Khusrau's horsemen, seemingly recognising Jahangir and Suleiman Beg, broke away from the fighting and galloped downhill to attack them, yelling '*Khusrau zinderbad*', Long live Khusrau! One made directly for Jahangir. As he approached, riding wildly, arms and legs flailing, Jahangir saw it was a younger brother of Aziz Koka. As the youth came closer he aimed a great swinging stroke at Jahangir with his curved sword but the emperor ducked and the blade cut through empty air two inches above his head.

As the impetus of his downhill charge carried the rider onwards, Jahangir twisted in the saddle and caught him with a hard backhand sword slash deep into the flesh and bone of his upper arm, almost severing the limb. Losing control of his mount, the youth careered downhill towards Jahangir's camp until he was knocked from his saddle by a well-aimed shot from one of Jahangir's musketeers, stationed by Ismail Amal behind the shelter of an overturned baggage wagon to protect the camp.

Looking about him with eyes now as sharply focused as usual, Jahangir saw that the other attackers had either been despatched or had retreated back up the ridge. Several bodies were strewn on the ground. Nearby, spreadeagled on his back, was a tall, saffron-robed man with a grizzled beard. A lance protruded bloodily from his belly. Jahangir recognised Tuhin Singh, one of his most loyal bodyguards — a Rajput from his mother's homeland of Amber. The man had guarded him for nearly a quarter of a century and now had given his life in battle for him. Only a few yards away, a slighter figure was twisting and writhing convulsively in the red dust, kicking his heels and clutching at his abdomen from which a skein of blue-red intestines was escaping. He was screaming in his agony for his mother. With a sharp intake of breath, Jahangir recognised the contorted beardless face as that of Imran, an even younger brother of Aziz Koka. He could be no more than thirteen years old and would surely never see another dawn.

Fury at Khusrau, Aziz Koka and their fellow conspirators for causing so many deaths in their reckless hunger for power before their due time overwhelmed Jahangir. With a shout to Suleiman Beg and his bodyguard to follow, Jahangir kicked the chestnut up the slope. Soon he was smashing into the fray, hacking and cutting around him. A spray of warm blood from the neck of a rider he had struck with the full impact of his sword Alamgir caught him in the face and temporarily blinded him again. Quickly wiping away the blood with the sleeve of his tunic, he charged further into the heaving melee, surrounded by shouts and screams and the clash of weapon on weapon.

The acrid smell of sweat and gunpowder smoke filled his nostrils and red dust in the air stung his eyes so that he could scarcely distinguish friend from foe. But he pushed onward with his bodyguard and Suleiman Beg in close attendance. With a final stroke of Alamgir, which caught one of Khusrau's men full on the kneecap, cutting deep into cartilage and sinew and almost jolting the sword from his hand once more, Jahangir was through the first line of battle. Looking up he saw that Khusrau's tents were now only four hundred yards away on the crest. However, as he watched, a large body of riders left them and disappeared down the other side of the ridge. As they went he saw – or thought he saw – Khusrau at their centre.

'After them. The cowards are fleeing,' he shouted to Suleiman Beg and his bodyguard, kicking the flanks of his chestnut mount as he did so. However, the animal was already blowing hard, nostrils flaring from its exertions in the previous fight, and unlike the fine white horse it had replaced it was not of the highest quality and stamina. By the time he reached the crest, Jahangir found that the fleeing group were already crashing into a line of his men stationed at the base of the ridge. After only a few moments, they burst through, losing only a single rider whose mount galloped on, reins dangling, after the rest who, still in close formation, were heading north across the plain.

Kicking the chestnut on again, Jahangir set off in what in his heart he now thought would be a futile pursuit. His son was going to escape. Why hadn't he allocated more of his reserve to forestall any break-out? Then to his intense relief he saw another band of horsemen with green Moghul banners – not the purple Khusrau claimed as his emblem – appear from the west on an interception course. Abdul Rahman too must have spotted the move and despatched them. They were closing fast on the escapees. Jahangir urged his tired horse on down the far slope of the ridge with Suleiman Beg and his bodyguards at his side. But even before

15

he reached the bottom, Khusrau's men had wheeled away from their pursuers and were galloping northeast, throwing up clouds of dust behind them. Then Jahangir saw four or five of Khusrau's rearguard turn and waving their swords charge back towards Abdul Rahman's force in a self-sacrificing attempt to buy more time for their comrades to escape.

Before he had gone more than a few yards one of these brave men fell, arms outflung, from his black horse, hit by an arrow from one of the mounted archers Abdul Rahman had astutely included among the pursuers and Jahangir could just make out standing in their stirrups to loose off their weapons. The mount of another of Khusrau's men crumpled to the ground moments later, pitching its rider over its head. The others continued their charge and crashed into Abdul Rahman's leading horsemen who opened their ranks to receive and surround them, scarcely slackening their pace to do so. Less than a minute later Jahangir's men were riding hard again, heads bent low over their horses' necks, the bodies of several rebels and horses left sprawling in their wake. Khusrau's followers had taken at least a couple of their enemies with them into the shadows of death, but their courage would not save Khusrau. Abdul Rahman's men were now almost upon the fleeing group and two more of the rearguard, one carrying one of Khusrau's purple banners, pitched from their horses, presumably the victims of the mounted archers. The foot of the banner-carrier caught in his stirrup and he was dragged through the red dust for a hundred yards, his purple standard fluttering behind him. Then the stirrup leather snapped and man and banner lay twisted and still.

As Jahangir urged on his chestnut, which, thin flanks

16

heaving, was blowing ever more deeply in pursuit of the action, he saw Khusrau's men swerve aside once more but then come to a sudden stop near an isolated clump of scrubby trees. At first he thought they had decided to stand and fight but then through the dust billowing around them he caught the glint of discarded weapons lying on the ground. Having sacrificed so many others, like Aziz Koka's young brothers and the brave men who had attacked Abdul Rahman's vanguard, they were surrendering in an attempt to save their worthless lives. They would come to regret their decision not to die like men on the battlefield, Jahangir thought grimly as he dug his heels into the chestnut to squeeze from it its last ounce of strength.

• ◆ •

'Bring them before me.'

With the sweat of the fight still warm on him and anger still hot in his heart, Jahangir watched from the shade of the clump of trees as his soldiers dragged Khusrau, his commander-in-chief Aziz Koka and his master of horse, Hassan Jamal, forward and pushed them to their knees in front of him. Though the other two did not dare raise their eyes to the emperor, Khusrau was looking imploringly at his father. Beyond them, hands already bound behind their backs with strips of cloth ripped from their garments or saddle blankets, were the thirty or so of Khusrau's men who had surrendered with him. Jahangir's soldiers were shoving them roughly to the ground. Among them Jahangir suddenly recognised a tall, muscular man, his beard dyed red with henna. He remembered glimpsing him during the battle, a smile on his face, thrusting tauntingly with his lance at a young soldier who, knocked from his horse,

17

was lying helpless and terrified in front of him, before finally impaling the youth through the abdomen.

Such a furious rage seized Jahangir that for a moment he could hardly think. When he could it was about how he could punish such callous rebels sufficiently harshly. Then it came to him. For generations the Moghuls had executed the worst of offenders – child murderers, rapists and the like – by impaling them on stakes. His great-grandfather Babur, the first Moghul emperor, had done it with rebels and robbers too – that was the punishment these men should suffer. Despite the chance to surrender they had continued in rebellion, impaling those who were little more than boys on their lance points. Let them understand what impalement felt like. Let them suffer terror and pain. It would be only just. Without reflecting further he yelled to his soldiers in a voice hoarse with anger, 'Cut stakes from these trees with your swords or battleaxes. Drive them into the ground. Sharpen them as best as you can or tie lances to them and impale these traitors on them. Do it and do it now! Leave only my son and these, his two chief accomplices. Let them watch their men's agonies before they learn their own fate. Anticipation of what is to come may instil into them a little understanding of the suffering they have inflicted on others.'

As his soldiers rushed to obey, some hacking at the trees with battleaxes, others digging at the ground with whatever implements they could improvise, including helmets, to make holes for the stakes while yet others seized hold of the captives and started hauling them across the ground, Jahangir felt Suleiman Beg's hand on his arm. Even before his milk-brother could speak Jahangir said, 'No, Suleiman Beg, it must be. They have brought it on themselves. They showed no mercy. Neither will I. I must make an example.'

Jahangir saw Khusrau, still on his knees, watching with an expression of abject terror. At the thought of his son's treachery, of the needless sacrifice of so many good men, it was all he could do not to fall on Khusrau with his bare hands. After what seemed only about five minutes four of Jahangir's men lifted the first of the wildly kicking and struggling prisoners – a thick-set, hairy man whom they had stripped of most of his clothing – high in the air. Then using all their strength they brought his body down on one of the hastily erected stakes and lances. As the hard point penetrated his soft flesh near his rectum, his screams – more animal than human – split the air. Spurting blood reddened the ground as, with Jahangir's men pulling on the prisoner's legs, the stake emerged near his breastbone. Then as more rebels were impaled the stink of ruptured guts and of the excrement of terrified men who, on the brink of death, had lost control of their bowels began to rise. But Jahangir, still burning with his own anger and intent on harsh justice, barely noticed.

Now was the time for Khusrau to witness close up the horrors for which his ambition was responsible. He strode forward and seizing his kneeling son by his shoulders pulled him roughly to his feet. 'See what you have done. These men are only suffering because of you. Walk through the stakes . . . go on,' he shouted, thrusting his face into Khusrau's. Then, releasing his son, he gave him a shove towards the stakes. But Khusrau, his arms wrapped tightly around himself and his eyes closed, attempted to turn away. Immediately Jahangir shouted to some of his bodyguards.

'Walk him past all the stakes and back again. Take your time. Make sure he looks at the bodies . . .'

Straight away two guards seized Khusrau by his arms and propelled him towards the stakes. With each step Khusrau's head drooped lower but every few paces his escort halted right in front of one of his dying supporters, writhing and kicking on a stake and in doing so impaling himself further, and one of the soldiers pulled back Khusrau's head by his hair, forcing him to look. But Khusrau had clearly had enough. Jahangir saw his son sag in the soldiers' arms and then collapse to the ground. He guessed he had fainted. 'Enough! Bring my son back here, together with Aziz Koka and Hassan Jamal.'

A few moments later, Jahangir surveyed the three men on their knees before him again. Khusrau's long dark hair was wet from the contents of the water bottle one of the guards had thrown over him to revive him. He was deathly pale, trembling violently and looked about to vomit. Raising his voice to make himself heard over the shrieks of agony still rising from the surrounding stakes where the remaining rebels were still being impaled, Jahangir spoke. 'You are all guilty of the worst crime a subject can commit against his emperor – armed rebellion. You—'

'I am not just a subject . . . I am your son . . .' Khusrau pleaded, his once handsome young face a mask of absolute terror.

'Silence! Ask yourself whether you have behaved like a son before you claim the rights of a son. You deserve no better treatment than those creatures for whose torment you, not I, are responsible, or the two men beside you. Aziz Koka, Hassan Jamal, you once swore loyalty to me but you broke your bond.' They stared up at him helplessly, their eyes rolling

20

in fear as he went on, 'Expect no mercy, for I have none to give. You have acted with the treachery and heedless ambition of men but also with the blind stupidity of beasts. To symbolise your base animal natures, you will be taken to Lahore where in the bazaar you will be stripped naked and sewn into the freshly flayed skins of an ass and an ox. Then, seated backwards on the backs of asses, you will be paraded through the city streets in the heat of the day so that my loyal subjects may witness your shame and understand how ridiculous were your pretensions to overthrow me.'

Jahangir heard the two men gasp. The idea for their punishment had come to him in a flash of inspiration only moments before he spoke. He knew his grandfather Humayun had prided himself on devising novel and sometimes bizarre ways of fitting punishments to the crime. Now so had he. However, he had no further time to waste on accomplices and so turned towards Khusrau who, his hands clasped in supplication, was sobbing brokenly and muttering something Jahangir couldn't catch but which sounded like gibberish. He drew himself up, preparing to utter the words that would send his son to his doom.

'Khusrau, you raised an army of disaffected traitors with the sole intention of overthrowing me – your father and the lawful Moghul emperor – and seizing my throne for yourself. You are responsible for the blood that has been spilled and in justice you should pay for that in blood.' The harshness of his voice was real and he meant every word he said. Khusrau knew it as well and in his fear lost control of his bladder. Jahangir saw a dark strain spreading through his cotton trousers and urine dripping on to the ground to form a yellow pool.

A wave of pity for the state to which Khusrau had been

reduced washed over him. Though moments earlier he had had every intention of ordering him to be beheaded, suddenly he no longer desired his death. There had already been so much bloodshed, so much suffering . . . 'But I have decided to spare you,' he heard himself say. 'You are my son and I will not take your life. Instead you will be kept in prison where over the months and years ahead you will have time to reflect on the transgressions that caused you to forfeit your liberty and your honour.'

As Khusrau, Aziz Koka and Hassan Jamal were led away Jahangir turned to his milk-brother, who was still standing nearby. 'Suleiman Beg, order our soldiers to cut the throats of any impaled prisoners who are still alive. They have suffered enough. Have their bodies disposed of in a common grave, the stakes taken down and fresh earth spread over the ground. Have those wounded in the battle – whether friend or foe – treated by our *hakims*. Let all the dead have the funeral rites of their religion. I want to forget how much blood has been spilled today.'

◆

A week later, in the fortress of Bagrat which he had made his temporary headquarters while his forces recuperated and reorganised, Jahangir studied the long letter he had just received from the Governor of Lahore reporting the fate of Aziz Koka and Hassan Jamal. As he read, Jahangir could picture the scene – the two struggling noblemen, all their dignity stripped from them, being stitched into the reeking bloody hides. The animals' heads had still been attached, the governor reported, and flopped about grotesquely with every desperate movement the prisoners made inside as they were paraded through the

22

city while the population jeered and threw rotting vegetables and stones at them. Aziz Koka, sewn into the ass's skin, had suffocated as the hide had dried and contracted in the intense heat. Hassan Jamal had still been alive if almost unconscious when pulled from the ox skin. He was now in Lahore's dungeons. At the end of his letter, the governor asked whether Jahangir wished Hassan Jamal to be executed.

Jahangir walked over to the casement and gazed out at the drear, sandy landscape. Now that he had had time to reflect on it, he was a little ashamed of the savagery of the punishments he had meted out even if they had been merited and would serve to deter other rebels. He had acted in the heat of the moment when his anger had been overflowing. Now he was calmer he was starting to wish he had behaved differently. Only a weak ruler need be afraid to show mercy . . . He had intended Hassan Jamal to die. It was only by some sort of miracle that the man had survived but it gave him a chance to show clemency that might begin to heal the rifts among his courtiers that Khusrau's rebellion had opened up. At once he summoned a scribe and dictated his reply to the governor. 'Hassan Jamal has been punished enough. Let him live.'

He had given his son a harsh lesson, Jahangir mused as soon as he was alone again, but would Khusrau have learned it? He was headstrong, conceited and above all ambitious. Ambition wasn't easy to suppress, as he himself should know. Hadn't he spent nearly twenty years of his own life tormented by the fear that his father Akbar might deny him the throne he craved? Hadn't he rebelled himself? Just as he had done, Khusrau would have to wait to know whether he would name him, his eldest son, his heir despite

23

his rebellion. And such a decision could wait. God willing, he had many more years left.

But what about his other sons? His disputes with his father had kept him apart from them for long periods. On his return to Akbar's court he had found it difficult to rebuild ties as close as those between a father and his sons should be. Jahangir frowned as words spoken to him long ago by Shaikh Salim Chishti, the Sufi mystic who had foretold his own birth, flashed through his mind. As a young prince uncertain of what the future held he had sought out the old man. 'Watch those around you. Be careful whom you confide in and take nothing on trust, even from those bound to you by blood . . . even the sons you will have,' the Sufi had said. 'Ambition is double edged. It drives men to greatness but can also poison their souls . . .' He should heed that warning. After all, much that the Sufi had predicted had already come to pass. He had indeed become emperor and ambition had indeed corrupted one of his sons.

Perhaps that was why his anger at Khusrau had burned so fiercely. He remembered how just two days before his battle with Khusrau, his army had occupied a small mud-walled village. Here the grizzled headman, after prostrating himself before Jahangir, had produced from a pocket of his grubby brown robe three small bronze coins which he claimed had been given to him by a party of Khusrau's scouts. With visibly trembling fingers he had handed them over to Jahangir in token of his submission. Inspecting them, Jahangir had seen that each of the seemingly hastily struck coins bore the image of Khusrau and the script encircling it had proclaimed Khusrau as the Emperor of Hindustan. Jahangir had been so overcome with anger that he had

24

ordered the headman to be flogged for daring to retain the coins, the coins themselves to be immediately defaced by the farriers and a proclamation to be issued that henceforth anyone found with such coins would lose the fingers of his right hand as punishment for handling them. The headman's scrawny body had already been roughly stripped to the waist and bound to the only tree within the village compound while Jahangir's most muscular bodyguard made the air hiss as he practised the lashes with his seven-tailed whip before Suleiman had with difficulty persuaded Jahangir to pardon him. How fortunate he was to have Suleiman Beg by his side as he had since his youth – a loyal friend who instinctively sensed his moods and was now proving a wise adviser.

But what would Parvez and Khurram – at sixteen and fourteen not so much younger than Khusrau – think about their half-brother's attempt to depose him and the punishment he had inflicted? Parvez's mother came from one of the old Moghul clans while Khurram's, like Khusrau's, was a Rajput princess and Khurram himself had been brought up by Akbar, who had shown him special favours. Both princes, but in particular Khurram, might think their claims to the throne as good as Khusrau's. At least he need have no worries yet about the ambitions of his youngest son Shahriyar, still living with his concubine mother in the imperial *haram*.

As soon as possible he must return to Agra and his younger sons. He had demonstrated by his treatment of Khusrau and his followers that as emperor he could brook no dissent. But he would also show them that he was still a loving father, that it was only Khusrau's treachery that had forced his ruthless acts . . .

25

Chapter 2

The Assassin

'You are sure you understand what to do?' Jahangir looked hard at the Englishman standing before him. This was only his second meeting with Bartholomew Hawkins but it had been enough to convince him that he was well fitted to the role of assassin. Hawkins spoke a crude, halting Persian picked up while serving as a mercenary with the Shah of Persia's army in Isfahan but enough for Jahangir to have been able to test him to his satisfaction.

'I will give you five hundred gold *mohurs* now for your journey to Bengal and back. When Sher Afghan is dead, I'll pay you another thousand *mohurs*.'

Bartholomew Hawkins nodded. His broad face, reddened by the sun, looked satisfied. Even though he was standing some ten feet away Jahangir could smell the man's almost animal reek. Why didn't these foreigners wash? More and more were arriving at his court at Agra. Englishmen like this one, Frenchmen, Italians, Portuguese and Spanish, and all of them, whether missionaries, merchants or mercenaries, seemed to stink. Perhaps it was the clothes they wore. Hawkins's broad, sweating body was encased in a tight black leather jerkin, pantaloons that fastened with dark red ribbons just above the knee and dun-coloured woollen stockings. On his feet was a pair of scuffed riding boots.

'You don't mind how I kill him?'

'No. All that matters is that he dies. If you merely injure him that's no use to me.'

'Once I get to Gaur, how will I find this Sher Afghan?'

'He is the city's governor and commands the garrison in the Gaur fort. Wait and watch and you will soon see him as he goes about his daily business. Any further questions?'

Hawkins hesitated a moment. 'Will you give me a document – a letter with your seal perhaps – proving that I am in your service?'

'No. Nothing must connect me with Sher Afghan's death. I am paying you to use your ingenuity. You told me you had undertaken sensitive missions for the shah.'

The Englishman shrugged bulky shoulders. 'Then I have nothing further to ask. I'll leave tomorrow.'

When he was alone Jahangir walked slowly out on to the balcony of his private apartments overlooking the Jumna river. Would Bartholomew Hawkins succeed? He seemed tough enough and, unlike most of the other Europeans at court, could speak some Persian. But one of his main reasons for choosing him was that he was a foreigner. If he'd sent his own men, they might have talked, albeit only to a friend or relation, and news of what he was planning might have reached Sher Afghan, giving him time to flee. That would be less of a risk with Bartholomew Hawkins, who had no clan or family loyalties to anyone in Hindustan and owed no man anything. He hadn't even asked why Jahangir wanted Sher Afghan dead. Such a lack of curiosity was an excellent thing . . .

Jahangir had told no one the purpose of his meetings with the English mercenary. He would have confided in Suleiman Beg but his milk-brother was dead from the spotted fever. He had died as together they had returned from a short campaign against some of Khusrau's followers who had fled into the jungles southeast of Agra. Jahangir shuddered even now as he recalled Suleiman Beg's last moments lying in a humid, airless tent while the monsoon rains beat down from leaden skies on its roof only twelve short hours after he had fallen ill. He had quickly become so delirious that he had not even recognised Jahangir. His lips, covered in a scum of white saliva, had stretched into a scream while his sweat-soaked body had twitched and convulsed beneath the thin sheet that covered it. Then he had been still, leaving Jahangir no chance to bid him goodbye or to tell him how important his wise and restraining words had been throughout his rebellion against his father or during the recent dark days of Khusrau's revolt.

To lose the companion he had trusted above all others just when everything was going so well seemed especially hard. In the ten months since Suleiman Beg's death there had been no further insurrections – not even the merest whiff of dissent. His empire was secure. The only threat had come from the belligerent ruler of Persia Shah Abbas who – if the reports brought by Abdul Rahman's scouts were true – was scheming to retake Kandahar from the Moghuls. However, the strong army equipped with twenty bronze

28

cannon and two hundred war elephants that Jahangir had at once despatched to the northwest had made the shah think again. His crimson-capped troops had withdrawn long before Jahangir's forces were even within sight of Kandahar's high mud-brick walls.

He still missed his milk-brother badly. Despite his wives and his remaining sons, his powers and his possessions, he felt alone – isolated even – in a way he had not while Suleiman Beg was alive. His boyhood had been filled with uncertainty, trying on the one hand to live up to the expectations of his father Akbar, a man who had never known failure, while on the other remaining loyal to his Rajput mother who had hated and despised Akbar as the barbarian subjugator of her people. Had it not been for his grandmother Hamida, always ready to listen to and encourage him, he would indeed have been lost. Suleiman Beg had been the only other person who had come anywhere close to occupying such a place in his life – a loyal and wise friend whose advice however unpalatable he had trusted among the self-serving counsel of his courtiers, vying for promotion and reward.

Only yesterday he had gone to inspect progress on the domed sandstone tomb he had ordered to be built for Suleiman Beg near the Agra fort. As he watched the labourers chisel away at the slabs of stone his loss had struck him anew, and he had spent the evening alone with his thoughts. Suleiman Beg's death had reminded him as little else could have done of the transitoriness of life. No man however young or in however good health or good spirits knew the number of his days. Before death overtook him he must achieve all that he could but he must also enjoy life – as much or as little of it as remained – and why not use his power to allow him to do so? His musings had finally persuaded him to send for Bartholomew Hawkins and entrust him with his secret mission without further delay.

Jahangir looked up at a sky that every day grew heavier and darker with rain clouds. In a very few weeks the monsoon rains would begin again. He hoped they wouldn't hamper Hawkins's journey down the Jumna and then the Ganges to Bengal. Though the rivers would soon be in full spate enabling the boats to make swift progress, the currents would become more hazardous. It wasn't an ideal time for such a mission but he was impatient. If Bartholomew Hawkins succeeded, he could take possession of the one thing – or rather the one person – that would make his life complete, even if the cautious Suleiman Beg might have questioned his methods of obtaining it.

◆

Bartholomew Hawkins slapped at a mosquito that had just bitten him on his jawline. Looking at his hand he saw that it was smeared with dark red blood. Good, he'd got the bastard, though it was only a small victory against one of the armies of biting insects that were making his life such a trial. The horse he had purchased for the last stage of his journey to Gaur was old, its ribs sticking out bony as a camel's, but even the finest animal would find it hard to make much progress in the thick ochre mud. Only the thought of the thousand *mohurs* was keeping him going. Since leaving Agra he'd had two prolonged bouts of fever – his sweat had soaked him, his garments and his bedding – and one of such ring-stinging liquid diarrhoea and agonising

stomach cramps that he'd vowed – and meant it – to take
the first ship he could find when he reached the coast and
sail home to England. But at least when he'd had his last
bout of fever he'd still been on a riverboat and an old white-
clad, white-haired Hindu priest with kind brown eyes had
looked after him. Yet when Bartholomew had tried to press
a coin into his hand the man had recoiled. He'd never
understand this country.

Peering ahead in the fading light, he could just make out
the rear of the Gaur-bound mule train that he had attached
himself to. Preoccupied with driving their laden beasts over
the boggy ground, none of the merchants had shown any
interest in him which was good although he had his story
ready – he was a Portuguese official on his way to the trading
settlement of Hooghly near the mouth of the Ganges to
enquire into the prospects for increasing trade in indigo and
calicoes. He looked nothing like an official – nor, come to
that, a Portuguese given his curly red-gold hair and pale
blue eyes – but these people didn't know that. Or that in
his saddlebags were two very fine steel daggers: one a Persian
weapon with a blade so sharp it could split the hair of a
horse's tail and the other a Turkish one with a curved blade
engraved – or so he'd been told by the Turkish armourer
who'd sold it to him – with the words *I will kill you but
whether you go to Paradise or to hell is God's will.*

The emperor's demeanour had suggested he'd far rather
Sher Afghan went to hell but he'd revealed nothing about
why he wanted the man dead. Bartholomew reached for his
leather bottle and took a gulp of water. It was warm and
fetid-tasting but he'd long ago ceased to worry about such
things. All he prayed was that he wouldn't be seized with

31

another attack in his bowels. Restoppering the bottle his thoughts returned to Jahangir, how intent the dark eyes in that handsome fine-boned face had looked as he'd given Bartholomew his orders. Despite his fine brocades and the glittering rings on every finger, Bartholomew had detected a man perhaps not so unlike himself . . . a man who knew what he wanted and was prepared to be ruthless in pursuit of it. He had also noted the whitened scars — one on the back of Jahangir's left hand and another running up his right brow into his hairline. The emperor knew about the art of killing too.

Suddenly Bartholomew heard men shouting to one another up ahead. Instinctively he felt for his sword in case robbers — *dacoits* the local people called them — were falling on the mule train. Such attacks often happened at dusk when the enfolding darkness gave cover to the robbers and the merchants were growing tired. Three nights ago at that time Bartholomew had saved a puny carpet seller. The man had stopped in drizzling rain to redistribute the load from a mule that had become lame among his other beasts. He had been struggling with a rolled carpet almost as large as himself when two bandits had trotted up out of the darkness. Jumping down from their ponies, one had kicked the carpet dealer to the ground while the other had begun gathering the reins of the mules, preparing to lead them away. Both were so preoccupied they never saw Bartholomew, galloping out of the murk, until it was too late. Drawing his Toledo steel sword he had almost severed one man's head from his shoulders and split the other's skull like a ripe melon. The carpet seller's gratitude had been overwhelming and he'd tried to force a rug on him. But Bartholomew had already been regretting his actions. If he was to carry out his mission and win his reward, he must not attract attention.

But now the reason for the shouts wasn't *dacoits*. The cries were of relief and joy, not fear. Ahead of him Bartholomew could see watchtowers silhouetted against the remnants of the sunset – it was Gaur. Bartholomew let go of his sword hilt and gave his sweating horse a pat. 'Not long now, you wretched old nag.'

· ◆ ·

What was all that commotion in the courtyard at this hour? Bartholomew wondered irritably as he lay on the straw-filled mattress in the small room he'd rented in a caravanserai just inside the walls of Gaur by the main gate. He sat up and scratched vigorously then clambered to his feet and without bothering to pull on his boots went outside. Though it was barely dawn, merchants were laying out their wares on a great stone platform in the centre of the courtyard ready to begin trading: sacks of spices, bags of rice, millet and maize, rolls of dun-coloured cotton and of garish silks. Bartholomew surveyed them without interest but as he turned away he found the carpet seller he had rescued looking up at him.

'Gaur is a fine city, sir.'

'Very fine,' Bartholomew said mechanically. He was about to go back to his room – he could do with an hour or two's more sleep – but then a thought struck him. 'Hassan Ali – that is your name, isn't it?'

The man nodded.

'Hassan Ali, you know Gaur well?'

'Yes. I come here six times a year and two of my cousins are traders here.'

'You said you wanted to repay me for my help. Be my guide. I don't know this place and my employers in Portugal wish me to send them a full report of it.'

An hour later Bartholomew followed Hassan Ali across the square courtyard of the caravanserai and out through its high arched gateway into the streets of Gaur. At first with its narrow, refuse-strewn streets it looked a mean place but as Hassan Ali, walking with surprising speed for such a small man, led him towards the centre the streets began to broaden and the houses – some of them two storeys high – to become more handsome. Bartholomew also noted the many groups of soldiers they passed. 'Where are they going?' He pointed to a double row of twenty green-sashed, green-turbaned warriors marching by.

'They were the detachment guarding the city's gates during the night but they have now been relieved and are returning to their barracks.'

'Where are they?'

'Not far. I will show you.'

A few minutes later Bartholomew looked up at a tall square fortress-like building with a parade ground in front of it. Built of mud bricks, its walls rose about fifty feet. As he watched, a group of horsemen, doubtless returning after exercising their mounts, trotted through the heavy metal-spiked gate that was the barracks' single entrance. 'It's a fine building.'

'Yes. It was built by the Emperor Akbar – may his spirit rest in Paradise – after his conquest of Bengal. He also re-inforced the city walls and built the fine caravanserais that we have here. He was truly a great man.'

'I'm sure. Who commands the Moghul troops here? He

34

must be an important man to be so favoured by the emperor.'

'I don't know his name. I'm sorry.'

'It's not important. I was merely curious to know who was entrusted with such a task. Hindustan is so huge compared with my own country. There, it is far easier for a monarch to control his lands and to know what is going on . . .'

'It is true. Our empire is without parallel in the world.' Hassan Ali nodded complacently. 'Come. Let me take you to the great bazaar where much trading is done in addition to that in the caravanserais.'

They were just turning away when the harsh metallic blaring of a trumpet made them halt. Moments later twelve soldiers splendidly mounted on matching bay horses cantered out of a side street and across the parade ground towards the barracks. One of them was holding the short brass trumpet he must have just sounded to signal their arrival. They were followed by three further riders – two in domed helmets riding on either side of a tall man who was looking to neither right nor left and whose long dark hair flowed from beneath a white-plumed helmet.

Bartholomew's pulses quickened. He glanced around for Hassan Ali and saw him conversing with a melon seller in a grimy dhoti. Bartholomew listened hard but couldn't understand what they were saying. It must be a local language, he thought. It certainly wasn't Persian. The melon seller seemed to have a lot to say. He had emerged from behind his mounds of cylindrical yellow-green fruits and was talking vigorously and pointing to the barracks into which the man with the plumed helmet and his escort had now disappeared.

'Sir,' said Hassan Ali, 'the commander of the garrison is called Sher Afghan. That was him we just saw. The melon seller told me he is a great warrior. Two years ago the late emperor sent him to the jungles and swamps of Arakan east of here to deal with the pirates living there. It is a terrible place, infested with crocodiles, but Sher Afghan triumphed. He captured and executed five hundred pirates, throwing their bodies on to pyres of their own burning boats.'

'Does he live in the barracks?'

'No. His mansion is in a large garden to the north of the city, by the Swordmaker's Gate. Now, let us go to the bazaar. You will find much to interest you there . . . last time I was here I saw a painted wooden figure of one of your Portuguese gods. It had golden wings . . .'

• ◆ •

Bartholomew bided his time. Every day the rains still came, hot and heavy, the drops bouncing up from the paved court-yard of the caravanserai. In between the showers he put on the hooded dark brown robe he had purchased in the bazaar to make his appearance less remarkable and walked around Gaur until he had fixed in his mind every twist of every street, every alley, in the area between the barracks and Sher Afghan's house. He also observed his intended victim's move-ments which, apart from the odd day's hunting or hawking when the weather allowed, seemed surprisingly regular. Nearly every afternoon, Sher Afghan spent several hours in the barracks. On Mondays he reviewed his troops on the parade ground, watching their displays of musketry practice, and on Wednesdays he inspected some part of the city's defences.

During the long journey from Agra Bartholomew had pondered how best to find an opportunity to kill Sher Afghan. He smiled to think he had even contemplated trying to pick a quarrel with him as if Gaur were an English town where he and Sher Afghan might meet and brawl in a tavern. Now he had seen not just the muscular strength of the man but that a bodyguard accompanied him everywhere the idea had less to commend it. Whatever he did must be by stealth. It might be possible to find a vantage point from which to aim an arrow or hurl a dagger but the chances of even wounding him, let alone of killing him outright, were slender. Jahangir had made it absolutely clear that he wanted Sher Afghan dead.

But on a clear day when the rains seemed finally to be easing and there was a new freshness in the air, the solution came to Bartholomew. It was so obvious and simple – though not without danger to himself – that he grinned as he wondered why he hadn't thought of it before.

• ◆ •

Two weeks later, towards eleven o'clock in the evening – an hour before the caravanserai's gates would be locked for the night – Bartholomew slipped out of his room, giving a parting kick to the sweat-stained straw-filled mattress on which he'd spent so many uncomfortable nights. Beneath his dark robe, his sword in its scabbard was suspended from a steel chain round his waist as were his two daggers, the Turkish blade on his right side and the Persian weapon on his left. He had cut slits in the coarse cloth of his robe to ensure he could reach for them quickly.

Bartholomew swiftly crossed the caravanserai's courtyard and went out through its arched entrance past the sleeping gate-keeper who was supposed to keep watch for late arrivals seeking a bed for the night for themselves and stabling for their animals. Once outside he glanced swiftly around him to make sure he was alone. Then he set off through the quiet, narrow streets. He'd walked this precise route many times and knew exactly where it was taking him as he headed across the parade ground and past the barracks towards the north of the city. Reaching a small Hindu temple where tapers burned in a brass pot before the image of an elephant god, Bartholomew turned down an alley where the overhanging upper storeys of the houses were so close they almost touched. He caught the soft sound of a woman singing from one house and the crying of a baby from another. Here and there the orange light of oil lamps flickered through the carved wooden *jalis* covering the windows.

Suddenly Bartholomew's foot caught something soft. It was a dog whose reproachful whimper followed him as he continued his leisurely progress. There was no need to hurry and anyway a man in a hurry always attracted more attention. The alley was broadening out, and as it curved round to the left it gave on to a large square. Bartholomew had seen it at every time of day and night. He knew how many neem trees shaded the stallholders peddling their wares in the heat of the day, how many other streets and alleys led into it and how many men would be guarding the tall house directly opposite him at the far end of the square. Pulling his hood still lower over his face, Bartholomew peered cautiously round the corner into the square. The new moon was shedding hardly any radiance but the glow from braziers burning on either side of the house's metal-bound gates showed that

– just as on other nights – four guards were on duty. It also showed that a green banner was flapping from a gilded pole above the gates – the sign, as he had discovered from Hassan Ali, that the commander was at home. All seemed very quiet. Had any sort of party or feast been in progress he would have had to postpone his plan . . .

Having seen what he wanted, Bartholomew drew back into the shadows of the alley and, turning, began to retrace his steps. After a hundred paces or so he came to a small street branching off to the left. In the daytime it was full of vegetable sellers raucously pressing their own wares on passers-by and deriding their competitors' produce, but now it was silent and empty. Bartholomew walked along it, the leaves of rotting vegetables slippery beneath his feet and the air reeking of their decomposition, but his mind was on other things. This street curved round behind the square. In a few hundred yards it would pass close to the western wall of the fine gardens behind Sher Afghan's house.

The wall was quite high – at least twenty feet – but there were enough foot- and handholds in the brickwork to make climbing it possible, as he knew. On the past two nights he had hauled himself over it, choosing a place where a tall clump of bamboo was growing on the other side, to drop down amongst the dense vegetation. Crouching amongst the leafy bamboos he had listened and watched. Through the swaying stems he had been able to make out a courtyard with a bubbling fountain and beyond it the dark walls of the house. Metal gates identical to those at the front led inside the house but with two important differences. They were kept open – beyond them he had glimpsed an inner courtyard – and they were also only lightly guarded. At night, a watchman – no more than a youth as far as Bartholomew could tell from his slight frame – sat on a wooden stool just inside the gates. He appeared to have no weapon – only a small drum to beat to rouse the household in case of danger.

But what danger could Sher Afghan be expecting? He was the commander of a garrison in a quiescent – albeit distant – part of a peaceful and powerful empire. The soldiers guarding the front gate were probably more for show than anything else. Once again Bartholomew found himself wondering why the emperor wanted this man dead and why – all-powerful as he was – he had chosen this way of getting rid of him. If Sher Afghan had committed some crime why didn't Jahangir just execute him? He was emperor after all. But then that was none of his business. All that mattered were the thousand *mohurs*.

Reaching the wall without incident, Bartholomew glanced about him to make sure yet again that no one was around. Satisfied, he hitched up his dark robe and began to climb. This time for some reason, perhaps nerves or impatience to get the job done, he didn't choose his handholds so well. When he was already about fifteen feet up, the corner of a brick he was grasping in his right hand crumbled and he nearly fell backwards to the ground. Digging his toes hard into crevices between the bricks and hanging on with his left hand – he could feel blood oozing from beneath his nails – he managed to steady himself. Stretching his right arm higher he probed the rough surfaces until he found a place that felt secure. With one more big heave he was on top of the wall.

Brushing the sweat from his face he carefully lowered himself down the other side, letting go when he was still ten feet above the ground to drop into the space he had found among the bamboos. Squatting down, heart pounding, he listened. No sounds, nothing. That was good. It must be after midnight now but it was still too early to make his move. He shifted a little to make himself more comfortable. He felt some small creature – a mouse or a gecko – run over his foot and heard the familiar whine of mosquitoes. Frowning slightly, he focused his mind on the task ahead.

It was about one in the morning when Bartholomew began moving slowly towards the house, keeping under cover of the bamboos and then of the spreading branches of a thickly leaved mango tree. In the moonlight, he could see the watchman, young head slumped on his chest and clearly fast asleep on his stool. Beyond him the inner courtyard, lit only by small torches burning in brackets on the wall, was quiet and still. Bartholomew darted across the garden past the still playing fountain to the wall of the house, choosing a place a little to the left of the gates that was overshadowed by a projecting balcony. Flattening his back against the wall he closed his eyes for a moment as he steadied his breathing.

Then he began edging towards the gates. Reaching them he paused and peered inside. He was so close to the watchman that he could hear his light snores. But there was no other sound. Tensing his muscles, he sprang forward through the doors, grabbed the youth from behind with both arms and hauled him out into the garden, right hand clamped firmly over his mouth. 'One sound out of you and you're dead,' Barthlomew whispered in Persian. 'Do you understand me?' The youth's eyes were wide with fright as he nodded. 'Now take me to where your master Sher Afghan is sleeping.'

The youth nodded again. Gripping the nape of the young watchman's neck with his left hand so firmly that his nails dug into the flesh, and with his right drawing his curved-bladed Turkish dagger from its oxhide scabbard, Bartholomew followed him across the inner courtyard, through a doorway in the corner and up a flight of narrow stone stairs to a long corridor. He could feel the youth trembling like a frightened puppy beneath his grip.

'Here, sir. This is the room.' The boy halted outside a chamber with highly polished doors of some dark wood inlaid with brass tigers. Bartholomew thought he could smell some spicy perfume – frankincense perhaps – and tightened his hold on the youth, who looked round, brown eyes terrified. Without warning he opened his mouth to cry out an alarm.

Bartholomew didn't hesitate. In two rapid movements he jerked back the boy's head with his left hand and with his right raised his bright-bladed Turkish dagger and drew it across the smooth-skinned throat. As the youth's last breaths bubbled through the gaping wound he laid the limp body down. In other circumstances he might have spared him, but not here where he could so easily lose his own life if he made a mistake. Instinctively he wiped the bloody dagger on his robes. All his thoughts were on what he would find on the other side of those dark doors with their gleaming tigers. He'd heard it said that 'sher' meant 'tiger' – if so he was in the right place and Sher Afghan was just a few feet away.

Still holding his dagger in his right hand, with his left Bartholomew carefully raised the ornate metal latch – again fashioned like a tiger – on the right-hand door and gave a gentle exploratory push. To his relief the door opened smoothly and quietly. When it was about six inches ajar he stopped. A shaft of pale golden light told him the room he was about to enter was not in darkness as he had hoped.

Perhaps Sher Afghan had already seen the door swing open and was even now drawing his sword . . .

Bartholomew hesitated no longer but pushed the door wide and stepped inside. The large room was hung with red silk embroidered with gold thread. Soft thick carpets were beneath his feet and a spiral of smoke was rising from some crystals glowing in an enamelled incense burner. Wicks were burning in oil-filled bronze *diyas*. But Bartholomew's gaze was on none of these things. He was staring through the almost transparent pale pink muslin curtains drawn across the room to divide it in two. Through the fabric he could see a large low bed and upon it two intertwined naked bodies, a man and a woman. The man at least was so absorbed in his lovemaking that Bartholomew could have probably kicked the door open without his noticing. The woman was on her back, slender legs hooked around the man's muscular hips as he thrust and her view of the door obstructed by her lover's body.

Providence could not have given him a better opportunity, Bartholomew thought as he came nearer. Carefully, he slipped through the muslin curtains and treading softly approached the bed. He was now so close he could see the sweaty sheen on the man's body and smell the salty tang of it but both he and the woman, whose head was turned aside, her eyes closed, were still oblivious of his presence. Close to climax, with each thrust Sher Afghan was joyously throwing back his head. As he did so, Bartholomew leapt forward, grabbed him by his thick black hair, yanked his head back even further and neatly severed his jugular. Bartholomew was a skilled killer. Just like the gatekeeper, Sher Afghan made not a sound as his hot red blood pumped from the gaping wound.

Bartholomew grabbed hold of the heavy body, stared for

43

a moment into the still open eyes to reassure himself that it was indeed Sher Afghan, then pushed it to the floor and turned his attention to the woman who had now opened her eyes and was sitting up, knees drawn up defensively. Her lover's blood was running down between her opulent breasts and her dark eyes were fixed on his face as if trying to predict what he would do next. 'Don't make a noise and I won't hurt you,' he said. Slowly, her gaze never leaving his face, she pulled up a sheet over her but said nothing.

He was relieved – he didn't want to kill a woman any more than he had wanted to kill the young watchman – but at the same time he was surprised. He'd have expected someone in her situation to scream hysterically or shout abuse but she didn't look as devastated as she might have that the man who just moments earlier had been passionately and vigorously making love to her was lying in a pool of congealing blood on the floor. Instead her expression was almost one of curiosity. He realised she was taking in every detail from his dark, grubby robe and blood-smeared hands to the stray curls of red-gold hair slipping from beneath the length of dun-coloured cloth he'd wound round his head.

He turned to go. He'd stayed too long already. Backing away just in case she had a weapon concealed somewhere, he reached the doors, expecting any moment to hear her scream out for the guards. But he was through the door, down the corridor and hurling himself down the stone steps into the silent and now empty courtyard before, at last, he heard a woman's shrill cry of 'Murder!' As he ran through the dark gardens he heard a commotion break out behind him – men's voices, the sound of running feet – but he was nearly at the wall now. Forcing his way through the tough bamboos, not caring how he scraped or scratched himself, he flung himself at the wall and scaled it, this time without difficulty.

Back in the street he paused for a moment. Taking his Turkish dagger, still stained with Sher Afghan's gore, he kissed it lightly. The thousand *mohurs* were his.

Chapter 3

The Widow

'We have prepared and washed your husband's body ready for burial,' said the *hakim*. 'I thought that before we laid him in his coffin you would wish to assure yourself that everything has been done exactly as you instructed.'

'Thank you.' Mehrunissa stepped closer and stared down at her husband's corpse. 'Leave me, please . . .' When she was alone she leaned over the body and scrutinised Sher Afghan's face, which looked surprisingly peaceful for a man who had met such a violent end. She could smell the astringent odour of the camphor water with which the *hakim* and his helper had cleansed him.

'I'm sorry you died in such a way,' she whispered, 'but I'm not sorry I'm free of you. If the killer had struck me down instead of you, you wouldn't have cared.' For a moment she touched her husband's cheek with her fingertips. 'Your flesh is cold now, but you were always cold to me and to our daughter, who meant nothing to you because she was not born a boy . . .'

Mehrunissa felt tears welling, but not for Sher Afghan. Though she despised self-pity they were for herself and her wasted years with a man to whom, once he had secured her dowry, she had become only an object on which to satisfy his lust and to demonstrate his power. She had been barely seventeen when she had married him. Nothing had prepared her for what became his callous indifference or – if she ever dared complain – his casual and vicious brutality. She turned away, feeling sick and a little giddy. It was barely six hours since the assassin had struck. The whole scene was raw and vivid in her mind: the murderer's eyes – pale blue like a Persian cat's – as he had stood over the bed, the silver flash of his blade, the warm red blood spurting from the cut in Sher Afghan's throat over her naked flesh, the utter astonishment on her husband's face in that moment just before life left him. Everything had happened so fast that she'd had no time to feel afraid, but now the thought that the killer might well have turned his bloodied dagger on her was making her shake. He hadn't scrupled to kill the young watchman . . .

Soldiers were already ransacking the town for the murderer. Her description had been enough to confirm that whoever he was, he was a foreigner. There had already been reports of a blue-eyed man – a Portuguese, some said – who had been staying in one of the caravanserais but now seemed to have vanished . . . Wrapping her arms around herself to feel warmer even though it was a summer's day, Mehrunissa turned her back on her husband's corpse and began to pace as she liked to do when she wished to think. Who the murderer was mattered less to her than his motive. Had the killing been

47

the prelude to some wider rising? Might Gaur itself soon come under attack? If so, her own life and that of her daughter might yet be in danger.

Or had Sher Afghan's murder been the result of some personal grudge? Her husband had made plenty of enemies. He had boasted to her about how he had embezzled imperial money as well as extorted higher taxes than authorised to enrich himself. He had also told her he had taken bribes from bandit chiefs to the north of Gaur in return for not suppressing their activities, and she knew that just before the start of the last monsoon rains, in response to pressure from the authorities in Agra to whom some wealthy merchants had complained, he had gone back on his word, pursuing the bandits relentlessly and cementing the heads of those he killed into towers as a warning. Many a man would be glad Sher Afghan was dead, but who would have dared to kill him in his own bedchamber?

Hearing voices outside – perhaps the coffin makers coming to measure the body – Mehrunissa hastily put such thoughts aside. In the hours and days ahead she must watch for any threat to herself and her daughter but now she had her part to play as a grieving widow. It was a matter of family honour. She would scrupulously observe the mourning rituals and no one would suspect that in her heart she felt no sorrow, only release.

· ◆ ·

A travel-stained, dusty-haired Bartholomew Hawkins was shown into Jahangir's private apartments. Though it was approaching midnight, learning of the Englishman's return Jahangir had been impatient for his news.

'Well?'

'Majesty, it is done. I slit his throat with my own hands.'

'Did anyone see you?'

'Only the woman he was with.'

Jahangir stared at him, face suddenly aghast. 'You didn't harm her?'

'No, Majesty.'

'You are absolutely certain?'

'I swear it on my life.'

Jahangir could see the puzzlement on Bartholomew's face. Clearly the man wasn't lying. He began to breathe more easily. 'You've done well. One of my *qorchis* will bring you your money in the morning . . .' He paused as an idea came to him. 'What do you intend to do now? Return to your own land?'

'I'm not sure, Majesty.'

'If you stay at my court I will find you further tasks. If you serve me as well as you have already, I will make you rich enough to purchase your own ship to take you home.' For all his tiredness Bartholomew Hawkins's eyes were suddenly agleam in his sunburned face. People were not so hard to understand as he had once believed, Jahangir thought.

• ◆ •

Despite all the cushions and the fur rugs to protect against the cold, the bullock cart carrying Mehrunissa up through the Khyber Pass towards Kabul was uncomfortable. She'd be glad when the long journey from Bengal was ended. Her daughter Ladli was sleeping, head resting in the lap of Farisha, her Persian nurse, who had tended her since birth. The child had enjoyed the river journey westward along the Ganges and then northwards up the Jumna, but since they had disembarked near Delhi to travel the last six hundred miles overland she had grown fretful. The interior of the bullock cart, enclosed by thick curtains, was stuffy and dark. At almost six years old Ladli was still too young to understand that the curtains must be drawn to preserve them from the common view. The only time of day she enjoyed was when camp was pitched and she could run around the area separated off for the women by high wooden screens.

But at least they were making good progress. They should be beyond the passes before the first snows fell. Winter in Kabul was harsh. Mehrunissa could recall the icicles thick as a man's arm hanging from the eaves of her father's house and how little moved beyond the city walls except the occasional hungry wolf patrolling the white expanses in search of a meal. Yet there had been many times in the hot, humid air of Bengal when she'd longed to feel the chill wind on her cheek and to breathe out spirals of frosty air.

Sher Afghan's murderer had still not been found by the time she left Gaur and there had been no clues to the motive behind the killing. To her relief everything had remained peaceful, but all the same she was glad Gaur now lay far behind. She had expected her father to make the arrangements for her long journey, and had therefore been surprised to receive his letter informing her that imperial troops from the fort at Monghyr, west of Gaur along the Ganges, would accompany her all the way to Kabul. *The emperor grieves for you in your sad situation. He wishes you to return swiftly and in safety to your family*, her father had written. *The emperor is good to us beyond anything I could have expected. Bless you, daughter.* The letter had been signed *Ghiyas Beg* and fastened with the great seal of the Treasurer of Kabul.

During the long journey, Mehrunissa had often pondered her father's words. Presumably the emperor's generosity to her family stemmed from those months he had spent in Kabul when his father, the Emperor Akbar, had exiled him there. According to rumours circulating even before the prince's arrival, Jahangir had greatly angered Akbar. The wife of Saif Khan, the Governor of Kabul, had explained to Mehrunissa's mother what had really happened – the prince had been caught with one of his father's concubines. His punishment had been banishment but the woman's had been death . . .

The prince had become a frequent visitor to her father's house. She could still recall the preparations when messengers brought word that he was on his way from the citadel – how her mother would order precious incense to be set alight in the burners, how her father would don his best robes and hurry to the entrance ready to greet him. Above all she could remember the night her father – who had given her no hint of what he intended – had summoned her to perform one of the classical dances of Persia for his guest. As her attendants brushed out and perfumed her hair she'd felt nervous but also excited. She had performed the dance of the golden tree, the tiny golden bells in her fluttering hands symbolising the falling of its gilded leaves in autumn to lie on the forest floor, ruffled by the chill breezes of the coming winter.

She had been so intent on getting the movements right – it was an intricate dance that she had spent many hours with her instructor trying to perfect – that at first she hadn't looked directly at the prince. When, confidence growing as the spirit of the dance began to possess her, she had raised her eyes to his, she had felt the intensity of his gaze. For some reason she hadn't understood at the time and now, after so many years, was even further from understanding, she had allowed her veil to slip. For three or four moments – no more – she had let him see her face and knew that it had pleased him.

Not long after, Akbar had ordered his son to return to Agra. By then her head had been filled with thoughts of her approaching marriage to Sher Afghan. It had been a good match for the daughter of a Persian nobleman who had come penniless to the Moghul court. Even though her father had grown rich enough in the service of the emperor, and through trading ventures with merchants passing through Kabul, to give his daughter a large dowry – ten thousand gold *mohurs* – he had no lands, no great estates. Sher Afghan on the other hand belonged to the old Moghul nobility – his great-grandfather had ridden with Babur, the first Moghul emperor, on his conquest of Hindustan. In her preparations for her coming marriage she'd pushed the prince – or the emperor as he now was – to the back of her mind: a sweet fantasy of what might have been.

The cart gave a great judder. One of the front wheels must have hit a boulder, Mehrunissa thought. She would be heartily glad when this journey came to an end.

• ◆ •

Mehrunissa laid aside the volume of poems by the Persian Firduz that her father had purchased for her from a merchant recently arrived from Tabriz, got up and stretched. Feeling the need for some activity, she climbed up to the flat roof of her father's house, enjoying the warmth of the shallow stone steps beneath her bare hennaed feet. Stepping on to the roof, she looked northwards. There against a backdrop of snow-dusted mountains was the forbidding citadel, perched on a barren crag overlooking the city.

She had thought of it often during her time in Gaur – how the tiny apertures in its strong walls resembled eyes keeping watch over Kabul. Although it was the governor's residence, her father had told her it was far from luxurious – a draughty stronghold built even before the time of Babur, who had launched his invasion of Hindustan from there. All the same she wished she could see inside a place where such grand ambitions had been nurtured. What must it have been like to see the Moghul army stream out of the citadel and away across the plains on a war of conquest that would change the lives of millions of people? What must it have been like for Babur to see his ambitions become reality?

And could she ever really understand? If she'd been born a man like her elder brother Asaf Khan, now an officer in the imperial army and on campaign over a thousand miles away to the south in the Deccan, or her younger brother Mir Khan, serving in the imperial garrison at Gwalior where the emperor's son Prince Khusrau was confined, she would have seen so much more of the world, understood so much more . . . Perhaps too her father would never have abandoned her to die straight after her birth on his perilous journey from Persia to Agra, however reluctant he had been to do so and however pleased he had been when fate and a friendly merchant had allowed him to recover her. The thought that expediency had overcome his love for her – and she knew both her parents loved her – was something that had remained with her. Together with her experiences in Bengal it had left her, she knew, with a cynical attitude to people and their motives. In a crisis the thoughts of few extended far beyond themselves.

Besides, a woman's life, her life, was anyway so confined, whether here in her parents' house or later in Sher Afghan's *haram* in Gaur. Ever since she began to grow up she'd felt curious about so much . . . about her family's homeland of Persia to the west and how the shah ruled that empire; whether the domes and minarets of Samarkand to the north-east really sparkled blue, green and gold as she'd heard tell. Her father – when she could prise him from his ledgers – tried to answer her questions but there was so much more she wanted to know. Reading helped quell her frustration. In Gaur the few manuscript volumes she had acquired had made life with Sher Afghan more bearable after the first disillusionment had set in. Yet at the same time they had fed her restlessness, her dissatisfaction. Everything – the accounts of travellers, even poems – stimulated her already vivid imagination, suggesting life was laden with possibilities far beyond loveless couplings in the commander's *haram* in Gaur or the domestic pleasantness of her parents' home.

Suddenly she heard a commotion in the square below. Walking swiftly across to the red and orange cotton screen that shielded the area of the roof bordering the square from passers-by, Mehrunissa peered down. A line of mounted imperial soldiers led by an officer and a banner-bearer was entering the square. As the soldiers dismounted her father's grooms hurried outside to take the reins and moments later the tall, thin figure of Ghiyas Beg himself appeared. Briefly inclining his head and touching his breast with his right hand, he led the officer inside. What did they want? she wondered.

The other soldiers began strolling around the square, talking and laughing and nibbling walnuts they had bought from the old vendor – his features as wrinkled as the nuts he sold – who habitually sat there. But however much she strained she couldn't catch their words. As time passed and the officer remained with her father, Mehrunissa descended again to the women's courtyard, sat down on her stool and picked up her book once more. The shadows were lengthening and two attendants were lighting oil lamps when Mehrunissa heard her father's voice. Glancing up, she saw he looked agitated.

'What is it, Father?'

He gestured to the attendants to withdraw then squatted beside her, long fingers twisting the gold-set amethyst ring that for as long as she could remember he had worn on the third finger of his left hand. She had never seen her father – normally so calm and controlled – like this. He hesitated briefly, then began in a voice that was not quite steady. 'Do you remember the letter I wrote to you in Gaur? That I was surprised by the emperor's goodness in sending imperial soldiers to escort you home . . . ?'

'Yes.'

'I was not being entirely frank with you . . . I did have an idea what the emperor's motive might be.'

'What do you mean?'

'Some years ago something happened here in Kabul – something to do with you. I never told you because I thought it better you shouldn't know. Had events turned out differently I alone would have taken the knowledge of it to my grave . . . When the emperor was still a prince, banished here to Kabul, he and I found much to discuss. Though I was only his father's treasurer, I think he appreciated me as an educated man – even came to regard me as a friend. That was why one night I asked you, as my only daughter, to dance for him. My single thought was to pay him the greatest compliment within my power. But soon afterwards – perhaps even the next day, I'm not sure – he came to see me . . . Do you know what he wanted?' Ghiyas Beg's look was penetrating.

'No.'

'He asked for you as his wife.'

Mehrunissa stood up so abruptly that her stool toppled sideways. 'He wanted to marry me . . . ?'

'Yes. But I had to tell him you were already betrothed to Sher Afghan – that I could not in all honour break that contract . . .'

Mehrunissa began to pace the courtyard, hands clasped. Her father had refused Jahangir . . . Instead of being the wife of the cold, brutish Sher Afghan in the fetid heat of Bengal she could have been a prince's wife at the Moghul court, close to the heart of everything that mattered. Why? How could he? What could have motivated him to cut her off from so much? He would have benefited, as too would all the family . . .

'You are angry with me and perhaps you are right to be. I know your marriage to Sher Afghan was unhappy, but I couldn't have predicted that. I felt I had no choice except to act as I did. After all, the prince had been exiled by his father. He would have needed his father's permission to marry you

56

and was unlikely to obtain it. At that time he was as likely to have been executed as to become emperor. To be associated with him by the emperor would not have been good for our family.' Ghiyas Beg paused.

To Mehrunissa there seemed something self-contradictory in her father's torrent of exculpation. Had her father refused Jahangir for honour or for expediency? But he was continuing.

'Listen to what else I have to tell you and then perhaps you won't judge me so harshly. The emperor has appointed me his Comptroller of Revenues and ordered me to Agra.' Her father's eyes were suddenly full of tears – something Mehrunissa had never seen before. 'For the past twenty years and more – ever since we first came here – I've thought about the moment when my qualities would be recognised and I would be given some great appointment. I had given up hope and schooled myself to be content . . . But there is still more. The emperor writes that you are to be lady-in-waiting to one of the Emperor Akbar's widows in the imperial *haram*. Daughter, I believe he has not forgotten you. Now that you are a widow and he is an emperor, he is free to do what he could not when he was only a prince and you were pledged to another man.'

• ◆ •

Six days later, Mehrunissa lay back in her palanquin as the eight Gilzai tribesmen on whose broad shoulders the palanquin's bamboo poles were resting carried her and her sleeping daughter Ladli swiftly down through the narrow rock-strewn Khoord pass on the first stage of the descent to the plains of Hindustan. The pink brocade curtains enclosing her fluttered in the breeze allowing her glimpses of the steep, scree-covered slopes dotted with holly oak bushes. The bearers were keeping up an even rhythm, singing as they half ran. She hoped her father was right about Jahangir's intentions. She wanted him to be but as she knew from experience men could be changeable. Sher Afghan had been an attentive husband, a tender lover in the first months of their marriage until he grew tired of her . . . Also she might no longer please Jahangir. Men liked young flesh. Then she had been a girl of sixteen; now she was a woman of twenty-four.

The crackle of musket fire and urgent cries of alarm from the back of the column broke into her thoughts. The palanquin began swaying violently as her bearers stopped singing and picked up speed. Putting a protective arm around Ladli she lifted a corner of one of the curtains and peered out but could see nothing but grey rocks and scree. All the time the yells and sounds of musketry grew louder and nearer. Then a rider galloped by from the rear of the column, so close that she could smell the sweat of his horse and the dust raised by its hooves stung her eyes and made her cough. He was shouting, '*Dacoits* are attacking the baggage train! Three men and two baggage camels are down. Get more troops back there quickly!'

Rubbing the dust from her eyes Mehrunissa looked back but a sharp bend in the track hid the baggage train from her view. These passes were notorious for the wild Afridi tribes who preyed on small groups of travellers, but to attack a party protected by an escort of imperial troops was surely reckless. They couldn't know who they were taking on . . . or maybe they did. Perhaps the news that the wealthy Treasurer of Kabul was on the road had tempted them. The shadows were lengthening. In an hour or two the sun would disappear below the peaks of the surrounding hills. Perhaps the attack on the baggage wagons in the rear was intended to hurry them deeper into the narrow Khoord Pass where a bigger ambush awaited in the dusk? The thought of the danger to herself and Ladli – and to her parents, travelling ahead of her in the column – chilled her for a moment, then she began to think. How would she defend herself and her daughter? She had no weapons. Ladli had awoken and she pulled the child closer to her. Sensing her mother's tension Ladli started to whimper. 'Hush,' Mehrunissa said, keeping her voice bright. 'Everything will be all right. Besides, crying never helped anyone.'

Just then someone shouted an order to halt. Her bearers stopped so abruptly that Mehrunissa tumbled forward. She lost her grip on Ladli and banged her forehead on one of the curved bamboo hoops that formed the frame of the palanquin so hard that for a moment she was dazed. Collecting herself, she pushed Ladli to the floor of the palanquin. 'Stay there!' Next she craned her head right out of the curtains to see that ahead of her the entire column had stopped. Musketmen were dismounting and, weapons slung across their backs, were scrambling up the scree-covered slopes, dislodging grit and pebbles as they did so, towards some tumbled rocks that would provide them with cover. Then a detachment of imperial horsemen swept past her palanquin heading towards the rear of the column where the sounds of fighting were intensifying. The track was so narrow that they had to drop into single file as they passed her. The last of them was a young officer mounted on a black horse, face anxious and sword already drawn.

Should she break purdah and run with Ladli to her parents' cart, Mehrunissa wondered, but then dismissed the idea. It would only expose them both to any marksmen in the rocks above. There was no point in making any move until the progress of the fighting was clearer. Instead she closed the curtains around the palanquin again. Time passed slowly in the semi-darkness. Conscious all the time of the sounds of muskets – sometimes seeming nearer, sometimes further away – and of curt shouted orders for soldiers to advance or fall back, as well as of the pain in her forehead, on which a large bump was now rising, she forced herself to sing Persian folk songs to Ladli.

At last the cries and shooting from the back of the column subsided, but what did that mean? Then she heard approaching hoofbeats, victorious whoops and answering cheers from bearers and soldiers near her palanquin. The raiders must have been beaten off . . . Looking out once more she watched the victorious imperial soldiers returning. Several, including the young officer she had seen, had the heads of those they had slain dangling by their hair from the pommels of their saddles, blood dripping from their roughly severed necks. But it was the last rider who caught her attention as he approached. He was oddly dressed in a short tight-fitting leather jacket and on his head, instead of a pointed Moghul helmet with a fringe of chain mail to protect the neck, was a plain round one. As he drew abreast of her, he turned his head. A pair of pale, cat-like blue eyes looked directly at her.

Chapter 4

The Imperial Haram

'Madam, it is time. My name is Mala. I am His Imperial Majesty's *khawajasara*, his superintendent of the imperial *haram*, and have come to escort you to the apartments of Fatima Begam whom you will serve.' Mala was a tall, stately looking woman in late middle age. Her long ivory staff of office carved at the top in the shape of a lotus flower added to her dignity. Mehrunissa sensed a formidable personality behind the smile.

She returned her gaze to her parents, standing side by side in the courtyard of the spacious apartments within the walls of the Agra fort allocated to Ghiyas Beg's household. Her mother was holding Ladli by the hand. Mehrunissa knelt and kissed her daughter. She had looked forward to this moment with enormous anticipation but now that it had come, three weeks after reaching Agra, she felt apprehensive, even reluctant. Parting from the child who had been such a consolation to her was hard, even though Ladli would be in the care of her grandparents and nursemaid Farisha and would be allowed to visit her in the *haram*.

Conscious that the *khawajasara* was watching, Mehrunissa forced herself to suppress her feelings, something her life with Sher Afghan had taught her to do well, and to keep a calm face. Giving Ladli one final hug she rose, turned to her parents and embraced them also. As she stepped back from them, Ghiyas Beg's face was full of pride. 'Our thoughts will be with you. Serve your mistress well,' he said.

Mehrunissa followed the *khawajasara* out of the courtyard and down a sandstone staircase that gave on to the steep ramp leading into the heart of the Agra fort. A few yards away six female attendants dressed in green waited beside a silk-decked palanquin. They looked tall and broad. She had already heard about the muscular Turkish women who helped guard the *haram*, but as she drew closer she gasped to see that the attendants were not women but eunuchs with large hands and feet and strangely smooth faces, neither masculine nor feminine. All were wearing rich jewellery and the eyes of several were rimmed with kohl. She had seen eunuchs before, employed as servants or dancing and playing for crowds in the bazaar, but never dressed as parodies of women like this.

'Madam, the palanquin is for you,' said the *khawajasara*. Mehrunissa stepped inside and sat cross-legged on the low seat. Hands twitched the silk curtains into place around her and the palanquin rose as the eunuchs lifted it on to their shoulders. As it began its slow swaying progress up the ramp, carrying her to a new life, she found she was clasping her hands and her heart was beating so fast that her blood seemed to pound in her ears. So much had happened in such a short time . . . In the shadowy half-light she tried to recapture Jahangir's lean, handsome face, the way he had looked at her as she had danced for him in Kabul . . . Was he really to be her future as her father claimed and she so desired? Soon she would know.

• ◆ •

'What do you wish to tell me, Majesty? I came from Fatehpur Sikri as soon as I received your summons.' The Sufi's voice was gentle but his gaze was penetrating. Now that the moment had come, Jahangir felt reluctant to speak. The Sufi, whom out of respect to his status as a holy man he had invited to sit on a stool close by his own in his private apartments, seemed to sense his awkwardness and continued, 'I know that when you were only a boy you opened your heart to my father. I don't presume to have either my father's powers of prophesy or his insight, but if you will trust me I will try to help you.'

Jahangir thought back to that warm night in Fatehpur Sikri when he had run from the palace to the house of Shaikh Salim Chishti hoping to find answers. 'Your father was a great man. He told me not to despair, that I would be emperor. His words sustained me through many difficult times as I grew to manhood.'

'Perhaps my words can also give you solace.'

Jahangir looked at the Sufi – a much bigger man than his frail-looking father had been. He was as tall as Jahangir and well muscled as a soldier, but physical strength wouldn't make him any more forgiving of moral weakness, Jahangir thought . . . He took a breath and began, choosing his words with care. 'When my father exiled me to Kabul I saw a

63

woman there, the daughter of one of my father's officials. I knew instinctively that she was the woman I had been seeking. Though I already had several wives I was certain beyond any doubt that she would be my soulmate – that I must marry her. But there was a problem. She was already promised to one of my father's commanders and though I begged my father he refused to break their betrothal.'

'The Emperor Akbar was a just man, Majesty.'

'Yes, but not always where members of his own family were concerned. He refused to accept how important this woman was to me. He wouldn't understand that I felt as my grandfather Humayun must have done when he saw his wife Hamida for the first time. He broke with his brother Hindal, who also loved Hamida, in order to have her. He even hazarded his empire because of his love for her. Some might say he was foolish . . .' Jahangir glanced at the Sufi sitting silent by his side, hands resting on his knees and white-turbaned head slightly bowed, 'but he was right. After they married he and Hamida were rarely apart. She sustained him through all the dangerous years until finally he won back the Moghul throne. After his sudden death Hamida had the strength to make sure my father Akbar inherited the throne.'

'Your grandmother was a brave woman and a worthy empress. You feel that the woman you wished to marry would have been as good a companion to you?'

'I know it. My father forced me to relinquish her but when I became emperor I knew the time had come when I could be with her.'

'But you said she was promised to another. Did she marry that man?'

'Yes.'

'Then what has changed? Has her husband died?'

'Yes, he is dead.' Jahangir paused for a moment then stood up and paced about before turning to face the Sufi. He could tell by the man's expression that he already knew what he was about to say. 'His name was Sher Afghan. He was my commander in Gaur in Bengal. I had him killed and ordered his widow to be brought here to the imperial *haram*.'

'To murder a man so you can take his wife is a great sin, Majesty.' The Sufi was sitting up very straight on his stool and his expression was stern.

'Was it murder? I am the emperor. I have the power of life and death over every one of my subjects.'

'But as emperor you are also the fount of justice. You cannot kill on a whim or to suit your convenience.'

'Sher Afghan was corrupt. The commander I appointed in his place has provided me with ample evidence of how much imperial money he stole. Thousands of *mohurs* sent him from my treasury for the purchase of horses and equipment went into his own pocket. He also had wealthy merchants executed on false charges so that he could seize their property. I have enough evidence to have had Sher Afghan executed ten, twenty times . . .'

'But you knew nothing about his crimes when you ordered his death?'

Jahangir hesitated, then said, 'No.'

'In that case, Majesty – and forgive me for speaking plainly – you should not try to justify your actions. You acted out of a selfish passion, nothing more.'

'But are my actions so different from my grandfather's? Is my crime so much worse than his? He stole a woman

65

from a brother who loved him and was loyal to him. If he hadn't alienated Hindal, Hindal himself would never have been murdered.'

'Your crime is far worse because you had a man killed for your own ends. You have sinned not only against God but against the family of the woman you desire and the woman herself. In your heart you know it, otherwise why send for me?' The Sufi's clear brown eyes were fixed on his face. When Jahangir said nothing he continued, 'I can't absolve you from your sin . . . only God can forgive you.'

Every word the Sufi had spoken was true, Jahangir thought. The need to confide in someone had been growing intolerable and he was glad that at last he had done it, but he had been deluding himself in hoping the holy man would condone his actions. 'I will try to win God's forgiveness. I will treble what I give to the poor. I'll order new mosques to be built in Agra, Delhi and Lahore. I'll—'

The Sufi raised his hand. 'Majesty, that isn't enough. You said you've had the woman brought to your *haram*. Have you lain with her yet?'

'No. She is not a common concubine. As I told you, I want to marry her. At present she is lady-in-waiting to one of my stepmothers and knows nothing of any of this. But soon I intend to send for her . . . to tell her what I feel . . .'

'No. Part of your penance must be personal. You must exercise self-control. Wed this woman now and God may exact a terrible price. You must subdue your desires and wait. You must not bed her for least six months and in the meantime you must pray daily to God to forgive you.' So saying,

66

the Sufi rose and without waiting for Jahangir to dismiss him walked from the apartments.

• ◆ •

Fatima Begam's broad face was lined and dry as parchment and a large mole on the left side of her chin sprouted a trio of luxuriant white hairs. Could she ever have been beautiful – beautiful enough to have made Akbar eager to make her his wife? Mehrunissa wondered, watching the elderly woman lying dozing on a low bed piled with plump orange cushions. She thought she could guess the answer. Though he had chosen his concubines for his physical pleasure, Akbar had used marriage as a means of contracting political alliances. Fatima Begam's family were rulers of a small state on the borders of Sind.

Mehrunissa stirred restlessly. She wished she could read but Fatima Begam liked the lighting in her apartments to be kept subdued. Muslin hangings over the arched windows filtered the sunlight. She rose and went over to one of the windows. Through the curtain she glimpsed the amber waters of the Jumna river sweeping by. A group of men were cantering along its broad muddy bank, their hunting dogs running behind. Once again she envied men their freedom. Here in the imperial *haram*, this self-contained city of women, her life felt even more constricted than it had in Kabul. Despite the beauty of its flower-filled gardens and terraces, its avenues of trees and shimmering scented fountains, the rich furnishings – no floor was ever left bare, and colourful swathes of glowing silks and sensuous velvets draped windows and doors – the *haram* seemed like a prison. Rajput soldiers guarded the great gates leading into it and within it was

67

patrolled by female guards and by the bland-faced but knowing-looking eunuchs whose presence, even after eight weeks, she still found unsettling.

Yet most unsettling of all was that as yet she had heard nothing from the emperor . . . she hadn't even caught a glimpse of him though she knew he was at court. Why hadn't he sent for her or even come to visit Fatima Begam where he would know he would be sure of seeing her? Could it be that her hopes – and those of her father – had no foundation after all? She must be patient, Mehrunissa told herself as she turned away from the window. What else could she do? If she was to prosper here instinct told her she needed to understand this strange new world. She must explore the *haram* whenever Fatima Begam had errands for her. She had already discovered that the honeycomb of rooms built around three sides of a square paved courtyard where Fatima Begam had her quarters housed dozens of women related one way or another to the imperial family – aunts, great-aunts, the most distant of distant cousins.

She had also seen enough to know that her estimation of Mala's importance and character had been correct. The *khawajasara* rigidly controlled every aspect of the *haram* from the preparation of perfumes and cosmetics to checking the accounts, purchasing the stores and monitoring the kitchens. The officious but efficient Mala knew the names of every one of her small army of assistants and servants down to the female scavengers employed to clean the underground tunnels into which the latrines emptied. It was she who gave permission for female visitors to enter the *haram*. It was also the *khawajasara*'s job – so Mehrunissa had heard – to keep a detailed account of every woman the emperor made love to, including his wives, and the date in case a child was conceived. Watching through a tiny screen set high in the walls of each chamber for just such a purpose, she even noted the number of couplings.

Jahangir's wives, so Mehrunissa had learned, lived in grand quarters in a separate part of the *haram* she had not yet seen. If only her father had agreed to Jahangir's request all those years ago, she might have been one of them. What kind of women were they and did he still visit their beds? It was difficult for her, a newcomer, to ask directly but gossip was one of the *haram's* main pastimes and conversation was easy to steer in the direction she wished. She had already heard that Jodh Bai, mother of Prince Khurram, was a humorous good-natured woman and that the Persian-born mother of Prince Parvez had grown very fat through eating the sweet-meats for which she had a passion but was still so vain that she spent hours studying her face in one of the tiny pearl-rimmed mirrors mounted on thumb rings that were so fashionable.

She had also learned that since Prince Khusrau's rebellion, his mother Man Bai had kept to her apartments, spending her time alternately condemning Khusrau and accusing others of leading her son astray. According to the gossip Man Bai had always been highly strung. It was sad to think of a woman whose love must be torn between husband and son, but Man Bai should show more strength . . . Mehrunissa was still so deep in her thoughts that she started as the doors opened and Fatima Begam's niece Sultana, a widow in her early forties, bustled in.

'I'm sorry. Fatima Begam is sleeping,' Mehrunissa whispered.

'I can see that. When she wakes tell her I'll come back later. I have a pressing business matter about a cargo of indigo to discuss.' Sultana's tone was cool and her expression unfriendly as she turned to leave.

Mehrunissa had grown used to the coldness, even hostility, of some of the inmates of the *haram*, and to their curiosity. She had overheard two elderly women speculating why the widow of the murdered Sher Afghan should have been made a lady-in-waiting. 'She's young and good looking enough. What is she doing here? You'd have thought they'd have married her off again,' one had said.

It was a good question. What was she doing here? Mehrunissa wondered. On the opposite side of the chamber, Fatima Begam shifted position a little and started to snore.

·◆·

'The *khawajasara* has ordered everyone to the courtyard immediately,' one of Fatima Begam's maids, a thin, wiry little woman called Nadya, said. 'Even you must come, madam,' she added, bowing her head respectfully to her elderly mistress.

'Why? What has happened?' Fatima Begam didn't look best pleased at having her early evening meal disrupted, Mehrunissa thought.

'A concubine has been caught with one of the eunuchs. Some say he was more of a man than he pretended, others that they were just kissing. She is to be flogged.'

'When I was young such a crime would have meant death.' Fatima Begam's normally mild face was disapproving. 'What about the eunuch?'

70

'He has already been taken down to the parade ground to die under the elephant's foot.'

'Good,' said Fatima Begam. 'That is as it should be.'

Following Fatima Begam, Mehrunissa saw that the court-yard was already packed with chattering women, some looking apprehensive while others were curious and trying to manoeuvre for a better view of the centre of the court-yard where five female *haram* guards were erecting a wooden frame like a small gallows. 'Stand behind me,' Fatima Begam ordered Mehrunissa, 'and hold my handkerchief and scent bottle.'

One of the guards was now pushing with her strong bare arms against the punishment frame, testing its strength. She stepped back and nodded to another guard who put a short bronze horn to her lips and blew a shrill metallic blast. At the sound Mehrunissa saw the *khawajasara*, clad entirely in scarlet and walking with her customary slow, dignified pace, enter the courtyard from the right, the women parting to allow her through. Behind Mala, dragged along by two more female guards, was a plump young woman whose eyes were already streaming with tears and whose abject posture showed that she knew there would be no mercy. As the *khawajasara* approached the wooden frame she said, 'Strip her. Let the flogging begin.'

The guards who had been holding the woman pushed her forward on to her knees and roughly pulled off her silk bodice and long, full muslin trousers, tearing the delicate fabric and sending pearls from the tasselled fastenings rolling across the courtyard. One came to rest against Mehrunissa's foot. As the guards dragged her naked to the frame the woman began screaming, her body bucking and straining and her full breasts swaying as she struggled, but she was no match for their muscular strength and they had soon bound her ankles to the bottom corners of the frame and her wrists to the upper corners with hide thongs. The woman's hair was very long, falling to well beneath her buttocks. Drawing her dagger, one of the guards hacked it off just beneath the nape of her neck and let the shining mass fall in a coil to the ground. All around her, Mehrunissa caught a collective gasp. For a woman to forfeit her hair – one of her greatest beauties – was in itself a terrible, shaming thing.

Two of the female guards now stepped forward, stripped off their outer tunics and from the broad, studded leather belts round their waists pulled out short-handled whips with knotted cords. Taking their place on either side of the frame they raised their arms and began, first one, then the other, to lash the prisoner's already trembling, quivering body. At each blow they called out the number – 'one', 'two', 'three' – and each time the hissing cords bit into her soft smooth flesh the woman screamed out until her cries became one continuous almost animal shriek. Desperately but futilely she tried to twist her body out of reach of the whips. Blood was soon running down her back and spine and between her buttocks and speckling the paving stones beneath her. All around her Mehrunissa realised the courtyard had fallen silent.

'Nineteen', 'twenty' called out the guards, their own bodies now glistening with a sheen of sweat. By the fifteenth blow the limp, bleeding figure dangling from the frame had ceased its terrible screaming and looked unconscious. 'Enough,' said the khawajasara. 'Take her naked as she is and throw her out into the streets. She will find her natural place in the

72

whorehouses of the bazaar.' Then holding her staff of office out in front of her she made her way from the courtyard as a babble of voices broke out behind her.

Mehrunissa was trembling and she felt a little sick. She needed space and fresh air. Telling Fatima Begam that she felt unwell, she half ran to a fountain in the far corner of the swiftly emptying courtyard and sitting down on its marble rim splashed her face with water.

'Are you all right, madam?' She looked up to see Nadya.

'Yes. It's just that I've never witnessed anything like that. I didn't know that punishments in the *haram* could be so brutal.'

'She was lucky. Far more terrible things can happen than a flogging. Surely you've heard the story of Anarkali?'

Mehrunissa shook her head.

'She was bricked up alive in the dungeons of the imperial palace at Lahore. They say if you pass by at night you can still hear her sobbing to be let out.'

'What had she done to deserve such a death?'

'She was the Emperor Akbar's most prized concubine but took his son, our present emperor Jahangir, as her lover.'

Mehrunissa stared at the maid. Anarkali must be the name of the concubine whose embraces had caused Jahangir's exile to Kabul. What a terrible price to pay for a few moments' human frailty . . . 'What actually happened, Nadya?'

The maid's face lit up. It was clearly a tale she enjoyed telling. 'Akbar's passion for Anarkali was greater than for any other. She once told me that when they were alone he liked her to dance for him naked except for the jewels he gave her. One night at the time of the great Nauruz festival he gave a feast where he ordered Anarkali to perform before him and his nobles. Akbar's son Jahangir was one of the guests. He had never seen her before and her beauty so overcame him that he determined to have her even though she was his father's. He bribed the woman who was then the *khawajasara* to bring Anarkali to him when Akbar was away from court.'

'And they were discovered?'

'Not at first, no. But as Jahangir's lust for Anarkali grew, so also did his recklessness. The *khawajasara* became frightened and confessed everything to the emperor. Her reward was a quick rather than a slow death. Then the emperor ordered Anarkali and Jahangir to be brought before him. My uncle was one of Akbar's bodyguards and saw everything. He told me Anarkali pleaded for her life, her face wet with kohl-streaked tears, but Akbar was deaf and blind to her. Even when Jahangir shouted that he, not Anarkali, was to blame the emperor told him to be silent. He ordered Anarkali to be walled up and left to starve to death.

'As for the prince, my uncle said everyone was certain from the emperor's expression that Akbar was going to order his execution. As soon as Anarkali had been dragged away a deep silence fell on the assembled courtiers. But whatever his original intentions, however violent his rage, at the last moment Akbar could not bring himself to have his own son killed. Instead he exiled him with only his milk-brother for company.'

Mehrunissa nodded. 'I know. He was sent to Kabul while my father was treasurer there.'

'But that wasn't quite the end of Anarkali's story, at least I don't think it was . . .'

'What do you mean?'

'Within the *haram* it was whispered that Jahangir had persuaded his grandmother Hamida to ease Anarkali's suffering and that somehow before the last bricks of her prison were in place Hamida found a way to get a phial of poison to her so she could escape the torments of a long and agonising death.'

Despite the warm early evening air Mehrunissa shivered. First the flogging and now this horrible story. 'I should return to Fatima Begum,' she said. As she walked with Nadya across the courtyard, where the wooden frame had now been taken down and the blood washed from the paving stones, her head was still full of the tragedy of Anarkali. Had Akbar been a harsh and callous man? That wasn't how others spoke of him and was certainly not how her father remembered him. Ghiyas Beg had always praised the late emperor and the tolerance and justice with which he had governed. Perhaps in the heat of his anger Akbar had forgotten who he was and had lashed out as a man whose pride had been wounded rather than as an emperor who should be above inflicting such a vicious revenge on a weak woman with little power over her own destiny.

Jahangir . . . surely he had been the most to blame? What did the story tell her about his character? That he could be reckless and impulsive and selfish but also that he was capable of great passion and had courage. He had tried to shield Anarkali and take the blame on himself. When that failed he had done what he could to save her from further suffering. Mehrunissa thought of his fine physique, the compelling look in his eyes that had prompted her to drop her veil as she danced for him. It was strange, but the story of his doomed desire for Anarkali hadn't diminished him in her

75

eyes – almost the reverse. How exciting it could be to share life with a man like that, so full of virile energy and with so much power to wield.

Yet almost at once other more sober thoughts began to intrude. Weren't there disturbing similarities between Anarkali's story and her own? Jahangir had seen Anarkali only once and that had been enough to convince him he must have her and he had been ruthless in his pursuit of her. He had also seen her, Mehrunissa, only once and not so many months after Anarkali's death and had wanted her as well. It wasn't quite the same, she tried to convince herself. Jahangir had openly and honourably asked her father for her hand. When her father refused him, he had accepted it. Or had he?

Mehrunissa's brain was now working feverishly. Unbidden she saw before her once again the blue-eyed man riding past her during the descent through the passes from Kabul. At the time, she'd asked Ladli's nursemaid Farisha, a notorious and accomplished gossip, to find out who he was. Just two days later she had reported triumphantly that there was indeed a foreign soldier with blue eyes among the bodyguard – an Englishman whom the emperor had recently appointed. At the time that information had persuaded Mehrunissa she had been mistaken. Sher Afghan's murderer was said to be Portuguese. Also, as she'd continued to tell herself, these foreigners often looked alike and she'd only seen her husband's assassin for a few moments in dim light and in terrifying circumstances. Yet in her heart she had not been satisfied. How could she forget the look in those pale eyes as he had drawn his dagger across her husband's throat or mistake them when she saw them again?

But now Mehrunissa wondered whether she might be coming closer to the truth. Jahangir had wanted Anarkali and had allowed nothing to stand in his way. If he desired her, Mehrunissa, why should he be any less ruthless? For a second time Mehrunissa shivered but now it was for herself rather than for the dead concubine. It excited her physically to think that Jahangir wanted her so much, but Anarkali's fate showed that too intimate a contact with the imperial family could bring danger as well as reward . . .

Chapter 5

The Meena Bazaar

Jahangir felt his opponent's curved sword grate on the steel
mesh of the mail coat protecting his thigh before sliding off
to cut deep into his gilded leather saddle. Pulling hard on the
reins of his black horse he aimed a slashing sword cut at his
enemy's arm as the man struggled to pull back his own weapon
for another swing. However, he missed as the other rider reined
in so hard that his grey horse reared up. One of the animal's
flailing front hooves caught Jahangir's mount in the belly. The
other struck Jahangir's upper calf. It was a glancing blow but
it turned his lower leg numb and his foot slipped from its
stirrup.

As his horse swerved away whinnying in pain, Jahangir
lost his balance but quickly recovered, steadied his mount
and managed to get his foot back in the stirrup. Then the
other man was upon him again. Jahangir ducked down on
to the sweating neck of his black horse as his opponent's
sword hissed through the air just above the plume on his

helmet. Even if a rebel, the raja was a true warrior who had had the courage to pick him out in the charge, Jahangir just had time to think as he wheeled his horse again to face him. Both men dug their heels into their mounts' flanks and simultaneously charged forward. This time Jahangir aimed his stroke at his enemy's neck. First it caught the rim of a steel breastplate but then bit into flesh and sinew. At the same time Jahangir felt a stinging pain as the raja's curved sword sliced through his long leather gauntlet into his own sword arm and blood began to flow. Turning quickly, he saw his opponent slowly collapse sideways from his saddle and then hit the dusty ground with a thud which dislodged the sword from his right hand.

Jahangir leapt from his saddle and half running, half limping because of his damaged calf propelled himself towards the fallen man. Although crimson blood was streaming from the wound in his neck into his thick, curly black beard and down on to his breastplate, he was still trying to struggle to his feet.

'Surrender,' Jahangir demanded.

'And end my life in your dungeons? Never. I will die here on the red earth that has been my family's for so many generations – so many more than yours have claimed our land.' As the words mingled with blood bubbling through his lips he used his remaining reserves of strength to pull a long serrated-bladed dagger from a scabbard inside his riding boot. Before he could even draw his arm back to make his thrust Jahangir's sword cut into his neck once more, this time just above his Adam's apple, almost severing his head from his torso. He fell back, his pumping blood crimsoning the dust. His body twitched once or twice and then he lay still.

Jahangir stood over the lifeless corpse. His own blood was still running from the wound in his forearm down his hand into the fingers of his gauntlet where it was collecting, warm and sticky. Sensation was quickly returning to his calf but the sensation was pain. Pulling his face cloth from around his neck with his uninjured hand he dabbed roughly at the calf wound, where the flailing hoof had penetrated not only the skin but also the layer of creamy fat beneath, exposing the purple-red of his muscle.

He could easily have been killed, losing his life and his throne before he had even begun to fulfil his ambitions. Why against all the advice of his counsellors had he decided to lead in person the campaign against the Raja of Mirzapur who now lay sprawled dead before him? Why had he himself led the charge against the raja's forces, outdistancing his bodyguard just as he had done in the battle against Khusrau? The raja had after all been no real threat to his throne, merely a recalcitrant vassal, the ruler of a small state on the borders of the Rajasthani desert who had refused to pay his annual tribute to the imperial treasury. Part of the answer was the one that he had repeated to his counsellors – to show that he would brook no defiance from any of his subordinates however mighty or humble and that he would rely on no one else to deal out punishments to rebels.

However, he could admit to himself that there was an additional reason for leading the expedition in person. It was a distraction from his thoughts of Mehrunissa, removing him from Agra and the almost irresistible temptation to call her to him despite the Sufi's prohibition. Feeling suddenly faint from heat and loss of blood Jahangir called to his men for water. Then the world began to spin before him.

A few minutes later he came back to consciousness to find himself lying on a blanket on the ground while two serious-faced *hakims* bent over him as they worked to staunch and bind his wounds beneath the desert sun. With returning consciousness came a sudden thought. Now the raja was dead and the campaign over he would be easily back in Agra in time for the New Year's celebrations. Surely they would provide an opportunity for him at least to meet Mehrunissa once more without breaking the Sufi's strictures to take no specific initiative to do so. Despite the sharp prick of pain as one of the *hakims'* needles went through the skin of his forearm, as the man began to stitch the two sides of his wound together Jahangir could not suppress a smile.

· ◆ ·

'Well, what do you think of the Agra fort?' Mehrunissa asked her niece as they sat in Ghiyas Beg's apartments. How beautiful Arjumand Banu was, she was thinking. She hadn't seen her since she was a young child in Kabul. She was fourteen now but had none of the clumsy awkwardness of many girls of her age. Her face was a delicate oval, the brows finely arched, and her thick dark hair fell almost to her waist. Her looks came from her Persian mother who had died when she was only four but her eyes, like her father's, Asaf Khan's, were black.

'I've never seen anything like it – so many attendants, so many courtyards and fountains, so many jewels. As we entered the fort they beat drums in the gatehouse in my father's honour.' Arjumand was still sparkling with the novelty of it all.

Mehrunissa smiled. How she wished she were that age again . . . 'Ever since Akbar's reign, the drums have been sounded to honour the arrival of a victorious commander. I was very proud to hear them as well.'

Some weeks previously Mehrunissa's father had written joyfully that her elder brother Asaf Khan had so distinguished himself while fighting away to the south in the Deccan that the emperor had summoned him to Agra to command the garrison here. Asaf Khan had reached the city two weeks ago. It had taken Mehrunissa this long to obtain leave first from Fatima Begam and then from the officious *khawajasara* to visit Ghiyas Beg's apartments and she was eager to see her brother.

'Where is your father? I've only permission to remain here until sunset.'

'He is with the emperor discussing plans for some new fortifications but he promised he would come as soon as he could.'

Mehrunissa could hear her mother singing to Ladli in a room just off the courtyard. The child had adjusted quickly to her absence and though she knew she should be glad it still hurt a little to realise that her daughter didn't really miss her. Her family was thriving. Ghiyas Beg's duties as Imperial Treasurer were keeping him very busy, so her mother told her, while Asaf Khan was clearly high in Jahangir's favour. It was only she, Mehrunissa, who was the failure. She had still heard nothing from the emperor and the monotony of serving Fatima Begam was growing daily more irksome.

'What is it, Aunt? You look sad.'

'It's nothing. I was just thinking what a very long time it's been since we were all together.'

'And the emperor's women? His wives and concubines, what are they like?' Arjumand persisted.

Mehrunissa shook her head. 'I haven't seen them. They live in a separate area of the *haram* where the emperor eats and sleeps. I live where the women, like my mistress, are nearly all old.'

Arjumand looked disappointed. 'That's not how I imagined the imperial *haram*.'

'Neither did I—' At that moment Mehrunissa heard footsteps in the corridor, then Asaf Khan strode in.

'Sister! The attendants told me I would find you here.' Before she had quite risen from her seat he had enfolded her in his arms, almost lifting her from the floor. He was as tall as their father but broader and square jawed. He was smiling at her. 'You've changed. You were just a girl when I last saw you – not much older than Arjumand, and a lot more gawky. But look at you now . . .'

'It's good to see you too, Asaf Khan. When I last saw you, you were only a young officer with spots and spindly legs,' she countered. 'Now you command the Agra garrison.'

Asaf Khan shrugged. 'The emperor has been good to me. I hope our brother is as fortunate. If I can I will get Mir Khan transferred here from Gwalior so that the family can really be together. It would please our parents, especially our mother . . . But more news. The emperor has invited our family to attend the Royal Meena Bazaar in the Agra fort next month.'

'What is it?' Arjumand turned puzzled eyes on her father but Mehrunissa answered.

'The bazaar is part of the Nauruz – the eighteen-day New Year celebration the Emperor Akbar introduced to mark the sun entering into Aries. Fatima Begam is always complaining that two weeks before it starts all you can hear in the *haram* is the sound of workmen hammering and banging as they erect the pavilion in the fort's gardens.'

'And the Royal Meena Bazaar?'

'One of the festival's most important events. It's like a real bazaar except the only customers are royalty and nobility. It takes place at night in the fort gardens. The courtiers' wives and daughters – women like us – spread out trinkets and swathes of silk on tables and play the part of traders, bantering and bargaining with their would-be purchasers – royal matrons and princesses and, of course, the emperor and his sons. The festival is so intimate that all the women go unveiled.'

'Father, I can go, can't I?' Arjumand was suddenly looking anxious.

'Of course. Now, I must leave you again. I've more military business to attend to but I'll be back soon.'

After Asaf Khan had left, Mehrunissa sat with Arjumand Banu trying to answer the girl's eager questions. But her mind was elsewhere. Fatima Begam had told her all about the bazaar but she had not been approving and had said things Mehrunissa certainly couldn't tell her niece. 'The Meena Bazaar is a meat market – no more, no less. Akbar started it because he wanted a chance to select new bedfellows. If any unmarried woman caught his eye he would order the *khawajasara* to prepare her for his pleasure.' Looking at the frown on the old woman's usually genial face, Mehrunissa guessed that long ago something had happened

84

at the bazaar to offend her. Perhaps she had resented Akbar's promiscuous sexual appetites. Deep down Mehrunissa felt as excited as Arjumand – the bazaar was one place she could be sure of seeing the emperor. But would Fatima Begam allow her to attend?

·◆·

As the evening candles were being lit in Fatima Begam's claustrophobic apartments a week later Mehrunissa had her answer. Ever since she'd told her of the invitation the old lady had equivocated. Now, even though Mehrunissa had dressed herself in her finest clothes and put on her best jewels, Fatima Begam had assumed a stubborn expression Mehrunissa knew well.

'I have decided. You are a widow. It would not be seemly for you to attend the bazaar. And I am too old for such things. Read some Persian poetry to me instead. That will be pleasanter for us both than all that noise and vulgarity.'

Biting her lip, Mehrunissa picked up a volume of poems and with fingers trembling with frustration slowly undid the silver clasps on the rosewood covers.

·◆·

The great courtyard of the Agra fort had been transformed, thought Khurram as, to three trumpet bursts, he and his elder brother Parvez entered it behind their father Jahangir, all three dressed in cloth of gold. Candles burning in globes of coloured glass suspended from the branches of trees and bushes and from artificial trees of silver and gold cast moving jewel-bright shadows – red, blue, yellow, green – in the soft breeze. Around the walls he could see the velvet-draped

85

stalls heaped with trinkets and the women waiting behind them. It looked as splendid as in his grandfather's time. He could vividly recall Akbar's pleasure in the whole Nauruz festival. 'Being wealthy is good – indeed it is a necessity. But showing that you are wealthy is even more important for a monarch.'

Akbar had understood the meaning of magnificence. Some of Khurram's earliest memories were of sitting by his grandfather's side in a glittering howdah as they rode through the streets of Agra. Akbar had always believed in showing himself to his people and they had loved him for it. Akbar had been like the sun and some of his radiance had fallen on himself, Khurram thought. Yet his father Jahangir who, sparkling with diamonds, was now moving among his nobles had been kept in the shadows. Even as a child Khurram had sensed tensions all around him – between his father and his grandfather and between his father and his eldest half-brother Khusrau who, instead of being here to share in the first Nauruz of their father's reign, was incarcerated in a dungeon in Gwalior. Khusrau had been a fool as well as disloyal, Khurram thought, following his father towards a dais draped in silver cloth that had been erected in the centre of the courtyard beneath a canopy of the same material, which shimmered in the light of the torches burning on either side of it.

Jahangir mounted the dais and began to speak. 'Tonight is the climax of our Nauruz celebrations when we hail the new lunar year. My astrologers tell me that the year ahead will be one of even greater glory for our empire. Now is the time to honour the women of my court. Until the stars begin to fade from the heavens they, not us, are the masters here. Unless we can persuade them otherwise, what they demand for their goods we must pay. Let the Royal Meena Bazaar begin.'

Jahangir descended from the dais. It seemed to Khurram that his father stopped for a moment and looked round him as if seeking someone in particular, and then an expression of disappointment crossed his face. But Jahangir composed himself and made his way towards a table spread with maroon velvet presided over by a smiling matron Khurram recognised as one of Parvez's milk-mothers. Parvez followed close behind but Khurram held back. The woman was garrulous and he wasn't in the mood for long stories about himself and his brother as children. His tight-fitting coat was heavy and uncomfortable. He flexed his broad shoulders beneath the stiff cloth and felt a trickle of sweat run down between his shoulder blades.

Instead of following his father, Khurram wandered towards a quieter part of the courtyard where he guessed the more junior women had their stalls. Perhaps there would be a pretty face among them, though for the moment a round-hipped, high-bosomed dancer from the Agra bazaar was absorbing most of his energies. Then Khurram noticed, almost in the shadows of a luxuriant sweep of white-flowered jasmine growing on the courtyard wall, a small stall on which were displayed some pieces of pottery. Behind the stall stood a tall, slender girl. He couldn't make out her face but he caught the gleam of pearls and diamonds in the long, thick hair that swung around her as she rearranged her goods. Khurram came closer. She was humming to herself and wasn't aware of him until he was standing just a few feet away. In her surprise her black eyes widened.

Khurram had never seen such a perfect face. 'I didn't mean to startle you. What are you selling?'

87

The girl didn't answer but held out a vase painted in vivid blues and greens. It was pretty enough but ordinary. However, there was nothing ordinary about those sparkling, thickly lashed eyes shyly watching him. Khurram felt stupid and tongue-tied and fixed his gaze on the vase, trying to think of something to say about it.

'I painted it. Do you like it?' the girl said. Raising his eyes to her again he saw she was looking a little amused. She must be about fourteen or fifteen, he thought. Her skin had the soft sheen of the pearls brought to the court by Arab traders and her wide lips were soft and pink.

'I like it. How much will you take?'

'What will you give?' She put her head on one side.

'Anything you ask.'

'You are a rich man, then?'

Khurram's green eyes flashed in surprise. Hadn't she seen him enter the courtyard and stand by the dais while his father spoke? Even if not, surely everyone knew the emperor's sons . . . 'I'm rich enough.'

'Good.'

'How long have you been at court?'

'Four weeks.'

'Where were you before then?'

'My father Asaf Khan is an officer in the emperor's armies. He was serving in the Deccan until the emperor promoted him to command the Agra garrison.'

'Arjumand . . . I hadn't meant to leave you on your own for so long . . .' A woman elegantly dressed in honey-coloured robes whose fine-boned face bore an unmistakable resemblance to the girl's came hurrying up. She was a little out of breath but when she saw Khurram she drew herself up

88

and inclined her head, saying quietly, 'Thank you for visiting our stall, Highness. Our goods are simple but my granddaughter made them all herself.'

'They are very fine. I will buy them all. Just name your price.'

'Arjumand, that is for you to say.'

Arjumand, who had been studying Khurram earnestly, looked uncertain, then said, 'One gold *mohur*.'

'I will give you ten. *Qorchi*, I need ten *mohurs*,' Khurram called to his squire, standing a few feet behind him. The *qorchi* came forward and held out the money to Arjumand. 'No, give it to me.' The squire poured the stream of gold coins into his right palm. Slowly Khurram raised his hand and offered the money to the girl. The breeze was rising and Arjumand looked as if she were bathed in every colour of the rainbow from the glass globes swaying all around. She took the coins from him one by one. The feel of her fingertips brushing against his skin was the most sensual thing he had ever experienced. Shocked, he glanced at her face and saw in her black eyes the proof that she felt the same. When the last coin was gone he lowered his hand again. He had wanted the feel of her flesh against his to go on for ever . . . Suddenly he felt confused, uncertain what he was feeling.

'Thank you.' Turning, he walked quickly away. It was only when he was back among the noisy laughing crowds around the main stalls that he realised he hadn't taken his purchases and that she hadn't called after him.

• ◆ •

Jamila ran her fingers teasingly across Khurram's sweat-soaked chest. 'You were a tiger tonight, Highness.' She nibbled his ear and on her breath he could smell the cardamom she loved to chew.

'Stop.' He pushed her hand away and gently disengaging himself stood up. Through the wooden screen that separated the cubicle where she slept from the room next door where she and the rest of the dancers ate, he could see an old woman vigorously sweeping the beaten earth floor with a broom of dry twigs. She made a good living from the fees the girls charged their customers.

Khurram stooped to splash some water from an earthenware dish resting on a metal stand on to his face.

'What's the matter? Did I displease you?' Jamila said, but her confident smile showed that she had few doubts about her performance.

'No. Of course you didn't.'

'Then what is it?' Jamila turned on her side.

He looked down at the round pretty face, the plump voluptuousness of the woman who had been his plaything for the past six months. He enjoyed the raucous atmosphere of the bazaar and the girls – so free and easy – seemed less intimidating than the concubines the *khawajasara* could have procured for him in the Agra fort where so many eyes were constantly upon him. Jamila had taught him all about lovemaking. He had been fumbling, over-eager, but she had shown him how to please a woman and how giving pleasure could enhance his own. Her warm pliant body, her inventiveness, had enthralled him. But no longer.

He had thought making love with Jamila would cure him of his obsession with Arjumand but it hadn't. Even while he was possessing Jamila's body it was Arjumand's face he saw. Though it was two months since the Royal

90

Meena Bazaar, he couldn't get Asaf Khan's daughter out of his head.

'Come back to bed. You must have some energy left and I have something new to show you . . .' Jamila's coaxing voice cut into his thoughts. She was sitting up, the nipples on her henna-tipped breasts erect, and he felt the familiar stirring in his groin. But it would be just one more coupling. He and Jamila were like mating beasts, hot and hungry for the moment with no real feeling for each other. If he didn't come to her she would find others, and if she and her dancing troupe left Agra he would easily find a replacement. Their frenetic love-making, driving one another beyond control, was no more than the satisfying of an itch. Now, with thoughts of Arjumand constantly in his mind, it was no longer enough for him.

• ◆ •

'Father, I want to ask you something.'

'What is it?' Jahangir put down the miniature painting of a nilgai that he had been examining in his private apartments. The court artist had captured every detail, including the bluish tinge of the antelope's coat, the delicate shape of its eyes . . .

Khurram hesitated. 'Could we be alone . . .'

'Leave us,' Jahangir ordered his attendants.

Almost before the doors had closed behind the last of the servants, Khurram blurted out, 'I'd like to take a wife.'

Jahangir looked at his son – nearly sixteen and already tall and muscular as a grown man. Few of his officers could beat Khurram at wrestling or in a sword fight.

'You are right,' Jahangir looked thoughtful. 'I was around

91

your age when I took my first wife, but we need not rush. I shall consider who would make you a suitable bride. The Rajput ruler of Jaisalmer has daughters and an alliance with his family would please our Hindu subjects. Or I could look beyond our empire. A marriage with one of the Shah of Persia's family might make him more willing to give up his ambitions to take Kandahar from the Moghuls . . .' Jahangir's mind was racing away. He would summon his vizier Majid Khan and perhaps some of his other councillors to discuss the matter. 'I am pleased you have raised this with me, Khurram. It shows your maturity and that you are indeed ready to take your first wife. We'll talk again when I have thought further about it – but it will be soon, I promise.'

'I already know the woman I would like as my wife.' Khurram's tone was emphatic and the expression in his green eyes serious.

Jahangir blinked in surprise. 'Who?'

'The daughter of the commander of your garrison in Agra.'

'Asaf Khan's daughter? Where did you see her?'

'At the Royal Meena Bazaar. Her name is Arjumand.'

'How old is she? Asaf Khan is young to have a daughter of marriageable age.'

'Perhaps a little younger than me.'

Jahangir frowned. His first impulse had been that this was just some youthful infatuation – perhaps it still was – but it was strange. The young woman who had caught Khurram's eye must be Mehrunissa's niece and thus the granddaughter of his treasurer Ghiyas Beg. Something his grandmother Hamida had said to him many years ago when Ghiyas Beg had first arrived penniless and despairing at Akbar's court came into his mind. What was it? Something like, *So much that happens appears random, yet I have often discerned patterns running through our existence as if at the hand of a divine weaver at the loom . . . one day this Ghiyas Beg might become important to our dynasty.* Hamida had had the gift of second sight. Only a fool would dismiss her words.

'Khurram. You are still very young but I can see that your mind is made up. If your heart is set on this girl, I will not object and I myself will slip the betrothal ring on her finger to signal the alliance between her family and ours. All that I ask is that you wait a while before you marry.'

Jahangir saw the surprise on his son's face — clearly he hadn't anticipated such an easy victory — but then it gave way to a smile of delight and Khurram embraced him. 'I will wait and do whatever else you ask . . .'

'I will summon Asaf Khan. There are things he and I should discuss. Until that time, be discreet. Say nothing about this even to your mother.'

When he was alone, Jahangir sat for a while, his head in his hands. His interview with Khurram had sparked many thoughts. Unlike Khusrau, whose treachery he could still not forgive, Khurram had been nothing but a loyal son of whom any man would be proud. He wished he could have been so confident at Khurram's age and also that he knew his son better, but Akbar's extreme partiality for his favourite grandson had made that difficult. Khurram had been brought up in Akbar's household. It was his grandfather — not his father — who had led the procession taking the prince to school for the first time. But that was all past, and in recent months father and son had been spending more time together.

All the same, he had surprised himself by agreeing so

readily to Khurram's request. A prince of the Moghul empire could take his pick of wives. Though Arjumand came from a noble Persian family it wasn't a match that would ever have occurred to him. But as he knew only too well, choice didn't always come into it. It hadn't with Humayun and Hamida. He hadn't asked to feel as he did about Mehrunissa so he could hardly blame his son for falling so precipitately in love. The women of Ghiyas Beg's family seemed to possess power to bewitch the men of his own, but like Khurram he too must wait . . .

Chapter 6

The Executioner's Sword

'Madam, wake up.' Someone seemed to be shaking her shoulder vigorously and Mehrunissa wondered whether she was dreaming, but opening sleepy eyes she saw Nadya leaning over her.

'What is it? Why have you woken me?' The maid had placed a lighted oil lamp on the marble table next to her bed and in the warm draughts blowing through the open casement it cast a flickering orange glow.

'A note has come for you. The messenger who left it at the *haram* gates said it must be delivered immediately.' Mehrunissa could see the maid was almost quivering with curiosity. Heart thumping, she sat up and took the sealed paper Nadya was holding out to her. News that came in the hours of darkness could only be bad. Her fingers shook a little as she unfolded the letter and recognised her niece's flowing hand. The note had been written in haste. There were uncharacteristic blots and several words had been crossed out.

Aunt, something terrible has happened. My father is away in Delhi on military business and my grandmother and I have no one else to turn to. Tonight while I was at my grandparents' apartments in the fort, guards came to arrest my grandfather. They claim he is part of a plot directed by Prince Khusrau from his prison cell in Gwalior to kill the emperor and that Khusrau had promised to reward him for his help in seizing the imperial treasuries by making him his vizier. You know what my grandfather is like — always so calm, so dignified. He went quietly, telling us not to worry, but I could see how shocked he was and also that he was afraid.

There was more, but Mehrunissa could scarcely absorb what she had already read. Her father Ghiyas Beg, who had served Akbar and then Jahangir so loyally for over two decades, arrested for plotting to kill the emperor . . . it was incredible. For a moment she wondered whether she wasn't still asleep and this wasn't some outlandish nightmare, but the high-pitched droning of a mosquito hovering somewhere close, and the strong musky scent of the perfume Nadya always wore, were undeniably real.

'What is it? Not bad news, I hope?' asked Nadya, eyes bright.

'It is a family matter. You may go, but leave the lamp so I have light to read by.'

When she was certain the maid had gone Mehrunissa pushed her long hair back from her face and looked again at Arjumand's note, her blood chilling in her veins as she took in its full import. Her father's life was at risk and their whole family faced ruin or worse. The idea of Arjumand marrying Prince Khurram now was laughable, and as for

96

her own hopes . . . For a moment she couldn't help glancing fearfully towards the still-swaying brocade hangings, expecting any moment to see the fragile fabric swept aside as eunuchs and *haram* guards rushed to arrest her also.

She must stay calm. Holding Arjumand's note tightly she read on. *As they were taking my grandfather away one of the guards told him, 'Your son Mir Khan was arrested on the same charge in Gwalior two days ago and brought to Agra in chains.' My grandmother is ill with worry. Please help us, Aunt. Tell us what we should do.* The note ended with a scrawled *Arjumand*.

Mehrunissa rose from her bed and folding the note placed it carefully on the table beside the oil lamp. Then she walked over to the casement and leaned her hands on the still-warm sandstone ledge. Below she could see two female guards patrolling the *haram* courtyard, their torches of pitch-dipped rags sending shadows leaping around them. From nearby she heard the court timekeeper, the *ghariyali*, striking the hour – once, twice, thrice . . . Glancing up at the sky she saw the patterns of bright stars splashed across its inky depths. Somehow the stars' cold remote beauty, so far removed from the troubles of the world, gave her strength, calming her and helping her to think more clearly.

Her father Ghiyas Beg, honourable and loyal to a fault, was guiltless, she was certain. Any accusations against him must be the result of misunderstanding or jealousy. But what about her younger brother, Mir Khan? She could not be so sure. They had grown up together in Kabul. She had always known he lacked her intelligence or that of Asaf Khan – or their inner strength. Mir Khan was vain and didn't recognise his limitations. He was also easily led, as she well knew. Time and again when they were children she had coaxed him to

97

some rash act to her benefit not his. She still blushed to recall how once she had persuaded him to climb along the rotting limb of an apricot tree to gather fruit for her. The branch had broken and he had fallen to the ground.

That was a long time ago. Mir Khan should have learned sense and discretion, but the advancement that had come early to Asaf Khan would never be his. Had frustration, jealousy of his elder brother and sugared promises of great rewards prompted him to join some wild scheme? She had no way of knowing. Her younger brother could be as innocent as Ghiyas Beg. She shouldn't rush to judge him. What mattered now was deciding coolly and rationally what to do. Her own and her family's fate – even their lives – were hanging in the balance. She mustn't be rash, but failure to act could be as fatal . . .

She could write to Asaf Khan in Delhi. Indeed, he might already have learned what had happened and be galloping back towards Agra. Together they could decide how best to try to save their family. Yet maybe he too had been implicated in the plot and was even now under guard. No, she couldn't wait to discover Asaf Khan's fate. She and she alone must act.

After an hour restlessly pacing her small apartment, with the thin, pale light of dawn creeping over the horizon Mehrunissa sat down cross-legged at her writing table. Dipping her pen into her green onyx inkpot – a present from her father – she penned a few swift words to Arjumand. *Wait quietly with my grandmother for your father to return and do nothing until you hear from me again. Trust in me.* As soon as she had finished she sprinkled fine sand over the wet ink to blot it, folded the paper and after warming the end of a stick of wax let it drip on to the join and stamped it with her seal, which was engraved with the eagle emblem used by her family in Persia for centuries. She seldom used the seal but did so now because the sight of the haughty eagle, recalling her family's long, illustrious past, gave her courage to take the step she had decided upon but had not revealed to Arjumand.

Reaching again for her inkpot she began to write a letter to Jahangir. *Majesty, I would not dare address you were it not for my love for my family and the duty I owe them to preserve their honour. Please, Majesty, grant me an audience. Mehrunissa, daughter of Ghiyas Beg.* Again she folded her letter and reached for the wax, and after a few moments the soft blood-red drops began to fall.

• ◆ •

The day had passed with painful slowness. Dusk would soon be falling. Everyone must know what had happened, Mehrunissa thought. Fatima Begam hadn't summoned her. In fact, no one had come near her, not even the ever-curious Nadya. They must fear the contagion of coming too close to Ghiyas Beg's family, not that she cared. Yet over twelve hours had passed since she had sent her letter to Jahangir, bribing the servant who had taken it with gold and telling her to make sure she gave it straight into the hands of a servant of Jahangir's vizier Majid Khan with the message that it was from Ghiyas Beg's daughter. From what she had learned of him Majid Khan was a just man who had in recent months become a regular visitor to her father's house, but maybe even he would now distance himself from Ghiyas Beg. She imagined the vizier holding her letter in the flame of a candle, turning her last hopes to ashes.

'Come with me at once.' Mehrunissa spun round. She hadn't heard the *khawajasara* enter and it was a shock to find Mala barely four feet away. The woman's expression was cold as she gestured towards the door with her staff of office. Mehrunissa had dressed in her finest blue silk robe embroidered with irises in silver thread in case the emperor should call for her, but looking at Mala's disdainful face she doubted whether that was why the *khawajasara* had come. More likely she was being ejected from the imperial *haram*, in which case she certainly wasn't going to leave without her favourite possessions like her inkpot and especially her jewels. She picked up a fine Kashmir shawl, a gift from Asaf Khan, and was reaching for her jewel casket when the *khawajasara* snapped, 'Leave everything. Come exactly as you are now. Just veil yourself.'

Mehrunissa put down the shawl, fastened her veil and lowered her eyes submissively. And so my life goes full circle, she thought, following Mala's tall, green-clad figure out of her apartment, along the passage and across the *haram* courtyard where the evening candelabras had already been lit. As she saw the sidelong glances, heard the ill-concealed remarks, tears pricked her eyelids but she drew herself up proudly and took her time. Though the *khawajasara* was walking quickly she would not be hurried from the *haram* like some whipped dog.

But then she realised that Mala wasn't leading her towards the *haram* gates directly in front of them. Instead she had turned sharply to the left and was ascending a flight of shallow stone steps leading up to a part of the fort

Mehrunissa had never seen. Her heart juddered against her ribs. Where was Mala taking her? The *khawajasara* paused at the top of the steps and looked back over her shoulder. 'Hurry up.' Mehrunissa gathered up the skirt of her blue robe and began to climb. Reaching the top she found herself on a broad terrace. Directly opposite were tall double doors covered in shining silver leaf inlaid with semi-precious stones. Mala was conversing rapidly with four red-turbaned Rajput guards posted outside them and gesticulating towards Mehrunissa.

The guards flung the doors open. Mala waited until Mehrunissa had caught up, then grasping her by the wrist marched her through into a wide corridor lined with brocade hangings. The air was heavily perfumed from the incense and spices smouldering in gold burners fashioned like male peacocks, the outspread tails set with emeralds and sapphires. Ahead were two further doors even higher and wider and made of gold inlaid with ivory and tortoiseshell. Outside these were stationed ten Rajput guards standing to attention with steel-tipped spears. 'Where are we?' she whispered to Mala.

'This is His Majesty's own entrance into the imperial *haram*. Through those doors are his private apartments.'

'You are taking me to the emperor?'

'Yes. No doubt he will decide what is to be done with you.'

Mehrunissa wasn't listening. In the few precious moments that remained she was running through the speech she had practised over and over in her mind since despatching her letter to Jahangir. Those great golden doors were opening now. Mala was standing to one side and she must go forward alone. Raising her head, she stepped through the doors.

The emperor was seated on a low dais at the far end of the room. Mehrunissa had expected to see *qorchis*, attendants, guards even, to protect the emperor's life against the daughter and sister of supposed traitors, but she was alone with him. Lengthening shadows falling through the casement and the effect of the flickering candlelight made it hard for her to distinguish Jahangir's expression. When she was still about fifteen feet away, just as she had planned she flung herself face down before him, her loose hair flowing out around her. Also as she had planned she didn't wait for Jahangir to speak.

'Majesty, thank you for your great goodness in granting me an audience. I am here to plead before you on behalf of my father, Ghiyas Beg. I swear on my life that he would never do anything to harm you, his benefactor, who has given him everything. My father would never plead for himself so I must do it. I only seek justice.' Mehrunissa did not move, face pushed into the thick carpet, arms outstretched on either side of her.

But from the man on the shadowy dais before her came not a sound. She resisted the temptation to raise her head, but just when she felt she could no longer bear not to look at him, his strong hands were under her arms, raising her to her feet. She closed her eyes. Now that he was so close to her she could not look into his face for fear of what she might see – condemnation not compassion. His hands dropped from her shoulders but then she felt him unfastening one corner of her veil. She opened her eyes and for the second time in her life looked into his. There was the face

102

she remembered from all those years ago in Kabul. No longer unlined but even handsomer except for the hard, cold expression which, as she took it in, made her suddenly feel sick and faint. Jahangir was looking at her intently but not a muscle betrayed his thoughts. After a few moments he turned away, remounted his dais and sat down again. 'Your father and your brother have both been questioned.'

'My father is innocent of any crime,' Mehrunissa said, struggling to keep her voice calm and controlled. 'Who accuses him?'

'The governor of the Gwalior fortress. His spies overheard my son discussing with your brother Mir Khan whether the Shah of Persia might be persuaded to send troops to help overthrow me if he was promised Kandahar. Your brother replied that Ghiyas Beg still had influence at the Persian court . . . he implied he might be induced to join in the plot.'

Mehrunissa flushed with anger. She could just picture Mir Khan so puffed up with conceit at being the confidant of a prince that he would say or do anything . . . She raised her chin. 'Such an idea is beneath contempt. Mir Khan was just trying to impress. My father left Persia before I was born. He cut all his links with his homeland when he became an official of the Moghul empire which he has served so well. Even if he could be bought – which he could not – what sense would it make when his granddaughter is about to marry Prince Khurram for him to support another of your sons against you?'

Jahangir was regarding her steadily. If he still retained any feelings for her, he was hiding them well, she thought.

'You speak soundly, but even before you argued with such

103

passion I had already decided that Ghiyas Beg had no know-ledge of the plot,' he said at last. 'I have known him a long time and believe he is a man of integrity.'

My father is safe, thought Mehrunissa. For a moment everything seemed to go dark around her and she put her hand to her eyes, willing herself to be strong.

'But the same isn't true of your brother . . .'

'My brother . . .'

'The evidence against Mir Khan is overwhelming. Even though at first he denied everything, after some . . . let's say persuasion . . . he has confessed that my traitorous son Prince Khusrau offered him great rewards to join a plot against me and that he agreed.'

Mehrunissa said nothing.

'You came here seeking justice. You have just shown me what a logical mind you have. What would you do if you were me?'

She stared down at the richly patterned carpet woven with a design of blood-red flowers against a dark blue back-ground as memories of Mir Khan as a cheerful, thoughtless child edging his way along the rotten bough of the apricot tree, laughing and reaching out his hand to pluck her some fruits, pierced her with an almost physical pain. 'Majesty.' Her voice was cool and controlled, with not the slightest tremor. 'You have no choice. Mir Khan is a traitor. Execute him. That is what I would do if I were you.'

'In your letter you spoke of your love for your family. Is it the act of a loving sister to counsel the death of a brother?'

'In Persia there is a saying: "If a tree produces bitter fruit cut it down to save the rest of the orchard." Mir Khan has betrayed the duty he owed to you as his emperor and the duty he owes to his family. He is the diseased tree. The rest of his family are the orchard.'

'Very well. Let it be as you advise.' Leaning down Jahangir picked up a large brass bell beside him and rang it vigorously. Its metallic clang had barely sounded more than two or three times before a *qorchi* entered through a side door to the right of the dais.

'Majesty?'

'Bring the traitor Mir Khan before me.'

Neither Mehrunissa nor Jahangir, sitting motionless on his dais, spoke as the minutes passed. She was steeling herself for the next stage in what had been the longest ordeal of her life. It must be about seven o'clock in the evening – fifteen hours after Nadya had woken her with Arjumand Banu's terrified note. Though mentally exhausted she must not let her resolve weaken. Only by keeping strong could she get through this and save herself and her family.

The sound of male voices and approaching footsteps jerked her out of her thoughts. The *qorchi* came into the apartment through the same side door, then stood to one side of it and called, 'Bring in Mir Khan.'

Two guards entered dragging a third man between them. As they approached the dais in the flickering candlelight, Mehrunissa had to force herself not to look away. The guards halted level with where she was standing and pushed the man forward on to the ground. Mir Khan fell unresistingly. Indeed, he looked barely conscious. As he had tumbled forward she had seen his battered, bloodied face. His clothes were ripped and through the rents she saw what looked like raw, red burn marks on his back, perhaps made with a hot iron. She told herself Mir Khan must pay for his mistakes

105

– that he must be the sacrifice that would save the rest of them – but it was almost more than she could bear to see her tortured younger brother lying on the floor beside her. Conscious that Jahangir's gaze was fixed on her and not on Mir Khan, she strained to maintain her composure. After a moment the emperor turned to the prisoner.

'Mir Khan, what do you have to say for yourself?'

Mir Khan's whole body was shaking convulsively. One of the guards seized his long black hair and pulled back his head. 'Answer His Majesty.'

Mir Khan muttered something incomprehensible and the guard pulled back his booted foot and kicked him hard in the pit of the stomach. This time he managed to force out a few words. 'Forgive me, Majesty.'

'There can be no forgiveness for treachery. You deserve a traitor's death. Even your sister has advised your execution.' Mehrunissa flinched as Mir Khan turned his despairing eyes on her. 'I should have you crushed beneath the foot of the execution elephant or impaled as I did my son's supporters in his previous revolt whose fate you were too stupid to learn from.' Jahangir's tone was chill. It was all Mehrunissa could do not to throw herself down beside Mir Khan and despite her former words plead for mercy for him. However, Jahangir went on, 'For the sake of your sister who has shown a courage you could never possess I will spare you the slow and agonising departure from this life you deserve. Have you anything to say before you die?'

Mir Khan struggled to his knees but when he spoke his words were for his sister, not the emperor. To her intense relief they were not of anger nor of reproach. 'Mehrunissa . . . forgive me . . .'

'I forgive you, brother.' Her mouth was so dry the words came slowly.

'And ask our father and Asaf Khan to forgive me too. They knew nothing about the plot . . . and tell our mother I love her and not to grieve.' Mir Khan was sobbing now, tears dissolving the dried blood on his battered face.

'Send for the executioner,' Jahangir ordered. The man must have been waiting outside for almost at once a tall black-turbaned man in a metal-studded leather tunic holding a double-headed axe and with what looked like a rolled length of animal hide beneath his other muscular arm entered.

'Majesty?'

'Behead this man.'

Hearing Jahangir's words, Mir Khan collapsed to the floor again. The executioner unrolled the hide, then pulled back the carpet in front of the dais and spread the skin out carefully on the stone flags. When he was ready he nodded to the guards. Mir Khan was still sobbing as the guards grabbed hold of him and dragged him forward on to the hide. 'Stretch out your neck,' the executioner ordered. As one guard pulled his right arm out from his body, which was now shaking convulsively, and the other guard extended his left one, Mehrunissa watched her brother in what must have been a supreme act of courage slowly extend his own neck. The executioner brushed his dark hair from his exposed nape then, satisfied, stepped back and picked up his axe. After carefully balancing the weight of it in his hands he looked enquiringly over his shoulder at Jahangir, who gave a brief nod.

Mehrunissa saw the curved blade gleam in the candlelight

as the executioner swung the axe high above him. She felt the rush of air against her cheek as he brought it down, then heard the thud of steel on flesh and bone as the blade sliced cleanly through her brother's neck and saw the bright spurt of blood as his head hit the floor with another duller thud. For some moments Mehrunissa was numb. Then came a comforting realisation – the executioner knew his business. Her brother hadn't suffered. She had saved him from a slow death. She watched the executioner swiftly cocoon Mir Khan's head and torso in the hide and with the help of one of the guards carry them from the chamber. Only a few drops of blood on the flagstones betrayed that just moments ago a life had been taken.

'It is over,' Mehrunissa heard Jahangir say. 'Go back to the *haram*.'

All power of thinking and feeling seemed to desert her. She obeyed blindly, stumbling towards the great golden doors at the far end of the chamber that were already opening to receive her.

Back in her apartment in the *haram* that she'd thought never to see again it was some minutes before Mehrunissa at last allowed the tears to flow. Watching her brother's execution had been hard. Her palms were bleeding from where she had dug in her nails in an effort to control herself. But Mir Khan had brought his fate on himself. He was guilty and justice had been done. There was nothing she could have done to save him and had she tried she might have endangered herself and her entire family. Just as her father had been prepared to abandon her as a baby to die in the desert to give the rest of his family a chance to survive, so she had had to sacrifice Mir Khan. Her act of expediency hadn't meant she didn't love him, weak and foolish though he was.

But what now? The meeting with Jahangir she had fantasised about for so long had finally happened but in very different circumstances from those she'd imagined. What did the future hold for herself . . . or for her family?

Chapter 7

Absolution

The sound of his horse's hooves rhythmically pounding the dry earth as he rode towards Fatehpur Sikri was satisfying, Jahangir thought. It told him that after months of waiting he was finally taking action. Ever since seeing Mehrunissa he had rarely been able to keep her from his thoughts. The courage with which she had stood before him and defended her father to him had confirmed what he had sensed all those years ago – that she was an exceptional as well as a beautiful woman. Others would have wept and wailed but she had retained her dignity. At the end of their encounter he had had no doubt that of all her family Mir Khan had been the only traitor. He had also known that the feelings she had roused in him all those years ago were still there. He wanted her more than ever.

However, dealing emphatically with Khusrau's latest treachery, hatched from within his prison cell in Gwalior, had had to be his first priority. With every passing day he had learned more of the group of hotheads, young men

110

like Mir Khan, who had pledged their allegiance to Khusrau, dazzled by promises his ambitious son had no right to make. He had acted quickly, ensuring that Khusrau's confederates were arrested before they could flee, interrogated to reveal the names of further conspirators and then executed.

Khusrau's fate was far more difficult to decide. He had been merciful in the past but what had been the result? Khusrau had repaid his generosity with further deceit. No, he could expect neither repentance nor gratitude from him. Whatever punishment he inflicted on Khusrau must be sufficiently harsh to ensure he could never rebel again. Yet he need not rush . . . For the present he had ordered Khusrau to be imprisoned in a dungeon cell in Gwalior and kept completely isolated.

He could trust Yar Muhammad, the stern old disciplinarian from Badakhshan whom he had recently appointed Governor of Gwalior, to make sure his orders were carried out. As for the previous governor, he had clearly been lax, allowed Khusrau too many privileges. He was to blame for making it possible for the prince to plot and that was why, fearing Jahangir's ire, he had tried to make amends for his negligence by providing information about the plotters, even implicating the innocent like Ghiyas Beg to save himself. Jahangir had not hesitated to strip him of his post and estates and banish him.

He smiled a little grimly. It should be a long time before anyone else was rash enough to consider rebelling against the emperor. And now with the crisis drawing to its close he was free at last to turn his mind to more personal matters. Last night, as thoughts of Mehrunissa had again kept him awake, he had begun to wonder whether Khusrau's revolt had subtly altered the situation between himself and Mehrunissa's family. Only the Sufi seer could answer that question. That was why he had decided to ride out to visit him as soon as his daily council meeting was over.

Ahead of him in the fast descending twilight, Jahangir could make out the lights of cooking fires. Fatehpur Sikri wasn't far now. He urged his horse into a faster gallop, taking his *qorchis* and his bodyguards by surprise. Behind him he could hear them encouraging their own horses onwards as they tried to keep up.

Fifteen minutes later, he jumped down from his horse in front of a low mud-brick house outside the main walls of the now mostly abandoned sandstone city of Fatehpur Sikri. The house looked smaller and meaner than he remembered from when as a boy he had visited the Sufi's father, but time played tricks with the memory. 'Wait here, all of you.' Peering through a small window to the right of the door he could see the apricot glow of an oil lamp. He removed his riding gauntlets and tapped on the rough wooden door, then pushed it gently open. Hearing no sound from within he tapped again and ducking beneath the low lintel stepped inside.

The room with its floor of hard beaten earth spread with a few thin rugs and a string charpoy in one corner was much as he remembered it, but of the Sufi himself there was no sign. For a moment Jahangir's heart sank, then he heard voices outside and moments later the Sufi entered, stooping like Jahangir to avoid scraping his white-turbaned head on the lintel.

'Majesty, I'm sorry I wasn't here to greet you. I was gathering firewood.'

'I'm the one at fault for coming here without warning.'

'Please, Majesty . . .' The Sufi gestured to one of the rugs, and when Jahangir had settled himself cross-legged sat down opposite him. 'What has brought you here in such haste?'

'I need your guidance once again.'

'On the same matter?'

Jahangir thought he detected a faint hardening of the Sufi's jaw. 'Yes. The situation has changed.'

'In what way?'

'You told me that not only had I sinned against God but I had wronged the family of the woman I love and wish to make my wife – Mehrunissa daughter of my treasurer Ghiyas Beg – by murdering the husband they had chosen for her. Because of that wrong you warned me not to risk God's anger by rushing to take what I wanted but to do penance and to wait.' The Sufi nodded but said nothing and Jahangir continued, 'My son Khusrau has once again plotted to seize my throne and take my life. Among the principal conspirators was the younger son of Ghiyas Beg – Mehrunissa's full brother. He confessed and I have had him executed. The question I have for you is whether his crime against me wipes out my transgression against his family?'

The Sufi's eyes were half closed and he was resting his chin on his folded hands but still he said nothing. Jahangir waited. Perhaps he should have simply sent for Mehrunissa, but his respect for the Sufi and even more for the Sufi's long-dead father had prevented him.

At last the Sufi spoke. 'There is some truth in what you say. Almighty God will be your ultimate judge, but you are no longer the only sinner in the relationship between your families. I believe that the account has been balanced. But remember that whatever happiness awaits you, the step you took to gratify your desires was unworthy of you as a man and as an emperor.'

'I know.' Jahangir bowed his head. The Sufi was right. He should not have had Sher Afghan killed. That had been the act of a jealous lover not an all-powerful emperor. But overriding all such thoughts was the joy the Sufi's words had brought him. Mehrunissa could be his at last. 'Tell me, Sufi, what does the future hold? Will this woman be the partner of my heart I seek?'

'That I cannot answer, Majesty. As I told you before, I am not a mighty soul as my father was. I don't have his gift of prophecy. But if you love her as you say you do – and can make her love you – then all things are possible.'

'Thank you. You have brought me great happiness. How can I reward you?'

'I spoke from my understanding of God and his purposes, not for reward, but say a prayer at my father's tomb before you leave Fatehpur Sikri. Repent again before God of all your sins and excesses, not just the murder of Sher Afghan. Perhaps from his place in Paradise my father can bless you and smooth the path that lies ahead of you.'

• ◆ •

'No, that's not quite right. Listen . . .' Salla read the verse aloud, translating from her native Armenian into Persian as she went. Mehrunissa shook her head. She would take a long time to master the language but she was glad of the distraction. Each day was like the one before and doubtless the one to follow. Even though she was again living in Fatima Begam's household, she was being ostracised. All the time came news of fresh arrests of those suspected of conspiring with Khusrau. The execution of her brother was enough to make the occupants of the *haram* wary of her. However, Salla, whose scholar father was employed in the imperial library, seemed to have no such inhibitions. She had recently been appointed attendant to Fatima Begam and Mehrunissa was glad of her company. As well as Armenian, Salla had also offered to teach Mehrunissa some English, a language which her father, who in his youth had spent three years as *munshi* or secretary to an English merchant, had taught her.

Salla's long dark hair, so thick she struggled to drag a brush through it, was hanging round her earnest face as she repeated the translation Mehrunissa had had such problems with: 'Do not fear when the night grows black as pitch. It is only a passing cloud blotting the radiance of moon and stars. Their light will return, all the more beautiful because once lost.'

The words touched Mehrunissa. 'Who wrote it?'

'One of our greatest poets – Hagopian from Yerevan.'

'How long ago . . .' But Mehrunissa got no further as Nadya burst into her apartment.

'Madam, you are to come at once. The *khawajasara* is waiting for you.'

What now? Mehrunissa wondered, rising to her feet. Ever since her audience with Jahangir she had been expecting to be told to return to her parents' house. The letters she had sent them and her brother Asaf Khan had been guarded. She was certain that any communications passing out of the *haram* – particularly addressed to a family implicated in treason – would be carefully scrutinised.

Following Nadya out into the bright courtyard – according to the shadow falling on the curved marble sundial it was just approaching midday – Mehrunissa saw Mala awaiting her. Behind the *khawajasara*'s tall figure half a dozen attendants in plain dark green robes were standing hands folded, eyes all fixed on her. Three were eunuchs and three were women.

'You sent for me.' Mehrunissa addressed the *khawajasara*.

'Yes, madam.'

'What is it you want?'

'I am not permitted to say in this public place. Please follow me.'

The *khawajasara* strutted ahead staff in hand like some great officer of state, which in a way she was. Next went the attendants and finally Mehrunissa. The little procession headed across the main courtyard past the turning leading, as Mehrunissa now knew, to the entrance to Jahangir's private apartments towards the gates of the *haram* itself. So she was being ejected after all . . .

But then Mehrunissa noticed another small arched entrance to the left of the gatehouse. Reaching it, Mala vanished inside. Following the attendants through the arch Mehrunissa found herself in a narrow passage winding down and sharply to the left. For one wild moment she wondered whether she was being taken to some dungeon but then she noticed that the air was getting warmer. Moisture was trickling down the sandstone walls and she could smell not the dankness of a prison but perfume – rosewater, sandalwood, ambergris. There was another sharp bend and Mehrunissa saw light ahead. A few more steps and she was in a tiny rectangular courtyard with high walls on all sides. Looking up all she could see of the sky was a small rectangle of metallic blue. A fountain bubbled in the centre of the

116

courtyard and through an opening in the wall directly opposite was the source of the moist, fragrant steam – a *hammam*.

'Please undress,' the *khawajasara* said.

Mehrunissa stared.

'The protocol of the *haram* forbade me from telling you
before we reached this private place, but the emperor has
sent for you. Tonight if you please him you will share his
bed. There is no argument. You will do as I say.'

Mehrunissa was so shocked that she stood unresisting as
the attendants began undressing her – untying the pearled
tassel of her enamelled belt set with polished chunks of rose
quartz, sliding her pink silk robe and underskirt from her,
taking her silk slippers from her feet. Before she realised it
she was standing naked in the bright shaft of sunlight falling
in the little courtyard and the *khawajasara* was appraising her
body with the dispassionate eye of the slave merchants she
had seen in the Kabul bazaar. She shook her long dark hair
around her to cover her breasts and turned away, still trying
to take in what Mala had said. So Jahangir had sent for her
at last but not, it seemed, to be his wife. She was being
prepared for his bed as a common concubine.

'Come,' said the *khawajasara*, gesturing through the opening
into the *hammam*. Inside, the heat of the steam rising from
the hot stones on to which scented water was flowing down
a marble chute stung her eyes and she could feel the perspiration breaking out on her skin. She had always enjoyed the
hammam but now she felt her body tense as the long process
began. First, lying on a slab of marble as attendants poured
yet more water on the hot, sizzling stones, she felt the sweat
truly begin to flow, cleansing her skin and making it feel
soft and supple as silk. Next, in an adjoining room she

immersed herself in a small tank of water so cold that crystals from the ice brought from the fort icehouse to fill the pool were still floating on its surface. Then she was led to a third, larger room. There was no natural light but the glow of many oil lamps set in niches around the wall revealed the delicate floral frescoes covering the plastered walls and high arched ceiling. Here a Turkish woman with large strong hands massaged her with scented oils as she lay face down on a marble bench.

Pungent incense smoking in a brass burner in one corner of the chamber was beginning to make her head spin. She had lost all sense of time when, her massage complete, a eunuch wrapped a muslin robe so fine it was almost transparent around her and led her to a low stool. Sitting her down, he began to brush her hair, sprinkling it with perfume and interweaving strings of gems into it. Another eunuch, frowning in concentration, plucked her eyebrows and then smudged kohl around her eyes, further darkening her already long black eyelashes. Then, taking an alabaster jar of carmine paste, he reddened her lips. When he stood back his pleased grunt told her he was satisfied with his work. The third eunuch approached next with a jade saucer of henna paste. With a fine brush he painted delicate designs on her arms, hands and feet. Disorientated, she watched him working as if from afar — as if he were preparing some little doll that was nothing to do with her. But his next words made her realise it was indeed her body. 'Open your robe, madam.'

Mehrunissa looked up at his smooth, slightly petulant face. His voice, even though he was a eunuch, was deep as a man's. 'What did you say?'

'Open your robe please,' he repeated. When she still didn't move he leaned down, slid his hands inside the neckline of her muslin robe and gently eased it over her shoulders until her breasts were exposed. Then, lips pursed, he applied the tip of his brush to her breasts, darkening her nipples which stiffened under the brush's touch and sketching a tracery of tiny flowers on the paler flesh around them. When he had finished he closed her robe again and called, 'Khawajasara, she is ready.'

Mala appeared beside him and together they studied her. Then Mala nodded. 'Excellent. You've done well.' To Mehrunissa she said, 'Come outside into the courtyard again.' Torches were now burning in sconces in the courtyard and in the little window of sky above she could see the first stars already pricking the night sky, telling her how long the preparations had taken.

'Eat.' The *khawajasara* gestured to a dish of almonds, pistachios and dried fruits that had been placed on a silver stand near the fountain but Mehrunissa's stomach felt knotted tight and she shook her head, feeling the weight of the jewels with which it was threaded. 'As you wish.' The *khawajasara* clapped her hands and the three female attendants came forward with a loose amber-coloured brocade robe, gold-hued satin slippers, and strings of yellow cat's eyes to hang round her neck and tie about her slim waist. 'Please turn so that I can satisfy myself all is as it should be,' said Mala when they had finished. Obediently Mehrunissa slowly revolved. The sense that her destiny had been taken out of her hands had been growing ever since Mala had revealed what the night ahead held for her. It wouldn't be long now until she was before Jahangir once more. Last time she had had clear ideas of what she must say and do. This time she had no idea . . .

'Enough!' Mala said. 'Come. It is time.'

'*Khawajasara* . . . advise me, guide me.' Even as she made the appeal Mehrunissa despised herself for it, but she couldn't help herself.

Mala smiled a tight-lipped smile. 'It is your task to please the emperor. That is all you need to know.'

• ◆ •

It was one of the eunuchs who led Mehrunissa back to the main courtyard and up the flight of stairs leading to the emperor's apartments. Through the gleaming gauze of the gold-spangled veil Mala had arranged carefully over her head, things looked muted and insubstantial – the silver doors flung open by the Rajput guards to allow her and the eunuch to pass through, the great golden doors into Jahangir's private apartments, seemed to shimmer like soft fabric rather than hard cold metal.

Just inside the golden doors waited a female attendant Mehrunissa had never seen before, but it was obvious that she and the eunuch knew one another. The eunuch bowed, saying, 'As ordered by His Majesty, I have brought Mehrunissa.'

'Thank you, Khaled,' the woman replied and then, as the eunuch withdrew and the guards outside pulled the golden doors shut behind him, she took Mehrunissa by the hand. 'I am Asa, the captain of His Majesty's female bodyguards, and it is my task to ensure that every woman who passes into the imperial bedchamber is unarmed. Please raise your arms.' Quickly and thoroughly the woman ran her hands over Mehrunissa's body. 'Good. Come this way.'

120

Mehrunissa followed Asa to the far end of the long chamber, past the dais where Jahangir had sat in judgement on her brother and on through a door concealed by a hanging some fifteen feet behind the dais. It led into a wide passageway at the far end of which stood yet more Rajputs protecting the approach to a small square door. Even through her veil Mehrunissa could see the fiery light shed by the gems with which it was studded. Halting by the door, Asa addressed the guards. 'This woman has been sent for by the emperor. Open the door.' The Rajputs rushed to obey. Mehrunissa felt Asa's hand between her shoulder blades gently propelling her forward into the darkened chamber beyond.

As the door closed behind her, Mehrunissa stood still. Jahangir was standing just a few feet away in a brocade robe fastened at the throat with a ruby clasp, his dark hair loose.

'You sent for me, Majesty.' The control she'd fought so hard to maintain in their last encounter had deserted her and she could hear the tremor in her voice.

Jahangir came closer. 'Take off your veil.' Slowly she raised her arms to pull off the piece of spangled gauze and let it drift to the ground. 'I have waited a long time for you, Mehrunissa. I want to spend the night with you, but first I must know whether you are willing.'

'I am, Majesty,' she heard herself say.

'Come then.' He turned and walked over to a large low bed covered with a flowered silk sheet and nothing else, no cushions, no bolsters. Tall candles in silver candelabras burned on either side of the bed, casting shadows over its smooth surface. Jahangir undid his robe and it fell to the floor. His oiled, muscled body shone in the faint light. He watched as she slowly took off her own clothes to reveal her nakedness. The sensation of his eyes taking in every curve, every crevice of her body was more arousing than if he had taken her roughly in his arms as her husband Sher Afghan had loved to do. Whether what was about to happen was the start of a lasting relationship or merely a transitory episode in their lives suddenly seemed unimportant compared with the physical need welling within her. She had always believed the mind ruled the body but now she realised it wasn't always so.

Without waiting for Jahangir to say anything she came slowly towards him and raising her arms pressed her perfumed body against him. She could feel her nipples harden against his chest and that his arousal was no less. He cupped her buttocks with both hands and she knew instinctively what he wanted her to do. Gripping the hard ridges of his shoulders, she wrapped her legs around his hips. His grip on her buttocks tightened as he supported her and she shuddered as she felt him enter her and begin to thrust. As he pushed deeper and deeper inside her, she arched her back and began to cry out, her nails digging into his skin urging him on.

'Wait,' he whispered. Carrying her towards the bed he laid her down and without breaking the rhythm of his thrust stretched out on top of her. His mouth was on her right nipple, teasing it with his tongue and nipping the soft flesh around it with his teeth. Their gasps were growing louder. She could feel Jahangir's back tauten. He was on the brink of climax but was managing to hold back, waiting until she could join him. With one final great thrust he brought her there. She heard their mingled cries as his sweat-soaked body collapsed against hers and they lay in each other's arms, hearts racing. As the passion that had ripped through her began slowly to diminish she pushed her hot face against his chest and felt his fingers lightly caress her long hair.

· ◆ ·

Six hours later Mehrunissa sleepily opened her eyes and saw the pale dawn light lancing through the half-open casement. She also saw what had woken her. Asa was standing by the bedside. Hastily Mehrunissa pulled part of the silk sheet over her naked body.

'Majesty,' Asa said, looking at Jahangir still fast asleep on his back, one arm over his chest, the other stretched out above his head. 'Please wake.' Jahangir opened his eyes. 'Majesty, it's time for your appearance on the *jharoka* balcony.'

Jahangir got out of bed at once and spread his arms for the silk robe Asa was already holding out to him. Bending his head he allowed her to place on it a green silk turban ornamented with an egret feather secured by a diamond starburst. Then, after quickly checking his appearance in a bronze mirror held out to him by Asa, he went outside through the fluttering green silk curtains on to the *jharoka-i-darshan*, the balcony of appearance, which overlooked the Jumna river.

Getting out of bed, Mehrunissa slipped naked across the room to look through the curtains. Jahangir was standing there as he did every morning to prove to his people that the Moghul emperor still lived. To the beat of the great *dundhubi* drum in the gatehouse he raised his arms. As Mehrunissa listened to the responsive roar of the crowds lining the river-banks below the fort, excitement surged through her. That was real power when whether you lived or died mattered to a hundred million people. Trumpets were sounding now from the battlements – all part of the emperor's daily ritual.

The emperor . . . Feeling suddenly a little chill Mehrunissa got back into bed and covered herself with the silk sheet, still warm from their bodies. Last night she had given herself without a moment's hesitation to a man of flesh and blood with a passion of which she hadn't known she was capable. They had made love three times, each encounter more shatteringly intense than the one before. But now daylight had come and her lover was no ordinary subject but a ruler who could have his pick of women. Why had he sent for her? To sate a lust that had bothered him itch-like ever since he had seen her in Kabul? Simple curiosity?

What could she hope for? To share the emperor's bed from time to time? To be his concubine? Perhaps having had her he would no longer be interested in her. He could choose women ten years younger . . . She was still musing half an hour later when Jahangir returned. He had bathed – wet strands of dark hair hung around his face. His expression was, as she had found before, hard to read.

'Shall I return to the *haram*, Majesty?' she asked, preferring to voice the question herself than to be dismissed by the man in whose arms during the hours of darkness she had felt every bit an equal.

'Yes.'

Mehrunissa swung her slender legs over the side of the bed and stooped to pick up her amber-coloured robe. Jahangir had come up behind her. She felt his hand on her breasts and his lips on the nape of her neck. Then he pulled her up and swung her round to face him.

'You don't understand,' he said, 'and I'm not sure I understand it myself . . .'

'Majesty?'

'My decision to summon you here last night wasn't a whim. I wanted you the moment I saw you in Kabul and have never ceased thinking about you. When I learned your family was implicated in a plot against me I feared it would put you out of my reach for ever. A monarch cannot, must not, tolerate dissent . . . sedition.' His strong jaw tightened. 'When you begged to see me I didn't know what you were going to ask. In Ghiyas Beg's case, it wasn't difficult. As I told you then I already believed him innocent. All the same, you defended him bravely when, for all you knew, I had already condemned him. But it was your behaviour over your brother Mir Khan that impressed me most. I know what it is like to have a traitor in the family . . .' he smiled a little grimly, 'I know how hard it is to subdue family love. You had the strength to do it – to see me execute your brother so that the rest of your family could survive.'

Mehrunissa's eyes filled with tears as he tilted up her chin to look hard into her face.

'My grandfather Humayun found his soulmate in his wife Hamida. I think I have found mine in you. I want you to be my empress and first of all my wives. When I have finished dealing with my son's rebellion we will marry – if you will accept me.'

'I could accept no other.' She felt him wipe away her tears.

'But there is something I must tell you. I couldn't be easy in my mind if I didn't. I ordered the death of your husband Sher Afghan. I sent an agent from Agra to Gaur to kill him.'

Mehrunissa gasped, seeing those pale blue eyes before her once more. 'Was the killer an Englishman?'

'Yes. His name is Bartholomew Hawkins. He is now one of my bodyguard. I have since discovered your husband was

125

guilty of many crimes – extortion, bribery, cruelty – but I didn't know that at the time. I had him killed simply because he stood in my way. Mehrunissa . . . can you forgive me?'

Mehrunissa raised her fingertips to his lips. 'There is no need to say more and nothing for me to forgive. I hated Sher Afghan. He was cruel to me. I was glad to be released from him.'

'Then nothing stands in our path.' Jahangir bent his head and kissed her long and hard.

· ◆ ·

As attendants pulled aside the curtains for him to enter his private audience chamber, Jahangir saw the broad figure of Yar Muhammad, his newly appointed Governor of Gwalior. Seeing Jahangir, Yar Muhammad threw himself forward, prostrating himself arms outspread in the traditional obeisance of his central Asian homelands.

'Rise, Yar Muhammad. Have you rid the world of those who conspired with my traitorous son against me?'

'Majesty, I believe I have identified and dealt with them all. As you ordered, I gave those who confessed a quick and easy death by the executioner's sword. Only one, Saad Aziz, refused to admit his guilt even under torture with the hot irons. I think he hoped to outwit us and evade justice but one of the other conspirators, as he himself was being led to execution, showed me a letter from Saad Aziz – I think to clear his conscience before he died. In the letter Saad Aziz pledged support to Prince Khusrau. When I confronted him with it, he had the effrontery to claim that it was a forgery.

'So all should know the reward of treachery I condemned him to one of the old Moghul punishments from the steppes.

126

I had the garrison and townspeople assembled on the great parade ground beneath the Gwalior fort. As the drums beat from the gatehouse I had each of Saad Aziz's limbs tied to wild stallions. Guards released the horses and whipped them into a gallop so that each of Saad Aziz's limbs was ripped from his body. I had a limb placed above each of the four gates of the fortress and his head and torso displayed in the market place.'

Yar Muhammad's thin face with its livid scar on the left cheek was expressionless as he delivered his report. For a moment Jahangir inwardly questioned the governor's severity, but he had been right to act as he did. Saad Aziz had had the opportunity to confess. If the pain and shame of his death banished others' thoughts of rebellion it would be worthwhile. Indeed it was good to know that within just three months he had utterly crushed his son's rebellion. Nevertheless he found it difficult to ask his next question.

'And Prince Khusrau?'

'The punishment was carried out exactly as you ordered. The *hakim* you sent, who indeed proved skilled in such matters, first gave him opium to dull the pain. Then four of my strongest men held him down while a fifth gripped his head and kept it still as the *hakim* stitched his eyelids tightly together with a strong silk thread. The prince can see nothing of the world around him and is no longer a threat to Your Majesty and the peace of the empire.'

It was hard to think of his handsome, dashing son reduced to such a condition but Jahangir told himself he had brought it on himself. Blinding was another traditional punishment carried by the Moghuls from Central Asia into Hindustan. It enabled a ruler to neutralise unruly members of his family without killing them. His vizier Majid Khan had reminded him that that was how his grandfather Humayun had dealt with the most rebellious of his half-brothers, Kamran. The more Jahangir had thought about it, the more it had seemed the most appropriate punishment. In Kamran's case his eyes had been pierced with needles and salt and lemon juice rubbed in to destroy his sight for ever. By only having Khusrau's eyelids stitched, if his son one day showed true repentance he could order the *hakims* to open his eyes once more.

A sudden noise caused Jahangir to turn to see a nervous-looking *qorchi* standing in the entrance to the room.

'Majesty—' he began, but got no further.

'I gave orders that I didn't wish to be disturbed, that I wanted to be alone with Yar Muhammad.' Jahangir glared at the youth.

'I have an urgent message from the *haram*.'

'What is it?' Had something happened to Mehrunissa, Jahangir wondered, suddenly anxious.

'It is Her Majesty, Man Bai. Her attendants have found her lying on her bed dressed in her wedding finery. A bottle of opium water was on the table beside her. They think she took an overdose – only dregs remained in the bottle.'

Jahangir felt irritation as well as pity. Man Bai had always been unstable, sometimes hysterical, and as his first wife once insanely jealous of those he had married later. On more than one occasion she had inflicted harm on herself to gain his attention. She must have just heard of her son Khusrau's blinding. One of the attendants who had accompanied Yar Muhammad from Gwalior must have spoken of the punishment and the news would have spread quickly. Her devotion to her son had made Man Bai refuse to acknowledge the

128

seriousness of his faults. All she saw was a disobedient, high-spirited youth. She had never understood the murderous depths of Khusrau's ambitions and the lengths to which he was prepared to go to achieve them. In recent weeks she had been pleading with Jahangir to pardon Khusrau, alternately vehement and tearful. Swallowing the opium would have been her immediate reaction to the news – an expression both of grief and of protest. It was his duty to go to her even if he could foresee her scalding reproaches as she recovered. But just as he could take no satisfaction from Khusrau's blinding, he could not regret it either. If punishment did not follow treason, chaos would.

'I will come at once. Forgive me, Yar Muhammad,' he said, and walked swiftly from the room.

Nearing Man Bai's apartments in the *haram*, he heard a sudden outburst of wailing. As he entered, her Rajput attendants were clustering around the form which lay perfectly still on the divan, one arm thrown out. Jahangir had no need for any words to know that his first wife was dead.

For some moments he stood still, his mind in a turmoil of grief, doubt and self-reproach. Memories of Man Bai as he had first known her – young and hungry for love and life, before her demons overcame her – flooded his mind. He had been fond of her once and had never wished her harm, let alone a death like this. Tears formed in his eyes but he brushed them away and straightened his back. Her suicide could not, must not be laid to his account. Khusrau had ruined many others' lives as well as his own, and he and he alone had caused his mother's death by his reckless and selfish ambitions. Jahangir's expression hardened. Never again would he allow one of his family to threaten his rule or disrupt his empire.

'Give orders for the funeral pyre to be built. Cremate Man Bai according to the rites of her Hindu religion but also with all the deference due to the wife of the emperor,' he said solemnly, before turning and without a further word retracing his steps.

Chapter 8

'Light of the Palace'

Jahangir stretched languorously then turned his head to look at Mehrunissa, lying naked beside him on the morning following their wedding. The pearlescent sheen of her skin tempted him to stroke the curve of her hip, half turned towards him, but he didn't want to wake her. He enjoyed watching her as she slept — the rise and fall of her breasts, that full mouth, small straight nose and wide brow. He would never tire of gazing at her face, he was certain. Their marriage, following quickly as it did after the crushing of Khusrau's second rebellion and the death of Man Bai, would, he was determined, mark a new beginning in both his life and his reign. With her at his side he would fulfil all the ambitions he had for himself and his dynasty.

Suddenly Mehrunissa's large eyes opened and looked straight into his.

'I have a promise to make to you,' he said.

'What is that?'

'That I will never marry again. Though I have other wives you will be the last.' Mehrunissa stretched to kiss him but before she could do so he went on, 'Wait, I have something else to tell you. To mark our marriage you will be known from now on at court as Nur Mahal.'

Mehrunissa sat up. *Nur Mahal* meant Light of the Palace. 'It is a great honour . . .'

'Don't talk to me like one of my courtiers, flattery on their tongues and deceit and ambition in their hearts.' She looked as if she thought he was teasing her but he wasn't and continued, his tone serious, 'I don't want your gratitude. I chose this title because you have brought light into my world. One of the court jewellers is already carving you a seal with your new name – an emerald set in ivory . . . It will show the place you occupy in my heart and in my court. But to me you will always be Mehrunissa. I still remember standing behind a column in my father's audience chamber listening to your father relate the story of his journey from Persia – of how, almost as soon as you were born, he abandoned you because he was in such desperate circumstances, and how he could not bear the thought of leaving you to the cold and the wolves and came back for you . . . It seemed to me then, though I was only a boy, that destiny had taken a hand in your life. You and I are similar. Destiny has also governed the lives of my family. My great-grandfather believed it was his destiny to found an empire here in Hindustan. It is my destiny and that of my sons to build on that legacy.'

'I will help you,' Mehrunissa said, meaning every word. Fate was giving her an opportunity for power and influence that came to very few of her sex and she would grasp it.

132

Jahangir sat up and shaking his dark hair from his shoulders smiled at her, his mood lightening once again as his eyes took in her naked form. 'This is our marriage bed. I've been talking about serious matters too much. For the moment we are just a bridegroom and his bride, and all I want is to make love with you again.'

Mehrunissa opened her arms to him.

• ◆ •

Mehrunissa closed her eyes as Salla brushed out her long hair. She was pleased she had been able to make the Armenian one of her ladies-in-waiting but nothing had been so satisfying as getting rid of Mala. Three weeks after her wedding she had summoned the *khawajasara* to her new and luxurious apartments in a tower overlooking the Jumna river – rooms that had once belonged to Jahangir's grandmother Hamida.

'Leave everything. Go exactly as you are,' Mehrunissa had said, repeating almost exactly the words Mala had spoken to her. The *khawajasara* had looked at her blankly.

'But you can't dismiss me. I have carried out my job honestly and conscientiously.'

'You enjoyed your power too much.'

The *khawajasara*'s eyes had glittered. She had seemed about to snap back a response but had clearly thought better of it and shaking her head had turned to go.

'You have forgotten something.'

Mala had paused, and when she turned her head again Mehrunissa had seen that her eyes were shining with tears of anger. 'What is that, Majesty?'

'Your staff of office.'

Mehrunissa had held out her hand, elaborately

henna-patterned from the wedding ritual, and reluctantly Mala had passed her the carved ivory staff still warm from her touch.

'Majesty – shall I weave some of these jasmine flowers in your hair?' Salla asked, holding her ebony brush in mid-air.

Mehrunissa nodded. As Salla's nimble fingers went to work, she allowed her mind to drift away down even more pleasurable avenues. How different her wedding night with Jahangir had been from the one she had endured with Sher Afghan. She had been so young then, so inexperienced, especially in the ways of men. To Sher Afghan only his gratification had mattered. Jahangir was a skilled lover but, more than that, in his every caress she felt his passion. He sent her gifts every day and had said to her, 'If there is anything you want, you only have to ask and it will be yours.' It was satisfying to reflect that, as an empress, she could have the best of everything. She would do justice to her place in this sumptuous court.

But what would that place be? How could she become the soulmate Jahangir seemed to crave? He had spoken of the close relationship between his grandparents. To her, Hamida and Humayun were just names, but she would find out more about them, try to mould herself to become what Jahangir wanted her to be and through him to fulfil her own restless ambitions and longings. Above all she must keep his love. Without that nothing else would matter . . .

Yet for the moment the possibilities for herself – and her family – appeared limitless. Jahangir had not only reinstated her father as Imperial Treasurer but heaped fresh honours on him including the title *Itimad-ud-Daulah*, Pillar of Government. Before long she would do something about

Arjumand's marriage to Khurram but not too quickly . . .
it mustn't be said that no sooner was the new empress
installed than she was trying to advance her own family.
Though everyone now treated her with deference in the
haram, she knew her marriage to Jahangir must have
displeased many. She wasn't of noble birth like Jahangir's
other wives. Khurram's mother, Jodh Bai, was a Rajput
princess while Sahib Jamal, the mother of his elder brother
Parvez, came from the old Moghul nobility. At her only
meeting with them so far – both had made a courtesy visit
to her apartments – she had detected both a wariness and
a disdain beneath their pleasantries and formal politeness.

'It is a remarkable thing that your father came penniless
to the Moghul court from Persia,' Jodh Bai had said, a smile
on her round face as she picked at the dish of silvered
almonds Mehrunissa had offered her.

'My father was a nobleman on whom fate did not smile
in our own homeland. He was fortunate to find favour with
the late emperor.'

'Indeed, one might say your whole family has been fortunate.' Jodh Bai's smile had seemed to harden a little.

'True, though such things lie in God's hands, not man's,'
Mehrunissa had responded and turned the conversation to
Khurram, praising his good looks.

Jodh Bai, proud, doting mother that she was, had unwound
a little but had then said, looking Mehrunissa straight in the
eye, 'It is important that my son marries well. The blood of
the greatest Rajput clans as well as of the imperial Moghuls
runs through his veins.'

Mehrunissa had politely agreed but she had known exactly
what Jodh Bai meant – that she disapproved of Khurram's

desire to wed Arjumand. She was now all the more determined to make sure the marriage proceeded.

Parvez's mother had been less talkative. In Sahib Jamal's
thickly lashed dark eyes Mehrunissa had detected a certain
haughty curiosity, but her questions had been few. She had
spoken almost entirely of herself and her family – of how
her ancestors had ridden at Babur's side in his conquest of
Hindustan. She had made it clear that Mehrunissa could
expect no intimacy with her. 'I lead a quiet, retired life,'
Sahib Jamal had murmured. 'My health is delicate and my
circle of friends necessarily small.'

Of course, some of their animosity had simply been the
natural envy of two ageing women of a younger, better-looking
rival. Mehrunissa smiled as she looked at her reflection. The
jasmine did become her . . . She wouldn't let their hostility
bother her and she was already making a friend of Yasmina,
the concubine mother of Jahangir's youngest son, Shahriyar.
From what she had seen, the boy, though unusually good
looking, was a spoiled brat prone to cry and run to his mother's
side whenever anything went wrong and – if his teachers
were to be believed – poor at his lessons. It was time he was
taken from the *haram* and given his own household. But she
had said none of this to Yasmina, who clearly doted on him.

As Salla finished her hair, Mehrunissa felt beneath her
robe for the slender steel dagger in a red velvet scabbard she
wore concealed there. She had heard many stories of jealousies and feuds in the *haram* from Nadya while living with
Fatima Begam. One was of a beautiful young concubine
pushed to her death from a stone terrace by a eunuch bribed
by a rival. Another was of a junior wife of Akbar who died
in screaming agony after an enemy stirred ground glass into

136

her food. No, it wasn't foolish to take measures such as carrying the dagger or, indeed, employing the food taster who sampled the marriage gifts of fruits and sweetmeats that were still arriving daily. Of course, when she ate with Jahangir she was safe. The precautions surrounding the preparation of the emperor's food were elaborate, from the special short-sleeved robes worn by the imperial cooks so that their hands were visible at all times in case they tried to sprinkle poison into the food to the sealing of the dishes with flour paste in the kitchen under the eye of Jahangir's steward before they were carried to his table. It was when she was alone that she must be on her guard.

• ◆ •

Half an hour later, descending the ramp of the Agra fort in a high-domed silver howdah, Mehrunissa felt both excitement and deep satisfaction. When she had first suggested joining him on a tiger hunt, Jahangir had looked astounded. 'No royal Moghul woman has ever done such a thing,' he had said.

'But why not? Why shouldn't I be the first? I want to be with you whenever I can and share your pleasures. Besides, I'd find it exciting.'

'I'll think about it,' he had replied, but she could tell her request had intrigued him. The next day he had given her a matched pair of muskets with ivory- and ebony-inlaid stocks and told her that he had commissioned this special hunting howdah for her. It had wide openings on all sides, and though there were thin gauze curtains to conceal her from view they hung from large brass rings and at the critical moment of the hunt could be quickly swept aside to allow her to aim her weapon.

Jahangir had been her tutor as she had practised her musketry. The fact that he had chosen to join her in the closed howdah instead of riding on his own elephant added to her delight. Behind them sat two *haram* eunuchs, trained to load their hunting muskets as quickly as possible.

'You look happy.' Jahangir's lips brushed the side of her neck.

'I am. I mean to make my first kill today.'

'We may be unlucky. The tigers my huntsmen saw this morning may have moved away by now.'

At first it seemed that Jahangir might be right. The huntsmen, galloping ahead, could find no trace of the tigers. Three hours after leaving Agra Jahangir would have given the order to return but Mehrunissa begged, 'Please. Let's just go a little further. Look, we're almost into the hills where the tigers were spotted this morning . . .'

Jahangir smiled. 'Very well.'

At first the sandy, dune-like terrain with its few spiny bushes looked unpromising. There was insufficient cover for a tiger. But then the ground began to climb towards some large grey rocks among which tamarind trees were growing. Suddenly the elephant halted and Jahangir leaned down to catch the words of a huntsman.

'They've found fresh tracks. They're going to place a goat carcass they've brought near the rocks,' Jahangir whispered moments later. 'We'll wait here, downwind.'

As the minutes passed a light breeze ruffled the tamarind trees but there was no other sound or movement. Then Mehrunissa smelled a strong, musky scent and Jahangir whispered once more, 'They're coming . . . see . . . two of them, among the rocks.

'Pass us the muskets and have the tapers ready,' he ordered the eunuchs and swept aside the howdah curtains. Mehrunissa quickly balanced the engraved steel barrel of her weapon on the edge of the howdah for support and checked the short thin length of fuse. Then, crouching forward as Jahangir had taught her, she squinted along the barrel. Sure enough, just emerging from the rocks were two black and orange shapes. The tigers, heads low between their massive shoulder blades, were moving slowly and cautiously towards the dead goat. She was about to reach behind her for the lighted taper when Jahangir said, 'No, not yet. If you're too quick you may frighten them off.'

With the blood pounding in her ears it was torture to wait. The tigers had reached the carcass and as they sank their teeth into the flesh she sensed their caution was leaving them.

'Now!' Jahangir said. 'You take the one on the right, I'll take the left.'

Grabbing the smouldering taper from the eunuch behind her Mehrunissa aimed at the broad, goat-gore-covered chest of her target. She heard the sharp crack as she fired, and then her tiger slumped sideways, fresh red blood crimsoning its white throat. Almost simultaneously Jahangir's tiger collapsed with a great roar and after shuddering for a few moments lay still, pink and black tongue lolling from its half-open mouth. A new visceral thrill ran though Mehrunissa. Lips parted and eyes bright, she turned to Jahangir.

But at that moment from behind their elephant came a high-pitched whinnying and a young qorchi on a bay mare panicked by the sound of the muskets rushed past. The elephant raised its trunk in alarm and shifted its feet but the *mahout* steadied it. The youth, elbows and ankles flapping wildly, sawed futilely at the reins. Mehrunissa was about to laugh when he was thrown clean over the mare's head to land a few yards from the dead tigers and lay there dazed. Suddenly some instinct told Mehrunissa to look not at the prone youth but into the rocks above. Something orange and black was moving there.

'My other musket – quickly!' Dropping the first she seized the new weapon from the eunuch and with two swift movements rested it on the rim of the howdah and trained the barrel on the rocks. She was only just in time as a tiger even larger than the first two leapt in a great arc towards the squire, who was still on the ground. Mehrunissa fired. In her haste she'd not braced herself properly and as the musket discharged the kick sent her tumbling backwards. Scrambling up she saw the tiger sprawled half across the body of the squire, who was struggling to extricate himself.

'That was some shot. Are you all right?' Jahangir asked. She nodded, breathing hard. 'You never cease to astonish me.' He was looking at her with utter admiration. 'Your speed of reaction was faster than my own.'

'The tiger was a threat. I reacted instinctively.'

'Could you have fired if it had been a man?'

'Yes, why not, if he was my enemy . . . or yours.'

• ◆ •

Khurram should be pleased with this gift of a painting of his bride-to-be, Jahangir thought as he scrutinised the portrait that Mushak Khan, his leading court artist, had placed on a carved rosewood stand in his apartments.

The ruler of a small, far-away realm called England had

recently sent gifts to the court including paintings of himself and his family. Although they looked outlandish in their tight-fitting clothes and high-crowned, curly-brimmed plumed hats, the idea of capturing the images of those around him had pleased Jahangir and he had commissioned several portraits. The mullahs didn't like it, claiming such man-made images were blasphemous in the eyes of God the creator, but some courtiers, eager to please him, now even wore tiny jewelled portraits of their emperor as turban ornaments.

Studying Arjumand's face carefully, Jahangir traced a resemblance to Mehrunissa, though to him his wife's face had a charismatic strength lacking here that in the six months since their marriage had continued to fascinate him. With Mehrunissa he felt complete as never before. Her love enveloped him. Not only did she understand his moods but she could change them. If he felt sad she could make him laugh. If he was anxious she could soothe his worries not just with pretty words but with practical prudent suggestions – never strident and always pertinent. He was spending as much time listening to her advice as to that of his vizier Majid Khan and the rest of his council, from whose words he had to disentangle the wise from the personally motivated. In a month's time he would be acting as she suggested by allowing the marriage of his son Khurram to Arjumand Banu. Jodh Bai had tried to tell him such a match was unworthy but seeing his determination had fallen silent.

He had already chosen the day – 10 May 1612, a date his astrologers assured him would guarantee the couple's perfect happiness. All that remained was for him to arrange the most magnificent wedding the Moghul court had ever witnessed. He would do so not only for his son but also for the pleasure it would give Mehrunissa to see her family so honoured.

· ◆ ·

In the bridal chamber Khurram, wearing only a green brocade robe secured round his waist with a narrow gold belt, stood alone close to the gauze curtain behind which Arjumand Banu's attendants were readying her for the consummation of their marriage. He looked down at his hands, painted earlier that day by his mother with patterns of henna and turmeric to symbolise good luck. He was still wearing the marriage tiara of glistening pearls that his father had tied on his head just before he had set out from the fort on an elephant wearing a diamond-studded headpiece that blazed like white fire in the summer sunshine to follow the immense wedding procession winding its way to Asaf Khan's mansion. Ahead of his elephant had marched trumpeters and drummers, then rows of attendants bearing golden trays piled with spices, then Khurram's friends and milk-brothers on matched black stallions.

The ceremonies and celebrations had seemed endless – the solemn incantations of the mullahs, Arjumand's whispered agreement to the marriage, the ritual rinsing of his hands in rosewater and the drinking of a goblet of water to confirm the union, all followed by feasting and exchanges of gifts. Glancing at Arjumand seated beside him concealed beneath layers of glittering veils he had wondered what was going through her mind. Soon he would know. She was so nearly his . . .

His heart was pounding and to his surprise he realised how uncertain he felt, even nervous . . . his expectations were so high he was afraid they couldn't be matched. What if making love to Arjumand Banu was not, after all, so special? His own mother, usually so good humoured, had warned him not to expect too much, but he knew he must trust to his own instincts. Jodh Bai resented Mehrunissa and didn't welcome her son's alliance with another woman of her family. When she was told that Mehrunissa had complimented Jahangir on his strength and on the sweetness of his breath he had heard her snap that only a woman with experience of many men could make such comparisons.

At last an attendant twitched back the curtain. Arjumand was lying naked against a bolster of ivory silk, her long hair combed out over her shoulders. Her body gleamed with the fragrant oils which had been rubbed into her skin – a ceremony intended not only to render the bride more desirable to her husband but also to stimulate and prepare her for sexual intercourse. The *haram* servants had done their work well. Khurram saw the rise and fall of her high round breasts, the tautness of her small dark nipples and the lustre in her eyes.

'Leave us,' he ordered the attendants, aware that their eyes were observing him a little slyly from above their filmy veils. Then he slowly approached the bed and unfastening his belt let his robe slide to the floor. He lay down beside his bride, very close but not touching her. Before he possessed her there was something he must say if he could find the words. Raising himself on one elbow he looked into her shining eyes. 'Arjumand. Whatever happens, for the rest of my life I will love and protect you. For as long as God gives us together your happiness will matter more to me than my own. I swear it.'

'And I swear I will be a good wife to you. When my father first told me you wanted to marry me I was afraid . . . you were so far above me, from a world I didn't know . . . but when my uncle's treachery brought disgrace on our family you didn't give me up. That was when I knew you must really love me. Tonight I give myself to you as completely and as trustingly as any woman can.' Her lovely face looked almost sombre as she made her declaration.

'No more words,' Khurram whispered, and pulled her to him.

• ◆ •

'Highnesses. The bedding of Prince Khurram and his bride has been inspected. The marriage has been consummated and Arjumand Banu was indeed a virgin.' The keeper of Khurram's *haram* bowed low before Mehrunissa and Jahangir before offering the traditional prayer for the fertility of the young couple. 'May God bless them with many children so that the bride becomes as a mine teeming with the gems of royalty.'

Mehrunissa smiled fondly at Jahangir. She was an empress and her niece the wife of his favourite son. The future had never looked so promising . . .

Chapter 9

Life and Death

'Marriage agrees with you, Khurram.' It was true, Jahangir thought as he contemplated the marble chess board, plotting his next move. Khurram did look content. To have a woman for whom you cared above all else was a gift from heaven. He was glad his son had such happiness just as he did himself.

Khurram smiled but said nothing. After a few more moments' reflection he pushed one of his rooks two squares forward. Jahangir could tell from his satisfied look that he believed he had made a clever move. In fact, he had made a mistake. Two more moves and he himself would be the victor.

'Happiness is making you careless. You haven't lost to me in many months but tonight you will.' Ten minutes later the game was over and a defeated and slightly crestfallen Khurram was standing, ready to call for his horse. But Jahangir had something he needed to say. He wasn't sure how his son would react so soon after his marriage to Arjumand and he knew he had been postponing this moment. But Khurram was a Moghul prince and must understand where his duty lay . . .

'Khurram . . . before you leave I have something to tell you.'

'What, Father?'

'Sit down again and hear me through. What I am about to say is for the good of both our dynasty and our empire.'

How quickly the mood could change, Jahangir thought a little sadly, noting Khurram's suddenly watchful expression. A few moments ago they had been just a father and son enjoying a game of chess on a hot Agra night. To be a ruler was to carry a heavy burden . . . to be marked out from ordinary men and subject to pressures unknown to them . . . but he could not wish his position to be otherwise. From his earliest years, as soon as he had understood who he was, he had wanted the throne. So too, he was sure, would Khurram. With such ambitions came responsibilities to the dynasty, however unwelcome or disruptive they might be personally. Drawing a deep breath, Jahangir began.

· ◆ ·

Arjumand lay beneath a silk canopy on a divan piled with cushions in the walled garden of the *haram* in Khurram's mansion, which was built along the half-moon curve of the Jumna near the Agra fort. The hot searing summer winds were beginning to blow. She was protected from them here and did not envy those who lived in the city, in the simple airless houses built of clay or mud. Sometimes the winds whirled sparks from cooking fires high into the air, igniting the tinder-dry thatch of the roofs. Her maids had told her that three days ago two houses had burned to the ground killing the women inside, who had been too afraid of breaking purdah to flee the flames by running out.

But this was no time for sombre thoughts – not when she was so happy. Her hand lay protectively on her smooth flat stomach where new life was stirring. She was eight weeks pregnant. Her love for Khurram was as complete as she knew was his love for her. She could not now imagine life without him – without the excitement she felt when the evening drew on and she knew that soon, released from his duties, he would come to her. Shy though she had been on their wedding night, her physical passion now matched his own. The abandonment she found in his arms ought to have made her blush but instead she felt pride, knowing the equal pleasure she brought him.

Suddenly she heard horses canter up the ramp into the palace courtyard beyond the tall wooden gates that separated it from the *haram* garden. Perhaps Khurram had returned early. A short blast of trumpets told her she was right. As the doors at the far end of the garden were flung open to reveal him, she ran towards them down the path of black and white tiles that felt warm beneath her bare feet. He caught her to him but instead of kissing her held her to him with an urgency that, as much as his earnest expression, told her something was wrong.

'Khurram, what is it? What's the matter?' she asked when finally he released her.

'There's something I have to tell you.' His voice had an edge but she saw nothing but love for her in his face. Whatever it was couldn't be too bad . . .

'My father says I must marry again.'

'No . . .' Instinctively Arjumand's hand went to her stomach.

At her gesture, Khurram took her in his arms again and pulled her close. 'Don't look so stricken, Arjumand . . . please . . .'

'Who is she?'

'A Persian princess offered by the shah as a royal bride as a gesture of goodwill to the Moghul empire. My father thinks it would be foolish to refuse.'

'But why you, Khurram? Why not Parvez? He's older than you.'

'Exactly what I asked my father. He told me that of all his sons, I am the best fitted to succeed him. Khusrau is a traitor, Parvez loves wine and opium too much and young Shahriyar is timorous and shy. He said that if I indeed become the next Moghul emperor he wants my throne to be as secure as possible. An alliance with the shah's family will help.'

'What answer did you give?'

'What could I say? I am an imperial prince, and I wish to be my father's heir . . . I cannot simply please myself. I replied that I had no desire for further wives – that you are the wife of my heart – but I would obey.'

Arjumand pulled away from him. 'When will you marry her?'

'The court astrologers will determine the precise date but it won't be for some months to allow time for the dowry to be agreed and for the princess to travel to Agra in due state. My father plans to send an escort to meet her and her entourage at the Persian border.'

'And will I have to watch from behind the *jali* screen as they paint her body with henna and perfume and oil her body for the marriage bed?' Arjumand's whole body was trembling now and she didn't care whether he saw her tears.

'You and I are lucky. It's not often that people in our position in life can marry for love, and my father could have prevented us. I can't forget the duty I owe to him and to the empire. But I promise you this – you are my whole life. You are *mumtaz* – the most special to me of any woman in the universe – the woman I wish to be the mother of my children. This princess will never mean anything to me, I swear it. She won't live here but in a separate palace.' His voice shook a little and she saw him rub the back of his hand across his eyes.

That one small gesture told her more than any words that he meant it. But to Arjumand the world seemed suddenly a less perfect place.

◆

She had never known pain like it – not only the physical agony that her body was suffering as under the direction of the two midwives she tried dutifully to push as they told her to but also the mental torture of knowing that less than half a mile away within the Agra fort Khurram was marrying another woman. Sweat was pouring from her body and the contractions were coming more and more frequently but all she could think of was Jahangir tying the marriage tiara on his son's head and the Persian princess sitting beneath her veils. What if she were beautiful? How could Khurram promise not to love a woman he had never seen?

'Highness, lie back.' Firm hands forced her back on to the wet cotton sheet on which she was lying. Without realising she had tried to get up, anxious to get over to the open casement and watch for the celebratory fireworks to shoot up into the night sky. When they did it would mean that the hour of the new marriage's consummation was at hand . . .

'Try to relax your body. Wait for the contractions.' One of the midwives had mistaken her attempt to sit up as a desire to force the birth. Arjumand told herself to lie still, to do as the midwives were telling her.

'Push, Highness, now!'

Summoning up her last reserves of energy, and with the midwives on either side supporting her shoulders, Arjumand thrust as hard as she could. Everything went shadowy around her. She was falling back against the mattress. What was that high-pitched wail she could hear? Was it her making that awful noise? She closed her eyes and had the sensation of drifting weightlessly off . . .

'Highness . . .' A hand gently touched her shoulder. It must be one of the midwives, she thought, and tried to pull away. It was no good – she could do no more. Any moment the pain would begin again and she had no strength left to fight it.

'Leave us, please,' said another voice, louder and male. A door opened and closed. She opened her eyes. The dawn light filtering in through the casement opposite made it difficult to see at first.

'Arjumand, have you nothing to say to your husband and your daughter?' Khurram emerged from the dazzle. In his arms was a bundle wrapped in a piece of green brocade. Kneeling beside her, he placed the baby in her arms.

• ◆ •

As the sun sank on a cool winter's evening and he walked quickly towards his council chamber, the waters of the Jumna looked to Jahangir as if they were flecked with gold, just as he imagined did the Zarafshan – the so-called Goldbearing River that flowed past the walls of Samarkand and that he had read about in the diaries of his great-grandfather Babur. Babur had fought hard to win the empire for the Moghuls and there would always be those who hoped to dislodge them from it. War had come many times since they had planted their green banner in Hindustan's red earth and now it had done so again. He had called his war council together to discuss disturbing news from the empire's southern borders.

The rich Muslim sultanates of the southern Deccan plateau – Golconda and especially Ahmednagar and Bijapur – had always been fiercely protective of their independence and even more so of the immense wealth of their gem mines and had long been a problem to the Moghuls. Though sometimes these kingdoms waged war on each other, on occasions they joined forces against their common overlords. He could remember Akbar telling him how he had forced them to submit to Moghul suzerainty and how, when the rulers of Ahmednagar and Bijapur suddenly refused to send tribute, he had cowed them by sending troops to annex some of their territories.

Now, though, these southern kingdoms were again a crucible of resistance to the Moghuls. The enemy's general was an unlikely one – an Abyssinian, Malik Ambar. Brought

151

to India as a slave he had, incredibly, achieved high office under the sultans of Ahmednagar and was now being employed by the rulers of both Ahmednagar and Bijapur to wage a guerrilla war on their behalf against the Moghuls. To rise as he had from his humble beginnings, Malik Ambar must possess immense strength of character, determination and ambition as well as being a clever and effective fighter. Certainly cleverer than Parvez, Jahangir thought, whom on first learning of Malik Ambar's activities six months ago he had despatched to the Deccan with orders to crush the rising.

As he entered the council chamber Jahangir saw the intent faces of his generals and advisers as they rose to greet him. Among them the tall figure of Iqbal Beg, one of the most senior officers he had despatched with Parvez, caught his attention. His face was lined with exhaustion. His arm was bandaged and in a sling. A trace of blood on the bandages betrayed that his wound had not healed properly.

'Iqbal Beg, give us your report,' said Jahangir, taking his place at the centre of the circle of counsellors.

'Majesty, I regret Malik Ambar has inflicted a disastrous defeat on our forces. We were ambushed and over a thousand of our men killed and many more wounded. We lost a lot of territory.'

'Tell me what happened in detail,' Jahangir ordered, taking care his expression conveyed none of the mixture of anger and anxiety he felt.

Iqbal Beg, however, looked visibly distressed, twisting the hem of his tunic with his unwounded hand as he recounted his story. 'Early one morning as our men clustered around their cooking fires in our camp in a narrow valley among

152

the Deccan hills, warming themselves and eating their break-
fasts of chapattis and dal, Malik Ambar's horsemen swept
down on us. Scattering the few pickets your son had ordered
us to post like chaff before the threshing flail they rampaged
through the camp, killing and wounding many as we rushed
for our weapons and equipment or tried to fight back against
swords and lances with burning brands pulled from the
campfires.'

Jahangir saw tears wet Iqbal Beg's face as he went on. 'A
group of horsemen cornered my son Asif and a few of his
companions against some baggage wagons as they tried to
protect the money and valuables contained in chests within
them. Although he and his comrades resisted bravely they
were on foot and had only their swords. They could not get
close enough to the horsemen to wound them. Instead, one
of Malik Ambar's men spitted Asif on the sharp steel point
of his lance. It transfixed him, penetrating so deep into the
wood of the baggage wagon that its owner could not retrieve
it. Asif died before I could reach him . . .' Iqbal Beg's voice
tailed off into a series of quiet sobs. Jahangir knew Asif had
been his only surviving son.

After another pause during which Iqbal Beg wiped his
tears with his face cloth and slowly regained his composure,
he continued. 'Having forestalled any organised resistance,
Malik Ambar's men then divided themselves into three
groups. The first concentrated on killing as many of our
war elephants as possible, thrusting lances deep into their
mouths or simply slashing through their trunks, without
which they can't live. The second group carried off the
money from the baggage wagons my son had died defending
as well as as much equipment as they could, and the third

153

fired our tents using brands from our own cooking fires. Then they withdrew as quickly as they descended. We had lost too many men and in truth too much confidence to pursue them. We could do nothing but pull back to recoup our strength.'

'How were you so easily surprised?' Jahangir asked sternly.

'They attacked over hills that we thought were impassable to large bodies of men.' The officer dropped his eyes. 'I must confess, Majesty, they knew the terrain much better than we did.'

'And my son, Parvez?'

'He was still in his tent when the attack began. His bodyguard were alert and armed as they are at all times. They defended your son's quarters well. Besides, Malik Ambar preferred easier targets. We should have done better . . . I am truly sorry, Majesty.'

'I know that you are and I grieve with you for your son. What is past is gone. We must turn our minds to revenging ourselves on Malik Ambar and driving him from our lands. Let each of us consider how best this can be done. We will resume our discussions in the morning.'

As the war council broke up, Jahangir called Khurram back. 'This defeat is an insult that must be avenged. If it is not, other neighbours or even rebellious vassals may take their cue from it. I am recalling Parvez. He has no head for war, and although Iqbal Beg is too honourable to mention it, if the reports from some of my other officers are true, he seldom has a sober moment. I fear his failure to post sufficient pickets and his lingering in his tent when his men were already awake and outside may both have had their cause in his drinking. He begged me for the command and

I gave it to him, hoping the responsibility would be good for him, but I was wrong.'

Khurram said nothing. Though only two years separated him and Parvez, they had been brought up in different households and had never been close. Jahangir continued, 'I have decided to send you in his stead to command the imperial armies. The empress says, and I agree with her, that you are far more able. Prove yourself against Malik Ambar and more honours will follow.'

'I won't fail you, Father,' Khurram said, hardly able to contain his excitement at being given his first independent command.

'Good. From now on until you depart – which I wish to be as soon as fresh forces and equipment can be made ready to accompany you – I want you to attend every meeting of the war council.'

• ◆ •

Khurram's euphoria lasted all the way from the Agra fort to the gates of his own mansion, where at the thought of what he must say to Arjumand it evaporated. Their daughter Jahanara was barely two years old. The idea of leaving them both was almost unbearable. And what would Arjumand say? But this was the chance for which he had been hoping and he must seize it. If he couldn't face Arjumand how could he face the enemy? he asked himself as he headed towards the *haram* apartments.

Arjumand was waiting for him as usual. She was wearing a pair of diaphanous blue trousers and a tight-fitting *choli* which left her midriff bare, and in her navel glinted a blue topaz set with diamonds. He thought he had never seen her look more beautiful, though perhaps that was because he knew that very soon he would be denied the luxury of looking at her.

He kissed her lips then took her hands in his. 'Arjumand. My father has conferred a great honour on me. He has appointed me commander of the imperial forces fighting the rebels in the Deccan. If I do well I think there is a good chance he will publicly name me his heir . . .'

For a moment she was silent but then said gravely, 'I am very proud of you. You will exceed your father's expectations. When must you go?'

'Soon. That is my only regret . . . that I must leave you and our daughter behind.'

Arjumand stared at him. 'Why must you?'

'I can't take you all that way – over five hundred miles, maybe more – into heat and danger and discomfort. You should stay here where I know you are safe.'

'Khurram, when you said you must take another wife – that it was your duty – I accepted it. Now I tell you that I must come with you – that it is my duty – and you must accept it. My grandfather and grandmother stayed together through the direst of circumstances. They knew that to be parted would be worse than anything else that could happen. Look at the emperor and Aunt Mehrunissa – they are never apart. Even when he goes on hunting expeditions she goes too. She is a better marksman and tiger killer than he is. She even rides on horseback with him when they're alone. If he went to war, so would she, I'm certain of it. Why should I be any different?'

'You're not strong. Jahanara's birth was difficult . . . you need to be here where the best *hakims* are, should you become pregnant again . . .'

156

'The best *hakims* can come with us. Khurram, I'm not a doll. I enjoy the comfort of my life here in the *haram* but none of that matters compared to being with you. I'd follow you barefoot carrying Jahanara in my arms if I had to and I'd be glad.' She gripped his arm and he could feel her nails sharp in his flesh. He had never seen her look so determined, her gentle face almost pugnacious.

'Perhaps my father should send you into the field against Malik Ambar – you look fierce enough.' He grinned, hoping to coax an answering smile from her, but her expression didn't alter. What should he do? His father was giving him the chance to prove himself fit to be the next emperor . . . Yet though he had been trained for war, had spent hours with his tutors studying the strategies of past Moghul campaigns, could fight with sword, dagger, mace and musket, he had never conducted a campaign before. He must allow nothing – no one – to deflect his focus. Nevertheless to part from Arjumand would be to leave a part of himself behind. Maybe he would think more clearly, fight more effectively, if he knew that at the end of every day she would be there waiting for him. He would certainly be happier . . .

'Khurram . . .' Her nails dug even harder.

Suddenly everything became very simple. They would not be parted and he would do whatever he must to keep her safe. 'Very well. We go together.'

'And always will.' Her voice was firm.

Chapter 10

'Lord of the World'

The stark outline of the sandstone fortress-palace at Burhanpur, 450 miles southwest of Agra, was reflected in the wide slow-flowing waters of the Tapti river. Khurram had reached the city – the Moghul command centre in the Deccan – a month ago and was now leaving it again to begin in earnest his campaign against Malik Ambar. A procession of war elephants already clothed in their overlapping steel plate armour was being led down the twisting ramp from the four-storeyed elephant stables, the *hati mahal*, to the parade ground beside the fortress's high walls. Here their drivers, sitting behind their ears, tapped the great beasts with the iron rods they held in their hands to make them kneel, and other attendants lifted gilded howdahs on to their backs. Once these had been secured with leather straps Khurram's chief generals and their *qorchis* and bodyguards clambered aboard, usually three men to a howdah but in the case of the biggest elephants four. Sweating labourers clad only in grubby white loincloths

158

lifted the small-calibre cannon, the *gajnals*, into the howdahs of others.

When all were loaded the main gates of the fortress opened and Khurram's own war elephant emerged. Larger than any of the others, it bore a green-canopied howdah in which Khurram himself was already sitting, immaculately dressed for war in an engraved steel breastplate studded with turquoises and wearing a gilded helmet on his head. Four other elephants followed his. The first had the embroidered muslin curtains of its howdah tied shut with golden ribbons to conceal Arjumand Banu from any prying gaze; the remaining three each contained four orange-turbaned Rajput warriors, the most trusted of Khurram's bodyguard, ordered by him on pain of death to protect Arjumand Banu from any insult. Each Rajput was heavily armed not only with the latest design of musket but also with the quicker-firing if less deadly bow and arrow as well as a sword. Their expressions beneath their luxuriant wide moustaches were stern. Their alert eyes were even now relentlessly scanning the small crowd which had formed around the gate for any sign of trouble, any lurking assassin that Malik Ambar might have sent to deprive the Moghul army of its leader or that leader of his beautiful wife. However, the only movement from the crowd was a respectful bowing of heads and the waving and clapping of weaponless hands.

The other war elephants formed up behind Khurram and Arjumand and their bodyguards. Together they moved slowly along the dusty parade ground past the intricately engraved bronze cannon on their heavy wooden limbers and the teams of oxen and bullocks already yoked to them. The teams designated to pull the largest cannon numbered as many as thirty animals with horns painted Moghul green, with one whip-equipped driver for every three beasts to ensure that none shirked their work. Interspersed with the cannon were the eight-wheeled ammunition wagons, some pulled by camels, others by mules, which contained the bags of powder for the cannon, well covered with oiled cloth to protect against rain or damp, and beside them the large stone or iron cannon balls.

Eventually Khurram's elephant and its companions took their places behind a vanguard of his elite horsemen drawn up in ranks of twelve abreast and on Khurram's orders all dressed alike in gold cloth with white egrets' feathers fluttering at the peaks of their turbans of the same material. They were mounted on dark horses and at the tops of their lances fluttered green and gold pennants. 'When the news of our battle array reaches Malik Ambar through his spies, as I'm sure it must,' said Khurram to his *qorchi* beside him, 'he'll realise he'd be wise to fear a commander whose attention to detail goes beyond that to weapons and stores to matters of appearance.' Then, full of pride and confidence, Khurram shouted the order to move out. Bronze trumpets blared from the fortress walls as well as from mounted trumpeters in the vanguard. Large bass drums ten feet in circumference sounded from the gatehouse and the side drums of mounted bandsmen beat a steady tattoo to the accompaniment of which the column swung slowly into motion.

As it made its way south up the sandy banks of the Tapti and away from the fortress, it was joined by more regiments of horsemen and then by the less well-clothed and shod but still well-armed ranks of infantry. Next followed the carts of all sizes carrying the main baggage. Finally, as with any

160

army on the march, choking in the dust of those who went before, came a disorganised and unruly mass of camp followers eager to service the army's needs and provide entertainment and relaxation. There were tailors and cobblers ready to renew clothing and footwear worn out by the march. There were sweetmeat and liquor vendors. There were fire-eaters, acrobats and magicians as well as a troupe of whirling dervishes. To provide more private release and solace, scores of whores had joined the column, not all young and not all pretty, but all eager to give themselves for the price of a meal of rice and lentils.

• ◆ •

Six weeks later Khurram opened his eyes in the bed he was sharing in the *haram* tent with Arjumand and found her already awake. She caught him in her arms, begging him to take care in the day's fighting. Promising that he would and that all he intended was a raid on Malik Ambar's forces to weaken them, he kissed her on her full warm lips. Then he gently disengaged himself from her arms and threw aside the bed's embroidered blue wool coverlet. Standing up, he folded a green silk robe around his muscular naked body and ducked out of the *haram* tent just as the first light of dawn was gilding the low hills surrounding the camp. After pausing for a few moments to breathe in the cool fresh morning air he crossed to a neighbouring tent where his *qorchi* was waiting to help him dress for battle. Soon Khurram was strapped into his engraved breastplate and was wearing his domed helmet with its iron mesh fringe hanging down his neck to protect it. He snatched a hasty breakfast of a chicken leg baked in the tandoor with spices and two pieces

161

of hot nan bread, then mounted his black horse and with his bodyguard around him rode over to where the raiding force of about five thousand of his best horsemen were waiting, their mounts restlessly pawing the ground, eager to be on their way.

'Let's go,' he said to Kamran Iqbal, the burly young commander of his cavalry, and they were off. As he was passing through the outer lines of the camp's strong defences Khurram took one final long look back at the *haram* tent. He was glad that Arjumand was there. Last night, once the plans for today's raid were complete, her calm presence had helped him relax and thus to get some sleep to prepare him for the day's action. Kicking his black horse forward he led his men across the dry countryside towards the spot about twelve miles away which, if his scouts' predictions were correct, Malik Ambar's forces should reach by mid-morning.

Around nine o'clock Khurram halted his men in the shadow of a low ridge which would conceal him from the sight of Malik Ambar's men if they approached from the direction he anticipated. Slipping from his high-pommelled gilded saddle he ran quickly towards the top of the ridge. Just before reaching the crest he dropped on to his stomach and peered over. He was soon joined by some of his officers. None could see any sign of movement other than that of a few goats. After three quarters of an hour of anxiously scanning the horizon while worrying that his scouts might have been wrong or that Malik Ambar might somehow have got to hear of his intentions and, eluding the scouts, changed his line of march or even decided to attack the Moghul camp, Khurram could still see nothing. He began to debate with himself whether he should send part of his force back to check that all was well at the camp but decided to leave it a little longer. To his great relief ten minutes later he saw a cloud of dust in the east – the direction from which he was expecting Malik Ambar to come. Only a few minutes later a member of his team of scouts, which had been ordered to keep watch on Malik Ambar's army in relays from a safe distance, rode up on his sweat-mottled chestnut horse.

'How far away are they?' Khurram asked. 'Distances can be deceptive in the heat haze.'

'About two or three miles, Highness.'

'That's less than I thought. What formation are they in?'

'They've got a screen of their own scouts riding about a quarter of a mile from the main column but the rest of the force look fairly relaxed as far as I could tell from where I was. The cannon and the powder wagons still have their covers on – that I'm certain of.'

'So they've no suspicion we're so close?'

'No, I think not, Highness.'

'Well, they'll know soon,' said Khurram, already turning to descend the ridge. He shouted to his officers, 'Let us attack straight away. Don't forget our main targets are the cannon. The more of them we can destroy or disable the more we can reduce our enemy's fighting power.'

A quarter of an hour later, Khurram was galloping towards Malik Ambar's column at the head of his men. The horses' hooves beat a tattoo on the dry ground while flying grit stung their riders' eyes and filled their mouths and noses. As he rode, Khurram could see through the thick dust that Malik Ambar's men had now realised the danger. Horsemen were wheeling to face the threat and gunners were hastily pulling the covers from the cannon and lashing the ox teams to turn the guns to face their opponents, while others were heaving bags of powder and cannon balls from the ammunition wagons. Archers were climbing into the howdahs of the war elephants. Musketeers were readying their weapons and setting their long barrels on tripods so that they could fire more accurately. Khurram could also see a group of men with glittering breastplates riding along the lines. Presumably these must be Malik Ambar and his officers, encouraging their troops and giving orders.

Arrows were beginning to plummet from the sky among his galloping men. The sound of musket balls hissing past his ear and the sight of flashes and puffs of white smoke from Malik Ambar's lines showed that at least some of the enemy musketeers were now firing. Only moments later a deeper bang and more billowing smoke left him in no doubt that one of Malik Ambar's cannon was also in action. No more than ten yards away Khurram saw one of his leading riders – a young Rajput banner-carrier – crash backwards out of his saddle to the ground, losing his grip on his large green standard as he fell. The horse of the following rider – another Rajput – stumbled over the body and then catching its legs in the banner fell too, pitching the Rajput over its head and bringing down yet another horse and rider into the dust. Only a quarter of a mile to go to Malik Ambar's lines, thought Khurram. The enemy could not do too much damage in the time it would take to cover that distance. Instinctively bending lower to his horse's neck, he twisted the reins to head more directly for Malik Ambar's cannon and kicked the willing black horse on.

Then he was in among Malik Ambar's column, slashing at a purple-turbaned musketeer deployed with his comrades in a line some yards in front of the cannon to protect them. He had fired once and was desperately trying to reload his weapon, pushing one of the lead bullets from the white cotton pouch at his side down the long barrel with a steel ramrod. He never completed his task. Khurram's sword, honed to perfect sharpness by the armourers that morning, caught him in the side of the face, almost severing his jaw and exposing his fine white teeth. Dropping the musket, he collapsed to the ground as, without a backward glance, Khurram charged onwards towards the cannon and the ammunition carts, his bodyguard around him. Only ten yards from Khurram a cannon fired with a deafening crash and billows of white smoke. The ball caught another of Khurram's bodyguards in the stomach, severing his torso and leaving his blood-spattered horse to gallop on with the bottom half of his body still in the saddle.

Coughing from the acrid gunpowder smoke, his ears ringing, Khurram urged his horse onwards again, slashing at another gunner who was struggling towards his weapon almost bent double under the weight of a heavy stone cannon ball. Struck in the back, the man dropped the ball and, blood soaking his grubby white tunic, slumped to the ground. In a minute or perhaps even less – time seemed to pass so slowly in battle – Khurram was on the other side of the column. Looking around him he could see that many other gunners were dropping their ramrods to abandon their posts and flee on foot. Most were doing so in vain since his own mounted men were catching them in the back with their swords as they ran or piercing them with their lances.

Quickly Khurram's men began gathering around him. 'Those of you issued with spikes hammer them into the breeches of the cannon,' he commanded. 'Those with mallets try to knock the wheels from the gun limbers. And those of you designated to set gunpowder trails to blow up the powder wagons as we depart, get to your work. The rest of us will hold off Malik Ambar's men while you do so.'

As his soldiers dropped from their saddles to begin their tasks Khurram heard a trumpet blow and through a gap in the billowing smoke – which he had already learned rendered battlefields such confusing places – saw a group of Malik Ambar's horsemen emerge from lower down the now dis-organised ranks of his column and charge determinedly towards his own position. 'Come on, let's meet them head on,' Khurram shouted, and urged his black horse forward.

He and his men could not get their horses into a gallop before the enemy was on them. Apparently recognising Khurram, one thick-set officer who had had no time to don either helmet or breastplate pulled on his reins to head directly for him. Khurram wheeled his horse, now blowing from its previous exertions, to meet him. However, it was his opponent who got in the first blow, aiming a swinging stroke of his scimitar which caught Khurram's breastplate and then skidded off, knocking Khurram off balance so that his own first stroke missed too, parting the air over the officer's head as he ducked. But then Khurram, recovering the faster, struck again, thrusting his sharp sword deep into the man's ample and unprotected stomach just below his breastbone. Dropping his weapon and his reins and clutching at his wound, the officer fell from his horse which, relieved of his weight, galloped away from the fray.

Looking around him while he caught his breath, Khurram saw that more and more of Malik Ambar's men were joining the fight and that several of his own soldiers were sprawled on the ground, dead or wounded. The raid had been as successful as he could have wished, eroding Malik Ambar's strength and his equipment. But now with their task complete it was time for him and his men to retreat while they still could. 'Mount up,' he shouted to those finishing disabling the cannon. 'Pick up any wounded or unhorsed men and ride two to a horse, but as you leave remember to set fire to the powder trails you've laid around the wagons.'

He watched as his dismounted men scrambled into their saddles, pulling comrades up behind. One tall Rajput was struggling to get a wounded companion on to his grey horse when two arrows thudded in quick succession into the body of the injured man and he fell backwards, clearly dead. 'Come on,' Khurram urged, and put his heels to his horse whose black coat was now covered with a scum of white sweat. He was among the last to leave. As he rode hard, twisting in his saddle to look behind him, he saw another of his men fall sideways from his mount, hit by a spear thrown by one of Malik Ambar's soldiers. The man's foot caught in the stirrup and he was dragged behind the horse for some distance before the stirrup leather snapped.

Suddenly, Khurram felt a blast of warm air sweep past him and a great boom deafened him again. At least one of the powder wagons had exploded. Another bang followed and Khurram felt a stinging pain in his left cheek near his nose and liquid running down his face on to his lips. It tasted salty and metallic on his tongue – blood. Putting his hand to his cheek as he rode he pulled out a sliver of metal. Perhaps part of a tin powder trunk, he thought.

Soon he was back on top of the ridge from which he had started the attack, where the rest of his men were regrouping. Patting the heaving flanks of his horse and looking behind him again, he saw that a few Moghul stragglers were still galloping away from Malik Ambar's disorganised column. The forelegs of one grey horse buckled as it ascended the slope and it collapsed, its rider, a burly, bow-legged man, leaping from the saddle just in time. Looking closer, Khurram saw that the horse had a great sword slash along its side. It had done well and bravely to get its rider so far.

Malik Ambar's men were not pursuing them. Just as had happened twice before in the two months since Khurram had left Burhanpur, his opponent had preferred to persist with a tactical retreat, accepting losses to his forces in hit and run raids like today's without attempting to follow his assailants when they broke off the action. Malik Ambar seemed determined to continue the withdrawal into the mountains bordering the Deccan plateau which he had begun on first hearing the news of Khurram's approach. Here his outnumbered force would be able to exploit familiar terrain in any battle.

Khurram wiped his bloody sword on a piece of saddlecloth and sheathed it once more in its jewelled scabbard, his emotions a mixture of satisfaction and frustration. Satisfaction that he had inflicted further damage on Malik Ambar's army, diminishing their firepower and numbers at an acceptable cost in Moghul lives, and frustration that Malik Ambar still would not commit himself to a conclusive battle. However, he comforted himself that such an encounter could not be long delayed.

• ◆ •

'Here, let me see,' Arjumand ordered. It was less than five minutes since Khurram had galloped back into the camp on his exhausted black horse. Heedless of convention she had run from the *haram* tent to greet him, having spent the intervening hours ceaselessly pacing the hot interior, returning only the most perfunctory answers to the attempts of her attendants to distract her with titbits of court gossip or queries as to whether she might want refreshment. Seeing the blood on Khurram's face she had immediately taken him back into the tent.

'It's nothing. It's a scratch. It really is. The scab is forming already,' Khurram protested but Arjumand would not be thwarted, calling for an infusion of the leaves of the neem tree to clean the wound, a sure way she had been told to prevent infection from setting in. While a maid hurried off to find the neem water, Arjumand undid the straps of Khurram's breastplate and lifted it from him, saying as she did so, 'Thanks to God that you are safe.'

'I told you I would return . . . You look so worried. Are you sure that accompanying me on campaign is really good for you? Wouldn't you be happier in Burhanpur?'

'No,' Arjumand replied immediately, her tone firm. 'Here the wait for news is shorter. It would be much worse waiting for messengers to arrive and then scanning their faces for what news they brought. Here in the camp I can be with you and share your thoughts and your joy in your final victory, which I know to be inevitable.' As she spoke she embraced him, heedless of the acrid smell of the sweat which stained his tunic.

Even as he returned her caress, Khurram's mind began to turn to how best he could achieve the victory Arjumand thought so inevitable. Malik Ambar still remained a most dangerous adversary.

• ◆ •

'Highness, rather than confront us in battle on open ground Malik Ambar has retreated into a closed valley about five miles ahead,' Kamran Iqbal reported, beads of perspiration running down his fleshy face from his exertions in the heat as he rode up on his return from his scouting mission. 'His men are already blocking the entrance with overturned wagons, rocks and anything else they can find.'

At last, thought Khurram. Since the raid in which he had suffered the superficial wound to his cheek his men had maintained contact with Malik Ambar's forces as they headed back into the Sultan of Ahmednagar's territory. Through a further series of flanking attacks and harassing raids Khurram had pushed his enemy away from any strongholds where he might obtain more men. Now Malik Ambar, who seemed to have succeeded in the difficult task of maintaining his men's discipline in retreat, had clearly decided he must finally stand and fight. Even if the Abyssinian had chosen terrain well suited to defence, Khurram was confident of victory. 'What about the valley beyond that? Is it a dead end?'

'The valley is bottle shaped. The entrance is the neck or narrowest part. The sides are steep and strewn with rock and scree. The valley floor has a small spring-fed river running through it to provide Malik Ambar's men with water. Also it is well wooded. They will be able to cut down some trees to build barricades and still leave enough standing to break up any charge we may make.'

'What do you think? Should we attack now?' Khurram asked, impatient to bring on the final battle.

'No, Highness. Although it would be tempting, I think not,' said Kamran Iqbal. 'The entrance to the valley is narrow and easy to fortify. If we attack just with the horsemen we have with us we risk a serious setback. We must wait until the cannon and the war elephants catch up with us.'

Khurram knew that Kamran Iqbal was right. He would be a fool to take a chance after spending so many weeks in manoeuvring Malik Ambar's army into its present position. Malik Ambar was like a wounded lion in his lair, still entirely capable of despatching an over-eager or careless hunter.

◆

'Victory will be ours today,' Khurram had told Arjumand an hour earlier. Now he was watching from a vantage point on a hillock about half a mile from the valley in which Malik Ambar's army had barricaded itself. The entrance really was narrow — no more than at most two hundred yards across — and the cliffs at either side were so steep as to be impossible to climb, at least for a body of men under fire. Malik Ambar's troops had blocked the valley's entrance with rocks, felled trees and even bundles of the spiny bushes which grew thereabouts as well as with overturned wagons. The barrels of those of Malik Ambar's cannon that had survived Khurram's raids poked out at intervals along the barricade.

More than ever, Khurram was convinced that he had been right in his assessment at the war council the previous evening that the place where the river flowed out of the valley was a likely weak spot. Malik Ambar's men could not extend the barricades across the river without creating a dam which would quickly lead to flooding of the area behind them, making them impossible to man.

As agreed at the war council a group of his elephants was already advancing to the attack, plodding slowly but determinedly towards the neck of the valley. Khurram could see flashes from musket shots from some of the howdahs and from others came the crash and smoke of his small cannon – his *gajnals*. Behind the elephants, ranks of his horsemen were already massing to exploit any breakthrough. In his heart Khurram wanted to be with them to lead their charge but in his head he knew that Arjumand had been right and not just thinking of his safety when she urged him to follow his commanders' advice that he would be better employed directing operations at a distance from the battle and its swirling smoke and consequent confusion.

Cannon were now firing from behind Malik Ambar's makeshift barricades and Khurram saw one of his leading elephants stop and then slowly collapse, falling sideways into the river, crushing its howdah. Both the *mahouts* fell from the neck of another elephant, presumably hit by a volley of concerted musketry. The elephant turned away from the attack, its trunk raised in panic and fear. In its flight the sharp swords attached to its tusks sliced into the leg of one of the following elephants and it too fell. As it did so, Khurram could make out the *gajnal* crashing from its howdah to the ground. Another elephant stumbled over it, pitching forward and dislodging both *mahouts* from its neck as well as its howdah.

172

Some elephants were still advancing but they were finding it difficult to get round the bodies of their fallen comrades. It would be almost impossible for them to get up the necessary pace in a charge towards Malik Ambar's barricades to succeed in breaching them. Yet another elephant crumpled as Khurram watched, this time so slowly that the four occupants of its howdah were able to jump down and begin running back to safety. To Khurram's dismay one of the four fell, clearly hit by a musket ball, just moments later. The second turned back to help his comrade but was shot before he could get to him. The third was also hit but perhaps less severely wounded and began crawling back towards Khurram's lines. The fourth, who was running through the shallows of the river, had nearly got out of musket range when he too was hit, flinging his arms into the air and collapsing face downwards into the water.

In the meantime at least four more elephants had fallen while two or three others were turning away. One of them, badly wounded, staggered into the river where it fell with a great splash, the blood staining the fast-flowing water. Best to call off the attack now, Khurram thought, before his force took any more casualties, and he immediately gave the order to the waiting despatch rider at his side. All along he had known that Malik Ambar was a crafty, skilled and experienced opponent. He was sure the Abyssinian thought that if he defended the valley well he could inflict so many casualties on the Moghuls that either they would retreat, leaving themselves vulnerable to his counterattack in the process, or at the very least the conflict might drag on into a stalemate from which he might be able to negotiate a truce and safe passage for his army. Khurram could only imagine his

173

quick-tempered father's reaction if he allowed either of those things to happen and thus failed in his first major campaign. He must take time to think out a new strategy. Better to postpone further action for a day or two than launch another futile frontal attack later that afternoon.

'What were our losses?' Khurram asked his commanders later as they sat cross-legged in a semicircle around him.

'At least six hundred men killed or badly injured. The *hakims* have only time to attend to those they think may have a chance of survival. Perhaps as important, thirty of our best war elephants were killed or so badly wounded that it was a kindness to end their suffering,' Kamran Iqbal responded.

'That's a little worse than I feared. I think we must dismiss the idea of straightforward frontal attacks for the moment. Are we sure that there are no back routes into the valley and the valley sides are indeed as steep as we think?'

'Yes, as far as we can tell, Highness. The local people, who are so often a good source of intelligence, have either fled or are so frightened that they won't give much useful information. If we press them too hard they will just tell us what they think we want to hear and that will be worse than useless.'

'We have sent out some of our scouts, haven't we, to ride around the escarpment and investigate the valley from the rear?'

'Yes, but Malik Ambar seems to have lots of his own scouts out too. Knowing the terrain better than our men they have successfuly ambushed them on a couple of occasions. Besides, the survivors and those who completed their missions unmolested report that from what they've seen the

174

only way that numbers of armed men can get into the valley is indeed through that narrow front entrance.'

'Well then, how do you suggest we go about the assault?' asked Khurram, for a moment devoid of anything to put forward himself.

'Highness, what we need to do is to get the cannon into an advanced position where they can really damage the barricades,' said Walid Beg, a thin Badakhshani, the most senior of Khurram's gunnery officers and at least twice the prince's age.

'That's easier said than done. The gunners will have no protection and Malik Ambar will be able to pick them off before they can bring their weapons into action.'

'Why not use the corpses of the dead elephants to provide some kind of protection for the cannon emplacements?' suggested Kamran Iqbal.

'Yes, but we'd still have to get the cannon into position and we'd take too many casualties as we tried to do so.'

Suddenly a thought came to Khurram. When both his war council and Arjumand had advised him not to command from the front line, both had cited the confusion caused by the billowing smoke as one of their main arguments. Why didn't he exploit smoke to his own advantage? 'Couldn't we create a screen of smoke behind which our men could bring up the cannon and position them behind the elephants' bodies?' he asked. 'There is lots of scrub and grass around that should burn with plenty of smoke. It should only take a few hours for our men to collect enough.'

'That may work, Highness,' said Walid Beg thoughtfully.

'It will. We can order our men to tie strips of green or white cloth round their arms to aid them in identifying each other in the smother. Send the men out immediately to start collecting the brush for burning. We'll put it in place overnight and you, Walid Beg, should start moving the cannon up in the hour or two before dawn so darkness will give us some added cover.'

• ◆ •

Khurram was already dressed for battle at four o'clock in the morning as the first of the ox teams pulling his cannon began to make their way slowly towards the entrance to the valley with an escort of horsemen. The brushwood had already been stacked in positions where the wind would blow smoke into Malik Ambar's defences, obscuring his men's view. Khurram hoped against hope that the current quite strong breeze would not change direction nor fade away. After what he guessed was about twenty minutes, he heard shots. The oxen teams had already encountered some advanced pickets of Malik Ambar's forces deployed by him beyond the barricades. The Abyssinian is a good general, thought Khurram, but I will prove a match for him.

It was now first light and time to put his plan to use smoke into action. 'Fire the first bonfire,' he shouted, and a rider galloped off to ensure it was done. Walid Beg and his gunners already had orders to open fire when they got into a suitable position behind the protection of the elephant corpses. Only a minute or two later he heard the deep boom of the first cannon shots, quickly followed by the crackle of musketry. Battle was joined, and even from his position six hundred and more yards away from the main action Khurram could smell the burning brushwood. As the day dawned more fully he could see that most of the smoke was indeed blowing towards Malik Ambar's barricades.

Despite the pressure from his commanders, Khurram had decided that he himself would lead the charge of his horsemen to exploit holes blown in the barricades. If any were to be made it should not be long now. Calling for his groom, he mounted his black horse and trotted over to his waiting bodyguard and the mass of other horsemen led by Kamran Iqbal. After only about ten minutes a messenger rode up. 'Highness, it's difficult to be certain in the smoke but we think we've made a breach about twenty yards from the river where the barricade is mostly brushwood and overturned carts.'

'Well then, Kamran Iqbal, let's move forward,' said Khurram. He felt more nervous than he had before any other battle. His heart was beating fast, his pulse racing and his mouth dry. However, as he rode forward he forced himself to clear his mind and to concentrate on the task ahead. Soon he and his men were passing the first of the dead elephants and a whiff of the decay that was already setting in caught his nostrils. The smell together with the mass of opalescent black flies clustering around the body must be dreadful for the Moghul crew of the large bronze cannon firing from behind it. The stench from the next elephant corpse they passed was worse, vomit-inducing even for the hardiest stomach. Malik Ambar's men had been returning cannon fire almost blind into the smoke but a lucky shot had hit the dead beast in the abdomen, rupturing its already swelling intestines – hence the smell.

Swallowing deeply to subdue his rising gorge and wrapping his cotton scarf more closely around his face, Khurram ordered his men to quicken their pace. Through a gap in the swirling smoke he saw that Malik Ambar's barricade was only three hundred yards or so away but to his consternation he could see no breach in it. Then the smoke pall moved again and for a moment he glimpsed one some way to his left, nearer the river than he had been led to believe. 'There it is!' he yelled. 'Charge to the left!'

Following his own order he kicked his black horse into a gallop. Less than a minute later the barricade loomed out of the smoke which was enveloping everything once more. It had only been partially destroyed. Therefore relaxing his reins and leaning forward in his saddle Khurram urged his mount to jump the remnants, which looked about three feet high. Launching itself with all the power of its muscled hindquarters, the horse cleared the obstacle easily.

He was in the enemy camp, followed swiftly by many of his bodyguard. 'Try to cut down the gunners,' he shouted. Turning along the barricade amid the drifting smoke, he came upon a cannon which was about to fire. With one full swing of his heavy but well-balanced sword he beheaded the gunner at the firing hole. Feeling a spray of warm blood on his face, with two more strokes he despatched two other men, one holding the cannon's ramrod and the other a bag of powder ready to reload. Still with his bodyguard around him, he galloped further along the barricade, disabling or killing another cannon crew with their help. Next he turned along the pebbly margin of the swift-flowing river to penetrate further into the camp, intending to lure more of his enemy into battle and hence to their destruction.

Together with his men he cut down several musketeers who were already fleeing from the fighting around the barricades. But suddenly a phalanx of Malik Ambar's cavalry appeared through the smoke from the right, charging at the gallop into the flank of his own horsemen, two of whom fell under the initial impact of their assault. Khurram himself wheeled his black horse round to face his attackers, thrusting with his sword at two assailants as they passed. One of his opponents parried his stroke. The second collapsed from his saddle with a deep wound in his stomach.

Then, as Khurram tried to turn tightly to attack his first opponent again, another enemy thrust hard at him with his long lance. The point caught his breastplate and bounced off without penetrating but its force was so great that, hit while making his turn, Khurram was thrown sideways from his horse to land with a crash in the very edge of the river. He looked up to see the horseman with the lance bearing down on him again. Time seemed to stand still and it suddenly came to him how much he wanted to see Arjumand again and that if he did not get out of the way of the rider he would not. He waited until the very last moment to act, in fact until the rider was already drawing back his lance to make his fatal thrust. Then he rolled away through the water and across the pebbles. As he did so he pulled a throwing dagger from his belt and hurled it at his opponent. It missed the man but hit his horse in the rump and it reared up, throwing its rider backwards into the water to land with a great splash.

Khurram scrambled on all fours through the shallows to the winded man and threw himself on top of him. He seized him by the throat, pushed his thumbs into his Adam's apple and squeezed hard until he had extinguished all the life from the man and his body grew limp. Heaving it aside, Khurram

179

struggled to his feet and staggered out of the river, water dripping from his clothes and filling his boots, relieved to be alive. As he emerged he saw that one of his men had caught his black horse. The bodies of at least five of his guards were scattered motionless along the riverbank while two of his comrades were helping to bind the deep bleeding cut in the arm of another, a young Rajput, who was biting his lip to avoid crying out in pain as they did so. However, as he remounted Khurram was pleased to see that there were more bodies of his enemy than of his own men and that they had retreated, leaving that part of the battlefield to the Moghuls. 'Where have Malik Ambar's men gone to?'

'Back along the river towards the valley's end, together with many more of their companions.'

'Have we secured the barricades?'

'Yes, Highness,' said Kamran Iqbal, who had just ridden up, breathing heavily. 'There are a few pockets of resistance but we're mopping them up easily enough.'

'Well, let's pursue those retreating but take care. The fires are subsiding and the smoke is dispersing. We're more visible and easier targets for musketeers and archers hiding behind trees. Let's move fast and stick to the riverbank where there are fewer obstacles.'

As he spoke Khurram dug his heels into his horse's flanks once more and pushed on along the riverbank. Soon he and his men came upon a band of fleeing archers and infantry. Most had thrown down their weapons but one archer, perhaps knowing death was inevitable, crouched down and aimed his bow at Khurram. One of Khurram's bodyguards cut him down with a sword slash across his back but not before he had sent his black-feathered arrow hissing towards the prince.

It thudded into his gilded saddle, grazing his thigh as it did so. Khurram felt no pain but was aware of blood running down his leg. Ignoring it, he rode on for another few hundred yards until he came to some lines of tents in a clearing. All looked abandoned and several were burning, seemingly set afire by Malik Ambar's retreating men.

Leaving the camp behind, Khurram continued with his bodyguards along the river which was narrowing all the time as the valley itself grew steeper and more enclosed. Suddenly some shots rang out from among the trees and one of the bodyguards fell, hit in the forehead by a musket ball. Rounding a bend in the river, Khurram saw another barricade of tree trunks ahead from behind which some musketeers were firing. The track was too narrow to allow him to swerve so he kicked his horse on towards the barricade as several bullets whistled through the air around him. However, his luck held, and both he and his horse were unscathed as they jumped the tree trunks. Almost immediately the defenders scattered and ran into the surrounding brush and trees. But one officer, whose dark skin and features suggested Abyssinian blood like that of Malik Ambar himself, tripped over some gnarled tree roots and sprawled full length on the ground. 'Take him alive,' yelled Khurram. Two of his bodyguards leapt from their saddles to obey, pinioning the wiry dark man by his arms.

'Bring him here,' Khurram ordered. They did so, forcing him down on his knees before him. 'Where is Malik Ambar?' Khurram spoke in Hindi rather than the Persian he used at court and in discussion with his senior officers.

'You would not say where your general was if you were captured and nor will I.' But an instinctive glance upwards to the lip of the valley betrayed him. Following it, Khurram

181

saw some figures at the top of the scree-strewn slope. 'There's a way out of the valley, isn't there?'

The man had relaxed having seen the figures, and responded, 'If you call the system of ladders we built from tree trunks a way out, yes. But it will be useless to you. Horses cannot use ladders and our commander and those troops who have made their escape have mounts waiting on top and will be long gone before you can attempt any pursuit.'

'Check the truth of what he's saying,' Khurram ordered some of his bodyguards, 'but take care. There may be yet more ambushes along the track.'

• ◆ •

Later that evening Khurram lay in Arjumand's arms. The wound to his thigh had proved minor and was now bound with clean white cloth and he himself was bathed and refreshed. Outside, his men were celebrating victory ever more raucously. He had stayed with them for a while but then had made a round of the *hakims'* tents to visit the wounded before returning to Arjumand. His joy at victory in his first campaign as sole commander was tempered both by the suffering of the wounded and by the knowledge that the Abyssinian officer had been telling the truth – Malik Ambar had escaped. But a count of prisoners and of the enemy dead suggested he could have taken no more than a few hundred of his men with him. The Sultan of Ahmednager's army was defeated. He would have to negotiate a peace. Victory was Moghul.

• ◆ •

Khurram's armies were drawn up on the bank of the Jumna beside the Agra fort. The rows of war elephants were clad for the occasion in their steel plate armour but — since this was a moment of celebration, not war — had no sabres tied to their tusks, which their *mahouts* had painted gold. Wagons pulled by white oxen, whose horns were also gilded, and surrounded by red- and orange-turbaned Rajput guards held the sacks of booty Khurram's men had seized.

Khurram himself was sitting some twenty paces in front of the leading ranks on the black stallion which had served him so bravely in battle. Unused to its golden ceremonial headplate and the heavy green velvet saddlecloth that reached almost to the ground, it was fidgeting and tossing its head. 'Calm,' Khurram murmured, stroking its glossy, sweating neck. 'You must allow the people to rejoice at our safe return and pay tribute to our victory.' Suddenly the blast of many trumpets rose from all along the battlements as Jahangir emerged on to them and raised his arms to acknowledge the return of the triumphant Moghul armies.

On the opposite bank of the Jumna, at Jahangir's gesture a great roar rose from the crowds jostling and straining to get a better look. Suddenly Khurram was possessed by a crazy desire to swim his horse across the dark brown waters and ride amongst the admiring, cheering onlookers. Did victory and public acclaim always feel this good? But, looking up again, he saw that his father had withdrawn. It was time to go to him. Followed by his bodyguard Khurram trotted towards the steep ramp leading up into the fort. Here Arjumand was waiting in a sapphire-studded howdah on one of the imperial elephants, shrouded from view by silk curtains. Twelve mounted bodyguards — sent as a mark of esteem by Jahangir — were drawn up in pairs behind her elephant. In front were the soldiers Khurram had chosen for their courage in the fighting to escort his wife on her triumphal return into Agra. Ordering his own bodyguard to bring up the rear, Khurram took his place at the head and signalled with his gauntleted hand for his small entourage to advance up the ramp.

As they passed beneath the main gatehouse into the fort, drums boomed and attendants flung fistfuls of gilded rose petals and tiny gold and silver ornaments shaped like stars and moons that fluttered around them. As they continued up the steep, twisting ramp Khurram saw that every wall had been hung with swathes of green brocade. Soon they were passing through a further gateway and into the main courtyard, at the far end of which was his father's many-pillared Hall of Public Audience, open to the air on three sides. The courtyard itself was packed with courtiers but a wide channel down the centre, strewn with more rose petals, had been left clear. At the far end he could see the glittering figure of his father on his throne on the dais.

When Khurram was still thirty feet from where Jahangir was sitting, he raised his hand to halt the procession and dismounted so that he could approach his father on foot. He had taken no more than two or three steps towards the dais when he heard Jahangir call, 'Stop. I will come to you.'

From all around came gasps of surprise. For the emperor to descend the throne to greet a returning commander – even his own flesh and blood – was unprecedented. Slowly Jahangir rose, walked from his throne to the edge of the dais and descended the six shallow marble stairs. Khurram saw the egret plumes in his father's jewelled turban sway as he came towards him and how the diamonds in his ears, at his throat and on his fingers gleamed like white fire, but he was watching it all as if in a dream.

When his father was just a couple feet away, Khurram dropped to his knees and bowed his head. Jahangir touched his hair, then said, 'Bring it.' Glancing up Khurram saw an attendant approach with a small golden tray piled with something – he couldn't see what – and his father take it from him. Khurram looked down again and the next thing he knew his father was gently tipping the tray's contents over his head. Gold coins and jewels were showering down around him.

'Welcome home, my victorious and much loved son,' he heard his father say, then felt Jahangir's hands on his shoulders, raising him up. 'I wish all those present to know of my esteem for you both as a commander and as my son. As a mark of my pride in you, I hereby confer on you the title Shah Jahan, Lord of the World.'

Khurram's heart swelled with pride. He had set out on campaign full of hope but also a little nervous as to how well he would succeed. Now he felt the deep satisfaction of a job well done. He had shown his father what he was capable of and his father had appreciated it. Surely nothing now could stand in the way of his fulfilling his ambition to be named his father's heir.

Chapter 11

The Red Velvet Coach

Mehrunissa watched from beneath the silk canopy set up at one end of the terrace adjoining the emperor's private apartments. The effort had been worth it. Ever since the news had come of Khurram's victories in the south she had been planning this intimate celebration. The food had been exquisite, especially the dishes she had ordered to be prepared by her Persian cook – quails simmered in pomegranate juice, whole lamb stuffed with apricots and pistachios, rice cooked with saffron and dried sour cherries – and the sweet-fleshed, fragrant peaches and melons that Jahangir loved. Instead of having the latter served in dishes of crushed ice she had ordered them to be presented on a bed of diamonds and pearls. The dancers, tumblers and musicians had performed well, but now everyone had withdrawn and the four of them were alone.

Arjumand was looking especially beautiful, Mehrunissa thought, scrutinising her niece in the soft light of the oil lamps burning in tiny mirrored alcoves around the terrace walls. The ruby and emerald diadem Jahangir had given her to mark the birth of her daughter Jahanara became her. So did motherhood. Arjumand was pregnant again and her skin and hair seemed to have a special lustre. Mehrunissa looked down at her own smooth flat belly, left bare by her short tight-fitting *choli* above a pair of wide red silk trousers gathered at the ankles. Every month she still hoped for signs of a child but every month she was disappointed. She longed to have a child by Jahangir – especially a son. It wasn't that it would make him love her more, but it would bind them yet closer for the long term and give her greater status in others' eyes. It would have been good to think of her blood intermingling with that of the Moghul dynasty and descending down through the generations. But time was passing. Though her body was still slender and firm, last month Salla had found a white hair among her long dark tresses. It might be the first but it would not be the last.

Instead it was another and younger member of her family who might become the mother and grandmother of emperors – Arjumand. Her niece was showing Khurram the cream silk pearl-trimmed tunic fastened with ivory buttons that Mehrunissa had presented to her at the start of the feast. Glancing at Jahangir, seated by her side, she saw him watching his son and Arjumand with an expression of quiet pride. Earlier that evening he had said to her, 'You were right to advise me to send Khurram to the Deccan in Parvez's place. I wasn't sure he was ready for such responsibility but you saw what I didn't – that he has the brains for war as well as the courage.'

But now, as Khurram called out something to his father and a smiling Jahangir rose and went over to him, a sudden doubt crept into her mind. For the benefit of her family – as well as for her niece's happiness – she had done everything in her power to bring about Arjumand's marriage to Khurram. She had also never doubted that it would be a good thing for her family if Khurram managed to impress his father – that was why she had suggested to Jahangir that he give him the Deccan command. Yet what if her interests and the interests of her wider family diverged? She hadn't anticipated how brilliantly Khurram would perform, how impressed Jahangir would be . . . Earlier that day as she had watched through the *jali* screen to one side of the throne in the Hall of Public Audience she had been surprised to see Jahangir descend from his throne to shower his son with gold and gems. He hadn't told her he planned to make that gesture, nor that he was going to follow it, as he had, by conferring on Khurram the right to use a scarlet tent on campaign as well as the title of ruler of Hissar Firoz – both clear indiations that he intended to name Khurram as his heir.

Now that Khurram was back at court perhaps Jahangir might wish to involve him more in the running of the empire. Khurram, rather than she, might become the confidant to whom he most naturally turned. As emperor, Jahangir had many routine cares and responsibilities. With her energy and clear mind, she was sure she could take some of that weight from him – indeed she was already starting to prove it to him. Only a few months ago he had told her of complaints from merchants travelling northwest to Kabul of night-time attacks by bandits on their camps. He had been pleased by her sugges-tion that he order the building of further imperial caravanserais along the trunk routes where travellers could be sure of finding a safe bed for themselves and secure stabling for their beasts and goods.

It wasn't just on such prosaic matters she could help. She

had already perceived that big decisions weighed on Jahangir. If he didn't act immediately out of impulse or emotion – which he frequently regretted – he often put them off, and when especially anxious or perplexed he would take a little wine and opium to ease his mind. She knew enough about the running of the imperial government from her father and from listening to Jahangir's council meetings from behind the *jali* screen to be able to share the burden . . . and for her it would be not a duty but a profound satisfaction.

A loud burst of laughter from Jahangir cut into her thoughts. Khurram must have said something to amuse him and he was clapping his son on the shoulder. On the surface it was a happy family scene but to Mehrunissa it suddenly represented something potentially more ominous and she was angry with herself for not foreseeing it. Once again in her life, she would have to watch and wait but above all look to her own interests. She must make sure Jahangir understood how much he needed her and no one else.

· ◆ ·

'Majesty, the ambassador from England is waiting outside the Hall of Public Audience,' said the *quorchi* as late one autumn afternoon Jahangir sat with Mehrunissa in his private apartments.

'Excellent. Summon my attendants.' As his servants began to dress him, Jahangir was smiling. He was anticipating this meeting with some curiosity. News that an embassy from England had arrived at the port of Surat had reached the Moghul court eight weeks before. As the ambassador had been making his slow progress towards Agra he had sent gifts ahead. One of these, a fantastical gilded carriage shaped a little like a giant melon on high wheels – Jahangir had never seen anything like it – had pleased him greatly even though the red velvet lining was spotted with mildew – doubtless a result of the long voyage on the damp salty ship from the remote island from which the ambassador had set out. Mehrunissa too had been delighted with the carriage and he had given it to her while ordering his own craftsmen to make him an exact copy. But he needed to know how the carriages should be drawn – by oxen or by horses, and how they should be harnessed.

'What do you think this ambassador wants?' Mehrunissa asked as Jahangir studied his reflection in a tall mirror.

'Trading concessions, I expect, just like the Portuguese and the Dutch. Since I allowed his countrymen to establish a small base at Surat and to export a few basic products, they've been petitioning me for the right to trade in goods like indigo and cotton calicoes as well as gems and pearls. I have delayed an answer, so now the ruler of their country has sent someone to plead on their behalf.'

'You are wise not to respond too hastily. From what I've heard some of these foreign merchants are growing impertinent, quarrelling and fighting amongst themselves on our streets and offending the local people.'

'Trade brings wealth. But I agree. They must be kept under control.'

Fifteen minutes later trumpets sounded as Jahangir entered the audience hall and seated himself on his throne, his chief counsellors and courtiers grouped on either side beneath the dais and Khurram in the place of honour nearest to the emperor.

A further flourish of trumpets accompanied by the booming of drums announced the arrival of the ambassador. Jahangir

190

could scarcely restrain himself from laughing out loud. A tall figure with very thin legs encased in pale material beneath what looked like short, baggy trousers of dark purple, slashed to reveal bright red fabric beneath and fastened with scarlet ribbons just above the knee, was making his way slowly towards the dais. A tight-fitting bright yellow brocade jacket ending in a stiffened point just above his groin emphasised his extreme thinness. As he came closer Jahangir saw beneath his high-brimmed hat with its curling feather a bright red face – the effect of the sun on a pale skin? – made all the more startling by a wide circle of some hard-looking white material around his neck. The brown hair falling on his shoulders was sparse but extravagant curling moustaches compensated for it. It was hard to estimate the age of this eccentric figure but Jahangir guessed he must be in his late thirties.

Behind him followed a much younger man – barely more than a youth – dressed in the same fashion except that his clothes were all of some dark brown material and he was bare headed. He was of middle height with hair the colour of barley and bright blue eyes like those of Bartholomew Hawkins – who to Jahangir's regret had recently returned to England, chests bulging with new-found wealth – that were looking with some wonder at him on his golden throne. In his right hand was a leash attached to the collar of a long-legged, pale-coated dog so lean that Jahangir could count its every rib. It didn't look unlike the ambassador.

At a gesture from Jahangir's vizier, Majid Khan, the ambassador halted some ten feet from the dais and removing his hat, which he tucked beneath his right arm, extended one skinny leg straight out in front of him, bent the other and inclined his upper body forward from the hips while making a circling

191

movement with his right hand. It was a strange obeisance, and the young man who Jahangir guessed must be his *qorchi* did the same. He was about to wave forward one of his scholars who could speak some English to interpret when the ambassador himself began to speak in halting but still recognisable Persian.

'Great emperor, my name is Sir Thomas Roe. I bring greetings from my own king, James the first of England and sixth of Scotland. Hearing of your greatness as a ruler he wishes to present you with gifts from his country. I have already sent some of these ahead of me and I bring more – paintings, silver mirrors, fine leathers, maps of the known world, a drink from the north of our island that we call whisky, four fine horses that I will present to Your Majesty when they have recovered from the long sea voyage and are worthy to be seen by you, and this hunting dog from our country – in English we call it a greyhound. There is no swifter dog in the world.' Roe turned to the young man, who was standing just behind his right shoulder. The youth stepped forward and undid the dog's leash. Jahangir expected it to race off but it must have been carefully trained for this moment. It took a few steps forward, then extending its front right paw as Roe had extended his leg lowered its head, mimicking the ambassador's own obeisance.

'You are welcome at my court. I thank your master for his presents.' Jahangir gestured to one of his *qorchis* to take the dog away. 'I trust that your apartments in the fort are comfortable and I look forward to talking with you in the days ahead.'

Roe looked a little confused and the young man began to whisper into his ear. At a nod from the ambassador he said, 'My master apologises, Majesty. He has learned a little

Persian, enough to address you just now – and hopes to learn more – but his understanding of the language is still limited. I am his interpreter and his squire. My name is Nicholas Ballantyne.' After a further exchange of whispers Ballantyne continued, 'The ambassador thanks you for your kindness. His apartments are indeed comfortable. During the discussions he looks forward to having with you, he hopes you will look favourably on our desire to trade with your great empire. He wishes me to tell you that we not only have our own goods to offer you but also our ships to carry your pilgrims to Arabia. We are island people and our vessels are the best in the world. They can cross great oceans and their cannon can destroy the ships of any nation. Last year, as you may know, Majesty, the Portuguese dared to attack two English ships off your coast. We sank them.'

Jahangir's eyes widened – not just at surprise at the young man's near perfect Persian but at the bluntness of the proposal. A Moghul – or indeed a Persian – would have taken far longer to come to the point. But it was good to know what the English king had to offer beyond his gifts. Till now Arab and Portuguese ships had between them enjoyed a virtual monopoly in conveying Muslim pilgrims from the ports of Gujarat across the seas on the first stage of their journey to Mecca. The Arab ships were not always seaworthy – only three weeks ago one had foundered in a storm with the loss of all three hundred aboard. And the Arab sailors were no match for the pirates who preyed on the pilgrim ships.

As for the Portuguese, Jahangir had seen the permits they sold to their passengers engraved with the images of their gods – a bearded young man called Jesus and a pale-faced virgin queen whose name was Mary. The Portuguese ships were strong and their well-armed sailors put up a better resistance to the pirates, but the Portuguese in their trading settlement at Goa were growing ever more arrogant. Their priests were aggressively seeking converts among both the Hindu and the Muslim populations and even trying to persuade pilgrims waiting to take ship for Mecca that their beliefs were mistaken. The Portuguese were also asking increasing sums for the transport of pilgrims. The fact that the English king had sent an ambassador to court might make them moderate their demands.

'Tell your master I will consider his proposals and that we will talk further,' Jahangir said. He gave a brief nod to the trumpeter standing to the right of the dais and the man put his bronze instrument to his lips to sound the short blast signalling that the interview was over. As Jahangir rose, the ambassador again stuck out a leg and made his elaborate homage. When he straightened up again his red face was even redder and beneath the arms of his yellow brocade jacket were dark circles of sweat. Had he been nervous or was it just the unaccustomed heat of Hindustan?

• ◆ •

'Send in more wine,' Jahangir ordered his *qorchi*. Roe's face looked shiny with perspiration, the muscles slack – the result of the prodigious amount of alcohol he'd consumed over the past three hours. Jahangir had never met a man with such capacity, but wine didn't seem to dull Roe's wits – rather the reverse. The more he drank the more Jahangir enjoyed his conversation, relishing the information flowing from his willing lips. Roe was clearly an educated man though the writers he was fond of quoting – Roman and Greek philosophers, some

194

dead for nearly two thousand years, he said – were mostly unknown to Jahangir. During the four months he'd spent at court the ambassador's Persian had improved and, though Jahangir might have expected the contrary, wine seemed to give him added fluency. Only yesterday Jahangir had listened to him make a spirited case to one of his own scholars that belief in the existence of the philosopher's stone – a substance thought by some to have the power to change base metals into silver and gold and even to hold the secret of eternal life – was irrational nonsense. Jahangir, whose inclination was to be sceptical of anything which could not be proved, had agreed.

Spread out on the table before them was a book of maps created by a map-maker whose name according to Roe was Mercator, which he had presented to Jahangir soon after his arrival at court. Roe called the book an 'Atlas', explaining that was the name of the mythological man bearing the whole weight of the world upon his shoulders depicted on the cover. 'I know, Majesty, that on your accession you took the title "Seizer of the World", but see how much of the world there actually is,' the ambassador had said a little slyly but making Jahangir laugh. Fascinated, he had kept going back to it, carefully turning the heavy pages to examine the outlines of lands he had never even heard of, all the while his brain teeming with questions for Roe, which was why he had invited him yet again to his private apartments.

'According to what you yourself have told me, it seems that the Spanish, the Portuguese and the Dutch are better explorers even than the English? That man Magellan you were talking about the other day – the first whose ship sailed right around the world – he was Portuguese, wasn't he?'

Roe tried to settle himself more comfortably. With his long

thin legs he found sitting cross-legged for long periods difficult. 'Yes, Majesty. It is true that a few foreign adventurers were lucky in their voyagings, but our English sailors and ships are second to none. My countrymen have recently established the first settlement in the northern Americas at a place they have named Jamestown, after our great king.' Roe's unshakeable belief in the importance of his remote little island never failed to amuse Jahangir. The life the ambassador described with such enthusiasm, from the habits of ordinary people to the customs of the court, sounded primitive to Jahangir's ears, though of course courtesy and his growing liking for Roe prevented him from saying as much.

'If it is true what you say and if your country will indeed provide ships to carry our pilgrims I may grant you the trading concessions you wish, but there will be conditions.'

'Of course, Majesty.' Despite all the wine he had consumed, Roe's eyes were suddenly intent. Over the months since the ambassador's arrival, Jahangir had been sparing with promises though he had sent gifts to this King James of his, carefully chosen to be impressive but not of a magnificence to embarrass the English ruler, who so obviously lacked the wealth of the Moghuls. Though he himself had been pleased with a crystal box inlaid with gold, some of the other English gifts were already falling apart – the leathers were cracking, perhaps as a result of the heat, the gilt was peeling from the picture frames, and he had already had the musty-smelling lining of the coach replaced with fine green brocade from Gujarat. Yet Roe had brought what no other ambassador had – information about the wider world, like the maps, and descriptions of new plants and animals found in this 'new world' he was so fond of talking about. Soon after his arrival he had presented

Jahangir with a small cotton bag containing some hard, round vegetable tubers – 'potatoes', he called them – and claimed they were good to eat once baked or boiled.

The *qorchi* had returned. 'Majesty. This wine – scented with rosewater – is a special gift from the empress. She asked me to say that she prepared it with her own hands.'

'Excellent. Now, ambassador, let's see how the potency of this wine compares with that whisky you brought me . . . and I want you to send for that *qorchi* of yours to sing me some more of those English songs . . .'

'Majesty, the emperor is asleep.'

Mehrunissa looked up from the book she had been reading by the light of an oil lamp, though now that the early morning light was filtering in through the casement she no longer needed it. 'And the ambassador?'

'Also asleep, Majesty.'

'Order attendants to carry the emperor back here to his apartments and send for the Englishman's servants to take him to his quarters.'

This was by no means the first time Jahangir's drinking bouts with Roe had lasted until dawn and Mehrunissa knew exactly what the *qorchi* meant when he said that her husband was asleep: the emperor had passed out. These sessions with Roe had been growing more frequent. Jahangir's excuse was that they had so many interesting things to discuss, so many ideas to explore. Yesterday he had told her he wanted to explain to Roe about some of his experiments with new medicines, especially his discovery – using water in which the leaves of the plane tree had been fermented – of a salve to make wounds

197

heal faster. He had been testing the ointment on a *qorchi* who had been gored in the thigh by a stag while out hunting. But she knew from observing through a small *jali* screen a few hours earlier that Jahangir and Roe had soon turned to more frivolous matters, singing bawdy songs – Persian and English – that they had taught one another, and even attempting trials of strength which the far more powerfully built Jahangir invariably won.

They were more like a pair of boys than an emperor and the ambassador of a foreign ruler, but perhaps such carousing was common at the English court. It certainly had charms for Jahangir, perhaps as a contrast to the elaborate formality of his own court where he must behave as not so much a man as the image of power and wealth. When Roe had farted loud and long in his presence, Jahangir had laughed and clapped him on the shoulder. Though they drank so much these sessions were perhaps no bad thing. They relaxed Jahangir and, apart from the fact that on some nights they kept him from her bed, took nothing away from her. Indeed the reverse was true, since they allowed her to do more for him. She tended him when, head aching, he finally woke, rubbing his temples with aloe and sandalwood oils to drive away the pain.

Sometimes, still bleary eyed after the previous night's carousing, he found it difficult to concentrate on the matters that made up so much of the business of his council meetings – the raising of taxes, the granting of titles and estates to his nobles, the sending of orders to the governors of his provinces. Even at the best of time such things bored him. However, she, who never missed a meeting, sitting intent behind the *jali* screen in the royal women's gallery, absorbed everything and could remind him of the things he ought to know. More and more frequently she offered to read the official documents he found so tedious and tell him the gist of their contents and he readily agreed, delighted to shift some of the burden from his shoulders to hers. Just as she had hoped he would, he now often sought her advice, even joking that he had little need of his vizier Majid Khan. The boundary between influence and power wasn't so wide, and recently she had felt herself beginning to edge across it . . .

Her fears that Khurram might be the one to whom Jahangir turned had so far proved groundless. He had been delighted by the birth of a son, Dara Shukoh, to Khurram and Arjumand, but though he and Khurram were frequently together it was usually to go hunting or hawking or to test each other's skill at archery or watch an elephant fight. Since his return from the Deccan the prince had shown no inclination to become involved in the minutiae of government that she found so fascinating and had such appetite for. Others were noticing her growing influence. Only last week half a dozen petitions addressed directly to her had arrived in the imperial *haram*. Soon she would ask Jahangir whether, to save him effort, she could start issuing edicts under her own name. She would use the carved emerald he had given her, inscribed with her title, Nur Mahal . . .

The doors opened and four attendants, legs bowing slightly with the strain, entered carrying a bamboo litter on which Jahangir was lying on his back, arms outflung. She could hear his heavy, rhythmic breathing.

'Put the litter down over here, then leave us,' Mehrunissa commanded, pointing to a dark corner of the chamber away from the bright sunlight that was now shafting in through the casement. As soon as they were alone she dipped a silk handkerchief into a brass bowl of water, then went over to Jahangir and knelt down by his side. How deeply he was sleeping, she thought, looking at his face, which with the passing of the years was growing a little fuller fleshed but was still handsome. As she began to wipe his forehead, a tenderness for him swept through her. This man had given her – could give her – everything she had ever wanted.

He began to stir. Suddenly he opened his eyes and smiled a little ruefully. 'I think I drank too much of that wine of yours again.'

Chapter 12

The Poison Pen

'Majesty . . . forgive me for waking you . . .'

Mehrunissa opened sleepy eyes to see Salla leaning over the couch where she had been dozing. The Armenian was breathing hard, as if she had run to her mistress's apartments. Mehrunissa sat up, alarmed.

'What's happened? Is it the emperor?' An hour earlier, Jahangir had left her to watch a contest between one of his prize fighting elephants – a great scarred beast called Avenger, veteran of many battles with a broken but still highly effective right tusk – and an even more massive elephant sent as a gift by the Governor of Gwalior. Normally she would have watched the fight as well – she enjoyed the spectacle of these mountainous animals pitting their strength against one another and trying to guess which would win – but she had felt a little weary and decided instead to rest.

'It isn't the emperor, Majesty.'

'What then?

Salla held out a jewelled hairpin fashioned like a peacock, its enamelled tail feathers set with tiny emeralds and sapphires. It was one of Mehrunissa's favourite pieces and she had been wearing it earlier that day as she had sat behind the *jali* screen set in the wall to one side of the imperial throne in the Hall of Public Audience, watching and listening as an emissary from the Governor of Lahore reported progress on improving the fortifications there. The pin must have slipped unnoticed from her hair, but surely Salla hadn't disturbed her to report the finding of a trinket?

'It was on your chair behind the *jali*,' Salla was saying. 'I found it when I went to retrieve my own shawl which I'd left there, but while I was there I overheard something . . .'

Salla looked so troubled that instinctively Mehrunissa took her hand. 'Tell me what it was.' Though eager to know what had so disturbed her waiting woman, she kept her tone gentle.

'It was the English ambassador and his *qorchi*. They were alone in the Hall of Public Audience because all the courtiers had accompanied the emperor to the elephant fight. I heard the ambassador say to his *qorchi* that for once it was safe for them to talk openly. I was curious and so I waited – you know that I understand their language. The ambassador was leaning against one of the sandstone columns by the dais while his *qorchi* perched on the edge of the emperor's dais.'

Mehrunissa frowned. To sit on the emperor's dais was an almost unthinkable breach of etiquette but the two foreigners had clearly thought themselves unobserved. 'Go on.'

'The ambassader said that he wished to dictate a letter to be sent to England. He said it was time for his masters to know the truth about the emperor – that he is not only full of pride but in thrall to a woman. He said – forgive me, Highness – that in his country a woman like you would be put in a bridle to shame her.'

'What else did he say?' Mehrunissa's voice shook with anger.

'I don't know . . . I left at once to find you. Did I do wrong?'

'You were entirely right. Come with me. If the ambassador is still there I may need your help to understand what they are saying.' Though she had been taking pains to learn English – even, with Salla's help, reading some sonnets by an English poet called Shakespeare that Roe had presented to Jahangir – Mehrunissa knew her command of the language was still weaker than Salla's.

The two women walked quickly from Mehrunissa's apartments and along the narrow passage connecting them with the small, dark room behind the *jali*. Barely a couple of minutes later Mehrunissa, with Salla behind her, slipped quietly into the room. Sitting down on a rose silk-covered stool, Mehrunissa leaned towards the *jali* to look intently through one of the star-shaped holes carved into the sandstone. Roe, spindly frame dressed in a long crimson satin tunic, was standing just as Salla had described, propped against a pillar. Nicholas Ballantyne's golden head was bent low over a piece of paper over which he had just sprinkled sand. So the dictation was over. Mehrunissa leaned back, disappointed. Then she heard Roe say, 'Read it back to me in case you've misheard anything.'

'Your Gracious Majesty,' Ballantyne began, speaking slowly enough for Salla to whisper to Mehrunissa the meaning of any unfamiliar words. 'It is now eighteen months since I arrived at the Moghul court. I have written to you many times of the great luxury with which the emperor surrounds himself but last week he did me the honour of inviting me to visit one of his underground treasure houses. It is hard to find words to describe what I saw – candlelit vaults piled with rubies and sapphires bigger than walnuts, silk sacks overflowing with more pearls than you would imagine an ocean could provide and diamonds to outshine the sun. Of course, I did not reveal my astonishment but merely nodded as if used to such sights. But truly, Your Majesty, even the emperor's favourite horses and elephants and hunting leopards have more magnificent jewels than any our royal treasury possesses, and all set in shining gold.

'This glittering wealth is of great importance to the emperor, who has the pride of Lucifer in his dynasty, his empire and himself. He loves to show off his riches and it grieves me to report that his pride has recently taken a new direction. I have already told you how, entirely disregarding his mullahs' prohibition of the portrayal of men and animals – as I am told his father did before him – he much admires the portrait of yourself that you sent him. He has had his own likeness painted. He is much pleased with the portrait, in which the artist – a man called Bichitr – has depicted him sitting on a jewelled cup like a chalice with a great golden halo round his head. He is handing a book to a mullah while you, Your Majesty, together with the Sultan of Turkey and the Shah of Persia, are shown as small and insignificant figures squeezed into the corner. By this depiction the emperor in his arrogance is claiming to be the Lord of the World.'

Mehrunissa shifted her weight on the stool. How dare

Roe speak so slightingly and patronisingly of Jahangir? But the squire was continuing and she fixed her attention on him again. It was important she tried to understand every word, every nuance correctly.

'This portrait is an affront to Your Royal Majesty, though when the emperor showed it to me I merely said that the artist had made his image most true to life and made no comment about the portrait's composition. The emperor is so conceited that he did not notice my cool response, as I knew he would not. Indeed, I spend so many hours with him – he enjoys my company and never tires of asking me questions – that I have had excellent opportunities to study his character. I think that the time has come when I should attempt to explain his nature to Your Majesty so that you may understand why, although the emperor has granted us some minor concessions to trade in indigo, civet and cottons, he has still not given me an answer about allowing English ships to transport pilgrims to Arabia – a matter that I know from your last despatch is testing your patience.

'The emperor Jahangir is a complex man in whom I have observed many contradictions. He can be charming and good natured. He has an open, active mind and delights in observing the natural world. When a villager recently brought word that a giant almost molten rock had fallen from the skies and crashed into the side of a hill not far from Agra, he ordered it to be dug out while still smoking and swords fashioned from the hot metal extracted from it to test its strength. He has also commissioned a study of the intestines of a lion to see whether they offer any clues to the beast's bravery.

'However, the emperor can also be impulsive, impatient

and short tempered to a fault. Although tolerant in most matters, including that of religion – indeed it seems to me that he himself has little – he can be bizarrely cruel. Always a believer in the importance of outward show, he makes a pageant out of torture and execution. On occasion he seems to relish the sight of men being skinned alive or crushed beneath the feet of elephants. He says these are the punishments that have always been meted out. I don't doubt that this is true – or that they are merited – but it turns my stomach to watch. The emperor on the other hand observes some of these executions from close to as if they were the experiments of alchemists, noting how long it takes a flayed or impaled man to die and what their tortures reveal of the innermost workings of their bodies.

'But to my mind worst of all, your Majesty, the emperor allows himself to be ruled by a woman. This Mehrunissa, of whom I have written to you before, is, I am convinced, a malign influence on him and on the empire he rules. It is well known throughout the court that she is hungry for power and also that she encourages her husband's love of wine and opium to make him the more willing to give it to her. She is far more important here than any courtier – even the emperor's vizier. Of course I take care to send her presents and flattering messages but despite this I am convinced from what I hear around the court that she is not our friend. Every time I ask the emperor for his agreement to allow English ships to transport the pilgrims, he tells me smilingly to be patient. I suspect the empress's hand behind this procrastination. Courtiers tell me that, although a Persian herself, she distrusts all foreigners and suspects our motives, judging them as self-seeking as her own, I believe.

Therefore she aims, by the advice she whispers into her husband's ear, to play us off against each other and thus to maintain and increase her own power. Jahangir, instead of doting on her, should teach her not to meddle and to know her place. I am not alone in that view.

'But I do not despair of achieving our objective. The emperor considers himself my friend and if I am patient I may yet persuade him to favour our proposal about the pilgrims. I will write again when I have further — and I trust favourable — news.'

Nicholas Ballantyne looked up enquiringly. 'Good.' Roe nodded. 'In fact, excellent. I want this letter despatched to Surat tonight so that it catches the *Peregrine* before she sails for England in a week's time. Let us go to my room so I can put my seal to it.'

Through the *jali*, Mehrunissa watched Ballantyne fold the letter and place it in his satchel. Then the two Englishmen made their way slowly from the hall. Her earlier weariness had disappeared as fresh energy and determination coursed through her. She had understood enough to know that Roe was not her friend. What was more, he had spoken disparagingly of the emperor. With Salla silent by her side, Mehrunissa sat motionless for a long time.

· ◆ ·

'Ladli, read the first three verses to me.' Ten years old now, her daughter had, like herself, a quick mind, Mehrunissa thought as the girl began. But though the poem was one of her favourites, she couldn't concentrate. All the time she was wondering what was happening in Roe's apartments. It had taken her time to decide how best to take her revenge on him and, indeed, whether it was even worth it. As her anger had died she had thought more rationally about his letter. Like any ambassador who had ever lived, Roe wanted to show his king how much influence he had, how deep were his insights into the lives of the great, how well he was furthering the interests of his own country, how his lack of success was not his fault . . . Now that she was calmer she could forgive Roe some of that.

Yet she could not overlook his view of her. *It is well known throughout the court that she is hungry for power*, he had written . . . What if he was encouraging such talk among the many friends and acquaintances he had at court? She was annoyed with herself for misjudging the situation. For a long time she had encouraged Roe's intimacy with Jahangir, knowing not only that her husband enjoyed his company but that the more time he spent with the ambassador the less time he would have for the official matters that bored him and that she was so willing – and able – to relieve him of.

She could not, would not, allow Roe to undermine her position and all that she had achieved and the greater glories she aspired to. Now that she thought about it, only two weeks ago she had noticed an odd look on Majid Khan's face when Jahangir had told his vizier to send some documents about refurbishments at the Lahore fort to her for approval. Even more recently she'd overheard two old women in the *haram* – one a great-aunt of Jahangir's, the other a distant cousin of his father's – bemoaning the influence of her family. 'Ghiyas Beg controls the empire's finances, Asaf Khan commands the Agra fort and as for her . . .' She'd known very well whom they'd meant by 'her'. It had taken an hour of having her long hair carefully brushed by Salla

208

to restore her good humour and during that time she had come to a decision. Roe must leave the court.

And tonight was the night when she should discover whether her plan was going to work. Suddenly she realised that Ladli had come to the end of the verse and was looking up at her. 'Excellent. Well done.' Mehrunissa smiled, feeling a little guilty that she'd no idea how well her daughter had read.

· ◆ ·

Nicholas Ballantyne looked with some consternation at his master, his red face for once pallid, lying sweat soaked and naked on his bed. 'My bowels feel as though they're on fire though I've emptied them at least six times in the past hour,' the ambassador moaned, closing his eyes.

'When did this begin?'

'Not long after I had finished supper.'

It sounded like dysentery, Nicholas thought, something that sooner or later afflicted most foreigners in Hindustan. It certainly smelled like it – the stink in the room from the near-overflowing brass chamber pot beneath Roe's bed was disgusting. Calling for an attendant to empty it and bring a new one, Nicholas steeled himself to come closer to his master, whose thin chest was rising and falling as he clenched the sides of the bed with both hands as if he feared to fall out.

'I'll fetch a *hakim*.'

When Nicholas returned about twenty minutes later with one of the court doctors, a short stout man in a brown turban carrying his instruments in a leather satchel, Roe was vomiting copiously into a copper basin an attendant was holding for him. When eventually he had finished and had collapsed back on to the bed the *hakim* felt his forehead then rolled back first his right eyelid and then his left. 'Let me see your tongue,' he ordered. Roe opened his mouth and stuck out the tip, which Nicholas could see was coated with a yellowy film. 'More,' the *hakim* commanded. Roe feebly pushed his tongue out a little further.

'You have eaten something rotten. You must be more careful in the hot season.'

'All the ambassador's food is prepared in the imperial kitchens by order of the emperor,' said Nicholas. 'The greatest care is taken . . .'

'These symptoms could only be caused by tainted food. His body is purging itself from above and below of whatever has caused the problem.' Seeing that Nicholas still looked unconvinced the doctor added, 'Young man, if it were poison, your master would already be dead. As it is, I can tell you there is little risk to his life if he stays quiet, drinks plenty of water and for the next few days eats only a mixture of yoghourt and salt into which you must grind pellets of opium. I will prepare a portion now. Watch me carefully so that you know exactly what to do. Feed him two spoonfuls – no more – every hour until the diarrhoea and sickness stop completely. After that he must have nothing but water for a further three days. If there is any change in his condition send for me at once.'

Nicholas nodded. After the *hakim* had left, he summoned attendants to wash Roe, change the bedding and, seeing how he was starting to shiver, bring him a nightshirt.

'Perhaps I've been here too long,' Roe said. With his long moustaches drooping and dripping moisture from being sponged he looked thoroughly dejected. 'They say this climate is no good for Europeans and that few of us survive more than two monsoons.'

'Courage. You've been healthy till now. This could have happened anywhere . . . in England even . . . and you haven't accomplished your mission yet.'

'Perhaps you're right. You're a good boy, Nicholas, thank you. I won't forget how well you've served me.' Roe managed a weak smile but suddenly a spasm crossed his face as fresh gripes seized him. 'Leave me now . . .' he gasped, and levering himself out of bed he reached once more for the chamber pot.

◆

'I thought you planned to spend the evening with Sir Thomas?' Mehrunissa looked up as Jahangir entered her apartments and bent to kiss her.

'He sent a message that he's not well.'

'I'm sorry. I hope he recovers quickly.' Mehrunissa composed her features into a look of gentle concern but inside she felt a deep satisfaction. It hadn't been difficult to bribe an attendant to slip a little rotted meat into the highly spiced lamb pullao that she knew Roe particularly enjoyed. She felt no guilt – he deserved his sufferings for writing poison about her. She hoped she'd made him feel sufficiently ill to consider leaving the Moghul court. Probably not, but having found a way of attacking the ambassador through his bowels she could use it again and again until she'd weakened him sufficiently to achieve her objective of his departure. She'd never lacked patience.

'I would have come to see you anyway. I have something

I want to discuss with you. My agents in the south report that Malik Ambar is assembling a fresh army. I thought we had taught him a lesson, but his insolence and ambition – like those of the Deccan kings on whose behalf he fights – seem to know no limits.'

'Will you send Khurram again?'

'That was what I wanted to discuss with you. He did well last time. He will expect me to send him but I'm reluctant to put him in danger again. The more I see of him the more convinced I am becoming that I should name him now as my heir and keep him here in safety. I can teach him much about how to govern an empire. That will help him when the time comes for him to succeed me. I wish my father had done the same for me and I do not want to repeat his mistakes.'

Mehrunissa thought quickly. Her every instinct told her she must not allow Jahangir and Khurram to become too close. Even though Khurram was married to Arjumand to whom he was devoted and her family's position might be advanced by such proximity, her own could only suffer. This she could not permit, but what could she say? Then an idea came to her. 'I understand your reluctance to part from Khurram. But he is proud and will be offended if you don't send him against Malik Ambar once again. He will take it as a criticism that last time he failed to capture or kill Malik Ambar.'

'So you truly believe I should send him?'

'Yes. To him, dealing with the Abyssinian is unfinished business – I have heard him say as much – and to do anything else would belittle him. And when he returns – as I am sure he will, if you order him not to hazard his own life – there will be time enough to think about naming your heir. You are still young – you have plenty of time to consider such an important step. You mustn't forget you have other sons and how they will feel if you show too much favour to Khurram.'

'Parvez is a fool and a drunk. He can surely have no more expectation of the throne than Khusrau.'

'But there's also Shahriyar. He is growing up fast and I hear encouraging things about his progress. They say that he rides superbly and is a sure shot with either bow or musket.'

Jahangir smiled. 'You make me ashamed. You shouldn't have to tell me about my own son's promise. I admit I hardly see Shahriyar.'

'You should. Then you can judge him for yourself.'

She was right, Jahangir thought. There was no need to rush to name an heir. And she was also right that he should allow Khurram to deal with Malik Ambar.

'As always, your instincts are correct. You see things so clearly.'

'I only want to help you. And after Khurram has departed on campaign I'll hold a small party and invite Shahriyar so that you can see how well he is turning out. And perhaps I will also ask Ladli to join us. She too is growing up and is not without looks and accomplishment. I think you will be pleased with her.'

'Do so. But enough of business. You have eased my mind. Let's now enjoy the pleasures of the body.' Gently he began to unfasten the coral buttons of her low-cut bodice and smiled to see the answering light in her eyes. Jahangir was hers and she was his and nothing and no one should come between them.

Chapter 13

The Abyssinian

'My father has sent us to confront Malik Ambar once more. Undaunted by our previous victories over him the Abyssinian has once again invaded Moghul territories,' Khurram began. He was standing immaculately dressed in cream robes with a quadruple string of pearls as a belt and another lustrous pearl almost as big as a grape adorning his cream turban on the *jharoka* balcony of the Agra fort to address the serried ranks of his troops gathered on the parade ground below. Jahangir, watching from the chamber behind the balcony, wondered whether he could have spoken with the same confidence and authority at his age. At Khurram's words a ripple, like wind stirring wheat in a field, seemed to run through the rows of men and they began to cheer.

'This time we will not be content with defeating Malik Ambar's forces and expelling him from our lands as we did three years ago,' Khurram continued, holding up his right hand to command silence. 'We will demand that his masters, the sultans of Golconda, Bijapur and Ahmednagar, cede some of their lands and goods to us. The booty will be magnificent and I will make sure you all share in it.' Khurram lowered his hand and smiled as a great chorus of *Khurram zinderbad, Padishah Jahangir zinderbad* burst from his men. His ancestor Babur had been right when recording that the prospect of profit was the best way of ensuring the loyalty and bravery of an army, Jahangir thought.

When finally the shouting had died down, Khurram went on, 'Tonight, once our final preparations are completed, I have ordered our cooks to provide a special feast so that when we ride out from Agra tomorrow we do so not only confident in our ultimate victory but also with well-filled stomachs.' Another wave of cheering enveloped Khurram as he turned, followed by two tall bodyguards dressed in cream with steel breastplates and helmets polished to mirror bright-ness, and went inside to where his father was waiting.

'You spoke well,' Jahangir said, embracing him.

'Because I wish my men to fight well. My announcement of the feast will speed their final preparations.'

'Today I received more news of Malik Ambar's movements. It appears he is marauding through the area around Mandu, raiding some of the richer estates. He's also seized two district treasuries and a local armoury.'

'So he'll have amassed quite a bit of loot?'

'Yes, but that might work in our favour by slowing him down a little and making it easier for you to catch up with him.'

'That will be my biggest problem. Our forces outnumber his and are the more heavily armed. Though I've ordered our men to bring no unnecessary baggage or equipment, his troops will be more mobile and nimble. Also, they know the southern lands better than we do, as we found to our cost three years ago. They'll again be an elusive prey . . .'

'But I don't doubt your ability to succeed.'

Khurram's expression told Jahangir that his son didn't doubt it either. 'I'll set up my headquarters at Burhanpur on the Tapti river again. From there I'll march for Mandu to try to come up with Malik Ambar. I'll also send flanking detachments to the south to block his retreat. I intend to drive him further into our territory rather than out of it so that we can reduce his advantage in local knowledge. Once I have defeated him there – as God willing I will – I'll have a better chance of destroying the remnants of his army as they retreat towards his own lands and of capturing Malik Ambar himself, ending his threat once and for all.'

'Be careful. He is a wily enemy.'

'He won't escape me this time.'

'I know, but remember not to let youthful eagerness and confidence in your abilities, however justified, make you abandon prudence. Think your plan of battle through carefully with your commanders. Take no unnecessary risks yourself.'

'I will try to remember, Father.'

'Arjumand goes with you, despite her pregnancy?'

'She insists on it, as she did last time. She also refuses to be parted from our children, though once we reach Burhanpur they will remain in the safety of the fortress there. Forgive me, Father. If I may I must leave you. I've some last minute commissariat matters to attend to before the farewell feast.'

Jahangir opened his arms to his son and the two men

embraced again. 'God bless and speed you back to me victorious, my son.'

After Khurram had gone, Jahangir walked out on to the *jharoka* balcony. The soldiers on the parade ground had dispersed. Looking towards the Jumna he saw a string of war elephants being led from the *hati mahal* to make their slow way down to the brown waters to drink, but otherwise there was little movement on the riverbank. The sun was sinking, streaking the western sky crimson and purple. How often had a Moghul emperor stood here, contemplating such a scene? For a moment Jahangir imagined his forebears – Babur the warrior from the Asian steppes, Humayun the stargazer, his own father the great Akbar, so revered by his people – standing beside him. Their line was ancient, reaching back even beyond Timur to the warrior Genghis Khan . . . It made him proud to think of it, and even prouder that he had fathered such an able and loyal son as Khurram, about to lead the Moghul armies in defence of the empire their ancestors had bled for.

◆

'Highness,' reported Kamran Iqbal as the Deccan sun beat down on the fabric of the red command tent in which Khurram was sitting on a small low divan surrounded by his senior officers. 'Ever since we freed the area around Mandu, Malik Ambar's men have continued to retreat before our advance. They are still following the course of the Bari river, sticking close to its west bank as they make their way south. They're now less than twenty miles from their own territories.'

'Good. That means we've achieved something since

217

launching our pursuit from Burhanpur, but it's not enough . . . Are any of our forces between them and the range of high hills that mark the divide between our two lands?'

'No, Highness. Only a few detachments of scouts not strong enough to fight a delaying action.'

'I thought not. Malik Ambar has outmanoeuvred us yet again. Despite our best efforts we've never managed to get enough of our forces between him and the borderlands to compel him to fight us on ground of our own choosing. He seems to anticipate our every move.'

'But we've been victorious in nearly all the skirmishes we've fought with his men and we've kept him away from any sources of fresh plunder – and even recovered some of what he had taken before,' said Kamran Iqbal with a hint of pride in his voice, while several other officers nodded in vigorous agreement.

'True, but I wanted to do more than contain his threat. Now I fear that within a day or two he will be back in among the hills he knows so well and almost impossible to bring to a decisive battle', said Khurram, trying but failing to keep some of the frustration he felt out of his voice. It was almost as if Malik Ambar had a spy amongst his senior officers, he'd complained to Arjumand in their tent the previous evening.

'But in that case, wouldn't he have found an opportunity to surprise and defeat you, rather than retreat?' she had argued. She was probably right, he comforted himself.

'Highness, one of our most reliable scouts tells me that the river bends quite sharply to the west about ten miles or so from Malik Ambar's present position.' Kamran Iqbal interrupted Khurram's sombre musing. 'Couldn't we attempt to corner him in the river bend?'

'Perhaps, but it depends on the nature of the ground within the bend. It's not too marshy, is it?'

'No. There are some sandbanks which might have defensive potential but they're quite low and apparently there aren't too many of them.'

'It's probably worth the risk then,' said Khurram, his spirits rising. 'When is Malik Ambar likely to get there?'

'Around ten o'clock tomorrow morning – if he follows his usual pattern of making camp for about nine hours overnight.'

'Let's attack him there, then. Have our outlying pickets redoubled to stop Malik Ambar's scouts getting close enough to observe our preparations. We'll make the bulk of them after dark for added security.'

• ◆ •

The next morning Khurram felt the mixture of fear and excitement that he always experienced before a battle drive out all other emotions as he galloped across the sandy ground towards Malik Ambar's position in the river bend. His preparations the previous night had gone seemingly unnoticed by his enemies but an advance party of his war elephants had travelled only half of the ten-mile distance towards the ambush place in the river bend before they had encountered some of Malik Ambar's scouts. Although the musketeers in their howdahs had shot down three of the scouts at least two others had galloped away unscathed towards Malik Ambar's column, so he would have had nearly an hour's warning of their attack. Perhaps he had been wrong not to rely solely on his cavalry, thought Khurram, but then he would have lacked the firepower of the small cannon in the howdahs of his elephants, which were loping into the attack surprisingly quickly for such large cumbersome-looking beasts, only a short distance behind his horsemen.

In the time the scouts' warning had given them, Malik Ambar's artillerymen had got perhaps half a dozen of their cannon into position behind some of the sand dunes, which seemed more numerous if a little lower than Khurram had anticipated. Their first shots had fallen short, thudding harmlessly into the sandy earth. Now, however, two of the cannon balls fired in the second round landed close together among the leading wave of Moghul horsemen.

Khurram, who was galloping in the second wave the better to see and direct the action, saw the mounts of two of his leading men crash to the ground, pitching their riders over their heads. Other horses including that of one of the Moghul standard-bearers stumbled over the bodies and fell too, legs flailing in the air. The long green banner dropped by its carrier was blown by the wind towards Malik Ambar's lines for a few yards before becoming entangled with a small spiny bush growing on the side of one of the dunes.

Malik Ambar's gunners were well disciplined and drilled. More cannon shots boomed out and more horsemen fell from the saddle. Two horses, one missing part of its left foreleg and both of them riderless and neighing in pain, swerved away from the guns across the path of other Moghul horsemen. As they did so, the first wave of Moghul cavalry began to lose all impetus. Soon Khurram and the leading riders of the second wave were among the remnants of the first.

'Come on! Charge with us!' Khurram yelled as loudly as he could above the noise of battle to some of the faltering riders. 'Aim for the nearest cannon – those behind the low dune to the left. The distance is short – they can't reload fast enough to get more than one round off before we reach them.' Head bent low to his horse's neck and with his sword extended before him in his right hand, Khurram wheeled his mount to lead them directly towards the long low dune in the centre of Malik Ambar's line over which two cannon barrels peered.

Before he had covered more than half the distance, he heard a crashing explosion followed immediately by a second boom and felt a rush of hot air as shards of metal and a shower of sand and grit flew around him and acrid smoke billowed from behind the dune. The chestnut horse of the rider next to him collapsed with a jagged piece of metal embedded in its throat and its rider, a tall, orange-clad Rajput, hit the ground head first and lay still, his neck broken. Khurram kicked his horse on, ears ringing, brains scrambled and eyes and mouth full of grit and smoke. Even dazed as he was, he knew that the violent blasts were not the normal discharge of the cannon. The thought that it might be some sort of new weapon flitted across his mind for a moment but then as his black horse breasted the low dune and some of the smoke cleared he saw that one of the two large cannon behind the dune had exploded. Its barrel had been peeled back like a banana. The dismembered and mangled bodies of several of its crew were strewn around. There was a large crater in the sand nearby around which were some fragments of tin and white cloth. The second explosion must have been caused by some powder stored nearby and ignited by the first.

The explosion of the first cannon had blown the long

barrel of the second from its heavy wooden limber crushing two of its gunners beneath it. A third was trying to crawl away with a shattered left leg which ended in a bloody mess of flesh and bone halfway down his calf.

Looking down as he reined in his horse to allow his troops to gather round him again, Khurram saw that the lower part of his breastplate, his saddle pommel and a steel plate protecting his horse's head were all spattered with blood and small pieces of flesh that must have come from the body of one of the crew of the first cannon. He had been very lucky, he thought with a shudder. The explosion had occurred directly in front of him. If overuse or faulty manufacture had not caused that gun barrel to explode, more than likely the cannon ball would have cut him in two. He must not fail to exploit the opportunity fate had given him.

To his delight he and the men swiftly gathering about him were now in Malik Ambar's lines and the Abyssinian's artillerymen could not manhandle their remaining weapons into a position where they could fire at them even if, stunned as they must be by the explosions, they had the presence of mind to do so. Some of the war elephants had now come up, trampling through the soft sand of the dune. Khurram waved them forward towards the centre of Malik Ambar's position, where behind some more dunes he could see baggage wagons and beyond them a group of mounted men, and shouted to his horsemen to follow.

Malik Ambar's troops were beginning to recover from their confusion. As the elephants moved forward Khurram heard the crackle of musketry from behind some of the nearby dunes, followed by the ring of musket balls ricocheting off the elephants' heavy steel plate armour. One elephant, clearly hit in an unprotected spot, first slowed and then veered away but the rest plodded resolutely forward as if deaf to their comrade's trumpets of distress. Knowing that the problem with muskets as with artillery was the time required to complete the cumbersome loading process, Khurram immediately gestured to an officer on the flank of his party to gather some of his horsemen to cut down the musketeers before they could reload. The man obeyed and less than a minute later several musketeers emerged from behind one side of the nearest of the dunes as the horsemen rounded the other. The enemy threw down their weapons and as they ran they tried pathetically to protect their heads from the cavalrymen's sharp slashing swords with their hands. It was to no avail and soon all were lying sprawled in the sand.

Meanwhile the elephants were approaching the wagons. Suddenly Khurram saw a group of Malik Ambar's men straining to heave two small wagons aside, revealing as they did so two cannon and their leather-jerkined gunners. At once the artillerymen put their tapers to the firing holes. One of the leading elephants pitched forward, hit by a cannon ball which shattered one of its tusks and reduced its trunk and mouth to bloody pulp. The second shot luckily missed but sprayed sand as it embedded itself in the ground near the foot of another large Moghul elephant. The beast stopped immediately, perhaps blinded momentarily by the grit, and began to trumpet. Nevertheless, the other elephants moved round it, answering to the commands of their *mahouts* as obediently as if on the parade ground. Khurram saw a flash and a billow of white smoke from a howdah as one of his *gajnals* fired. The ball hit the nearest of Malik Ambar's

223

cannon, knocking off one of its metal-bound wooden wheels and destroying the axle, causing the cannon barrel to point skywards at a crazy angle. Musketeers from another of the howdahs had picked off two of the crew of the second cannon, one of whom lay on his back, heels drumming the sandy ground in his death agony. As Khurram watched, four of his horsemen surrounded the remaining two artillerymen, who threw themselves face down on the ground in token of surrender.

As he ordered his men to push on towards the riverbank, Khurram was delighted to see that Malik Ambar's men were pulling back towards the river. As he waved his men forward against his retreating enemy Khurram began to realise that, after little more than an hour, victory would soon again be his, although it had taken a stroke of great good fortune when the cannon had exploded to assure it. However, as he breasted another sand dune and for the first time got a clear view of the river, he saw that there was a large group of horsemen on the opposite bank and rafts carrying others were in midstream, being frantically poled towards the far side. As he reached the edge of the river a minute or two later a small figure wearing a breastplate which glinted mirror bright in the late morning sun waved his sword in a gesture of defiance before turning and leading his few remaining troops away. Malik Ambar had eluded him again, thought Khurram, but again he had lost most of his army and – if the abandoned wagons contained what he thought they did – most of his booty.

His father would be pleased when the news reached him. So too would his mother have been, but Jodh Bai had died three months ago. According to the reports that had reached him, her death though unexpected had been peaceful, in her sleep. He still thought of her often and found it hard to believe she was gone.

◆

The acrobat's lithe body, naked except for a short orange loincloth, gleamed with oil as, bracing his legs on the paving stones of the terrace of Jahangir's apartments, he leaned back and raised his right hand to insert the two-foot-long slim steel sword that Jahangir had just inspected into his open mouth. Jahangir gasped as the blade disappeared up to the hilt, expecting at any moment to see the tip burst through the man's muscular torso in a shower of blood. But as smoothly as he had swallowed it the man drew the blade slowly out again, bowed before Jahangir and Mehrunissa and placed the sword on the ground. He clapped his hands and two more acrobats came forward, each holding a long metal skewer around which cloth dipped in oil had been tightly bound and then set alight. Leaning back again, this time so far that his long dark hair brushed the paving stones, the man swallowed first one of the skewers, then the other, then both simultaneously. Just as there had been no pierced skin there was no smell of burning flesh. As the man stood upright again and taking deep breaths extinguished the still-burning skewers, Jahangir tossed him a handful of gold *mohurs*.

'I thought they would amuse you,' said Mehrunissa as the acrobats ran lightly from the terrace. 'They come from the hills of the far northeast where the tribespeople are skilled at such tricks.'

'They did amuse me. In the morning I'll summon them again and ask them to explain the secrets of their tricks.'

Mehrunissa smiled. She was always trying to find curiosities to divert Jahangir. She liked it when he sought his relaxation with her and the quiet of evening was one of the best times to talk.

Jahangir sipped the rose-scented wine she had prepared for him. 'I have had a letter from Shahriyar. He is still at Bhadaur but reports that he has found a good site for building a new fort. From what he says he seems to have examined the area diligently and to have some useful suggestions on how the fort should be constructed.'

'Good.' Mehrunissa nodded. She herself had suggested some ideas to Shahriyar after discussing Jahangir's desire to construct a new fort to protect the southern approaches to Agra with her brother. Asaf Khan's nose had, she sensed, been put a little out of joint by Jahangir's decision – at her behest, not that Asaf Khan knew that – to give the task to Shahriyar. As the commander of the Agra garrison her brother felt he should have at least accompanied the prince. In his chagrin he had told Mehrunissa everything he would have proposed for the new fortifications. She had smiled sympathetically, listened carefully and remembered everything. Then she had written to Shahriyar, subtly implanting some of the ideas into a mind that possessed few of its own.

'I wasn't sure Shahriyar was capable of taking on such a responsibility – after all he's only seventeen – but it seems you were right to suggest giving him the task.'

'And you did right to send him on his own. If you'd sent my brother with him as you originally proposed, Shahriyar might have felt you didn't trust him.'

'You understand people very well.'

'I've told you before, you underestimate Shahriyar.'

226

'I only wish you could advise me about Parvez. His marriage hasn't steadied him – indeed, quite the reverse. He reminds me of my own half-brothers Murad and Daniyal. Despite all my father's attempts to stop them they drank themselves to death. I worry that it is a curse afflicting our family.'

'Parvez is a grown man. He should master his weaknesses. It is not your fault that he seldom has a sober day. You don't allow such things to dominate you.'

Don't I, Jahangir wondered to himself. In his twenties he had been a slave to wine and opium, using them to console himself for his father's refusal to give him any position of responsibility. He too might have died except for the love shown him by his milk-brother, Suleiman Beg, who had helped him break his addiction. For a moment Suleiman Beg's face swam into his mind – not ravaged by fever as he'd last seen it but confident and cheerful. He had been a true friend and even after all these years he realised how much he missed him. What would Suleiman Beg say of him now? Of his growing indolence, his disinclination for the cares of state, his drinking sessions with the English ambassador – though regrettably these had become less frequent now that Sir Thomas so often seemed to be ill – and his liking for opium, which he had never completely thrown off and was growing stronger again.

Why did he indulge in wine and opium? When he was young he had used them out of a bitterness of heart to bring on oblivion from the frustrations of his life. Now that he was a mature man with a stable and wealthy empire and two sons of whom he could be proud, why shouldn't he use them for enjoyment? They helped him to relax, even to expand his mind. It was while he was in the pleasurable semi-trance that wine and opium together induced that he had some of his most insightful thoughts about the nature of the world around him . . . and some of his most stimulating discussions with Roe about everything from the eccentricities of the Christian religion to art. Mehrunissa had just said he didn't let them rule him, but if he were honest he himself was much less sure. If he went without them for more than half a day the cravings began and he rarely withstood them for long. Yet even if they did seduce him away from the day to day running of his empire, did it really matter? He had enough loyal people only too willing to shoulder the burden for him, Mehrunissa included. It amused him how she constantly sought fresh responsibilities, always taking care to assure him that she wished only to be his helpmate. That was true, he was sure, but he knew too how much she enjoyed it. Perhaps he didn't need to fight the wine and opium too hard with her at his side to guard him.

'You got a despatch from Khurram today, didn't you?' she asked, prompting him from his reverie.

'Yes. His campaign against Malik Ambar is going well. He is a good general. I'm glad to have given him the chances to prove himself in battle that my father would never give me. Just as the astrologers predicted at his birth, fortune seems to favour him. His family grows, too. He reports that his new daughter has recovered from the fever and is in good health. They have named her Roshanara.'

Mehrunissa was silent. It was nearly nine months since Khurram had departed for the Deccan. At first Jahangir had missed him and lamented his absence but under her prompting his interest in his youngest son had been growing. She had realised that it hurt Jahangir to know that of his two eldest sons one was a traitor and the other a drunk . . . it made him feel a failure as a father just as he felt his own father Akbar had failed him. That was why, just as he was eager to take pride in the capable and charismatic Khurram, he was equally disposed to find good in the handsome Shahriyar.

It was far better that there should be contenders for Jahangir's favour among his sons, she thought. Their rivalries and jealousies would allow her more scope to extend her influence than if Khurram were the undisputed favoured son.

Chapter 14

The Enemy Within

'Majesty, forgive me for interrupting you.' Majid Khan touched his hand to his breast as he entered Jahangir's apartments. 'An imperial post rider has brought another despatch from the Deccan. I have it here.'

Jahangir had had no firm news from Khurram for several weeks after the despatch reporting the recovery of Roshanara and he was eager to know whether the campaign was proceeding as successfully as Khurram had then anticipated. He reached for the letter and broke the seal. *Though I have not yet captured Malik Ambar I have defeated his army and seized his treasure,* Khurram had written in his bold hand. After detailing his confrontation with the Abyssinian's forces in the river bend, his final buoyant words were, *Our enemy has fled back into his own territories like a kicked dog. As soon as I have regrouped and resupplied my forces I will pursue him. I do not doubt my victory.*

Jahangir smiled in delight. 'Good news, Majid Khan. My

son has beaten Malik Ambar on the battlefield and he has fled. I must tell the empress.'

A few minutes later, he entered Mehrunissa's apartments. 'I have had a despatch at last from Khurram. Here, look . . .'

Mehrunissa read the letter carefully, but even before she had finished Jahangir began extolling his son's virtues. 'He has shown such maturity, such judgement . . . when he finally returns to Agra I will appoint him a full member of my military council. He's earned his place there.' As Jahangir continued to exult, Mehrunissa's thoughts were more sombre than the smile on her lips suggested. She hadn't anticipated that Khurram would achieve quite so much and certainly not so quickly. When he returned at the head of his victorious armies why should Jahangir any longer delay naming his heir? It would be the obvious thing for him to do . . .

'We must celebrate. Later this afternoon, when it is a little cooler, I will order a camel race along the banks of the Jumna. I've been meaning to try out those animals the Raja of Amber sent me. He swears the Rajput racing camels have no equal but I'm not so sure . . .'

'An excellent idea. I'll watch from my balcony.'

But later, as she watched Jahangir and his bodyguard trot along the baked mud of the riverbank to where soldiers had laid out a half-mile course for the race, her head was beginning to ache and the spectacle held no attraction for her. Usually she enjoyed camel racing – the sight of the snorting beasts, their necks outstretched, urged along by their riders, the roar of the crowds . . . Immediately after her marriage to Jahangir he had sometimes ridden races himself and often won. She remembered him coming to her afterwards, the sweat of victory still on his body . . .

She turned away from the riverbank just as trumpeters put their instruments to their lips to signal the first race and went inside. 'Salla,' she called, 'I have a pain behind my eyes. Please massage me – that always soothes me.'

As Mehrunissa settled herself against a red satin bolster, the Armenian went gently to work, expertly kneading the muscles of her neck. Slowly the throbbing pain eased and Mehrunissa's mind turned again to Khurram's despatch. Perhaps in persuading Jahangir to send Khurram south again she had misjudged . . . wanting to get him away from Jahangir all she had done was give Khurram the chance for yet greater glory. If Khurram succeeded in capturing or killing Malik Ambar – as he seemed certain he would – he would be back at court within months and would inevitably be looking for new honours, new responsibilities. He must have expectations . . .

Though her husband was only in his late forties, the growing indolence that made him so willing to succumb to her wine and opium mix and to allow her to help him with his responsibilities might also encourage him to hand over much of the running of the empire to the able son he was so proud of so that he could devote more of his remaining days to contentedly studying nature's oddities. The power and the passion that had so attracted and excited her would ebb from him. It wouldn't be good for Jahangir, she told herself. It would propel him too early into old age. And what would she become? The bored and ageing ruler of the *haram*. For a moment Fatima Begam's broad, lined face and inactive flabby body came into her mind. She would not allow that to happen to her. The *haram* was too small an empire for her. Jahangir was hers and no one else's – just as

232

he had said to her so often. Khurram's rise must be halted, not slowed, and perhaps even reversed . . .

'Majesty, I'm sorry, did I hurt you? I saw in the mirror that suddenly you frowned.'

'No, Salla, I was just thinking.'

As Mehrunissa continued to reflect, she felt something akin to panic. What could she do? Even in her bleakest moments she had always found a way. Hadn't she survived when as a baby her father had abandoned her to the wind and the wolves? Hadn't she saved herself and her family when her brother's treason had threatened to condemn them all? This wasn't the moment to waver . . .

She sat up. 'Thank you, Salla, my head is better. You may go. Please make sure I'm not disturbed.' Alone with the sounds of cheering and trumpets drifting in through the open casement, telling her that the camel races had not yet ended, Mehrunissa began to pace as she always did when she wanted to think. Her eye fell on a low marble table on which rested the ivory seal inscribed with the new title Jahangir had recently conferred on her. She was no longer Nur Mahal, the Light of the Palace, but Nur Jahan, the Light of the World. She was not only Jahangir's beloved empress but the adviser he trusted most . . . that was her most powerful weapon. Soon a plan began to form in her mind. It was bold and not without risk, but if it succeeded she — not her niece Arjumand — would become the grandmother and great-grandmother of emperors.

Dusk had fallen by the time Jahangir came to Mehrunissa's apartments. He looked happy and relaxed. 'Well, I was right — those Rajasthani camels aren't as fast as they look, and they've got a temper. Did you see that one unseat his rider and then kick out at him?'

233

'To tell you the truth I didn't watch the races. I've had something on my mind all afternoon – ever since I saw Khurram's despatch.'

'What is it?'

Her heart was beating fast but she forced herself to look composed, even a little sad, as she replied. 'I'm not sure whether I should tell you, yet I can have no secrets from you.'

Jahangir's face was now as grave as her own. 'Go on.'

'You know I study the routine reports from your officials in Khurram's camp. Mostly they're about the need for more supplies of food or new wagons or fresh tents – tedious things that needn't concern you. But recently amid all the detail I've begun to detect something else – hints that Khurram is growing arrogant . . . that in his war council he is impatient of the views of others, including officers older and more experienced than himself, such as Walid Beg, his gunnery officer. That is perhaps not so serious – after all Khurram's campaign has succeeded so far. But several recent reports also suggest that Khurram has spoken slightingly of you, boasting that he has achieved military success far younger than you did . . .'

Jahangir stared at her and she saw that his breathing had quickened. 'Are you sure? He would never be so presumptuous . . .'

'There seems little doubt of it. He is a fine commander but he knows it and is growing conceited. Of course, you can forgive a young man a lot who has enjoyed such success. It's only natural it should go to his head a little. Even the tone of his latest despatch shows how pleased with himself he is. I'm sure he won't contemplate any foolishness, like Khusrau, yet such behaviour if left uncurbed may become dangerous . . .'

'Who is making these accusations? Could it be men who have been justly passed over for promotion or rebuked for their failings by Khurram, and are disgruntled as a result?'

'I think not. I made a few enquiries. They're just junior officers – too insignificant for you to know their names or to have come to Khurram's direct attention. Though they probably thought they were doing their duty, they were mistaken in committing such thoughts to paper. If they were seen by the wrong eyes they could cause trouble so I have burned them . . . for your sake and for that of those unwise officers.' Mehrunissa gestured towards an incense burner in which were some charred fragments of paper.

Suddenly it wasn't Mehrunissa Jahangir was hearing but old Shaikh Salim Chishti uttering his warning all those years ago: 'Take nothing on trust, even from those bound to you by blood – even the sons you will have . . .' After the blinding of Khusrau, he had thought he had nothing left to fear from his sons – not from Parvez who most mornings didn't even have the will to get out of bed or from Khurram, so seemingly dutiful and to whom he had given everything he asked – including Arjumand – and certainly not from Shahriyar. But perhaps he had been wrong. Khurram was easily the most gifted of his sons – the whole world could see that – and so could Khurram. Mehrunissa had been trying to reassure him – she didn't want him to be worried – but how could he be sure that Khurram wasn't already contemplating rebellion just as Khusrau had done?

'Don't look so anxious. I warned you so that you can nip this early.'

'If you're right, what should I do?'

'I'm not sure.' Mehrunissa seemed to hesitate for a moment. 'You'll certainly need to restrain Khurram . . .'

'I suppose so, but how?'

'Well . . . perhaps with hindsight you were too generous in allowing him the right to pitch a scarlet tent. You did it, I know, because you wanted to reward him but it may have raised his pride and expectations too much . . . Why not write to him that you are withdrawing the privilege for the present. Perhaps say that although you rejoice in his victories you may have been a little premature . . .'

'He'd be bound to see it as an affront – I would.'

'Yes, but it would test him. Favoured by his grandfather above all his other grandsons and with his wishes indulged by you, he has come to regard unimpeded advancement as his right and not an honour and a gift which is yours to bestow. His reaction would show you whether he is still your loyal and obedient son or whether his ambition now exceeds his sense of duty. Remember you're his emperor as well as his father. And it would be for Khurram's own benefit. By acting now you'd be acting like a good father to prevent him from straying further.'

Jahangir nodded. There was truth in what Mehrunissa said. Khurram had never known the adversity he himself had faced as a youth. If Khurram responded well the scarlet tent could soon be restored.

• ◆ •

The doves – dyed in rainbow colours and with tiny jewelled collars – were fluttering back to the imperial dovecote as Jahangir stood with Mehrunissa at his side on the sandstone terrace of his private apartments. On the banks of the Jumna below herdsmen were driving their goats and camels down to the river to drink, and in the shallows slate-grey water buffalo were enjoying a final wallow for the day in warm brown waters.

Then, from the direction of the setting sun, Jahangir saw a small group of riders approaching the fort. As they came closer he recognised his youngest son Shahriyar at their head and behind him two huntsmen, hooded falcons on their wrists. By the number of dead birds dangling from the saddle of a third huntsman they had had a successful expedition.

'Did you know that Shahriyar sent Ladli a message in the *haram* boasting that his falcons would kill at least a dozen birds today?' Mehrunissa asked. 'My daughter replied she wouldn't be impressed unless he killed double that number. It looks as if he's succeeded. He is getting to be almost as good a sportsman as you.'

'Not to mention you . . .'

'You flatter me.' Mehrunissa smiled before adding, 'Soon I will teach Ladli to shoot a musket. She's fifteen now – quite old enough to accompany me in the purdah howdah on a hunt.'

Jahangir scanned the darkening sky for his one remaining dove. Shahriyar's hawks hadn't brought it down, had they? He had told Shahriyar never to go hawking close to the fort but he was unsure how much attention his youngest son ever paid. Besides, sometimes the doves strayed further away than they should. Then he saw the bird, feathers dyed the palest lilac, flying down to land on the stone balustrade near him. As he lifted the latecomer gently into the cote, Mehrunissa continued, 'I've been meaning to ask you – has Shahriyar ever said anything to you about Ladli?'

Jahangir thought for a moment. Shahriyar's handsome

head seemed more filled with hunting and hawking than with anything else. 'No, I don't think so. Why?'

'It may be nothing, but several times recently he's spoken admiringly to me of her – he's seen her a number of times and during the Nauruz celebrations they talked together.' She gave a little shrug. 'It wasn't so much what he said but rather the way he said it.'

'You think he has feelings for her?'

'I don't know. Perhaps . . .'

'I could talk to him.'

'Yes. You and he have grown closer recently. He'll reveal his feelings to you, I'm sure . . . And if he does care for Ladli, tell him to put an end to such thoughts.'

Jahangir blinked in surprise. 'Why shouldn't Shahriyar admire her . . . and come to that even marry her?'

'But I thought you intended to choose him a bride from one of the princely families of Sind?'

'I do. I've already discussed it with my council, as you know, but as something for the future. Shahriyar can still take a wife from Sind but nothing need prevent him from marrying your daughter first. After all, I permitted Khurram to wed your niece before he married his royal Persian bride . . .'

Mehrunissa's face lit up. 'If Shahriyar indeed wishes to marry Ladli, it would give me the greatest happiness – you know my regard for him.'

'Not always deserved, I fear . . . last week I had to rebuke him for forgetting to review with my master of horse how many new animals we need to purchase for the cavalry. But he is very young and will learn. Who knows, marriage might mature him. I will go and find him now.'

Standing alone by the dovecote, Mehrunissa relaxed. She hadn't thought it would be so easy. She knew what Shahriyar would say to Jahangir. She had groomed the prince for this moment, hinting to the naïve and suggestible youth of Ladli's admiration for him and his looks and making sure he in turn had plenty of opportunity to observe Ladli's undeniable beauty. It hadn't taken much effort to help Shahriyar convince himself that he loved her. As for her daughter, she'd brought her up to think an imperial prince was a good match.

The young couple would be happy – and so would she, especially when she convinced Jahangir to declare Shahriyar his heir and that might not take long. Mettlesome and unused to contradiction or setback, Khurram had responded angrily to his father's rescinding of the right to pitch the scarlet tent just as, knowing his character, she had anticipated. He had scrawled a hurt and indignant letter bereft of the usual exquisite courtesies that formed such an essential part of Moghul etiquette. It had greatly angered Jahangir, who had regarded their absence as an affront to his dignity. The suspicion with which he was beginning to view his once favourite son was growing. If she could achieve an open breach between them her own position would be unassailable. And that would also be in Jahangir's interests. After all, who had his best interests more at heart than she?

• ◆ •

A month later in his private apartments, hung with coloured lanterns for the occasion, Jahangir slid an emerald betrothal ring on to Ladli's slim finger then taking her hand placed it in Shahriyar's. 'By this act I give my blessing to your coming union. May it bring you happiness and prosperity

239

and many children.' Jahangir couldn't see Ladli's expression beneath her betrothal veils but glancing at Mehrunissa he saw her happiness. He knew it grieved her that she had not borne him a child – and after all these years of marriage probably never would – but as she had told him, to see her only child allied to one of his sons was balm to the wound. As for himself, the more he thought about it, the better pleased he was by the union. Though Shahriyar still had much to learn, he was a good and biddable son, with none of Parvez's vices or Khurram's emerging arrogance and pride.

At the thought of Khurram, Jahangir frowned. How would he react when he learned the news of Shahriyar's betrothal? Would he be affronted that his father hadn't written informing him of it? Well, let him be. It was no more than he deserved for his own lack of respect. Anyway, the announcement he was about to make would seem a far more serious snub. 'Shahriyar, as a betrothal gift I confer on you the *jagir* – the estates – of Badakpur which on the death of the previous holder have recently reverted to the crown.'

'Father, thank you.' Shahriyar knelt and Jahangir touched his head with his beringed hand, pleased to see him so overcome by his generosity. That was how a son should behave – with respect and humility. Shortly before Khurram had departed for the Deccan, Jahangir had promised him the rich and fertile estates of Badakpur. The news that he had instead conferred them on his younger half-brother should, as Mehrunissa had said, be a further salutary lesson and perhaps compel him to heel.

Chapter 15

The Homecoming

Two scarlet-headed Sarus cranes stood motionless on the sandy banks of the Chambal river. As Khurram's column drew nearer they took flight, slender legs trailing like ribbons from a kite. A pair of sleek-headed cormorants dived into the river for fish but the tranquil beauty of the scene was lost on Khurram. All the Chambal was to him was the final barrier on his long, hurried journey northward from the Deccan. Shading his eyes against the early morning light, he looked towards the ford where their drivers were already leading lines of camels laden with brushwood across. Though the monsoon was close the rains hadn't yet begun in earnest and the river level looked low. He and his party should have no problem crossing. With luck they would reach Agra before nightfall.

He had not wanted to break off his campaign against Malik Ambar just as he had been preparing to pursue him deep into his own territory to secure a conclusive victory, but he had felt he had no alternative. He had to know what was in his father's mind. To be told by message that he could no longer have the honour of pitching the scarlet tent was humiliation enough, but to learn after the event that Jahangir had given lands he had originally promised to him to Shahriyar was an even more disturbing blow to his peace of mind. But soon – maybe in just a few hours – he would see his father face to face and ask how he had offended him. Surely his father would not fail to respond to his pleas if he made them in person.

In fact the final stage of the journey took a little longer than Khurram had hoped. Soon after crossing the Chambal, purple-black monsoon clouds that had begun sweeping in from the west burst above them, turning the ground to a sticky mire in which the tired horses and pack animals slithered and slipped. But just before sunset Khurram made out torches guttering in the rain on either side of the gates of his mansion, which had been thrown open ready to receive them. A week ago he had sent messengers ahead with orders to prepare the house for his return. He had also after much deliberation despatched a short letter to his father designed to convey his injured innocence. *I could not stay in the Deccan without knowing what I have done to offend you. I have only tried to do my duty but you are acting as though I have defied you. When I reach Agra I will answer any question, any charge.*

Khurram trotted into the courtyard and jumping down from his horse threw his reins to his *qorchi*. The large curtained bullock cart in which Arjumand and the children were travelling was just trundling up. As it halted Khurram lifted the sodden curtain and peered in. Arjumand's face, though she managed a smile, was pinched and tired and her hand was on her belly. This latest pregnancy was proving hard.

242

Four-year-old Jahanara and her little sister Roshanara whom she was holding in her arms were, like their mother, awake, but their two brothers Dara Shukoh and Shah Shuja were fast asleep, bodies coiled around one another like puppies. As he looked at his young family anger welled inside Khurram that they should have had to endure the discomforts and hazards of this hurried journey. How different it was from his last return to Agra, when his father had rained down gold and jewels upon him and hailed him as 'Shah Jahan'.

• ◆ •

'Highness, you have a visitor.'

Khurram stood up. Glancing at the marble sundial in the courtyard he saw it was nearly midday. He had been waiting all morning for a response to the message he had sent to the fort at first light, requesting an audience with his father. To be kept waiting so long was yet a further snub, though it shouldn't be long now till he saw Jahangir. But at the sight of the visitor Khurram's face fell. Instead of his father's vizier Majid Khan or some other high official of the court, he saw the tall, spindly figure of the English ambassador. Even in his dismay he noticed how changed Sir Thomas Roe looked as he came forward. He was thinner than ever, the thighs protruding from his short striped breeches barely thicker than Khurram's upper arms, and his once ruddy face was pale. The whites of his eyes were almost yellow and Khurram could see that the long ebony stick in his slightly shaking hand, a gaudy ribbon round its handle, was not for dignity or decoration but support. The ambassador was leaning heavily upon it.

243

'Thank you for receiving me, Highness.'

Khurram gestured to Roe to seat himself on a low bench beneath a silk canopy and called for attendants to bring cushions. He had never liked the ambassador – he distrusted all the foreigners who clustered around the court and had been puzzled by his father's interest in this one – but the man's physical state demanded his courtesy. Roe lowered himself cautiously on to the seat and as he did so grimaced with pain and couldn't prevent himself from emitting a low moan. 'I'm sorry, Highness. My stomach has been troubling me.' Not only his stomach, the ambassador thought wryly. His bowels were still torture. Hardly a week passed without their turning to water, and now he was troubled by haemorrhoids – his 'emeralds' as he called them in his increasingly querulous letters to his wife at home in England. But of course he would say nothing about that to this haughty young prince. There were far more important matters to discuss. Ever since he had learned that Khurram was on the road back from the Deccan he had been debating whether to try to see him. This would be a difficult conversation but it was his duty to his own king, his own country, to have it.

'Highness, what I have to say is only for your ears.'

'Leave us,' Khurram ordered his attendants, and drew closer. 'What is it?'

Roe waited until he was certain they were alone. 'Forgive me for coming so soon after your return to Agra, Highness, but it was imperative that I see you. Though I am a foreigner at your father's court, while I have been here I have learned your language and been privileged to make many friends among the courtiers. For a time I also enjoyed your father's

244

favour. Indeed, I felt he had come to look on me as a friend . . .'

'It wasn't he who sent you?' The thought had suddenly struck Khurram.

'No. I am here on my own account, not his. Indeed, I have not had a private audience with him for some time. You may find what I am about to tell you incredible but I beg you to believe me.' Roe leaned forward, resting both hands on the top of his stick. 'Beware the Empress Mehrunissa. She is no longer your friend. Indeed, she is your enemy.'

'Mehrunissa?' Had the Englishman become sick in mind as well as body? Nothing else could excuse his bizarre accusation or his impertinence in making it. 'You are wrong,' Khurram went on coldly. 'The empress is my wife's aunt – the great-aunt of our children. Family ties as well as the love I know she bears my wife make such a thing impossible.'

'Listen to me, Highness. Very soon I will return home to England. My health can no longer bear the rigours of the climate here. If I stay I may die. But before I depart let me have the satisfaction of knowing that I tried to warn you even if you wouldn't listen. Remember that as a foreigner I dare tell you things a Moghul courtier might not. Ask yourself why your father has turned his face against you . . . Ask yourself why he is favouring Prince Shahriyar . . .'

The ambassador's bluntness took Khurram aback. 'There has been some misunderstanding between us,' he said stiffly.

'No. It is all the empress's doing. She thinks herself subtle but many around the court have noticed her scheming. While you have been away in the Deccan she has done all in her power to bring Prince Shahriyar to the emperor's attention.

I saw this happening and asked myself why. The prince has no special abilities or talents and – forgive me, Highness, for speaking so of your half-brother – I have even heard him called slow witted. When I heard he was betrothed to the empress's daughter, matters became clearer. The empress craves power. Perhaps you do not know how many decrees she issues, how many decisions she takes. Some even call her the Purdah Emperor. She means to encourage the emperor to declare Shahriyar – not you – as his heir. When your father dies she will rule Hindustan. Prince Shahriyar and her daughter will be no more than her puppets.'

Khurram stared at the ambassador's earnest face, beaded with sweat despite the shade provided by the canopy. What Roe was saying seemed impossible, and yet . . . 'My father would never permit his wife to manipulate him in such a way,' he said slowly, as much to himself as to the ambassador.

'Your father has changed. The business of government bores him. Ask any of his counsellors. The empress encourages him to take his ease, to follow the enquiries into the natural world that so absorb him, to drink wine and take opium . . . She has made him utterly dependent on her and abuses his trust for her own ends.'

'You said you were no longer in my father's favour. What happened?'

'I'm not certain. Once I was frequently in the emperor's company. When I first fell ill, he was most solicitous, suggesting remedies and even on one occasion sending his own *hakim*. But his interest in me waned. His invitations to me during times I was well became fewer and then ceased. The only times I have seen your father recently have been on public occasions.'

'Perhaps my father has tired of your demands for trading concessions.' Roe's expression told Khurram his remark had hit home and he pressed on.

'You spoke of wanting the satisfaction of warning me. Why, Sir Thomas? Why should you care which son my father favours?'

'It matters to me because the emperor has refused my request to allow English ships to join the Portuguese and the Arabs in shipping pilgrims to Arabia. My king will be very disappointed. Had your father agreed, many more English ships would have come to Surat and our trading settlement there would have expanded. Our ships would have brought more goods from England and as well as carrying pilgrims could have taken on board more goods from Hindustan to trade in Arabia or bring home to England. Trade must be the ambition of every civilised nation and England's trade with the Moghul empire could have been greatly enhanced.'

He would never understand these foreigners' enthusiasm for trade, thought Khurram. Roe was a nobleman yet his face when he talked of profits was as animated as that of any merchant in the bazaar. In his agitation the ambassador had dropped his stick, and he had to stoop to retrieve it before he went on.

'I came in the hope that my information will help you save yourself . . . that you will remember it was an Englishman who warned you and be grateful . . . that one day, when you become emperor, as I hope and trust you will, you will favour my country.'

'What do you mean, save myself?'

'Now the empress has set herself on this path she will

not stop until she has provoked an open breach – perhaps even war – between yourself and your father.' Seeing Khurram's still sceptical expression, Roe shook his head in frustration. 'Highness, reflect on what I have told you. I swear to you I'm not lying. Ignore my words and you will regret it.'

For the first time Roe's earnestness, the passionate conviction in his voice, penetrated the disbelief clouding Khurram's mind. Mehrunissa . . . Could it really be she – not an ambitious courtier or disloyal officer – who had turned his father against him? If she had indeed become his enemy every perplexing thing that had happened would start to make sense. 'I don't know whether I believe you, but I will think about what you've said.'

'That is all I ask, except for one favour. As I said, I will shortly be returning to England, but my page Nicholas Ballantyne wishes to remain in Hindustan. He is loyal and intelligent and would serve any master well. Will you take him into your household?'

'To spy and report back to you in England?'

For the first time Roe smiled. 'No. I tried as hard as I could to persuade him to return to England. But it is no matter. If you will not take him, Majesty, I will ask one of my acquaintances at court.'

· ◆ ·

Asaf Khan's usually animated face was very still as he listened. After Khurram had finished, he took a moment to respond. 'It's hard to say this of my own sister but I believe the ambassador is right. Mehrunissa has turned against you. She plans one day to rule through Shahriyar and you stand in her way. As the ambassador said, people at court have begun to talk about her love of power.'

Khurram struck the stone column against which he was leaning with his gauntleted hand. 'How can my father be so blind? Doesn't he know what's being said?'

'He does know but chooses to ignore it. Only a month ago, Mullah Shaikh Hassan used his sermon in the Friday mosque to criticise the emperor for allowing the empress to issue imperial decrees. He claimed a woman had no right to do so. He also criticised the emperor for drinking wine, blaming it for clouding your father's mind and making him fall asleep while attending the meetings of the religious council, the *ulama*. Mehrunissa wanted the mullah flogged but for once the emperor resisted her and simply ignored the outburst. The mullahs aren't the only ones to resent Mehrunissa. Some of the commanders – particularly the older ones like Yar Muhammad, the Governor of Gwalior – have complained to me that it is now her seal more often than his which is affixed to their orders, but they express their discontent privately. One of the few who said anything openly to the emperor found himself next day "promoted" to an outpost in the fever-ridden swamps of Bengal.'

It was early evening. After Roe's departure Khurram had waited in vain for a summons from his father to go to him in the fort. All day he had been turning Roe's words over and over in his mind, each time finding them more credible. He had been about to call for his horse and ride up to the fort to demand to see Jahangir when he had thought of consulting Asaf Khan. He better than anyone should have an insight into what might be in his sister's mind, and as Arjumand's father he could surely be trusted.

249

'In harming me Mehrunissa would harm Arjumand and our children. Doesn't that mean anything to her?'

'No. Having installed herself in Jahangir's affections, she thinks first of her own interests and then those of her daughter. She will brook no rivals . . . whoever they are. You have been away from court. You could not perceive what I have been unable to ignore. She isolates the emperor. Though I command the Agra garrison, these days I rarely see him. Even when I do, Mehrunissa is always there. She issues my orders as she does those of the other commanders. Her seal dangles from them, stamped with the new title Jahangir has given her. My sister is no longer merely "Nur Mahal", "The Light of the Palace" – your father has awarded her the title "Nur Jahan", "The Light of the World".'

'What does Ghiyas Beg say?'

'Even he has no influence over her. As the comptroller of the imperial revenues, he knew the Badakpur estates were promised to you. When he asked Mehrunissa why they were instead being given to Shahriyar she told him it was no concern of his. My father is a mild man. I never thought to see him so angry.' Asaf Khan fell silent, then asked, 'What will you do?'

'This must not continue. I will make my father see me, whether he wants to or not. I will make him understand that the empress has dripped poison in his ear and that I am still his loyal son. I have been away from court too long. When he sees me his love for me will revive.'

'Be careful, Highness. Act with thought as well as passion. If you let your heart rule your head you will be the loser. Heed the ambassador's warning. Beware Mehrunissa. She is as clever as she is fearless.'

'Don't worry, Asaf Khan. At last I know who my enemy is – and how formidable. I won't allow emotion to run away with me any more than I would in battle. I have never been defeated in my campaigns for my father. I will not let his wife defeat me now.'

· ◆ ·

'I'm sorry, Highness, the emperor left orders he was not to be disturbed.'

'Majid Khan, I know you are a loyal servant to my father. As his vizier you should have his interests at heart, as well as the best interests of the empire. A misunderstanding has sprung up between myself and my father that was not of my making. If I could only have a few moments with him I am certain that I could convince him of my loyalty and heal the rift between us.'

The vizier's long, thin face was thoughtful as he gazed at a point over Khurram's left shoulder. He knows I'm right, Khurram thought, but he's wondering whether he dare defy the empress. He took Majid Khan by the arm, turning him slightly and forcing him to look into his eyes. 'I've been waiting for three days now for my father to summon me. I'm no Khusrau. I've not plotted and schemed for my father's throne. Surely you know that, Majid Khan. I swear on the heads of my beloved wife and children that all I seek is justice. Look . . .' Khurram released the vizier and stepped back, pulling his curved dagger from his sash and pushing it into the hands of the startled Majid Khan. 'Take it – and my sword.'

'No, no, Highness.' The vizier looked thoroughly embarrassed. 'I don't doubt your intentions.' Then, looking around him as if fearful of being overheard even here in his private apartments in the fort, he lowered his voice and said, 'Highness, every evening at dusk the emperor has taken to going to his dovecote on the battlements to watch his birds return. He takes no guards or attendants with him for fear of alarming the doves. The empress sometimes goes with him but tonight she is holding a special entertainment in the emperor's quarters and will, I am sure, be supervising the details personally.'

• ◆ •

The sky was pinkening in the west as Khurram made his way to the battlements, choosing a steep, narrow staircase in the westernmost corner of the fort where as boys he and his brothers had once played at being attackers and defenders. The dust and cobwebs suggested that few people used it these days and he reached the battlements unchallenged, indeed unseen. About a hundred yards ahead he saw the conical dovecote and beyond it an arched door through which lay the wide staircase that he knew led down to the imperial courtyards. When he glanced around there wasn't even a sentry in view.

He went a little closer to the cote then drew back into the shadows and waited. In a courtyard below him he could hear attendants talking as they lit the torches and oil lamps. Then he saw a sudden glow against the darkening sky that meant that in the main courtyard by the Hall of Public Audience the great *akash diya* – a giant saucer filled with oil on top of a golden pole twenty feet high – had been lit. The sight cost him a pang. How familiar it all was, from the apricot glow of the lamps to the smell of incense drifting

252

on the night air. This was his world, the place where he belonged. Then a tall bare-headed figure in flowing robes emerged through the arched door and moved towards the dovecote.

'Father!' Khurram ran towards Jahangir, whose right hand flew immediately to his dagger. In the half-light Khurram caught the gleam of honed steel. 'Father . . . it's me, Khurram.' All his carefully rehearsed words vanished as he flung himself at his father's feet. He expected to feel Jahangir's hand on his head but there was nothing. He looked up to see the emperor's face taut with anger.

'How dare you leap out at me like an assassin?' Jahangir's voice was a little thick, as if he had been drinking.

Stunned by his father's rage, Khurram rose to his feet. 'I am no assassin but your son. It is surely my right to see you.'

'You have no rights.' Jahangir pushed his dagger back into its scabbard.

'It seems not. Since I reached Agra three days ago I have begged you again and again to see me. Why didn't you answer me?'

'Because I didn't wish to see you, just as I didn't order you to abandon your command in the Deccan. In your arrogance you behave just as you please.'

'I came to Agra to discover what I have done to offend you. I can't carry on when every imperial messenger delivers some fresh snub from you. Why have you sent Shahriyar against the Persians? Why have you given him my lands?'

'It is not for you to question me.'

'If you will not allow me to ask questions at least permit me to tell you what I believe the answers to be. I think that someone has turned you against me.'

253

'Who?'

Khurram hesitated, but only briefly. 'Mehrunissa.'

Jahangir took a step closer and Khurram was shocked to see how greatly his father had changed during the eighteen months he had been away. His eyes were bloodshot and the skin on his once firm jaw hung slackly. 'The empress is jealous of the love that you have – once had – for me,' he forced himself to continue. 'She fears my influence with you and seeks to replace me in your affections with Shahriyar who has no mind of his own. When he becomes her son-in-law her control over him will be as absolute as her control over her daughter . . . and over you!'

'Enough! Have you lost your senses? It was the empress who begged me to let you marry Arjumand Banu and to give you your first independent command. It isn't that she fears you but that you resent her influence and her love for me. My father was a great man but one of his mistakes was to make too much of you when you were a boy. You have grown up believing it is your right to be my heir.'

'No, but you encouraged me to think it. You gave me the title Shah Jahan and the right to pitch the scarlet tent.'

'But I did not name you as the next Moghul emperor. It is for me to decide which of my sons succeeds me. I have heard of your arrogant conduct in the Deccan, how you were already behaving as if the throne was yours . . .'

'From whom?'

'I told you before not to question me. Doesn't your conduct in riding to Agra and forcing yourself into my presence confirm everything I feared about your pride, your heedless, reckless ambition?' Jahangir's whole body was trembling. As Khurram looked at him it was as if his father had become a stranger. He had hoped to revive the love he had once had for him but his presence only seemed to be enraging him. A helpless, hopeless feeling that he had never experienced in battle was descending on him but he decided to make one last appeal.

'I came because I wanted to tell you to your face that I am your loyal son. That is all.' Had his words struck home? Jahangir's expression seemed to soften a little. 'I am also the father of sons.' Khurram tried to press home his advantage. 'In the years to come they may do things that don't please me but I hope I will always love them and strive to be fair to them. That is all I ask, Father – justice. You must—' But to his dismay he heard footsteps and then a *qorchi* holding a flaring torch in his right hand because it was now almost dark appeared through the arched door.

'Majesty, the empress says that the musicians are ready.'

'Tell her I will be there shortly.'

As soon as the youth had left Jahangir spoke. 'I will consider what you have said. Now go, and do not come to the fort again until I send for you.' Then he turned and disappeared through the doorway. Khurram stood for a moment listening to the cooing of the doves. He would go home and wait as his father had ordered. After all, what else could he do?

◆

'You look troubled. Did one of your doves fail to return?' Mehrunissa said.

'You know my every mood. No, it's not my birds that have upset me. Khurram came to me while I was on the battlements.'

255

'Khurram? How dare he!'

'That is what I said to him.'

'What did he want?'

'To ask why I hadn't sent for him and to know in what way he had displeased me.'

Mehrunissa frowned. An attendant came into the room, doubtless to ask whether she wished the musicians on the terrace outside to begin, and she waved the woman away. She hadn't anticipated that Khurram would find a way of making a direct appeal to his father. Her intention had been that in a further few days – the longer the better to make the humiliation of Khurram all the greater – Jahangir should summon him to the Hall of Public Audience and before all the court censure him for abandoning his campaign in the Deccan and order him back there. In such a forum there would have been no opportunity for Khurram to say the things that had clearly touched Jahangir. But she had underestimated the prince.

'Presumption is one of Khurram's faults,' she said.

'He seemed genuinely distressed.'

'Because he knows that his misdemeanours have been discovered. He was trying to rouse your sympathy.'

'He claimed he had done nothing wrong . . . that an enemy was trying to alienate me from him.'

'An enemy? Who?'

'You.' Jahangir raised his head and looked directly at her.

'But why should I be his enemy?'

'He claims that you crave power and fear he stands in your way.'

Mehrunissa felt her heart begin to pound but forced her expression to stay calm, even a little scornful. 'I hadn't thought his ambition would drive him to such lengths. He knows the love I have for you, how I try to take some of the burden of government from you so that you may concentrate on the important matters of state. That is why he attacks you through me.'

'But why should he do that?'

'Don't you see?' Mehrunissa took Jahangir's hands in hers. 'If that is what he dares say to you, imagine what outrageous things he will be saying to others! By claiming that a woman rules you he is suggesting that you are no longer fit to rule. He has invented these accusations against me as a pretext for seizing the throne.'

'But in that case why come to Agra, why come to me? He has an army in the Deccan that he could have mobilised against me.'

'It's all a part of his scheming.' Mehrunissa released Jahangir's hands and turned to pick up a glass bottle. She pulled out the stopper, poured some of its contents into a drinking cup and handed it to him. 'Drink some of this. It will soothe you.'

Jahangir took a swallow of wine in which he could tell from the slight bitterness opium pellets had been dissolved. It at once began to warm his stomach and after a few moments he took another, larger sip, enjoying the glow beginning to steal through his body. Sitting down on a divan and resting his back against a brocade bolster he stared into the contents of the cup, watching how the ruby liquid caught the light as he held it in his none too steady hands. 'Go on . . .'

'As I said, I think Khurram has plans to seize the throne. He didn't make his move while in the Deccan because he

257

wished to test opinion at court. Perhaps that is what he has been doing since he reached Agra – I know for a fact that he had an interview with Majid Khan. He's probably been using the opportunity to spread poison about both of us. The reason he sought you out may well have been so that he could say he had appealed to you but you would not listen. I'm sure that before too long his army will appear from the Deccan. With your other main forces away in the northwest with Shahriyar, you are vulnerable.'

Jahangir drank some more wine but said nothing.

'Khurram is cleverer than Khusrau at disguising his ambitions, but he wants the same thing.' Mehrunissa came and sat close to Jahangir. 'It is a terrible thing for a father when his sons are disloyal. It is a tragedy when families divide against one another when they should find strength in unity, but it is the way of the world. You have already had to face it once and now you must again.' Her tone was sad. 'Ambition can be a fine thing, but the thought of winning great honours can drive a man to dishonourable acts . . .'

She was right, Jahangir thought. Hadn't Shaikh Salim Chishti used almost the same words to him all those years ago? The Sufi had foreseen the disloyalty of Khusrau and Khurram and tried to warn him, just as Mehrunissa was trying to warn him now.

'What should I do?' Tears of self-pity were pricking his eyelids and he drained his cup.

'Arrest Khurram.'

◆

Khurram and Arjumand were sitting cross-legged before a low table spread with white cloth. The dishes of food laid

258

out before them – pheasant in a tamarind sauce, roasted lamb stuffed with dried fruits and breads still steaming from the tandoor – smelled appetising. Even so Khurram didn't feel like eating and looking at Arjumand knew she felt the same. His account of his meeting with his father had shaken her.

'You must eat something . . .' he was starting to say, but got no further. One of Arjumand's attendants had burst through the curtained doorway.

'Forgive me, Highnesses, but an urgent message has come for you from Asaf Khan.'

'My father?' Arjumand turned startled eyes on Khurram, who leapt to his feet, almost knocking over some of the dishes in his haste, and seized the note from the attendant's hand. Had Asaf Khan heard that Jahangir had relented, he wondered as he broke the seal and unfolded the letter. But as he took in the hastily scrawled words his blood seemed to turn to ice in his veins: *The emperor has commanded your immediate arrest. You must flee. The captain of the guard, who is my friend, showed me the written order. He will delay the despatch of horsemen to carry it out for a little while but dare not wait long. I pray that this note reaches you in time. Destroy it as soon as you've read it or its contents may destroy me and my friend the captain.* For a moment Khurram felt too stunned to say or do anything and just stared at the piece of paper as if he could somehow make the words vanish.

'Khurram . . . what is it?' Arjumand's voice recalled him to himself. Acting now as instinctively as on the battlefield, he held the note in the flame of an oil lamp. Then, taking Arjumand by the hand, he pulled her to her feet. 'My father has ordered my arrest. Fetch our children. We must leave at once.'

Arjumand's eyes widened but the urgency in his voice told her there was no time for questions and she at once hurried towards the children's rooms. Following her through the door and then out from the *haram* Khurram shouted to his bodyguards, 'Saddle every horse we have.' Fearing at any moment to hear the sound of soldiers at the gates, he ran to his room and, taking a key from around his neck, unlocked a painted chest. Grabbing a small casket of jewels and a bag of gold coins he shoved them into a leather satchel which he slung over his shoulder, then seized his sword and, buckling it round his waist, raced down to the main courtyard.

Arjumand was already waiting, a shawl thrown around her head. Beside her, Jahanara was gripping the hand of a bleary eyed Dara Shukoh and nurses held Roshanara and Shah Shuja. A groom had fitted saddle and bridle to the last of the horses and was bending beneath its belly to check the tightness of the girths. Once he had stood back, his task completed, Khurram shouted the order to leave and mounting a tall chestnut horse pulled Arjumand up to ride behind him. She held him round the waist as he kicked the horse forward, galloping through the gateway and out of his mansion. When would he see it again? Behind and riding with equal urgency were a dozen or so of his household. Dara Shukoh and Jahanara were being held on the pommels of their saddles by two of Khurram's *qorchis* while Shah Shuja and Roshanara were in straw panniers slung from either side of the broad-chested bay horse of Khurram's steward, Shah Gul.

Looking back over his shoulder, Khurram saw lights on the ramp leading from the fort. Could it be riders carrying torches? No, it was only the flickering flames from the braziers which normally lit the fort's approaches. He strained his ears for the sounds of pursuit. He was afraid not for himself but for his family. What would their fate be if he were imprisoned or executed? Then Arjumand gripped him more tightly as he heard a frantic barking and two large dogs ran from a shack by the road, leaping at Khurram's horse until they too were left behind. Soon there was no other sound in the enshrouding darkness but the hoofbeats of his desperate little party galloping southward along the Jumna. However, he still didn't feel safe. Bending low to his horse's neck, his mind was focused on only one thing – to ensure that by the time the dawn rose he and his family were as far from Agra as possible.

Part II

Outcasts

Chapter 16

Asirgarh

Alone rider on a black horse galloped across the plain, a pall of red dust hanging behind him in the still, late afternoon air. As he approached the base of the ridge on which the fortress of Asirgarh stood, Khurram, watching from the sandstone battlements, saw the rider slow his pace only a little as he began to ascend the steep track winding up to the fortress. As he came nearer Khurram noticed that despite the heat the man was wearing a steel helmet and a metal-studded leather tunic. 'Shall we shoot him down?' asked Kamran Iqbal, who was standing beside him.

'No. One rider can't harm us. Let's see what he wants,' replied Khurram, not taking his eyes from the horseman, who had reached the flat lip of land immediately beneath the fortress and was urging his now-blowing mount once more into a gallop. When he was about fifty yards from the gatehouse he took a bag that had been hanging from his saddle and, wheeling his horse to such an abrupt halt that it reared on its hind legs, whirled it above his head and flung it with all his strength towards the tall spiked gates of the fortress. 'A present for the traitor Khurram, may he rot in hell,' he shouted, then he turned his horse's head and galloped back down the track, bending low over his mount's neck and zigzagging slightly as if he expected the watching soldiers on the battlements to fire at him.

As the horseman descended swiftly to the plains below Khurram scanned the arid landscape, wondering whether his gesture in riding defiantly up to Asirgarh might be the prelude to an attack. But there was no sign of any other living thing except some vultures soaring on the air currents high above. 'Send someone to retrieve that bag,' he ordered, wiping a trickle of sweat from his face. It was early June and every day the heat grew more intense and the air heavier and more oppressive. Moments later he heard metal wheels grinding on each other in the gatehouse followed by a rattle of chains as the great grille protecting the wooden entrance gates began its shuddering ascent. Then a small door – barely four feet high – in the right-hand gate swung back. A tall, slim young man, his barley-coloured hair glinting in the sun, ducked through it and ran across to where the package had come to rest against a spiny bush. Thomas Roe had been right, Khurram thought, as Nicholas Ballantyne bent to retrieve the bundle. Over the past few months, the young Englishman had proved a loyal and resourceful *qorchi*. In the drama of his flight from Agra he had completely forgotten Roe's request to take the young man into his service. However, Nicholas hadn't. After seeing his master on to a ship bound for England from the port of Surat, he had made his way here to Asirgarh, on the northern rim of the Deccan plateau.

266

Khurram saw Nicholas suddenly recoil and almost drop the bag. Recovering himself, he gripped it in two hands and holding it well away from his body carried it carefully back up the ramp and into the fortress. Curious to know what the rider had left, Khurram hurried down the steep stone staircase to the main courtyard below. A group of soldiers was clustering around Nicholas and the stained jute bag on the ground at his feet. As Khurram approached, he caught a nauseous stench. 'Open it,' he ordered Nicholas. 'Quickly.'

Taking his dagger Nicholas cut through the thick cord securing the bag and then tipped it up. A blotchy, putrescent object rolled out. For a moment Khurram thought it was a rotten melon until he smelled the full sickly sweet stench of death. One of the soldiers, a gangling youth, turned away and started to retch and Khurram felt bile rising in his own throat as he realised what he was looking at.

Squatting, he forced himself to examine the bloated suppurating thing that had once been the head of Jamal Khan, one of his trusted scouts. Some weeks ago he had despatched him to the Governor of Mandu with a message asking for the governor's support in his breach with Jahangir. The scout's left eye had been gouged out and a pair of maggots were wriggling in the bloodied socket. From the gaping mouth with its broken teeth, pus-filled gums and bursting purple lips protruded a piece of paper bearing what Khurram recognised as his seal. It could only be his letter to the Governor of Mandu.

'Highness, there's something else in the sack,' he heard Nicholas say. Getting to his feet again he took the small leather pouch the *qorchi* was holding out, and desperately trying to suppress his rising gorge he stepped back a pace or two to open it. Inside was a letter addressed to *The Traitor Khurram*.

I am a loyal servant of the Emperor Jahangir. I have dealt with your messenger as he deserved. His end wasn't quick but serving such a master he didn't deserve mercy. In the agony of his last moments he confessed everything he knew – how many troops you have, how much artillery, what other messengers you have despatched soliciting treason and to whom. By the time you read this I will have reached the Moghul court to report your seditious approach to your father, His Imperial Majesty.

The letter was signed *Ali Khan, Governor of Mandu.*

'The note is nothing, merely a piece of insolence and bravado,' Khurram said with more confidence than he felt. 'Bury the head with due religious ceremony. It is all that we can do for Jamal Khan now.'

He turned and still holding the governor's note made his way to Arjumand's rooms on the fort's upper storey. Through the open door he saw that she was sitting by a casement, their new son Aurangzeb in her arms. For a moment he stopped and watched them. The child was doing well, though he would never forget the day, two months after they had left Agra and a full month before the baby was due, that Arjumand had gone into labour as their party was struggling up into the Vindhya mountains where, fed by the heavy monsoon rains, small streams had become hazardous torrents and the dripping branches of the trees provided the only shelter for their tents when they made camp.

With no *hakim*, and no midwife, only the two nursemaids who had accompanied them, Arjumand had given birth in

268

the curtained bullock cart. Standing in the rain, listening helplessly to her screams – willing them to stop but at the same time afraid of what it might mean if they suddenly did – he had never felt so powerless. Why had his life, which had started so well with the favour of his grandfather and then his father, marriage to a woman he loved and who loved him, and then his victorious campaigns, suffered such a reversal of fortunes? Were the fates testing him, he had wondered, arms clasped around himself for comfort, to see if his ambition would crumble at a setback? No, he had determined, dropping his arms to his sides and drawing himself to his full height as Arjumand's screams had seemed to reach their crescendo, his misfortunes would merely make him more resolute. Moments later Arjumand's cries had abated and been joined by the lusty yelling of a child.

Now, though, as he stood in the shadow of the doorway watching her with their son, the anxiety for them that never left him for long gripped him again. Leading an army into battle held few fears for him but protecting his family when everything seemed to be turning against him was another thing. He had hoped his army in the Deccan would remain loyal to him, but immediately after his family's flight and long before he could reach his forces Jahangir had sent imperial post riders ordering the abandonment of the campaign against Malik Ambar and recalling the army to Agra. Some of Khurram's officers – men like Kamran Iqbal – had disobeyed the order and sought him out at Asirgarh. Many more – conscious of where their own advantage lay as well as afraid of Jahangir's retribution – had dutifully returned to Agra where they had taken the public oath of loyalty to the emperor Jahangir had demanded of them.

Now had come this new blow – the killing of Jamal Khan. No man could withstand torture. Jamal Khan had indeed known some of his plans but he prayed that not too many of his supporters had been compromised by his forced confession. So far none of the important rulers and governors he had tried to attract to his banner had responded. Doubtless they preferred to wait and see which way the wind would blow and this would stand them in good stead if the news of his letters to them did indeed reach Jahangir. But it would make them even less likely to provide him with aid, even covertly.

He tried to look cheerful as he entered Arjumand's room but she knew him too well. Hearing his approach she looked up, but seeing his tense expression her smile faded.

'Khurram, what is it?'

He didn't answer at first but bent to kiss her then walked over to the casement to gaze again into the dry, shimmering landscape. Behind him he heard Arjumand call an attendant to take Aurangzeb. Then he felt her arms gently take hold of him and turn him to face her.

'Please, Khurram, whatever it is you must tell me.'

'You remember that I sent Jamal Khan to the Governor of Mandu as my emissary? Well, I have had my answer. No doubt hoping my father would reward him, the governor had him tortured to reveal what he knew of our plans and then killed. He has had the temerity to return his head to me, together with a contemptuous note. He must believe my father has entirely cast me off and that I have no chance of rehabilitation or he'd never have dared do such things. And he's probably right. During all the months we've been here I've not received one word from my father though I've sent him letters protesting my innocence.'

'But at least he hasn't yet sent an army after you. That must mean something.'

'Not necessarily. Like everyone else – like all those I'm trying to persuade to support me who don't answer – he may be simply waiting, letting time and his ability to offer rewards and threaten punishments, which I cannot match, fight his battles for him. My men are already starting to drift away. At the last count I had barely two thousand ... Who knows how many I'll have in a month's time, two months' time? We can't continue like this. How can I fulfil those ambitions to which my birth and abilities entitle me?'

'But what can you do?'

'Go back to Agra again, throw myself on my father's mercy once more and force him to listen to me ...'

'No!' Her vehemence startled him. 'Listen to me, Khurram. To do so would mean almost certain death. Blinding like that of Khusrau would be the very least you could expect. When you first told me Mehrunissa had become our enemy I couldn't believe it of my own aunt ... but then I started to reflect and to realise how little I really know her. While I was growing up, she was with her first husband in Bengal. After she became empress she seemed to become more distant, more preoccupied with herself and her position ... I hardly ever saw her alone. Now, with Ladli betrothed to Shahriyar, we have become obstacles to her ... I understand that now. And one thing I do know about my aunt is how clever she is, how deter-mined, how strong ... She used those qualities to save herself and our family when my uncle Mir Khan joined Khusrau's rebellion and she will use them to destroy us if she sees the need. Don't go back to Agra ... don't put

271

yourself in her power. I'm terrified of what she might convince the emperor to do. Promise me, please . . .'

Khurram heard the passionate conviction in Arjumand's voice. Usually willing to trust his judgement she seldom argued with him. She was probably right. However much he believed in his innocence and his powers of argument and persuasion, Mehrunissa, impregnable in Jahangir's affections, would be likely to prevent him even getting another interview with his father. 'Very well,' he said at last, 'I promise . . . I will be patient a little longer.'

· ◆ ·

Jahangir winced as the *hakim* bound his forearm tightly. The gash was the result of his own carelessness while out hawking along the Jumna. If he had worn his leather gauntlet the sharp yellow beak of his falcon, a favourite bird that he had trained himself, could not have ripped the old scar tissue on the arm he had wounded fighting the Raja of Mirzapur. As the *hakim* finished his work an attendant entered. 'Majesty, the Governor of Mandu wishes to see you. He says he has news that cannot wait.'

'Then bring him to me here in my apartments at once.' What did the man want? Jahangir wondered as the *hakim* packed away his instruments and departed. Mandu was many days' travel to the south and the stout and ageing Ali Khan wasn't given to unnecessary exertion. Five minutes later the governor made his obeisance. His sweat-stained robes and dusty boots suggested he indeed had something urgent to impart.

'What is it, Ali Khan?'

'Serious news I wanted you to hear from my own lips or else I feared you might not believe it.'

272

'Go on.'

'Your son Prince Khurram is raising your subjects against you.'

'What do you mean?'

'He wrote to me seeking my support if there should be an open breach between you. I, of course, refused and thought it my duty to come to you at once.'

'Show me his letter.'

'I no longer have it, but I had the messenger who brought it tortured until he confessed everything. Prince Khurram is trying to build a power base in the south from which to challenge you. I am not the only governor the prince has approached. See – I have a list of names . . .' Ali Khan smiled what Jahangir assumed was meant to be an ingratiating smile.

Jahangir took the paper Ali Khan was holding out to him. He had had cause to suspect the governor's loyalty as long ago as the time of Khusrau's last revolt. However, Ali Khan was both wily and well connected and Jahangir had never had sufficient grounds to act against him. Khurram would have known the man's loyalty was suspect and that was presuambly the reason he had approached him. It said something for the weakness of Khurram's position that Ali Khan, no doubt after careful calculation, had decided to betray him to his father.

Scanning the list of names Jahangir saw it was long. Suddenly, he felt weary and wanted to be alone. 'I will reward you well, Ali Khan. Leave me now.'

'Thank you, Majesty. You may depend on my loyalty.' Ali Khan beamed as he turned and headed from the room.

Once the doors closed behind the governor, Jahangir brushed the back of his hand across his eyes. How could the son he had once loved the most be so disloyal? Since their last brief meeting on the battlements, barely a day had passed when he had not brooded about Khurram, wondering what he was planning to do. Part of him had hoped that he might repent his defiance and submit. His letters from Asirgarh had at first encouraged those hopes, but as Mehrunissa had pointed out his words were no more than arrogant self-justification – there had been no apology, no recognition of any fault. At her suggestion he had not replied. But he had not sent troops to apprehend his son as Mehrunissa had also urged. Now it seemed she had, as usual, been right. He had been lax, allowing time to drift by without acting, which had encouraged Khurram to further defiance.

· ◆ ·

Dusk was falling as Jahangir approached Mehrunissa's apartments. He had just come from a council meeting at which Ali Khan, in clean green robes, had repeated his story. His counsellors' anxious questioning of the governor had shown they were as troubled as he was himself – or at least pretending to be. None of their names were on Ali Khan's list but had any of them been aware of Khurram's plotting? Jahangir's expression hardened at the thought. Mehrunissa had seen and heard everything through the grille in the rear wall of the council chamber. He wanted to hear what she had to say – but also to consult Ghiyas Beg and Asaf Khan, whom he had summoned to join them.

The evening candles had just been lit in Mehrunissa's apartments when he entered. His head was aching badly. She came to him at once, put her hands on his shoulders and pressed her lips briefly against his before turning wordlessly away to pour him a goblet of wine. He took a long swallow.

274

He needed the wine's comfort and its soothing warmth, he thought, as the doors opened again to admit the tall, now elderly figure of Ghiyas Beg and behind him the bulkier figure of his son Asaf Khan.

'Well, you all heard Ali Khan. What do you think?' he asked bluntly.

'Majesty, I hardly know what to say.' Ghiyas Beg shook his silver-haired head. 'I had not thought such a thing possible.'

'It is only too possible. It's just as I suspected. Khurram wishes to seize the throne. I was right to advise you to arrest him all those months ago. If only the guards had been quicker . . .' Mehrunissa said.

'But, Majesty, reflect a moment − all Ali Khan said was that Prince Khurram is trying to gather supporters. That does not mean he intends leading an army against you,' Ghiyas Beg protested.

'But why else take such a step?' Mehrunissa demanded.

'Because, daughter, he feels vulnerable. Forgive my plain speaking, Majesty, but you never told the prince how he had displeased you. That is why he risked your anger by coming to Agra to try to speak to you . . . Majid Khan told me of the prince's conversation with him that night. And if I am honest I and many others at court don't understand why you have turned against him. Prince Khurram did everything you asked . . . led your armies loyally and bravely to victory. Until recently he was your greatest pride . . . everyone expected you to name him your heir—'

'Exactly. Because the emperor was so open, so generous with his affections, he raised such expectations, but in the prince himself those expectations turned to something else − a greedy, impatient ambition . . .' Mehrunissa broke in.

'Young men are ambitious. But what proof have you that he ever intended treachery?'

'He abandoned his command in the Deccan and came to Agra.'

'But only because things had happened that he didn't understand. Like the awarding to Prince Shahriyar of lands Khurram believed he had been promised . . . and rightly, too.'

'The grant of those lands was the emperor's prerogative. It is not your place to question His Majesty's decision.'

'And it is not yours to interrupt me. You may be empress but I am still your father.' The old man took a moment to compose himself before continuing, 'Majesty, ever since your late father rescued me and my family from destitution I've tried to serve your house well. I speak from all my long experience when I urge you to be cautious. Take no hasty decisions you may later regret.'

Silence fell in the chamber. Mehrunissa had turned away. Jahangir could tell by her posture, the angle of her head, how angry she was. He had never heard her argue with her father before nor heard Ghiyas Beg, usually so gently circumspect, speak with such passion. Asaf Khan was looking from one to the other, a deep frown on his face.

'Asaf Khan, you stand there so silent and grave. Don't you have anything to say?' Jahangir asked. 'If Khurram ruins himself, he ruins your daughter also.'

'I believe my father is right, Majesty. You should not act until you know more. You need to find out what is really in Khurram's heart and mind. Send an envoy to him — I will gladly go if you wish.'

'Yes,' Ghiyas Beg put in. 'At least offer him the chance to

276

be reconciled with you before he drifts so far that reconciliation becomes impossible.'

'Perhaps he doesn't want to be reconciled.'

'You won't know unless you attempt it, Majesty. In any event, your subjects will praise you for seeking to avert war with your son,' Ghiyas Beg pressed.

Jahangir studied the dark dregs in his goblet. Ghiyas Beg's words had struck a chord. Had he been unfair to Khurram, just as Akbar had been to him? What would have happened had he listened longer to Khurram that night on the battlements? Could they have reached a better understanding?

But then Mehrunissa spoke again. 'Father, in an ideal world your suggestion might be right. But our world is not perfect. It is peopled with enemies within and beyond our borders, all longing to aggrandise themselves at the emperor's expense. Even now Khurram may be gathering his forces, soliciting allies among our foes.'

'Have you any evidence of that?'

'There are rumours. Every day that passes without our taking decisive action weakens the emperor and strengthens Khurram and he will know that.' Kneeling in front of Jahangir, she took his face between her hands. 'Listen to me. Haven't I always advised you well? You must act quickly. Hesitation is a sign of weakness. It's hard, I know, but you must move to crush Khurram. When he's brought before you as a captive, that will be time enough to talk. You may be a father, but you are an emperor first. Isn't your greatest duty to protect your empire?' For a moment her eyes held his, then she released him and stood up.

Ghiyas Beg was again shaking his head. 'Majesty, my

daughter's words are ill judged. You should do nothing rash. At least take a few days to consider . . .'

'You know you're only saying that because you favour my brother and his daughter over me and my daughter,' Mehrunissa burst out, voice trembling. 'And you, brother.' She swung round to Asaf Khan. 'Ask yourself where your true loyalties lie . . . to your emperor or to your daughter?'

Asaf Khan took a step back and glanced nervously at Jahangir, but Ghiyas Beg was not intimidated. 'Mehrunissa, how dare you make such accusations! We might equally accuse you of having personal reasons to promote the interests of your daughter and Shahriyar over those of Khurram and Arjumand.'

'You are growing old. Your mind is failing or you could not say such a thing . . . This is about the safety of the empire, not mere family interests.'

'You are insolent. You forget the duty of respect you owe me.'

'Duty? You speak of duty? Where was duty when you abandoned me as a newborn baby under a tree to die? How much respect did you show me then?'

'We were all close to death. I had no choice, as you very well know. And when fortune smiled, I came back to find you . . .'

'And now you're abandoning me all over again.'

'Enough of this!' Jahangir's head still ached. For once he even felt impatient with Mehrunissa, whose usually beautiful eyes were glittering with anger and whose lower lip was thrust out in an ugly pout. 'I wished to hear your views on this matter because it affects both our families, but the decision I take will be mine alone.'

'Of course.' Mehrunissa spoke more calmly. 'I'm sorry I was angry, but my anger was for you, because I wish to defend you from harm . . . as we should always do for those we love.'

Jahangir looked at the three of them – father, brother and sister. His was not the only family divided by recent events. 'I will think on what you've all said, but now I will return to my own apartments.' He saw Mehrunissa make a slight movement towards him, but he ignored her. Tonight he needed to be alone to reflect.

· ◆ ·

Jahangir sat in the darkness by the open casement, a cup of Mehrunissa's opium-laced wine by his side. As he sipped, the pain in his head was easing, but he still found it hard to marshal his thoughts. Disturbing images flickered across his mind, distorting as they passed – of himself as a boy watching his father Akbar and wondering whether he could ever win his approval, of running through the warm night to the house of the Sufi, Shaikh Salim Chishti, to reveal his fears and uncertainties to the old man, of his rebellion against Akbar. All Akbar's affection had been for Jahangir's sons, not for Jahangir, and what had that led to in the case of Khusrau? The screams of his eldest son's followers, spitted on stakes, echoed in his head, and Khusrau peered at him with sightless eyes.

Horrified by these phantom images, Jahangir pulled himself fully awake and tossed the metal cup into a corner, splashing the rugs with the dregs of the wine. He needed to think with a clear mind. Slowly, the soft breezes through the casement seemed to blow away the drug and alcohol fumes. If Akbar had been a better father to him and he a better father to his own sons, Khusrau's revolt and Khurram's disaffection might not have happened. Yet he had tried so hard not to repeat Akbar's failings towards him. Perhaps what had happened was inevitable – perhaps the inheritance the Moghuls had brought from the steppes of Asia made it so. It was in their blood to challenge for the throne, just as a young stag tests his strength against the leader of the herd. It was part of nature for fathers to teach sons harsh lessons.

Jahangir gazed deep into the starry darkness. His grand-father the Emperor Humayun had believed that the stars held the answers to all life's mysteries. Jahangir's lip curled. They certainly hadn't solved Humayun's problems – problems born of being merciful when he should have been ruthless, hesitant when he should have been decisive. That was why he had lost his empire.

That would never happen to him. He had waited too long for his throne . . . Mehrunissa was right, as always. Any delay, any hesitation on his part could be fatal. He must put sentiment aside and deal with Khurram.

· ◆ ·

At dusk the following evening, with his entire court standing beneath the marble dais in the Hall of Public Audience, Jahangir rose to address the rows of noblemen before him. Now that he had made his decision he felt his confidence grow, just as it had at his coronation when he first appeared to his people on the *jharoka* balcony. Among those nearest the dais were Ghiyas Beg, Asaf Khan and his vizier Majid Khan. He had told nobody, not even Mehrunissa, what he was about to say, but no one could doubt that he was about to announce something momentous.

He had ordered the hall's hundred sandstone pillars to be wrapped in black silk. All the fountains in the courtyard beyond had been turned off and more black silk had been thrown over the beds of bright flowers, banishing all colour. He himself was also dressed in black, a simple turban of the same hue on his head and not a single jewel. His courtiers were looking round uneasily. Jahangir waited, allowing the tension to build yet further, and then began.

'As you know, yesterday the Governor of Mandu reported to me that my son Prince Khurram is stirring up insurrection. He has written to many of my governors urging them to ally themselves with him against me. That is not his only crime. He abandoned his command in the Deccan and came to Agra without my permission. When I ordered his arrest he fled in the night. Even then I hoped he would see his error and return to the path of duty. In my fatherly affection I was patient, allowing him time to repent of his youthful arrogance; I sent no army against him. But ambition has corrupted him completely. He responded not with love but with further defiance. Now I can hold my hand no longer.'

Jahangir paused. The silence was absolute. His eye fell on Ghiyas Beg, whose head was bowed. Mehrunissa's father would not like what he was about to say but his own security, the empire's security, must come first. Speaking loudly and firmly to emphasise the importance of the moment Jahangir commanded, 'Bring me the imperial ledger in which I inscribed the name of the *bi-dalaut*, the wretch called Khurram, on the ill-starred day of his birth.'

An attendant holding a large green leather-bound volume stepped forward and laid it on a mulberry wood bookstand that another servant had already placed on the dais. Jahangir

281

opened the book and slowly turned the pages until he found the one he sought. Then, taking a pen from the attendant, he dipped it into a black onyx ink pot that the man held and drew a line through the page with a single decisive stroke. 'Before you all I declare that I disown the *bi-dalaut*, Khurram. Just as you have seen me strike his name from the list of my sons so I strike him for ever from my heart. From this day forward Khurram is no son of mine.'

Even while he was speaking, Jahangir heard shocked murmuring from his courtiers. Ghiyas Beg and Asaf Khan, standing just a few feet away, had horror on their faces while his vizier Majid Khan, eyes closed, was running his prayer beads through his fingers and rocking backwards and forwards. But he was not finished yet.

'I will not tolerate rebellion within my empire – whoever the perpetrator. Earlier today I signed and sealed a *firman*, an imperial decree, declaring Khurram an outlaw and placing a price upon his head – fifty thousand gold *mohurs* for any man who captures him. Furthermore, I am sending an army against him under the command of my general Mahabat Khan. It will march in a week's time.'

Jahangir turned and walked swiftly from the hall, a craving for Mehrunissa's opium wine to numb the harsh realities of an emperor's life, a father's life, gnawing at him once more.

Chapter 17

The Outlaw

The smell of rain falling on the hot earth – the unmistakable smell of the monsoon – seemed to grow ever more
pungent the further east they travelled through the fetid lands
of Bengal, Khurram thought as, riding at the head of the
column, he looked back over his shoulder at the force strag-
gling behind him. During the last months it had dwindled to
a mere five or six hundred men. The news that Mahabat Khan
had swept out of Agra at the head of a large and well-equipped
army – twenty thousand soldiers and three hundred war
elephants according to some reports – to hunt him down had
persuaded many of his own soldiers to desert.

Khurram had only met Mahabat Khan once at court but
had heard of his bravery in battle. He was a Persian who
had been in the service of the shah until, like Ghiyas Beg,
he had fallen from favour and come to the Moghul court.
By all accounts he was a risk taker, impulsive sometimes to
the point of recklessness, but always successful – at least until

now. His elite personal force of two thousand Rajputs were said to be devoted to him. He must indeed be a charismatic leader if as a foreigner and a Muslim he could so impress those fearless saffron-clad Hindu warriors, who believed themselves the children of the sun and the moon. Small wonder, Khurram thought, that some of his own men had slunk away. But better a small force of true supporters than a larger one with no stomach for a fight.

Feeling an insect bite the side of his neck, he slapped at it with his hand and glancing at his fingers saw that they were smeared with blood. He had seldom felt wearier or more dispirited. By declaring him an outlaw, his father had set every man in the empire against him. A feeling of help-lessness mingled with anger rose within him. How could his father have repudiated and humiliated him so brutally, so publicly, allowing him no chance to defend himself? How could the pride he had once had in him, his deeds and auspicious birth, have turned to such vindictive rancour? Whatever his father might choose to believe, he had become nothing more than Mehrunissa's puppet. She controlled Jahangir and she controlled his empire, feeding his weakness for wine and opium. And everything she wanted was coming to pass. According to a letter from Asaf Khan, whose messenger had followed Khurram's retreating force from Asirgarh, two months ago Jahangir had summoned Shahriyar and placing the imperial turban on his head had declared him his heir. And that wasn't all. The date for Shahriyar's marriage to Mehrunissa's daughter Ladli had been set by the court astrologers and would take place during the New Year festivities.

Meanwhile, he and his family were being forced to flee

for their lives, perhaps even beyond the borders of the empire. Mehrunissa had reduced him to a landless wanderer just like his great-grandfather Humayun and Babur before him. But she would not win. One day he would reign, like Babur and Humayun. Jahangir could do or say what he would but he, Khurram, was the only one of his four sons fit to be an emperor and his father had forfeited the right to his loyalty.

Hearing a sudden noise behind him, Khurram looked round. A wheel on one of the heavily laden baggage wagons had become bogged down in the mire. If his men couldn't free the wagon quickly they would have to abandon it. Food and equipment mattered less than putting distance between himself and his father's pursuing army. At least his small force could cover the ground faster than a large one with artillery to drag across a terrain made even more inhospitable by the monsoon rains that had been falling for the past two months, making the swamps and marshes almost impossible for a large army to negotiate. That was why he had chosen to come east. And, even if Mahabat Khan's army succeeded in following him into Bengal, he could take ship and seek sanctuary further south down the coast. Only two weeks ago he had received a surprising letter – an offer of alliance from Malik Ambar. 'You and I have been worthy adversaries on the battlefield,' the Abyssinian had written. 'Why shouldn't we now be brothers in arms?' Khurram hadn't replied but he hadn't dismissed the idea either. Malik Ambar and his backers, the Deccan rulers, would be bound to require substantial concessions in return for their support, but with it he would have the strength to confront his father. But could he really make common cause with the Moghul empire's external enemies, even if it seemed his only way to regain the position that was rightly his?

As his men pulled and heaved at the wagon Khurram felt himself boil over with frustration. Without even calling to his bodyguard to follow, he kicked his horse and cantered ahead over the squelching ground. After riding barely half a mile through the thinly slanting rain he glimpsed a ribbon of water. Brushing raindrops from his face he peered more closely. It must be the Mahanadi river at last . . . He was about to turn his horse to ride back with the good news when an arrow slashed through the air, just missing his head but shattering his peace of mind. Then another – black shafted and black feathered – thudded into his saddlebag, embedding itself in the by now mildewing gilded leather and missing his thigh by inches, while a third landed in the mud just by his mount's right foreleg. Dropping low over his horse's neck and dragging hard on his reins to turn it, he kicked the animal into a gallop back towards the column, every nerve tingling, all the time fearing that another arrow was about to strike him in the back and put an end to all his ambitions. As he rode he cursed himself for his recklessness. He should have sent scouts ahead.

Who could the attackers be? Had some henchman of his father's, attracted by the reward for his capture and riding fast and light, caught up with them? Could it even be Mahabat Khan and his troops? If so, he would sell his life dearly. After what seemed an age but was probably less than a minute he was approaching the column. As soon as he was within earshot he shouted, 'Archers up ahead. We're under attack. Halt the column. Our muskets will be useless in the rain. Ready your own bows and arrows.' Back among his men, he flung himself from the saddle, keeping his horse's body between himself and the direction from which the arrows had come.

As his men yanked on their reins and reached for their weapons, Khurram looked back towards the river but could see nothing. Perhaps the attackers had already made off . . . But at that very moment more arrows hissed through the air as if to disabuse him of such thoughts. One hit a young *qorchi* standing only a few feet from Khurram in the wind-pipe and blood bubbled through his fingers as he clutched at his throat. Another embedded itself in the neck of a pack mule and the animal began a piteous high-pitched braying before collapsing to its knees in the thick mud.

Khurram's overriding thought was to get back to Arjumand and the children. At least the thick hide hangings of the bullock wagons they were travelling in should be some protection from the arrows. Ducking behind a grain cart and half running, half crawling through the mud, he reached the wagon in which Arjumand and their daughters were riding. Reaching up he pulled aside the heavy curtains and looked in. Arjumand was huddled in a corner, arms tight around Jahanara and Roshanara, her mouth already forming into a scream until she saw who it was.

'We're being attacked, I don't know why or by whom,' Khurram gasped, breathing hard. 'Lie down on the bottom of the wagon and stay there until I return. Don't on any account get out.' Arjumand nodded. Dropping the hanging, Khurram ran, bent double, to the wagon containing the boys and their nurses. His sons looked at him with round eyes as he repeated the instructions he had just given Arjumand. As he did so, a piercing scream told him another arrow had found a target.

Mud soaked, he scrambled back to the protection of the grain cart and, heart thumping, looked about him. Two more of his men were sprawled face down in the viscous mire. Another – Nicholas Ballantyne, pale hands crimson with his own blood as he worked – was jabbing at his calf with his dagger, trying to cut out an arrowhead. Nearby another pack mule was lying on its side, legs threshing wildly. Before he had time to think more arrows skimmed over them, one striking a soldier in the back, another thudding into the hub of one of the wheels on Arjumand's wagon. Then, suddenly, the firing ceased. The rain was growing heavier all the time, splashing into the growing puddles and drenching everything. It would make it harder for the archers, already fumbling with wet fingers to fit arrows to sodden bowstrings.

What was happening? Warily raising his head, he made out through the downpour a cluster of riders approaching slowly at no more than a trot from the direction of the river. The steely veil of rain made it difficult for him to gauge how many there were. Probably they were having the same difficulty assessing the strength of his force. Well, they were about to find out, Khurram thought.

'Mount up and follow me,' he yelled to his bodyguard as he ran towards his horse and scrambled back into the wet saddle. 'The rest of you, protect the wagons and tend the wounded.' Within moments Khurram and his guards were charging towards their unknown enemy, mud and water raised by their horses' hooves flying around them. 'Keep down,' he yelled as he bent over his horse's neck, sword drawn and warm rain running off his face. Gripping hard with his knees in case his horse should stumble in the slippery soft mud, he narrowed his eyes, picking out his target.

As Khurram and his men emerged through the rain, they heard cries of alarm and surprise from their attackers. Instantly, their assailants were tugging frantically at their reins, turning their horses and fleeing away from them back towards the river. Urging his own horse on, Khurram passed a spiny bush on which a grimy length of turban cloth had caught. Rounding a bend in the track he saw the whole group properly at last: thirty or forty helmetless men, bows and quivers now slung on their backs, arms and legs working to push their horses along as fast as the mud would allow – but not fast enough to keep them ahead of the better-mounted Moghuls. They were his, Khurram thought with grim satisfaction as he and his men bore down on them. One man fell from his horse and Khurram heard his skull crack as the hoof of one of his bodyguards' horses caught it. Gaining fast on another whose small brown pony was labouring, Khurram struck hard, opening a great gash in the man's back. With a sweep of his sword he decapitated a second – a scrawny fellow in a rough dun-coloured tunic who had been foolish enough to slow in his flight to see how far his pursuers were behind him. The head splashed into a puddle and the torso slowly slipped from the saddle, and after a few moments also toppled into the mud. All around, Khurram saw his men cutting and stabbing with their sharply honed steel weapons, which their opponents had nothing to match. Everywhere, bright, fresh, crimson blood was mingling with the rivulets of muddy rainwater on the ground.

In less than five minutes he and his men had slaughtered nearly all of their enemies except for a very few who had managed to escape along the riverbank into the bush. Khurram was about to turn his horse and give the order to return to the main column when he detected movement beneath a jumble of dead branches thirty feet away. One of the attackers must have taken refuge there after being unhorsed. Pulling his bloodied sword once more from its scabbard Khurram quickly dismounted and moved quietly towards the branches, where all now seemed still. When he was about ten feet away he circled slowly round to the right. Ducking beneath the branches he saw a man crouching down with his back towards him, bow and arrows by his side and a serrated-edged hunting knife gripped in his right hand. He had no suspicion Khurram was there until he felt the prick of the steel tip of his sword in the small of his back.

'Get up and out of there,' Khurram ordered, speaking in Persian. He would soon know whether these were his father's soldiers or not. When there was no response he repeated his order in Hindi and jabbed the sword into the man's flesh, drawing blood that stained his already wet and torn cotton tunic. His enemy yelped and pushing the branches aside scrambled quickly to his feet before turning round, dagger clenched in his hand and eyes searching wildly for an escape route. He was short and wiry and in his left earlobe was a single gold hoop. 'Put down your dagger,' Khurram shouted. The man let it fall and Khurram kicked it away. 'Who are you? Why did you attack me and my men?'

'Why not? Anyone foolish enough to travel through these marshes belongs to us.'

So they were just local *dacoits*, albeit lethally dangerous ones, Khurram thought, remembering his dead and wounded men sprawled in the mud back up the track. This contemptible creature would pay, but not quite yet. 'Who is your leader? Where is your village?'

'We have neither. We are our own men. We roam these lands making camp where and when we choose.'

'How many of you are there?'

'We were just a small party hunting for the pot. We came upon you by chance. We thought you were a caravan of merchants. If we'd known how many of you there were we wouldn't have attacked you with so few men. But soon more of our brothers will come – hundreds of us, looking to revenge us on you. You won't realise they're there until it's too late. They'll be in your camp, killing your soldiers, taking your goods – and having fun with your women.'

As he spoke the man suddenly lunged to one side, trying desperately to reach his knife which was lying half submerged in a puddle. His fingers were just curling round the hilt when Khurram thrust his sword into his stomach. The man collapsed backwards into the mud and after thrashing about for a moment, blood bubbling through his betel-stained teeth and eyes bulging, lay still.

Remounting, Khurram made his way back up the track, pondering what the *dacoit* had said. Were there really many more of them – some kind of robber army – or had it just been a vainglorious boast? He couldn't take the risk. They must push on and cross the river before nightfall. How many more times before he could reach safety would he be at the mercy of bandits – vicious outlaws just as his father had declared him to be? Bitterness at what his father had done to him and how far he had fallen darkened his thoughts as he rode.

• ◆ •

Two hours later, after the dead had been buried and scouts had reported no further sign of bandits, the column advanced the short distance to the river. It was wide – about two hundred feet across – but in spite of the rains not especially deep, no more than four or so feet at a fording place the scouts had found. Nevertheless, it was flowing with some force and in midstream jagged rocks protruded. Khurram urged his horse into the fast-running water to gauge its strength. To his relief the animal was able to stand its ground – they should be able to cross it if they were careful. 'Send a detachment of soldiers across to secure the opposite bank,' he ordered the captain of his guard. 'Then we'll begin sending the wagons over.'

It wasn't long before Khurram saw a torch flare on the other side of the river – the signal that it was safe to begin the main crossing. The rain had ceased and there was even a patch of blue sky as the drivers urged the first teams of oxen hauling the baggage wagons into the water. The protesting beasts moved agonisingly slowly but reached the opposite shore without incident. Next Khurram sent the strings of pack mules, only lightly burdened as the heaviest loads had been transferred to the wagons. Though the rushing water came above their bellies and some of them had to be prodded into the river at the point of a lance, they too gained the far side where they shook themselves dry like dogs, the bells round their necks clanging.

Khurram relaxed a little. The remaining wagons held only people and were lighter than the baggage wagons. With luck,

292

the day's dangers were over. Glancing up at the sky he saw it was still quite light. They should be able to put two or three miles between themselves and the river by nightfall and he would choose a secure campsite and post pickets. Two wagons full of wounded men crossed first. Nicholas Ballantyne, the rough bloodstained bandage on his calf visible through the cut he had made in his breeches, was sitting beside the driver in the first, keeping an eye out for concealed rocks and floating driftwood, of which there was plenty. The wagon carrying Khurram's three sons and their nurses went next. After they had reached the far side, finally it was the turn of Arjumand's wagon.

As the four white bullocks pulling it entered the water, Khurram urged his horse into the river behind it, wanting to stay close in case of any mishap. Water surged through the great, metal-bound wheels as they slowly turned. The driver was doing well in avoiding the sharp rocks. But when the wagon was almost halfway across, one of the two leading bullocks slipped and half tumbled to its knees. Emitting deep bellows it managed to right itself and continue doggedly pulling. The next moment Khurram heard shouts of alarm from the opposite bank and was aware of men running down to the water's edge. Looking upstream to where they were pointing, he saw a massive fallen tree with widespread, densely leaved branches hurtling towards them in the foaming water. He barely had time to register the sight before the tree trunk slammed into the left side of the wagon. The spokes of the back wheel splintered and the wagon tipped slowly sideways into the water, the tree jammed on top of it for a moment until the sheer force of the current sent it rushing on its way downstream again.

Kicking his frightened horse nearer to the tumbled wagon Khurram saw that the wildly struggling bullocks were trapped beneath the water. 'Cut them from their yokes,' he yelled to the driver. Then, leaping from his horse, he managed to grab hold of one of the shattered spokes and haul himself on to what had been the left side of the wagon but which, protruding from the water, now formed its roof. Tearing his dagger from its scabbard he sawed a jagged cut in the thick hide covering and looked inside. With the gushing water almost up to her chin and her long hair streaming around her, Arjumand was clinging with her right arm to one of the wooden ribs of the wagon's frame and in her left was trying to hold Roshanara above the water. Jahanara was hanging on to one of the ribs with both hands.

Behind him Khurram heard voices – others were coming to his assistance. Jahanara was closest to him and he lowered his right hand towards her. 'Let go of the wagon and hold on to me instead', he said to the terrified child, who hesitated a moment and then grabbed on to him. He lifted her out and handed her to one of his soldiers who had managed to get his horse close to the wagon. Then he reached inside the wagon again. 'Arjumand, try to get a little closer so that I can take Roshanara from you.' In the semi-gloom he could see Arjumand's eyes and hear her laboured breathing as she slid her right hand along the wooden spar without letting go and held Roshanara out to him. Reaching down, he managed to grip his daughter's arm and though she cried out with pain he pulled her out of the wagon.

But as Khurram twisted round to hand Roshanara to another of his men, the wagon rocked violently again. He lost his footing and fell into the water, and felt the force of

294

the torrent tear Roshanara from his grasp. Managing to stand upright he looked desperately round. 'Roshanara!' he yelled, wiping the water from his eyes. 'Roshanara!' At first he couldn't see her but then he caught a glimpse of something scarlet in the flood – the colour of her tunic – and saw her being carried away.

Arjumand had heard his frantic cries and was hauling herself out of the wagon, blood running from a cut on her chin. 'Roshanara – where is she?' she screamed.

Khurram pointed downstream. 'Stay there. I'll get her.' But before he had even finished speaking Arjumand had flung herself into the river. She was a good swimmer – she had loved to swim in the pool in the *haram* of his mansion in Agra – but she would be no match for the strong current that was already bearing her away or the sharp rocks concealed beneath the surface.

Quickly Khurram made his decision. He struggled out of the water on the far bank where most of his force was now gathered and shouted for a horse and for men to follow him. Leaping on to the animal's back, he rode downstream as fast as the thick mud would allow, scanning the churning water all the while. A few hundred yards ahead the river took a sharp bend to the left amid some trees. The current should slow at that point, and he could see long branches overhanging the water well into midstream. His heart leapt as he made out Arjumand clinging to a piece of wood and a hundred or so yards ahead of her the red shape – barely bigger than a doll – that was Roshanara. He must get to the bend in the river before they did . . .

Tree branches whipped at his face as he galloped towards the bend. Wheeling his horse to an abrupt stop, he jumped

295

from the saddle and hauled himself up into one of the trees overhanging the river. Clambering on to a thick smooth branch, about three feet above the water, he edged his way along it as far as he thought it would bear his weight. Then, still holding on to it with one hand, he lowered his body into the torrent and turned to face upstream. He was only just in time. There she was, like a bundle of sodden red rags . . . Reaching out with his free hand he managed to grab hold first of Roshanara's tunic and then one of her arms. It took all his strength to tug her, one handed, out of the water and on to the branch, but he managed it, then pulled himself up. To his relief he could hear the child's ragged breathing. Her body was limp, but she was alive. One of his soldiers had climbed out on to a nearby branch and he handed her to him.

As Roshanara was being taken to safety, Khurram was already edging back along the branch. He could make out Arjumand being whirled towards him, still clinging to her piece of wood, but she was too far away for him to be able to catch hold of her. When she was almost level with him he leapt into the water and struck out towards her. The river was deeper here but, just as he'd hoped, the bend was reducing its force. Ten strokes brought him to Arjumand's side. Putting his left arm round her waist, he said, 'Let go of the log. I have you.' She did as he said and he began to make for the shore, striking out with his right arm and kicking as hard as he could with his legs. With so much water in his eyes it was hard to think of anything but the green blur of the bank and not letting go of Arjumand.

Then he saw something sticking out towards them. 'Grab the lance shaft, Highness,' a voice was shouting. Reaching out, his fingers made contact with wood. Then, gripping the lance handle hard, he felt himself being pulled in. Moments later, he and Arjumand were lying in the mud gasping for breath. Arjumand's right upper arm was scraped and bleeding heavily where she had caught it against some rocks and her cheek was gashed but her first words were, 'Roshanara . . . is she all right?' Khurram just nodded. Shivering, wet and muddy as they were, they clasped one another in silent gratitude.

Chapter 18

The Kindness of Strangers

T he oozing, evil-smelling brown mud still sucked at the wheels of the wagons as if unwilling to let them pass. Khurram felt close to despair. Over the weeks since crossing the Mahanadi river their progress had become painfully slow, sometimes no more than three or four miles a day, as they headed northeastwards towards the Ganges delta. The monsoon rains had ended but their legacy was still there, from the moist air to the thick carpet of rotting leaves and fallen branches and the glinting black water of the now-stagnating swamps they had fed. Though they had had no further trouble from bandits and had seen no sign of Mahabat Khan, hazards lurked all around. Venomous serpents slid through the undergrowth. Whirring, biting mosquitoes descended in swarms at dusk, hungry for warm blood. And now disease had begun spreading among his men – six had died in the last two weeks including his elderly steward, Shah Gul, who had faithfully fled with him into exile from Agra. Every morning his forces were fewer as men slipped away, preferring to take their chances on their own.

Locked in gloom, Khurram pushed aside one of the tangles of dank, ragged green moss that dangled from every tree. His greatest worry was Arjumand, again pregnant, and their children. The children all looked sickly and thin and Arjumand herself was haggard, with shadows beneath her eyes. The injury to her upper arm she had suffered crossing the Mahanadi had never healed fully. It still looked hot and puffy and occasionally oozed yellow pus. What should he do? He wished he knew the whereabouts of Mahabat Khan's army . . . whether, now that the dry season had come, it was on his heels or whether it had turned back during the monsoon. With no information it was impossible to plan. The scouts he had despatched ten days ago to search for any signs of pursuit hadn't yet returned and perhaps they wouldn't – the opportunity to desert might have proved too tempting.

His head ached and glancing down he saw how worn and mud-streaked his clothes were, like the dull coat of his once fine horse whose ribs now visibly protruded. Looking ahead again, he tried to convince himself that the vegetation was thinning. Surely they couldn't be far from the coast, or at least the network of waterways that made up the mouth of the Ganges. If they could only find one of those they could follow it downstream to the sea . . .

As if his thoughts had conjured them, Nicholas Ballantyne and another of his guards emerged from the green shadows ahead. He had sent them out early, as he always did after his experience with *dacoits* on the riverbank, to scout the way ahead. 'Well?' he called as soon as they were in range.

Then to his surprise he saw that they were not alone. Twenty yards behind them, mounted on a handsome white mule was a man in a long robe of coarse brown cloth whose strange, flat, wide-brimmed hat obscured his face.

'Highness,' said Nicholas, trotting up, his young face pink with sweat. 'That man is a Portuguese priest. We found him supervising a group of men cutting firewood about five miles ahead. He says we're not far from the Portuguese settlement at Hooghly.'

'Hooghly?' Khurram frowned. He had heard his father talk about the trading settlement. There had been stories at court that the Portuguese priests there were trying forcibly to convert the local people to their religion and even that Portuguese merchants were selling those who refused to the slave traders whose ships put in there . . . 'Does this priest know who I am?'

'No, Highness. All I told him was that you were a Moghul nobleman.'

'Tell him to approach.'

As the priest rode forward, he bowed his head in greeting. Beneath the brim of his hat, Khurram saw amber eyes in a long thin-nosed face with a close-clipped fringe of beard. 'I understand that you are a Portuguese priest from Hooghly.'

'Yes, Highness,' the man answered in Persian.

'You know me?'

'My name is Father Ronaldo. I visited your father's court some years ago. At that time your father was showing great interest in our religion – the true faith. He even spoke of appointing a Jesuit priest like myself as tutor to your youngest brother.'

Khurram nodded. He remembered now how interested

his father had been in the Jesuits — just as his grandfather Akbar had been. For a time the court had swarmed with priests and the mullahs had objected to their processions through the streets of Agra behind a great, rough-hewn wooden cross and their incessant clamour to be allowed to build their churches.

Father Ronaldo pursed his thin lips. 'The emperor allowed himself to be swayed by the dogma of his own priests, who were jealous of our influence and feared us as the revealers of the true path to God.'

Khurram said nothing. This was no time for a religious debate. He and his family needed help and this man might provide it. 'Do you know what has brought me to Bengal?' he asked, eyes fixed closely on the priest's face. The amber eyes flickered.

'We heard something of a disagreement between you and your father,' said Father Ronaldo after a moment.

'It is more than a disagreement. We are on the brink of war. I have brought my family here in the hope of finding a refuge for them while I regroup my forces. I still have many allies.'

'You really think it will come to war?' The priest looked shocked.

'I hope not but it may. My father is no longer his own man. He has given in to wine and opium and leaves the governance of his empire to his wife.'

'The Empress Mehrunissa? A recent decree granting our merchants the right to trade in indigo bore her seal. We were surprised, but assumed it must be because the emperor was ill.'

'No. She rules, not he. I will tell you more later, but

first I must know whether you and your fellow Portuguese will give my family sanctuary at Hooghly. We have travelled hundreds of miles, often in great danger. My children are young and my wife is ill and pregnant. She must rest.'

For the first time the priest smiled. 'It is our Christian duty to help you, Highness. If you will send your English squire ahead with me, I will speak to my brother priests and we will prepare quarters for you.'

· ◆ ·

A light breeze stirred the muslin hangings of the white-washed room in the simple one-storey, palm-thatched house sitting on stilts on the banks of the Hooghly river where Arjumand was lying on a low divan. For a moment her gaze rested on the dark painting of a man nailed to a wooden cross on the wall opposite her. He was so thin that every rib protruded and blood so dark it was almost black ran from beneath a wreath of thorns down his waxen face, which was twisted in agony. His eyes looked despairingly up to the sky, the pupils barely visible, just the veined whites. It was a horrible picture and at night she placed a cloth over it, but in the daytime she didn't wish to offend the Portuguese maids who attended her with such kindness. It was they who cooked and cleaned for the priests and had also taken over the care of her, Khurram and their small household here in the priests' walled compound, often serving them the salted fish of which the Portuguese seemed so inordinately fond. Khurram's soldiers were comfortably encamped on the banks of the Hooghly about a quarter of a mile beyond where the Portuguese trading vessels were moored.

302

Often her mind filled with memories of Agra and especially of her grandfather Ghiyas Beg, whom she would never see again. A Portuguese merchant who had called at Hooghly not long before she and Khurram had arrived had told the priests that the Imperial Treasurer was dead and the Moghul court in mourning. She could scarcely believe it. He had been such a presence in her life – in the lives of all her family. Inevitably, the news had also turned her thoughts to her aunt. Mehrunissa would surely be grieving . . . or would she? Because of Mehrunissa, the Moghul imperial family was split as so often in the past, father against son, half-brother against half-brother. Sometimes it seemed to her that their family troubles were like a canker in the heart of a flower, eating away unseen until it was too late.

Such disunity should never happen among her own children, she thought, listening to the shouts of her sons from outside. Khurram loved his three sons and they loved him. What was more, her boys were full brothers with a single loving mother to watch over them, not the sons of different mothers, brought up in different establishments so that the early bonds of fraternal love were never fully formed. And surely the dangers and hardships they'd faced – perhaps still faced – would bind them yet closer.

Feeling a kick inside her, she shifted. What would this child be? Another son? It was a big child – her belly had never been quite so swollen before. She usually felt well in pregnancy and with each child giving birth had come more easily. But this time she felt ill and a little afraid. All that she had endured, and the infection in her arm that had still not yet healed, had left her

303

feeling so weak . . . She gasped as a sudden sharp pain ran through her.

• ◆ •

As Khurram rode towards the Jesuits' compound after a pleasant few hours hunting along the banks of the Hooghly he saw a youth running towards him whom he recognised as one of the priests' servants. He was a Christian convert and instead of a cotton *dhoti* was wearing a European-style jerkin and trousers.

'Your wife has gone into labour,' the lad shouted as soon as Khurram was in earshot.

Khurram stared at him, one thought only forming in his mind – it's too soon . . . much too soon . . . Riding quickly into the compound, he dismounted and ran up the wooden steps to Arjumand's room. He paused outside the closed door, listening for the usual cries of pain, but instead there was silence and it chilled him. Then the door opened and one of the Portuguese maids came out. 'What's happened?' he demanded, but she looked at him uncomprehendingly. He pushed past her into the room. Arjumand was lying in a pool of blood and the midwife was wrapping something small and still in a piece of cloth.

Slowly he approached the bed, afraid of what he would see. Then he heard her voice.

'Khurram – I'm sorry. We've lost our son . . .'

It was a moment before he could speak and even then his voice trembled. 'All that matters to me is that you are alive . . . This is my fault. You should never have had to endure so much. I should have let my father arrest me in Agra rather than drag you and our children across Hindustan

304

till we became nothing more than hunted beasts with the dogs snapping at our heels.'

'No,' she whispered. 'Don't say such things. At least we are together, and as long as we are together we can hope.'

Khurram embraced her and said no more, but bitterness welled within him. His father was to blame for the loss of his son as surely as if he had killed him with his own hands. Had it not been for Jahangir's persecution of him and his family, Arjumand would never have had to flee, would never have suffered the accident in the river that had left her too weak to carry their child to full term.

· ◆ ·

'You cannot mean it.' Khurram's voice as he looked at Father Ronaldo was incredulous.

'I'm sorry. We have done our best. We have given you our hospitality for over three months and now you must depart.'

'My wife has just miscarried. She can still barely stand . . . she is in no condition to travel.'

'Charity and compassion made us hold our hand until your wife's pregnancy reached its term . . . we have already done more for you than we should.'

'I don't believe you. What has happened to turn you against us?' Khurram asked bluntly.

For a moment Father Ronaldo looked a little embarrassed, but then he drew up his thin frame. 'The emperor your father knows that you are here at Hooghly. Two weeks ago one of our ships brought a letter from the court. It told us that unless we expel you the emperor will send his troops against us and burn down our settlement. We cannot allow that to happen. We have God's work to do – souls to save from the darkness . . .'

'And profits to make,' cut in Khurram angrily. 'For all his faults my father had the sense not to be taken in by your hypocritical and self-seeking speeches. Where's the Christian charity you're always talking about, the loving mercy? You're asking me to set out into the wilderness with a sick woman who nearly died three days ago.'

'I'm sorry. The matter is out of my hands. The head of my order and the president of our merchants decided it at one of our council meetings.'

Without realising what he'd done Khurram found himself fingering the hilt of his dagger. How he'd like to silence that oily, self-justificatory voice. 'This letter you mention – was it signed by my father?'

'No.' The priest looked down at his dusty sandals. 'It was signed by the empress and bore her seal with the imprint of her title Nur Jahan, Light of the World.'

'I tell you this and you should remember it. The empress is no friend to you. She despises all Europeans as no more than pariah dogs vying with each other for scraps from the Moghul table. You may escape her ire by obeying her command but you'll have no reward. And when one day I sit on the Moghul throne – as I will – I won't forget your callous indifference.'

As soon as the priest had scurried away, no doubt to report the conversation to his colleagues, Khurram went straight to his camp, thinking quickly. His three hundred men should be enough to repel any assault by the Portuguese soldiers guarding the settlement if they were foolish enough to try anything – like attempting to take him prisoner so they could hand him over to his father. He would post a double line of pickets round the camp's perimeter, he decided, and tonight he, Arjumand and their children would sleep in the camp, not in the priests' compound. Later he must go to her and tell her gently what had happened, but first there was something else he had decided he must do.

After giving the necessary orders, Khurram made his way to his own quarters and sat down cross-legged in front of his low desk. After thinking for a while, he took a piece of paper, dipped his ivory-tipped quill pen into his jade ink bottle and began slowly to write, weighing every word with extreme care. When he had finished he reread what he had written several times. Then he stood up, and ordered one of his guards to send Nicholas Ballantyne to him. Five minutes later, the *qorchi* appeared, his bright hair concealed beneath the tightly bound black turban he had taken to wearing.

Khurram grasped him by the shoulder. 'Before he left Hindustan, your master Sir Thomas Roe told me that if I took you into my service you would be loyal and true. Was he right?'

Nicholas's wide blue eyes showed his surprise. 'Yes, Highness.'

'Listen to me – I am going to speak very frankly. We cannot remain at Hooghly. The Portuguese fear my father's retribution if they harbour us any longer and have told us to go. I also know we can't just go on wandering. It wouldn't be long until my father's armies caught and crushed us. We could take ship from the coast to Persia or some other country, but I don't want to be driven from my homeland. Also, my wife is frail. I must think of her. So I have decided to write to my father asking for a reconciliation. I don't know whether he will listen, but I must try. My question to you is, will you be my messenger? As a foreigner and also as one who served Sir Thomas Roe, who was my father's friend, you will be safer from my father's vengeance than any Moghul emissary. You also know the court and how it works. You will stand a good chance of getting the letter into my father's own hands.'

'Of course, Highness.'

Chapter 19

The Messenger

In the paradise world of Kashmir everything was purple – the fields of saffron crocuses stretching down to the Dal lake, the waters of the lake themselves glinting amethyst in the sunlight, the peaks of the encircling mountains . . . Jahangir was lying on his back among the crocuses, breathing in their sweet pungency and now and then plucking petals and throwing them into the air so that they drifted around him like snow-flakes. How contented he felt . . . he could lie here until the real snows began to fall, shrouding his body with their soothing icy flakes . . .

'Majesty.' A voice and reality intruded into his dream. Jahangir turned over with a groan on the cream brocade-covered divan on which he was lying in his private apartments in the Agra fort. Then he felt a hand gently shake his shoulder. 'Majesty, a messenger has come from Prince Khurram.'

At the mention of his son's name, Jahangir opened his

eyes and slowly sat up. The exquisite, softly muted world of his wine- and opium-fuelled dreams faded and he rubbed his eyes. In the shafts of light filtering through the carved *jali* opposite his bed everything looked too stark, too bright. His eyes fell on the jewelled cup on a low table by the divan in which some dark red wine still remained. Reaching for it with a shaking hand he took a sip, feeling the bitter liquid coat the back of his throat. He started to cough, and drank the water that the young servant who had woken him hastily poured out for him.

'What did you just say?'

'Your son, Prince Khurram, has sent a messenger. He is asking to see you.'

Khurram? Jahangir pondered for a moment. Sometimes in his richly textured dreams he saw his third son but always at a distance – on the opposite banks of a river, or high on the battlements of a castle or galloping on horseback amid a cloud of dust – always too far off for Jahangir to call to and seemingly oblivious of him anyway. Over the years since he had last seen Khurram he had often thought of him in his waking hours as well, hurt and anger at his behaviour mingling with regret for times past when the prince had been the loyal son of whom he had felt so proud that he had showered him with gold and jewels . . . Even with his mind fuddled with wine and opium he realised that a message from Khurram now, with Mahabat Khan and his army closing in on him, could mean only one thing – capitulation.

'I will come to the Hall of Public Audience,' he told the servant, his voice low. 'Summon the court and send word to the empress. She will wish to listen from the women's gallery to what the messenger has to say . . . And take this away,' he added, handing him the jewelled wine cup.

• ◆ •

Nearly an hour later Jahangir took his place on his throne and at his signal a trumpeter put his brass instrument to his lips to signal in a series of short blasts that the emperor was ready to give audience. Glancing up at the grille high in the wall to one side of the throne Jahangir thought he detected the gleam of dark eyes beneath a diadem of pearls. Good – Mehrunissa was there.

He watched as Khurram's messenger, preceded by four guards in Moghul green, slowly approached. Jahangir couldn't make out his face, half hidden as he was by the soldiers who, when they were twenty feet from the throne, moved smartly to either side. A little clumsily, as if he wasn't used to it, the man flung himself on the ground, arms outstretched in the formal salutation of the *korunush*. Beneath the black turban, Jahangir saw red-raw skin. The messenger was a European.

'You may rise,' he said, leaning forward for a closer look. As the man got to his feet and raised his head Jahangir saw a pair of blue eyes in a young sunburned face. It was familiar but his mind was still partially clouded and he stared at the man in puzzlement. 'Who are you?'

'My name is Nicholas Ballantyne. I was once squire to Sir Thomas Roe, ambassador to the Moghul court from the King of England.' As Nicholas finished speaking he made the low bow, right leg extended in front of him, that Jahangir remembered Sir Thomas so often making. What a long time ago all that now seemed . . . Jahangir thought fondly back to his evenings with Roe.

311

'I am now in the service of your son, Prince Khurram, who has entrusted me with a letter for Your Majesty.' Reaching into a red camel-leather satchel hanging from his shoulder, Nicholas took out the letter. Jahangir could see his fingers shaking a little with nerves though when he had spoken his voice, with its oddly accented Persian, had been clear and steady.

'I will read what the wretch has had the audacity to say.' Jahangir nodded to his vizier Majid Khan, who stepped forward from where he was standing to the right of Jahangir's dais and took the letter from Nicholas to hand to him. Slowly Jahangir broke the seal, opened it and glanced down at the close-written lines. His own father Akbar – unable to read or write himself – had been proud of Khurram's elegant calligraphy. In his mind's eye he suddenly saw Akbar leading the elephant carrying the four-year-old Khurram in triumphant procession through the streets of Lahore to his first day at school while he himself had stood to one side, excluded from the moment by both his father and his son.

His head was aching but he made himself concentrate on what the letter said, reading silently and slowly.

Father, for reasons that I do not comprehend I have had the misfortune to lose your love and to rouse your anger against me. You have disowned me. You have sent armies to pursue me, even declared me outlaw giving any subject in your empire the right to kill me. I do not question your reasons. You are the emperor and it is your right to rule as you wish. But I make this appeal to you as my father as well as my sovereign. I am sorry for anything I may have done to displease you and I throw myself on your mercy. My wife and children can no longer endure this life of wandering, never knowing where or whether we will find safety. For their sake, if not mine, I beg you to let us be reconciled. I will obey whatever orders you have for me — go to any part of the empire you choose to send me — but let this strife between us end. I swear on my life and the lives of my family that I am your loyal and obedient son. Bring me from the darkness back into the sunlight of your forgiveness.

Jahangir lowered the letter and stared ahead of him. The eyes of his courtiers were fixed upon him. He could feel the intensity of their curiosity. He looked down at the letter again. *You are the emperor and it is your right to rule as you wish.* Did Khurram really mean that?

'Prince Khurram seeks my forgiveness,' Jahangir said at last and saw a ripple run through the ranks of his courtiers, 'I will consider my answer.' To Nicholas, standing before him, head bowed, he said, 'I will send for you when I have decided.' Then, a little shakily, and still clutching Khurram's letter, he rose from his throne, descended from the dais and left the hall, mind and emotions in a turmoil.

•◆•

Alone in her apartments in the *haram*, Mehrunissa paced about waiting for Jahangir to come as she knew he would. What exactly had Khurram written? She burned to know but at the same time felt a little apprehensive. If only she could have intercepted the letter as she had those that Khurram had written in the early months of his breach with his father. Whatever Khurram had said, she had seen how his words had moved Jahangir. The hot anger against Khurram that had made it so easy for her to induce him to

313

declare him outlaw was ebbing. Jahangir was ageing mentally and physically. As the first cold winds of old age began to blow upon them, men sometimes yearned to put right things that had gone wrong in their lives while there was still time. Probably deep in his heart Jahangir hankered to be reconciled with Khurram.

The death two months ago of Parvez, shrieking in alcohol-induced delirium, had grieved him, causing him to be more careful about the amount of drink and drugs he consumed himself and perhaps softening his attitude towards his other erring sons. Several times recently he had spoken of making Khusrau's imprisonment less harsh . . .

Mehrunissa heard footsteps and voices calling 'The emperor approaches'. Then the double doors of ivory-inlaid polished mulberry were flung open. As Jahangir entered her apartments she ran to him and took his hands in hers. 'You look troubled and unwell. What has the *bi-dalaut* dared to write that has distressed you so much?'

'Read his letter for yourself.'

Mehrunissa took it from him and ran her eyes quickly down it. 'Khurram knows he has no chance against Mahabat Khan, that is why he has written to you so pleadingly. But even though he asks your forgiveness he still doesn't confess his guilt. See what he writes.' She pointed with her hennaed fingertip to the line *for reasons that I do not comprehend I have had the misfortune to lose your love.* 'He is still puffed up with conceit and pride. It is rather that he is forgiving you than the other way around.'

'But if he is sincere in wanting to be reconciled,' Jahangir countered, 'perhaps I should consider it. Mahabat Khan is one of my best commanders – that is why I chose him to pursue Khurram – and I would rather have his army ready to send against the Persians in case they attack Kandahar once more as our spies tell us they plan to do. As a Persian himself and a former officer of the shah he understands their thinking and tactics. Also, if my son is seen to bow to my authority again, accepting it voluntarily, it adds to my dignity.'

Mehrunissa looked sharply at her husband. She hadn't seen him so forthright for a long time. Although she believed that in the end she would be able to sway him in whichever direction she chose, perhaps he was right. Maybe the time had come for a change. Despite what she had just said to Jahangir there was no certainty that Mahabat Khan, able though he was, would catch Khurram, who as long as he remained a renegade would be a threat to Jahangir and to her and her plans for Shahriyar and her daughter Ladli. Khurram too was an able and experienced general and leader. There was always the possibility that he might be able to raise a large enough force to challenge Mahabat Khan. She had heard rumours that Malik Ambar had offered him an alliance against Jahangir. He might even flee the empire altogether to seek such an army. The Shah of Persia would doubtless be delighted to offer him troops in return for territorial concessions. What if Khurram offered the shah the city of Kandahar that he so coveted? Twice before her Persian countrymen had offered help to a Moghul ruler – first Babur, then Humayun – in return for something they wanted.

'What do you think? Should I agree?' Jahangir persisted, twisting the tiger-headed ring that had once belonged to his great ancestor Timur.

Mehrunissa's mind was suddenly racing but her expression

315

was composed as she said slowly, 'Perhaps you're right. This breach has gone on for too long and should be resolved. It has caused divisions within my own family too that have long been a source of pain to me. I know how happy my brother Asaf Khan would be if the rift were healed. But we must think very carefully. Come and sit by me.'

As Jahangir lay back against a bolster of turquoise silk beside her, Mehrunissa picked up Khurram's letter again as if wishing to reconsider it but really as a device to purchase time to reflect. An idea was beginning to form in her mind but she must take care how she considered every aspect. She couldn't trust Khurram if he returned to court knowing full well – as he did – that she had been the instigator and sustainer of his father's displeasure. Choosing her words carefully, she began slowly and softly.

'I have often thought what a pity it was that Khurram allowed himself to be seduced by ambition. He has since proved by his actions that he does not deserve to rule any more than Khusrau – or indeed poor Parvez who could never master his love of wine. Yet he has talents, and if he will indeed be obedient to you, why should they not be employed to the empire's benefit? And as you say, if you behave with generosity towards him it will only enhance your subjects' respect for you.'

Jahangir was nodding, clearly pleased. Encouraged, Mehrunissa continued. 'But it would be better – at least for the present – to keep him from the court. Find him some obscure place to administer. Make him prove himself again by hard work and diligence far from the seat of power. Then you will know whether his protestations to you are sincere.'

'I could send him to be governor of Balaghat . . .'

At the mention of this remote province in central Hindustan which yielded very little revenue – certainly not enough to equip a large army – Mehrunissa smiled. She couldn't have thought of a better place herself. 'An excellent idea,' she said. 'All the same, Balaghat isn't so far from the kingdoms of the Deccan which are always looking to create trouble for you. The rulers there might seek to entice him into rebellion against you. They say Malik Ambar has suggested to Khurram that they join forces.'

'Perhaps I should find somewhere else for him to go? Kabul maybe?' Jahangir smiled for a moment at the thought of his own exile there after his seduction of his father's concubine Anarkali. It had given him his first glimpse of Mehrunissa.

'No. It is too wealthy and important a place,' said Mehrunissa, unaware where Jahangir's thoughts had taken him. 'That would seem almost a reward for his insolence. Balaghat is far better. He will have to swallow his pride if he goes there. But we must find a way to be certain he isn't once again tempted into rebellion.'

'But how? Send spies to report on him?'

'No. Spies can be bribed. I think that Khurram himself may have provided the answer. In his letter he swore loyalty to you on his own life – but also on those of his family. Put that to the test.'

'How?'

'As a condition of your forgiveness, order him to send his eldest son Dara Shukoh to court – and perhaps one of Dara Shukoh's brothers to be company for him.'

'As hostages, you mean?'

'Yes, in a sense you could say so. Even Khurram would

317

never dare move against you if his sons were in your power.'

'I believe that . . . but would it be right to separate his sons from him? I know from my own childhood how important parents' love can be.' Jahangir sighed as if an old dark shadow was again crossing his mind.

'They would be well treated, and think of all the advantages they would have here at court near their grandfather. And if Khurram means what he says in his letter, there would never be any question of having to take measures against them.'

Jahangir was silent for a while. She knew her suggestion had surprised him, perhaps even shocked him, but as he began to reflect surely he would see the sense of it. The more she thought about it, the better she liked it, though she would have to ensure that in practice Jahangir did not see too much of his grandsons . . .

'I am only thinking of you,' she said after a while, moving a little closer to Jahangir and leaning her head against his shoulder. She felt him begin to stroke her long hair as he often did. 'Khurram's behaviour has caused you so much anxiety. By agreeing to a reconciliation you are being merciful as a great emperor should be, but you must be careful for yourself. Do as I suggest and all will, I am sure, be as you wish it to be. Khurram will have to accept your terms and you can withdraw Mahabat Khan and his army from their pursuit of him. You have already had enough to bear from ungrateful and rebellious sons. Let this be an end of it.'

Jahangir ran his hand across his eyes but then at last he smiled, though it was a sad wan smile. 'You're right, I'm sure.

318

You always are. Tomorrow I'll summon my council and tell them my decision. It will be good to be reconciled with Khurram. I will enjoy seeing my grandsons too. Dara Shukoh must have changed so much.'

•—◆—•

The next morning, Nicholas received a summons to go to Jahangir in his private apartments. Ever since arriving in Agra he had felt nervous, remembering Khurram's warning. But nothing untoward had happened and his letter was safe in Jahangir's hands.

As a *qorchi* ushered Nicholas into the room he saw Jahangir standing at its centre in his night attire with his grey hair loose. His drawn face still had some of its old authority as he acknowledged Nicholas's bow, but now that the Englishman saw him at close quarters he could see how he had aged since the days when he and Sir Thomas had been drinking partners, exchanging stories until dawn.

'Take this back to my son.' Jahangir held out an embroidered leather wallet. 'Inside is my reply to his letter. Guard it well. I have ordered fresh horses for you and your escort so that you travel quickly.'

'Thank you, Majesty.' Nicholas took the wallet, wishing he knew what Jahangir had written. He hesitated a moment, hoping Jahangir would give him some clue, but the emperor had already turned away and was rinsing his face in a silver bowl of water that an attendant was holding out to him.

Half an hour later, Jahangir watched from a casement as Nicholas and his soldiers trotted down the ramp from the Agra fort into the seething streets of Agra. How would

319

Khurram react to his letter? he wondered. And for the first time another thought struck him. How would Arjumand – a woman of the same stock as his beloved Mehrunissa – respond? Would she agree to yield her children or would she urge Khurram to resist?

Chapter 20

The Price

'**M**ahabat Khan will do everything in his power to defeat and capture you.' Azam Bahksh poked the brazier of charcoals and invited Khurram to draw his stool a little closer to the warmth. Autumn was approaching and chill winds were already beginning to blow off the mountains on the north-western horizon so that the two of them, sitting in the courtyard of the mud-brick fortress on the banks of the Gandak river where Azam Bahksh had offered sanctuary to Khurram and his family, were shivering a little.

'You know Mahabat Khan?' Khurram asked in some surprise. Azam Bahksh was an old man – well over seventy – and as a youth had fought in Akbar's armies.

'Only by repute. They say he is a born commander, dashing and ingenious, intelligent as well as ambitious. Such are his qualities that his Rajput horsemen have sworn loyalty to the death to him though he's not of their race.'

Khurram stared into the heart of the glowing orange

321

coals. The rumours brought by some of Azam Bahksh's men earlier that day that Mahabat Khan's advancing army was less than four weeks away had been a shock. He had hoped to be safe here for a while at least. The invitation from the old warrior Khurram remembered only vaguely from his boyhood to take refuge in his ancestral stronghold in the hills north of Patna had been a welcome surprise. Azam Bakhsh's steward had found Khurram's column a week after he had left Hooghly. The old man had written that he had learned of Khurram's plight and was offering his help in memory of Akbar, whom he had revered, knowing that Khurram had been Akbar's favourite grandson. Khurram had set out at once on the journey, which had brought him some two hundred miles north of Hooghly. But once again it seemed the refuge would only be temporary. This little fortress would be no defence against Mahabat Khan's armies. He would not put his friends at risk. But the real question was why Mahabat Khan's army was still pursuing him.

'I had hoped my father would call Mahabat Khan off. It's nearly two months since I sent my messenger to Agra.'

'Is your courier trustworthy?'

'Yes, I'm sure he is. But he would have faced many dangers on the road to Agra and perhaps he never reached it. The empress may have been warned of his mission and sent assassins to intercept him. Or he may have been killed by bandits or fallen ill. Perhaps I should not have sent a European. They are much more prone to sickness than we are. Certainly if all had gone smoothly he should have found me by now. My whereabouts are no secret if Mahabat Khan is on my track, and anyway many will have seen my column pass this way from Hooghly.' Khurram raised his head to look at the bright veil of stars across the night sky. How insignificant and transitory men's lives were compared to that mysterious and timeless expanse above them . . .

'Don't look so sombre.' Azam Bahksh's gruff voice cut into his thoughts. 'There is still time. My many years have taught me one lesson at least – patience. All may yet be well.'

Khurram nodded, but only out of politeness. He could not afford to be patient when the lives of himself and his family hung so precariously in the balance.

• ◆ •

But two days later, Azam Bahksh was proved right. Khurram was sitting with Arjumand when he heard drums boom from the small gatehouse to announce new arrivals. Leaping to his feet he hurried down a narrow flight of steps into the courtyard.

Nicholas Ballantyne was just dismounting. As he unwound his face cloth, Khurram saw he looked exhausted. He was hollow cheeked and his chin thickly stubbled. 'Majesty.'

As Nicholas made to kneel, Khurram said quickly, 'No need for that. Tell me what happened. Did you give my father my letter? What did he say?'

'I reached Agra without incident, although my journey was slower than I had hoped. The emperor received me in the Hall of Public Audience where he indeed read your letter. Next day he gave me this to bring to you.' Nicholas reached into his jerkin and extracted the leather wallet Jahangir had entrusted to him. Even while snatching a few hours' brief sleep on the road he had always been conscious of it, tucked into his shirt just inches from his heart. As he handed it to Khurram, he felt a weight drop from him.

Khurram opened the wallet with impatient fingers, pulled out the letter and began to read it. Watching him, Nicholas saw first joy, then bewilderment, then anger cross his features. He also heard Khurram's quick intake of breath and saw how his fingers were starting to crush the piece of paper. Then, suddenly aware again of Nicholas and his escort and of the other attendants in the courtyard, all watching him intently, Khurram seemed to gather himself together. 'Thank you,' he said quietly to Nicholas. 'You discharged a difficult task loyally and well. When you have rested we will talk more. I want to know everything that happened while you were at court, but first I must go to my wife.'

As Khurram turned away back into the shadows and began to mount the stairs leading to the upper storey, he looked to Nicholas a different man from the one who just a few minutes earlier had bounded eagerly into the sunlit courtyard. His head was bowed and he was moving slowly as if trying to delay reaching Arjumand's quarters.

She was waiting near the door. 'That was your messenger returning from the court, wasn't it?' Khurram nodded, and slowly drew the oak door shut behind him so they would not be overheard.

'Khurram, why do you look like that? What does your father say?'

He hesitated, then began. 'He will recall Mahabat Khan and his army provided I agree to withdraw my remaining men to Balaghat where I am to be governor. I must also agree not to go to court unless he summons me there.'

Arjumand's pinched face was suddenly radiant. She looked

324

again like the eager, happy girl he had first glimpsed at the Royal Meena Bazaar. 'But that's wonderful. He has agreed to be reconciled with you. It must mean he has decided to forgive you. We and our children will be safe at last after all these years of wandering.' She flung her arms round his neck, but when he failed to respond she let them fall and stepped back from him. 'What's the matter? Isn't this what we were hoping for? Why aren't you happy, Khurram? Tell me, please.'

Khurram thought of Jahangir's cold, brief, disdainful words – not a message of forgiveness from a father to his son but a list of conditions such as a ruler might send to an erring vassal. And of all those conditions the one he was still struggling to take in was the one he must now admit to Arjumand.

'As a guarantee of my good conduct, my father demands that we send Dara Shukoh and one of his brothers to him at the court.'

'What?' Arjumand whispered. Putting her hands to her head as if she'd received a physical blow, she crumpled to her knees on to the worn red carpet. Helplessly, Khurram watched as she began to weep. He should put his arms round her and hold her to him, but what could he say to comfort her when he felt the same despair?

'My father says the boys will be well treated but I can't hide the truth from you. They will be hostages in all but name.'

'Dara Shukoh is so young . . . I can't bear to even think of it. How could your father be so cruel? He once loved Dara . . . I remember the gifts he gave us when he was born . . .'

'I'm sure my father would never harm our sons. But . . .' He paused and looked at Arjumand, knowing she understood.

Wiping the tears from her face with the back of her hand and struggling to regain her self-control she managed one word.

'Mehrunissa?'

He nodded.

'You really think she might hurt them?'

Khurram reflected. Much as he hated Mehrunissa – and who knew what she might not be capable of in desperate circumstances? – could he really see her as the cold-blooded murderer of children? 'No, I don't think so,' he said at last. 'And after all, why should she? Having control of our sons is enough for her ends. She is also shrewd enough to know that any harshness towards them would cause outrage. Our tradition – going back even to the days of Timur – is that the lives of young and innocent imperial princes are sacred. It is only those who rebelled when older that have received the severest of punishments.'

Arjumand rose slowly to her feet and, pushing her loose hair back from her face, went to the casement. The sun was going down, pinkening the tips of the distant mountains. She could smell the pungent smokiness of dung fires being lit to cook the evening meal and see the first torches being lit in the courtyard below. Such normal scenes, she thought, and yet their whole lives had been turned upside down. As a mother what should she do? Surrender two of her children to secure the survival of the rest? The physical pain of childbirth was nothing compared to this mental agony she was feeling.

'We do have a choice. We don't have to accept my father's terms. We could go north, up into the mountains where it would be hard for Mahabat Khan to follow . . .'

But Arjumand's face as she turned away from the casement had hardened. 'No. Think what your father would say if you reject his offer: that your unwillingness to trust our sons to him – his own grandsons – means you never intended to remain loyal to him. He will ask why a supposedly obedient and dutiful son would refuse to send his children to their own grandfather unless he intended to rebel. He will redouble his efforts to capture you and what would happen to our children then?'

Though his initial instinct – both as a father and as a prince – was to reject his father's offer, wasn't she right? Khurram wondered, stricken by the truth and clarity of her words. What choice did they really have? He had barely three hundred men and no resources to recruit more. If he were alone he could fight on as his great-great-grandfather Babur had done, taking to the hills, leading hit and run raids, waiting for an opportunity to grab territory. But he had his family to think of . . .

Now that he was thinking more calmly he could see that Jahangir's offer was as subtle as a move on the chess board, leaving him nowhere to go except where his father wanted. Jahangir had once loved to play chess, but Khurram knew whose intricate mind had produced the idea of demanding he yield up his sons. He could picture Mehrunissa winding a strand of her dark hair around her finger and smiling as she wondered what choice he and Arjumand would make. Mehrunissa was like a spider that beginning with one or two simple strands begins to weave an ever more intricate web. His father had been caught in it long ago. One day, he promised himself, he would rip that web apart. He would free himself, his family and even his father – if he were not

327

already too far lost in Mehrunissa's toils – from her bonds, allowing the Moghul empire to prosper once more. But that satisfaction could only lie in the future. He must think of the present.

'You're right,' he said, a heaviness wrapping itself around his heart as he spoke. 'The truth – and you saw it more swiftly than I – is we have little option but to agree. But which of our other sons should we send with Dara Shukoh – Shah Shuja or Aurangzeb?'

'Aurangzeb,' Arjumand replied after a moment's thought. 'Though he's a year younger than Shah Shuja he's stronger – he's seldom had a day's illness – and he's fearless. He will even be excited at the thought of going to the court.' Arjumand's voice trembled a little. 'When must they go?'

'My father has instructed me to write immediately with my decision to the commander of Patna who will speed the letter to Agra by relays of imperial messengers. If we accept his terms, we're to send our sons under strong escort to Allahabad where my father will in turn send men to receive them. We must prepare them immediately. Dara Shukoh is old enough to have understood that my father and I have been at odds. We must tell him we have resolved our quarrel and that their grandfather is anxious to see him and one of his brothers. We mustn't let him see how troubled we are . . .'

Chapter 21

The Opportunist

Mahabat Khan took the leather message pouch from the hands of the weary-looking imperial post rider who five minutes earlier had caught up with his column as it advanced, enveloped in clouds of dust, towards its confrontation with Khurram. Opening the well-worn pouch Mahabat Khan took out the single letter it contained and broke the green wax seal. A brief glance told him all he needed to know. Although the seal was Jahangir's the writing was Mehrunissa's, as it so frequently was with his orders. Her message was terse: *The wretched one has seen sense and made terms, surrendering two of his sons to our good care as surety for his future behaviour. Your mission is aborted. Return to Agra to await our further instructions which will be despatched on our arrival in Kashmir. M.* There followed the date and the place of writing – Lahore.

Not a word of commendation or thanks, thought Mahabat Khan as he crumpled the paper in his hand. 'No reply,' he told the messenger, 'except the simple confirmation that I

329

have received the instruction.' Turning to the officer riding at his side – a young slim Rajput named Ashok, mounted on a chestnut horse – he said, 'The emperor – or rather the empress – has ordered our return. The campaign is over. We will halt here and make camp for the night.' Then, softening his tone, he added to one of his attendants, 'Make sure this messenger gets food and a chance to rest as well as a fresh horse before he begins his return journey.'

• ◆ •

That night, Mahabat Khan could not sleep, not just because his tent was hot and airless – which it was – nor because he had drunk quantities of the wine of his native Shiraz with some of his senior officers – which he had – but because he felt more than a little discontented at the summary manner of the recall of his army to Agra – and not even by the emperor, he mused, but by the empress. That she had been the authoress of the peremptory letter of command was an added cause of his discontent. Not for the first time he wondered why he should allow Mehrunissa to exploit his loyalty to the emperor by ordering him hither and thither as if he were a common soldier. Why on this occasion should she arbitrarily deprive him and his devoted followers of the rich booty that would have been theirs had he conquered Khurram and his allies? And she a mere woman too, albeit the most shrewd and calculating he had come across and a Persian like himself.

Even though she had reduced the emperor – supposedly the most powerful man in the world – to a mere henpecked lapdog he was himself her better or at least her equal in every way. Although both their blood was Persian, his was of a more noble family. She had no more right to wield power than he. She might be clever but she was no cleverer than he was. Unlike himself she commanded no armies and being a woman never would. The more Mahabat Khan debated with himself, tossing and turning in the heat beneath his simple cotton coverlet, the more it seemed to him that he should no longer tolerate Mehrunissa's domination. He was as good an arbiter of imperial power as she was with all her plotting against Khurram and her promotion of her dimwitted son-in-law Shahriyar as the heir, now that alcohol had finally killed Parvez. Perhaps he had been wrong not to have thought more earlier about joining forces with the young charismatic Khurram against his ailing father and his calculating, manipulative, steel-tongued chief wife? Their respective absences from court on campaign had meant that he had met Khurram only once, but he was by all accounts a good and generous leader and his skills as a general had been amply demonstrated by his ability to evade Mahabat Khan's own forces. Such was the loyalty that Khurram inspired that he still had many adherents at court and elsewhere, even if they were lying low at present. Perhaps he should switch sides now? His skirmishes and confrontations with Khurram's supporters in his long pursuit of the prince had been conducted within the conventions of warfare. There had been no massacres, no executions, no loss of close family members on either side to give rise to embittered hatred or blood feud.

As the night wore on and Mahabat Khan continued to toss around, his mind too active now to sleep, another thought came to him. Couldn't he create an independent role in the power struggle for himself? He knew from the messenger and others who had preceded him that now, in the early spring, the emperor and empress were making their way with a mass of courtiers and accompanying baggage – but no great army – towards Kashmir, in the happy assumption that with Khurram sidelined they had no threats to fear. What if they were wrong and he himself turned from being their loyal, even obsequious general, subject to their every command however tersely conveyed, into the arbiter of their destiny and that of the empire?

Wasn't he in a position to control them and not the other way round? What if he and his ten thousand men, all personally loyal to him, followed the emperor and empress and seized Khurram's children from them? Wouldn't that put him higher in Khurram's favour than making an alliance now? Even better, if more daring, wouldn't holding the opium-fuddled emperor and his wife hostage, as well as Khurram's children, allow him to dictate terms to either party? Let the emperor and Khurram outbid each other for his favour. How much more booty would he amass, how much more influence would he wield, than if he had either continued his campaign against Khurram or if he threw in his lot with him now. Such a strategy was no mere fantasy. His long military experience had taught him that the most novel and audacious plans often proved the most successful, probably because of the consternation and surprise created by their very novelty. It would be risky, he thought as he slapped at a whining mosquito, very risky, but sometimes he felt he was only alive when facing danger or planning how to overturn long odds. That was what had made him a soldier in the first place. In the morning he must sound out his men, but he had no doubt of their loyalty or their appetite for rewards. His mind was made up. He would capture the entire imperial party and play the emperor-maker and breaker. Within minutes of deciding, Mahabat Khan had fallen into a deep, untroubled sleep, oblivious of the heat and buzzing mosquitoes.

• ◆ •

Jahangir settled himself more comfortably against a brocade-covered bolster on the thickly carpeted floor of his tent. He was growing old, he thought. His muscles ached after eight hours in a howdah as the imperial column – nearly half a mile long – completed another day's slow march northwest. The sight of the foaming jade-green Jhelum river, the last great barrier before they reached Kashmir, had been welcome. So too had been that of the emperor's scarlet tents, which had been sent ahead and were already erected near the riverbank.

'How soon should we cross?' asked Mehrunissa, who was seated on a low stool close by him.

'My officers say it will take two days, maybe longer, for our whole column to do so. It won't be easy. As you saw, the Jhelum is in full spate with meltwater from the mountains. The bridge will take a little time to construct. They suggest we ourselves cross on the morning of the second day.'

'No matter. This is a good place to break our journey and we've no need for haste.' She pushed back a lock of her hair. 'You're tired. Soon I'll order the attendants to light the fires in the bathhouse so you may bathe.'

Jahangir nodded and closed his eyes. He was glad Mehrunissa had suggested they go to Kashmir. At least the crisis with Khurram was over and it was safe for him to travel so far from his capital at Agra. According to the latest despatch from Majid Khan, Khurram had reached Balaghat and quietly assumed his duties as governor. Time would tell whether, despite Mehrunissa's reservations, he would keep his side of the bargain as Jahangir hoped he would. Surrendering two of his sons must be some guarantee for his good behaviour.

And now that civil war had been averted he had less to fear from enemies beyond his borders who had been watching the discord within the Moghul empire hopefully, just as jackals sniff the blood of wounded animals from afar. Shortly before he had left Agra, a gift of six perfectly matched black stallions had arrived from the Shah of Persia, together with a letter professing eternal friendship. Yet Jahangir knew that had the shah scented the slightest opportunity he would have seized Kandahar, Herat or some other Moghul strong-hold close to the Helmand river and his borders.

After recent events, he felt the need of tranquillity and Kashmir's lakes and gardens would provide it. He had loved the place since the first time he had seen its misty purple fields of saffron crocuses after his father had conquered it for the Moghuls. There he had felt closest to Akbar. He would spend his days gliding about the shimmering surface of the Dal lake in the imperial barge or riding into the mountains in search of game while gradually regaining the ease of mind that Khurram had shattered. Perhaps too he would recover his physical strength and lose the persistent cough that in recent months had scarcely left him.

Suddenly he heard children's voices from somewhere outside. 'Is that Dara Shukoh and Aurangzeb?'

Mehrunissa nodded. 'I said that they could practise their archery down on the riverbank. They have so much energy . . . the journey doesn't tire them at all.'

'Sometimes I wonder whether taking them from their parents was right. It must be hard for them.'

'We had no choice. There must be peace within the empire and having them in our custody will help ensure it. We treat them well. They lack for nothing.'

'But they must miss their parents. They haven't seen them for at least three months. Aurangzeb seems cheerful enough but sometimes I see Dara Shukoh watching us and frowning and I ask myself what he is thinking . . .'

'He is only a boy. He's probably thinking of nothing more than when he can go hunting or hawking again.' Mehrunissa's tone was brisk and dismissive. 'Now, I think I will go to the bath tent myself to supervise the warming of the water. Last night's wasn't hot enough – the attendants are growing lazy and hadn't collected enough firewood. After that I'll prepare your evening wine.'

When she had gone, Jahangir stretched out again. He was fond of Dara Shukoh and Aurangzeb and sensed that their initial reticence towards him might be relaxing. The relationship between a grandfather and his grandsons should be less constrained than between a father and his sons . . . There could be no element of rivalry. Perhaps that was why his own father Akbar had taken such pleasure in his grandsons.

•◆•

'General, we've caught up with the imperial column. The emperor has been encamped for the last two nights on

335

the bank of the Jhelum river about five miles ahead of us while his men have built a bridge of boats across it. Many of his troops – I guess two out of the three thousand he has with him – crossed this evening before darkness began to fall and then I heard shouted orders to halt crossings for the night and begin to prepare the evening meal. I am sure that the imperial party will cross tomorrow,' a scout clothed entirely in dull brown to allow him to blend into the terrain reported to a relieved Mahabat Khan after dusk the following evening.

Just as he had known they would, Mahabat Khan's officers had given his bold and impulsive plan their immediate and unanimous support despite the obvious risks and dangers. So too had his entire loyal battle-hardened army of Rajputs. Moving at more than eight times the speed of the imperial caravan they had quickly gained ground on it. The few officials on the way who had queried their haste or their mission had easily been satisfied by Mahabat Khan's assertion that he wanted to report in person to the emperor on another successful campaign. Nevertheless he was glad that the pursuit was over and the time to put his plan into action was at hand.

'Does the camp have outlying pickets posted to its rear?' Mahabat Khan asked.

'No,' replied the scout. 'There are sentries, of course, but only a few of them and they're close around the perimeter of the camp itself and seem very relaxed. The only patrols I saw set off were those fanning out on the opposite side of the river presumably scouting the way ahead.'

Mahabat Khan smiled. Circumstances were conspiring in his favour. All he would have to do in the morning was wait until even more of the imperial troops had crossed, burn or block the bridge and then swoop on the camp and capture the emperor, the empress and Khurram's two sons. For safety's sake, though, he and his men would pull back a mile or two for the night and light no cooking fires which might betray their presence.

·◆·

The night was a cold one in the shadow of the hills and mountains surrounding the Jhelum river valley. When Mahabat Khan led out his mounted horsemen just after dawn a thick chill mist still enveloped the landscape. Luck was certainly on his side. The mist would allow him to approach the crossing unseen, he thought. But he must not rely on luck alone. He must stay calm and take nothing for granted. He had seen too many generals defeated because they thought everything was so much in their favour that they did not plan well or take sufficient care in their attack. Therefore he reminded his officers once more of the orders he had issued the previous night.

'Ashok,' he said to the young Rajput mounted on his chestnut horse at the head of his troops. 'Your task is to secure the boat bridge so that no imperial troops can return. Burn it if you have to. You, Rajesh' – he turned to an older, bushy bearded man who had a scar running diagonally across his face from hairline to beard and a flap of skin falling over the empty socket where his left eye should have been – 'you and your men surround the camp and make sure no one can escape south with news of our action. I will lead the rest of the men to capture the imperial family.

'Remember, all of you, avoid casualties if you can, not just of course to our men but also to the imperial troops. We will need as many of them to cooperate with us as possible. Above all, make sure that the imperial family come to no harm. Alive they are worth several times more to us than their weight in gold. Dead they will be weights dragging us down to hell, turning everyone against us and rendering compromise impossible. Do you understand?' His officers nodded. 'Now, let's take maximum benefit from this mist.'

Wheeling his horse, Mahabat Khan led the way into the enshrouding greyness. The next few hours would be crucial to his future. He would either be in effective control of the empire or, if his audacious bid failed, suffer a slow death – the emperor never allowed a traitor to die quickly or easily. He shuddered at the memory of those he had seen impaled or buried up to their necks in sand to die in the hot sun, or even while still living having their intestines pulled out inch by inch and wound around sticks by cold-eyed torturers. For his own sake and that of his men he must succeed, and he would. Grim faced, he urged his tall black horse forward.

Within an hour and without any incident or obvious sign of detection he and his men were breasting some low mud hills by the Jhelum river and looking down on the boat bridge. Though the mist persisted it had become thinner and patchy. Amid the gaps Mahabat Khan could see that more imperial troops were crossing the bridge together with some pack elephants whose weight and lumbering gait made the boats bob and sway in the swift-flowing waters, which were grey-green from the rock and silt they carried down from their source in the mountains and glaciers. Through another gap in the drifting mist Mahabat Khan saw that the scarlet imperial tents remained on his side of the river and that cooking fires burned adjacent to them – perhaps the emperor and empress were taking a leisurely morning meal. He knew from his appearances at court that the emperor, befuddled from his excesses of the previous night – whether opium, liquor or more usually a mixture of the two – often rose late and remained half comatose and not entirely coherent until midday. Pray that he did so today, but he could not rely on it.

Turning to his officers, Mahabat Khan commanded, 'No time to lose. Act now and act quickly. Make sure your men maintain their discipline. Have them unfurl our banners so that the imperial soldiers know who we are and we keep them uncertain of our intentions until the last possible moment.' With that he kicked his heels into the flanks of his black horse, which responded willingly and sent up clods of dirt as it rapidly descended the mud hills towards the camp.

• ◆ •

Five minutes later Mahabat Khan was galloping hard through the sparsely defended perimeter of Jahangir's camp. The first few guards seemed too confused to react until it was too late, and they were swamped by his own far more numerous men before they could draw their weapons. As he rode on towards the river he looked round and saw Rajesh's men wheeling to throw up an encircling cordon of their own around the camp and Ashok's horsemen heading at the gallop towards the bridge of boats, scattering cooking pots and other loose camp equipment as they went. He heard no shots and saw no arrows rise, so he pushed on towards the imperial tents. Soon they were before him and as he thundered down upon them several men scattered in panic. From their beardless faces and soft, brightly coloured garments they seemed to be the eunuchs who attended the *haram*. Pulling so hard on his reins

339

that his horse almost reared, Mahabat Khan brought his mount to a standstill and jumped from the saddle to fling himself on one of the eunuchs, a lithe young man who struggled and wriggled for a moment in an effort to twist himself from Mahabat Khan's grip, but, finding it futile, made no further resistance. Quickly, Mahabat Khan grabbed him by his shoulder and shook him. 'Where's the emperor?'

The eunuch said nothing but swung his head towards an area about ten yards off which was screened by wooden panels intricately painted with hunting scenes and laced together by leather thongs. Water was seeping beneath the panels. That must be where he was, in the *hammam* tents – the bath tents – washing away last night's debauch, Mahabat Khan thought. Throwing the eunuch aside, he ran over to the screened area and kicked down some of the panels.

The smell of rosewater filled the air. Steam was rising from the great stone bath carved from a single block that the emperor always carried with him on his travels, but the bath was empty of anything but hot water and the only people Mahabat Khan could see were two attendants, alarm and fear etched into their smooth faces. Suddenly he heard volleys of musket shots crackle out from the direction of the riverbank. Where was the emperor? Was everything going to go wrong? Even, heaven forbid, had one of his own men found an opportunity during the long journey to betray him, allowing Jahangir to set him a trap? Mahabat Khan turned and, heart thumping, ran from the *hammam*. 'Find the emperor!'

· ◆ ·

Shouts and the crash of steel on steel rose and fell in Jahangir's dreams. But then, coming suddenly nearer, they woke him.

340

Trying to collect his scattered thoughts he rose to his feet, and when there was no answer to his call to his *qorchi* he made his way towards the entrance of the tent.

Mind set on reaching his horse and riding for the river-bank Mahabat Khan didn't see the tent flap rise and only just prevented himself from colliding with the frail but straight-backed figure who emerged, still dressed in his night-clothes. He immediately recognised Jahangir, thinner and more hollow eyed than ever.

The emperor spoke first. 'What is all this commotion, Mahabat Khan?'

Mahabat Khan was lost for words for some moments, but finally answered, 'I have come to take you into my custody for the sake of the empire.'

'Custody for the sake of the empire? What rubbish! What do you mean?'

'The empress and your current advisers act in their own interests, not in yours. I am better placed to guide you than they are,' Mahabat Khan said awkwardly.

'How dare you!' Jahangir spoke with some of the old fire and temper in his eyes and his hand went to his waist where if his dressing had been complete his dagger would have been. Finding it absent he looked around for his guards, but the few he could see were squatting on the ground, hands already tied behind their backs, while Mahabat Khan's men were everywhere, swords drawn and glinting in the early morning sun. He let his hand fall back to his side and asked, 'Do I have a choice in this supposed change of counsellors?'

'In due course, Majesty, when you see how much better I can perform than the existing ones.' Despite his opium-dilated eyes, to Mahabat Khan the emperor seemed to be calculating his options. At last he nodded as if he realised that for the present resistance would be futile, and slowly turned and ducked back beneath the scarlet awning of his tent. Mahabat Khan looked at his men. 'Guard the emperor's tent but treat him courteously. He is our emperor.'

Inside the tent Jahangir struggled to make sense of what had just happened. What did Mahabat Khan think he could achieve? For the moment Jahangir knew he could do little. Where were Mehrunissa and his grandsons? He soon learned the answer from a shouted conversation outside.

'General, we have Khurram's children,' he heard. 'We found them under close guard in a tent set a little apart from the others. Dara Shukoh keeps asking when we will return them to their parents, insisting that we will be well rewarded when we do. I've told him not quite yet and to be patient. Aurangzeb has said little but I see defiance in his eyes.'

'That's good, Rajesh,' Jahangir heard Mahabat Khan reply. 'Khurram at least will be pleased to negotiate with us, then. Look after the boys well but keep them under close supervision. I wouldn't put it beyond them to attempt to escape. Where is the empress?'

'I don't know. Our men are searching everywhere in the camp but so far with no success. One of the eunuchs we found in the *haram* quarters spoke of her grabbing bow and quiver, flinging on a dark cloak, jumping onto a horse and riding off astride. But no woman would behave like that, General.'

'You have never encountered the empress. The heart of a tigress beats beneath her woman's skin.'

Jahangir smiled. Mahabat Khan was no fool. With Mehrunissa free all was not lost.

Outside, Mahabat Khan, his brow once more furrowing with tension and worry, turned quickly to remount his horse and set off for the bridge of boats. If the empress had indeed fled his plan had only half succeeded. It was no distance to the river and within only a couple of minutes he was dismounting again. There was no sign of life around the bridge, which was unburnt, but some of his musketeers were sheltering behind upturned wagons not far away. They had their weapons primed and ready on their tripods and were looking down the long steel barrels which were aimed across the river. Others including Ashok were bent over, tending what looked like musket wounds in two of their comrades. Elsewhere two bodies sprawled on the riverbank, clothes soaked in blood. It was clear now to Mahabat Khan where the sound of shots had come from, and with a heavy heart he could guess the cause. 'Ashok, what happened?'

'All went well at first. We secured the approach to the bridge. Those on it obeyed our instructions to continue their crossing on pain of being shot down if they resisted, turned back or even stood still. Those waiting to cross – mostly muleteers with their charges – surrendered readily enough although this officer supervising their transit drew his sword.' Mahabat Khan followed the direction of Ashok's pointing arm to see a stout figure with his hands tied behind his back guarded by two of Ashok's men. 'Before he could be restrained he wounded one of my junior officers but only slightly, thank goodness.'

'But then how did these other men come to be injured and killed?'

'It couldn't have been more than a couple of minutes later when I heard pounding hooves behind me and a cloaked figure came galloping at top speed towards the bridge. I shouted, "Stop, or we will fire!" The hood of the cloak flew back from the rider's head and I saw long dark hair stream out. For a moment I thought it was a woman but then I dismissed the idea. No woman would ride astride like that, urging the animal on with hands and knees. I was about to give the order to fire when I realised that I had been debating with myself so long that the rider had knocked two of our men guarding the entrance to the bridge out of the way, sending one tumbling into the water, and was already halfway across the bridge, which was swaying wildly under the impact of the galloping horse's hooves. Mindful of your order not to harm people who might have influence I decided to let the rider go. I couldn't but admire his courage. After his arrival upon the opposite bank the muskets started to open up and the first fusillade was the one that caused the casualties. We've been exchanging fire off and on since then.'

'You did well not to shoot. You don't realise whom you might have killed,' Mahabat Khan said. Then, thinking it strangely appropriate to his situation, he added, 'Burn the bridge so no one can return.'

Chapter 22

River of Blood

'You have disgraced yourselves before God, the emperor and the people. Through your negligence the unimaginable has happened. The emperor has been captured!' Mehrunissa raged as she paced up and down before the senior officers of Jahangir's bodyguard, entirely disregarding the rules of purdah. When she looked directly into their eyes it was they who looked away, face down like meek maidens. 'How are you going to redeem your honour? How are you going to rescue the emperor? You stood by while Mahabat Khan's men burned the boat bridge immediately after I escaped over it. Now how will we cross back? Cross we will even if we have to swim our horses and elephants over the river. Come on, answer me.'

A long pause followed. 'Majesty.' A tall, hawk-nosed Badakhshani eventually spoke, still contriving to avoid Mehrunissa's blazing eyes. 'When I was leading the advance party searching for the best way to cross the Jhelum four or five days ago we found a possible fording place about a mile upstream from here. We rejected it because the water was too deep for men to wade through without risk of being swept away by the current. Only horsemen and elephants could cross that way and even then the bed was uneven and rock-strewn. It was an easy decision to avoid the potential dangers and to build the boat bridge here where – although the water is deeper – the force of the current is abated as the river bends round the small hill on this side of the bank. However, if there is no alternative we could consider mounting an attack over the ford, Majesty.'

'Have any of the rest of you anything better to suggest?' Mehrunissa asked. There was no response beyond a silent shifting of feet and exchange of dismayed looks.

'Well then, the ford it must be – I cannot and you cannot leave your emperor in the hands of that renegade Mahabat Khan. How long will preparations to attack take?'

'A few hours to check what weapons we have and what has been left on the other bank, to tie muskets and powder in oiled cloth bags to give them what protection we can from water, to fit the few remaining war elephants with their armour – that sort of thing . . . We could be ready before dusk, but the morning would be better.'

'Won't Mahabat Khan move off rather than stand by while we make such preparations?' A slight young man with a neatly trimmed beard – one of the youngest officers – found his voice.

'No. Whatever else he is, Mahabat Khan is less of a fool than you,' Mehrunissa said. 'He knows that even if he has the emperor, having failed to seize me he has failed to seize power. Don't fear – he will wait to see my next move. We will attack in the morning so none of you incompetents can have any excuse that you had insufficient time to prepare. In the meantime, keep up occasional fire over the river so that Mahabat Khan's men have a disturbed night. Also, send out patrols in all directions to keep him guessing about our intentions.' Mehrunissa smiled grimly. She was almost enjoying herself. Mahabat Khan had given her the power to act directly and not as before through an intermediary. 'Have my elephant and its howdah prepared for war. Tomorrow I will lead you to redeem your honour and to rescue our emperor. Cowards though some of you may be, you will not dare hang back if a woman leads.'

• ◆ •

'Majesty, Mahabat Khan permits your grandsons to join you,' said a tall Rajput, sweeping aside the velvet entrance curtain.

Dara Shukoh and Aurangzeb entered hesitantly. None of what was going on would make any sense to them, Jahangir thought. Once they were alone, he knelt and took each by the hand. 'Don't be afraid. No one is going to harm you. I am here and will protect you. And it won't be long before the empress rescues us. She escaped from Mahabat Khan and even now will be rallying our troops on the other side of the river.'

Aurangzeb said nothing but Jahangir felt Dara Shukoh pull away. 'The empress isn't our friend – she's our enemy. That's what I overheard my father say.'

'He is wrong. Mehrunissa is your great-aunt and is concerned for your welfare. She will find a way to help us . . . help you . . .' Jahangir released Aurangzeb and stood up.

'My father says she only cares about herself,' Dara Shukoh continued. 'That's why she makes you so drunk – so she can give all the orders. He told me never to trust her . . . and I don't. My brother and I want to go home!'

'Enough! I asked for you to be brought to me because I was worried you might be afraid, and this is how you reward me. When we're free again I will try to forget what you said, Dara Shukoh. But I'm sad to find that my son has taught you to be as insolent and ungrateful as himself.'

Turning away, Jahangir took a deep breath. Dara Shukoh's vehemence had shaken him.

· ◆ ·

'General, they are moving down the riverbank,' shouted one of Mahabat Khan's junior officers the next morning, two hours after daybreak. Mahabat Khan had had his scouts monitor carefully the movements of the troops on the other bank as he tried to predict what Mehrunissa and the officers of Jahangir's guard would do next. He had discovered from questioning the prisoners – not under threat of torture but with the promise of reward under his new regime – that the imperial forces accompanying Jahangir numbered not three thousand as he had thought but more like six thousand, of whom he had captured perhaps fifteen hundred, together with a lot of equipment. With his ten thousand Rajputs he still theoretically had double the manpower of Mehrunissa but he knew that in practice he needed at least a quarter of these to guard the camp and his prisoners. In particular he had designated Ashok and two hundred of his most loyal and level-headed soldiers to keep Jahangir and his two grandsons safe but also secure in his hands at all times.

Although he had been confused for a time by the various patrols sent in random directions in accordance with

Mehrunissa's orders, it had become increasingly clear to him that the imperial troops were really concentrating all their efforts upstream around a small hill on their side of the river. Just before dusk one of his prisoners had volunteered that the imperial troops had previously considered but quickly discarded the idea of using a deep ford there as an alternative to a boat bridge for crossing the Jhelum. It had only taken Mahabat Khan a moment to realise that Mehrunissa had no intention of either yielding or trying to escape but meant to attempt to snatch her husband back by an attack over that same ford. He could not help but admire the courage of his fellow Persian. Indeed, she reminded him of his wife, and for a moment he found himself wishing for the comforting presence of that strong-willed woman. But at the beginning of his impulsive ride from the Deccan he had written telling her to leave Agra on the pretext of returning to visit relations in Persia and go to Rajasthan to the Aravalli Hills, whence he had recruited so many of his best troops and where he knew she would be safe.

Once he had become sure in his own mind that an attack was coming sooner or later over the ford, he had ordered a thousand of his best musketeers to take an extra musket each from a stock he had found among the captured baggage train so that they could fire two volleys quickly. He had also designated others of his men to act as their loaders, again to increase their rate of fire. In this way he hoped to make up for his lack of cannon apart from the three small bronze *gajnals* he had found among the imperial baggage train, which were equipped with only limited quantities of powder and shot. These he had ordered to be mounted in baggage carts and moved by ox teams under cover of darkness to some of the low mud banks near the ford, where he had also commanded some of his chosen musketeers with their two weapons and attendant loaders to conceal themselves.

Now the moment for action had come once more Mahabat Khan grew calm. He shouted to his musketeers and archers to hold their fire until he was sure their targets were within range and gave the order. Then they were to continue to fire as rapidly as possible. He ordered those manning the small cannon to do the same, although he knew that their inexperience with the weapons would make them slow to reload. Then he moved across to join the squadrons of horsemen waiting to attack any of the imperial soldiers who actually succeeded in crossing the Jhelum.

The first beasts Mahabat Khan saw enter the river, which at this point was around eighty yards wide, were a line of three large war elephants wearing overlapping steel plate armour to protect their bodies and heads with scimitars strapped to their red-painted tusks. Each had two drivers sitting behind its ears and trying to make themselves as small targets as possible in their exposed position. Five musketeers were crammed into open wooden howdahs on each of their backs. Two more war elephants followed them into the cold water and Mahabat Khan saw at least twenty or thirty more behind them. Perhaps, he thought, some were actually baggage elephants pressed into an unfamiliar role. There were also hundreds of horsemen massing on the riverbank and churning it into mud. Many were carrying long lances at the ends of which fluttered green Moghul pennants. The middle elephant of the first line of three had advanced only about ten yards into the river and Mahabat Khan's men were still holding their fire when he saw it stumble, perhaps in one of the deep potholes in the river bed the prisoners had warned of. It swayed so violently it shed two of the musketeers from its open howdah into the swift-flowing waters to be carried off downstream towards the burnt remnants of the bridge of boats.

Mahabat Khan knew that this was his opportunity and shouted the order to open fire. Within moments the musketeers and archers emerged from behind the mud banks and got to work. Some of the first shots hit both of the mahouts on another of the leading elephants and they too fell with a splash into the swirling waters of the Jhelum, leaving the driverless animal to try to turn in fright to regain the northern bank from which it had come. As it turned it too slipped, and its left shoulder dropped below the water level. Impeded by the heavy weight of its armour, it overbalanced completely and was carried away half submerged and drowning, leaving the musketeers from its howdah to swim as best they could for their lives. The remaining elephant of the front line continued to advance, however, as did those behind until a shot from one of the *gajnals* caught an elephant in the fourth rank in an unprotected portion of its face and it too fell, flecking the jade-green waters of the Jhelum with its blood.

Many of the imperial horsemen were now in the water and they and their mounts seemed to be making better progress, half walking, half swimming and overtaking the stumbling elephants. Some of the riders even stood courageously in their stirrups to loose off arrows or – astonishingly, to Mahabat Khan's mind – in one case managing to fire a long-barrelled musket. Two or three of Mahabat Khan's musketeers fell and by now others were reloading, so the fire from his side of the river diminished.

This allowed several of the leading imperial horsemen to complete their crossing.

'Charge!' Mahabat Khan yelled, and at the head of his riders he swept down on to the muddy river bank to attack the horsemen as they emerged. His first sword stroke glanced off the breastplate of one but his second caught the throat of a chestnut horse which instantly collapsed, throwing its rider. For a moment it lay kicking in the shallows, blood pumping into the water, but then it was still. All about him horsemen were clashing along the river's edge. Here a horse reared up and its imperial rider slipped from its back; there one of his own Rajputs was knocked from his saddle, spitted like a chicken for cooking by one of the imperial lances.

Elsewhere, two men were fighting in the shallows, rolling over and over as they grappled to hold each other's head under water. Then one managed to grab a dagger and stabbed his opponent beneath his breastplate. Blood flowed into the water again. The victor – who Mahabat Khan was relieved to see was one of his Rajputs – heaved aside the body of his dying opponent and, water sluicing from him, began to stagger from the river. But Mahabat Khan's relief turned to dismay when the man suddenly flung up his arms and fell backwards, to be carried away instantly in the current. Almost immediately another Rajput crashed from his horse so close to Mahabat Khan that cold water from the splash soaked him. He looked around for the source of the accurate fire and as he did so he heard another musket ball hiss past his head.

Then he saw where the fire was coming from – the gilded howdah on a massive elephant wading through the river about fifty feet away. In the howdah were four figures. The

352

one in front was wearing a dark cloak. The other three were attendants, two intent on loading muskets, pushing lead balls down the barrel with steel ramrods, the third handing a loaded weapon to the cloaked figure. The empress, Mahabat Khan realised at once. He knew instinctively that she recognised him too. Well aware of her skill as a tiger hunter he tried to make himself small, crouching low over the withers of his horse, his arms about its neck. But only a few moments later he felt a sharp pain and numbness in his right forearm and the horse pitched forward. Both he and his mount had been hit.

Immediately he was in the cold water, being whirled downstream by the flow. Although he had lost his helmet in his fall he was being pulled underwater by the weight of his breastplate. Water was in his nostrils and his ears and he struggled to close his mouth. His ears were bubbling now and his lungs felt fit to burst. He had to do something quickly to get his breastplate off or he would drown. Despite the wound he could still move his right hand and he groped for the dagger at his waist. Finding it, he closed his fingers carefully round the jade hilt before pulling it out of its scabbard to be sure it would not slip from his grasp. It came out fairly easily and he cut first one and then the other leather strap on the left side of his breastplate. As it came away the force of the water caught it and because the straps on his right side were still fastened he was twisted down further underwater, before he freed himself from it. He clawed his way up to the surface, and took in a gasping lungful of air, only to feel a sharp blow and then another in the small of his back.

He was becoming entangled with another floating body

– that of a dying horse kicking its hooves in its agony. Mahabat Khan dived again, this time beneath the horse, holding his breath and gripping a stone on the river bed to keep himself still while the current carried the animal's body away. Then he pushed back to the surface and made the mistake of trying to wade out of the river. His foot slipped on a slimy, algae-covered rock and he went under yet again. This time he struck out for the shore using his little skill at swimming. But he was nearly at the bend in the river and the current was decreasing. Using all his diminishing reserves of strength he was able to get himself into the shallows and scramble out, water pouring from his sodden garments and mingling with the blood from the wound in his right arm.

Sitting down on the muddy riverbank he inspected the wound. He could see some creamy fat and red muscle exposed but no bone. God be praised, only a flesh wound. He pulled off the yellow woollen cloth he had been wearing round his neck to stop his breastplate chafing. It was dripping water but using his left hand he managed to wring it out after a fashion and with the help of his teeth tied it roughly round the wound in his right arm. Then he saw the shadow of a rider approaching from behind. He realised he would have little chance if it was one of the imperial soldiers but when he twisted round he saw to his intense relief it was not. One of his own bodyguards had seen him fall into the river and followed him downstream in case he was washed ashore.

'Are you all right, General?' the man asked.

'I think so,' he said, although in fact he was beginning to shake with cold and shock. 'Give me your horse,' he added. He scrambled to his feet only for his knees to buckle, causing him to collapse once more. The rider dismounted, but before he could get to him Mahabat Khan was on his feet again. This time his knees held and he staggered over to the horse. With a little help from his bodyguard he clambered aboard. His feet were so cold he could barely feel them, but he pushed them clumsily into the stirrups and with a shout of thanks to his bodyguard headed back towards the fighting round the ford. It was no distance and he realised that probably less than a quarter of an hour had elapsed since he was hit and fell into the river. But that was a long time in the course of a battle.

As far as he could make out his men seemed to be gaining the advantage, as they should given their superiority in numbers and the fact that their opponents had had to ford the river under fire. Then he made out Rajesh and rode towards him, shouting out as soon as he was in earshot, 'What happened to the elephant with the gold howdah?'

'I was told by one of your bodyguards that soon after you fell into the water one of its *mahouts* toppled from its neck and the remaining one, perhaps wounded, was not able to control the beast properly. It turned back into midstream and the guards lost sight of it.'

'That was the empress,' Mahabat Khan blurted out, eyes sweeping the river for any sign of the huge beast or its gold howdah. 'We must find that elephant. We must know if she lives or dies.'

'I was abandoned at birth to die and did not. It will take more than you to kill me, Mahabat Khan,' came a voice from behind him. Mahabat Khan jumped in surprise and turned. Amid the sounds of battle and preoccupied with his scanning of the river he had not heard some of his

355

bodyguards ride up behind him with a prisoner. There was Mehrunissa, looking unperturbed.

'I am sorry I did not kill you, Mahabat Khan. I yield to you this time from expediency and not from fear. Now take me to my husband. I have already given orders for my men to surrender. Remember, your victory is only temporary.'

Chapter 23

A Parting of the Ways

'M ajesty, I am again most grateful to you for your agreement. Rajesh will make an excellent divisional master of horse – much better than Alim Das who was both corrupt and an incompetent judge of horseflesh.' Mahabat Khan bowed and then turned and left the audience chamber. He was surprised that Jahangir had agreed so easily to Rajesh's appointment. In truth Rajesh's knowledge of horses was little better than the previous incumbent's and he too had a venal streak and might seek to profit from his position. Few officials did not. But at least he was no worse, and the appointment was a fitting reward for one of his most loyal officers.

As he walked towards his luxurious quarters in Srinagar's Hari Parbat fort, Mahabat Khan mused over the events of the months since his capture of the imperial party. After much thought he had decided that they should continue the journey to Srinagar together. To do so would suggest that that there was nothing unduly untoward as well as freeing him from questions of how to handle other courtiers and officials if they returned to Agra or Lahore. The Governor of Kashmir was an old army colleague of his and a Persian from Tabriz. On both counts he had thought him likely to be sympathetic and so he had proved, particularly when offered a promotion and expensive presents.

The greatest difficulty he himself had had – and still had – was how to use his newly acquired power; how to make his control anything other than temporary. When he spoke to Jahangir or Mehrunissa they acquiesced in his suggestions. They had only objected when he raised the question of replacing some of their closest attendants or dismissing the remnants of the bodyguard who had accompanied them on their journey to Kashmir. He had agreed to their wishes for appearances' sake and both attendants and bodyguards remained with them.

Jahangir, however, was in poor health. He ate little but continued to consume opium and alcohol in considerable quantities. Mahabat Khan could see that they were taking their toll on the constitution of a man by now in his fifty-eighth year. In addition to being bleary eyed and scarcely coherent for much of the day, Jahangir was racked with bouts of coughing. Nevertheless he continued to claim that the mountain air of Kashmir would clear his lungs, but to Mahabat Khan the beneficial effect of the beautiful valley seemed slow in taking effect.

The emperor could still, however, surprise Mahabat Khan when, on the occasions he was relatively free from the effect of drugs, he commented wisely on military matters and tartly on the characters and failings of his courtiers and officers. What impressed the Persian most was the emperor's detailed knowledge about plants and animals and the other workings of the natural world in general and Kashmir in particular.

Once and only once had Jahangir commented to Mahabat Khan on his present situation. The two men had been riding side by side along the Dal lake, a little ahead of the bodyguards whom Mahabat Khan had thought it prudent to have always accompanying them both, in the case of the emperor to prevent escape and in his own to guard against assassination, when Jahangir had suddenly asked, 'Have you learned to be careful what you wish for yet, Mahabat Khan? I too wished for unrestrained power when it should not yet have been mine. And then when I obtained it, I found knowing what to do with it even more difficult, never being quite sure whom to trust even amongst those close to me.'

Mahabat Khan winced at the truth of this assertion but Jahangir did not appear to notice and continued, 'Power corrodes most men. I know it has me, and that is why I'm happy to drift away from it through the opium and alcohol my wife prepares for me. It's a great comfort to leave decisions to the empress, and now even she is relieved of that burden since you have taken it on yourself. I warn you, power is lonely – or I found it so.' Jahangir broke off for a moment before going on. 'Perhaps the time when I acquired it made it more so, for I already felt isolated. I had lost my grandmother Hamida – a great support to me – as well of course as my father . . . though to this day I don't know whether he loved me – and I soon lost my best friend, my milk-brother Suleiman Beg. I was close to none of my sons, nor my wives. For a while I gloried in my authority, sometimes – I now admit – using it brutally and capriciously. Then I married Mehrunissa. I loved her and still do. She, I believe, loved me . . . loves me, as well as my power. The more she wanted of it the more I let her have. Was I wrong . . . ?'

Jahangir's voice had become quieter and more introspective the longer he spoke and finally tailed off as he turned and gazed abstractedly into the middle distance towards the glinting waters of the Dal lake. Mahabat Khan had made no response and had known that none was expected or required.

What of the empress? he wondered. She was habitually present whenever he spoke to Jahangir and had dispensed with any pretence of keeping purdah before him, although otherwise she had reverted to the seclusion of the *haram*. Her eyes frankly met his whenever they met and sometimes the expression in them when she told him that she lay in his power, that she was his to command, had led him to imagine that she might even have dallied with the idea of seducing him as a means of regaining control. She was after all still only in her forties, only a few years older than him, and her flesh had not yet started to sag down her body like wax down a candle as it did so often as women aged or fattened. However he had put the idea of seduction firmly from his mind as fantasy, but still when they met it was he who averted his eyes. When she spoke softly and smiled he usually agreed, almost without thinking, to her requests, such as retaining the remaining members of the bodyguard.

Did she love the emperor? Yes, she probably did. Of course she fed him opium. Of course she enjoyed his power and was not coy about letting people know she wielded it. He had witnessed that on many occasions. However, when she wiped his brow or held the bowl for him to cough into when he was ill, he had seen love on her face. Perhaps her

360

motives were as mixed as his own. Everything would probably become clearer as they made the long journey back south again to Lahore, which could not be much longer delayed. The nights were becoming chill and autumn was drawing on. By then, too, he would need to decide what to do himself. Although he had planned his capture of the imperial party with care, he realised he had not thought enough about his next steps and had now become almost paralysed by indecision as to how to win new allies and secure a position in power for the long term. Since his arrival in Kashmir he had done little other than to send messages to Asaf Khan for onward transmission to his son-in-law, assuring Khurram of his sons' good health and good treatment, and of his loyalty to the imperial family in general as well as his understanding of Khurram's situation in particular. As he mused, Mahabat Khan made up his mind that they would start for the plains in a week.

• ◆ •

'I'll be sorry to leave Kashmir.'

'Even though we've been prisoners here?'

'Yes. Nothing can detract from the beauty of the place, and Mahabat Khan has been respectful to us.'

'That kind of respect costs him nothing. If he had asked you whether you were ready to leave Kashmir that would have been proper respect. Instead he just announced the date politely as if we were his servants.'

'To be fair to him, we couldn't have stayed much longer. In another couple of weeks the first snows will begin to fall in the passes.'

'True. Anyway, despite Mahabat Khan's presumption I'm

glad we're leaving. Our plans depend on our returning to the plains.' Mehrunissa rose and began to mix a little opium with rosewater for her husband. 'You will remember to remain acquiescent whatever Mahabat Khan requests as we descend from Kashmir, won't you? As the moment to act grows closer it's vital we do or say nothing to rouse his suspicion.'

'Of course. In any case, he asks very little.'

'And you must be discreet in front of your grandsons. Children are good at hearing things they were not intended to hear and then blurting them out to impress people.'

'I've said nothing.'

'Good. There's also the risk that they might deliberately use anything they overhear to persuade Mahabat Khan to send them back to their parents – especially Dara Shukoh. I've noticed how he enjoys going about with Mahabat Khan, listening to his stories of battles, and he's always asking questions.'

'He's an intelligent and curious boy. Besides, don't all children ask questions? I know I did. It's part of growing up.'

'Perhaps. But we must be careful, especially now we're getting nearer to achieving what we want.'

'Sometimes I wonder if we couldn't reach some sort of accommodation, some compromise with Mahabat Khan, rather than all this plotting of yours.'

'You speak as if Mahabat Khan could be trusted. We know nothing about what's really in his mind.'

'You don't think he means us harm?'

'He gives the appearance of being a decent man and he's certainly a good general, but never forget that above all he's a traitor who has seized power that can only be given by you, not taken. He's also taken huge risks, which — unless he's a complete fool — he must realise. If he perceives a danger to himself who knows what he might not be capable of? Besides, my "plots" as you call them go well.' Mehrunissa shook the opium and rosewater together in a pink bottle, then poured a little, handed it to him and pulled the soft, intricately patterned Kashmir shawl a little tighter around him. Jahangir was coughing more and the air was becoming colder.

'You will play your part just as I play mine, won't you?' she persisted. 'Mahabat Khan is wary of me, but he respects you . . .'

· ◆ ·

From the north bank of the Jhelum, seated in his golden howdah on his favourite elephant Thunderer, Jahangir watched Mahabat Khan and Ashok. The two men were sitting relaxed on their horses on a muddy hillock on the south bank, looking back towards the new bridge of boats that they had had constructed across the Jhelum on the latest stage of the return journey from Kashmir. The river was slower-flowing and narrower than in the spring and they had found it relatively easy to obtain enough boats to rope together to form the bottom of the bridge and then to fashion planking from branches and pieces of camp equipment to lay across them.

The weather had been kind and progress quick down through the passes and valleys. Here the leaves on the trees were turning red and gold as the local people completed their harvests of apples and pears and the drying of the grapes and apricots for which their region was famous throughout Hindustan. Farmers were stocking their barns with root vegetables, corn and straw to feed themselves and their animals through the long harsh winter. It had been an almost idyllic journey, soothing the minds of all. Mehrunissa had seemingly immersed herself in Persian poetry, only emerging from her quarters to give orders for attendants to leave the camp to collect autumn flowers and animal specimens for Jahangir who, she told Mahabat Khan, had been inspired by the autumn beauty to renew his study of the natural world with added vigour.

Earlier that day Mahabat Khan had told Jahangir that everyone should be over the Jhelum well before dusk, and that the next morning they should be able to set out for Lahore. Then he had crossed the bridge with Ashok and a vanguard of a third of his forces, leaving Rajesh – whose offer to command the rearguard that day Mahabat Khan had gratefully and unthinkingly accepted – to send over the imperial family and their escort when ordered to do so and finally to cross himself with the remaining men.

Switching his glance towards the bridge itself, Jahangir saw a tall, purple-turbaned Rajput mounted on a chestnut stallion, which skittered nervously as the bridge swayed beneath its hooves, crossing back to the north side. Presumably he was the messenger bringing the order from Mahabat Khan to Rajesh to bring the imperial party across. The Rajput did indeed ride up to Rajesh, sitting stiffly on his white horse only a few feet from Jahangir's elephant, and the emperor felt his heart beat a little faster as it had in his youth before a battle.

'Rajesh, Mahabat Khan commands you to begin bringing the emperor and empress across the river.'

364

Rajesh hesitated for what seemed an age. Then he said, voice tense and jerky with emotion, 'Tell Mahabat Khan I cannot . . . I mean I will not . . .' Jahangir relaxed. Mehrunissa's plan was going to work. All the long hours of plotting and persuasion including his own wooing of Rajesh under Mehrunissa's guidance were bearing fruit. What a woman she was. What an opponent she would have made if she had been a man.

Rajesh went on, his words coming more easily now the breach was begun. 'Tell Mahabat Khan that as a holder of an imperial office, at present that of divisional master of horse, my duty is to the emperor and the empress alone. The emperor has promised me and my men further advancement if we will answer only to him. I will take command of the detachments of loyal vassals who are even now hastening to the emperor's side. I regret I must sever all connections with Mahabat Khan, but out of past loyalty to him tell him I am returning you safe and unharmed and that I have persuaded the emperor to wait half an hour after you have crossed back before he gives the order to open fire against you and the other rebels against his rightful power.'

On the opposite bank Mahabat Khan had also been in deep thought. Although Jahangir and Mehrunissa had continued calmly to accept his authority he had got little further in his debate with himself about how to consolidate his position. The emperor had been right that to be in authority was to be lonely. He had felt unable to consult others or discuss his views with them, fearing that to do so might be taken as weakness or indecision. That in turn had led him into procrastination on the bigger issues, leaving

365

him to concentrate in too much detail on tangible topics such as food and supplies for the journey. Now he wheeled his horse and rode down the short distance to the boat bridge. The emperor and empress should begin crossing soon.

As he reached the bridge he was surprised to see the purple-turbaned Rajput riding slowly back across the gently swaying bridge of boats alone, and no sign that the imperial party was preparing to follow. What was going on? He jumped down from his horse and ran to meet the rider as he came off the bridge.

As the young Rajput stammered out Rajesh's message Mahabat Khan's face contorted with fury and he flung his riding gauntlets to the ground.

Mehrunissa had outwitted him. How could he have been made such a fool of? It suddenly dawned on him that when she had supposedly sent attendants out for plant and animal specimens they had actually been carrying letters or messages to and from supporters. He knew too that he was now paying the price for agreeing without proper thought to the couple's pleas not to dismiss the remnants of Jahangir's imperial bodyguard. How could Rajesh betray him? How had Mehrunissa won him over? How had he persuaded the men he commanded to join him?

Even to Mahabat Khan in his anger the answer to these questions became quickly obvious. For the venal Rajesh the promise of a pardon and promotion beyond that he himself had secured for him had been enough. As for his men, they were mostly from the small poor Rajput state of which Rajesh's father was the ruler. They owed their loyalty to Rajesh first. Whatever the reason for their betrayal of him, now was not the time to brood upon it. He must act and act quickly. The realisation energised him. 'Burn the bridge,' he yelled to Ashok, 'Rajesh has betrayed us. Bring brands from the noon cooking fires. I will set the first flame.'

As an astonished Ashok rode off, Mahabat Khan decided something else. Despite his anger and appetite for revenge he would not attempt to recapture the emperor and empress. He was made for battle where the distinction between friend and foe was clear and each action had a direct consequence, not for the amorphous and ambiguous world of court politics. Jahangir had been right. The achievement of an ambition for supreme power was its own punishment. He and his remaining men, outnumbered as they were, would withdraw to the hills. Once there he could consider his future . . . decide to whom he might offer his support, relinquishing to that person the supreme leader's responsibility for difficult decisions.

• ◆ •

'Your scheme worked. I congratulate you,' said Jahangir that night. Mehrunissa looked exultant. He had often seen just that look on her face after a successful kill during a tiger hunt. He smiled to think how she had played and outwitted Mahabat Khan — one of his best and most intelligent commanders — as if he had been little more than a fat trout in the Jhelum transfixed by her lure.

'I warned Mahabat Khan at the beginning of all this that his victory was only temporary. I hope he remembers my words.'

'I am sure he will. What do you think he'll do now?'

'I don't know. I doubt he does. But he would be wise to leave the empire, perhaps go home to Persia. He must know that a crime like his can't go unpunished and that once you've returned safely to Lahore you'll send armies against him.'

Jahangir nodded. She was right. Mahabat Khan had seen an opportunity and taken it. Unless he suffered for it others might be tempted to rebellion. But he should never have allowed the whole thing to happen in the first place. Perhaps he was growing old . . . At the thought a little of his triumph ebbed. When he returned to his capital he must demonstrate to all that his grip on his empire was as tight as ever. But now he told himself he should relax – tonight he and Mehrunissa should simply enjoy their new-found freedom and Dara Shukoh and Aurangzeb should join them to share their triumph.

'Bring my grandsons to me,' he called to a *qorchi*. A few minutes later the boys entered the tent and Jahangir embraced each in turn. 'This is a great moment,' he told them.

'Why, Grandfather?' Dara Shukoh asked.

Everything that had happened during recent months must have seemed strange to the child, Jahangir reflected as he replied, 'We have outwitted our enemy Mahabat Khan and regained our freedom.'

'Was Mahabat Khan our enemy?' Dara Shukoh looked surprised.

'Yes,' Jahangir answered. 'He held us against our will and wanted to dictate to me whom I should choose as my advisers and how I should run the empire.'

'But I thought . . . I mean the way you talked to him . . . you had become friends.'

Jahangir smiled. 'No. That was pretence. To gain what he wants a ruler must sometimes practise deception. You will understand that when you grow older. Now, taste some of these sweetmeats – and you too, Aurangzeb.'

He held out a silver dish of dried apricots stuffed with marzipan, but though Aurangzeb took a fistful Dara Shukoh didn't help himself. He still looked thoughtful, then said, 'Before he sent us to you my father told us things about you.'

Jahangir stiffened. 'What things?'

'That you are not only our grandfather and the emperor, but also a great man. Therefore we should always show respect to you. Was that what Mahabat Khan did wrong? Did he fail to respect you?'

Jahangir nodded, but his mind was elsewhere. Had Khurram really said that of him? If so, had he simply been trying to ensure his sons did nothing to annoy him, or had he truly meant those words?

• ◆ •

Jahangir looked up as fireworks lit the night sky above his encampment on the northwestern plains near the town of Bhimbaar. Two days ago Shahriyar and Ladli had arrived with their young daughter – born just before Jahangir had left for Kashmir – and ten thousand men to escort him the rest of the way back to Lahore. Several of his most senior courtiers and officials had accompanied them. With their security now beyond doubt, Mehrunissa had suggested holding a celebration to mark both their arrival and his deliverance from Mahabat Khan and he had readily agreed. As the last and greatest firework exploded, sending a mass of red and purple stars shooting across the heavens, Jahangir felt content. Despite Mahabat Khan's treachery, his grip over

369

his empire was still strong. Not only had his scouts reported that Mahabat Khan himself had not emerged from the hills into which he had fled a month ago but his officials had brought news that Khurram remained quiet in the south, that an insurrection in Gujarat had been swiftly put down by the Moghul governor there and that elsewhere in the empire all was peaceful.

As soon as the fireworks – purchased as a prelude to tonight's revelry from a caravan of Chinese travelling merchants passing northwards towards Peshawar and the Khyber Pass – were over Jahangir inspected the arrangements for the feast. He had ordered the imperial dais to be set up at the very centre of the vast encampment, about fifty yards in front of his scarlet tent, and covered in gold cloth. The low imperial throne and next to it an intricately carved stool for Shahriyar already stood on it. A little to one side, screened by green silken hangings embroidered with gold thread, was the area where Mehrunissa and her daughter Ladli were to eat. Attendants were still placing red velvet cushions trimmed with gold around a long, low table set with silver plates and drinking vessels for Jahangir's senior officers and high officials in front of the dais. Further back were tables set less elaborately for more junior officers and courtiers while other servants had created dining spaces elsewhere in the camp for the rest of his men.

The smell of roasting meats – deer and mutton, ducks, hens and peafowl – was already rising from hundreds of cooking spits set up over open fires. The portable tandoori ovens were being filled with meats more subtly prepared with yogurts and spices. Cooking pots with dishes flavoured with dried Kashmiri fruit – apricots, cherries and sultanas – as well as spices were already simmering. Dough was being prepared so that bread could be made and brought to the tables hot when required. Puddings of rice and rosewater and of ground almonds and cream, some topped with gold leaf, had been prepared and covered with cloths. Yes, everything was as it should be. Jahangir grunted with approval and returned to his tent where his *qorchis* waited to dress him for the feast.

An hour later his officers were in their places as to the blare of trumpets the awning of the imperial tent was raised again and four palanquins, each carried by four bearers, emerged. The first two stopped in front of the dais. The second two, which were closed, were carried to its rear so that Mehrunissa and Ladli could enter the screened area unobserved by onlookers. To a final flourish of trumpets Jahangir slowly descended from his palanquin, to be joined by the slim figure of Shahriyar from the second. The prince helped his father mount the dais and cross to the throne.

Before he seated himself, Jahangir glanced for a moment into the twinkling stars in the velvet darkness above. Was he being fanciful or were they shining particularly brightly tonight, honouring his celebration by their silver radiance? Then he motioned for silence and spoke, his voice firm. 'We feast here today to celebrate both the arrival of my beloved son Shahriyar and our escape from the domination of the treacherous Mahabat Khan. His crime is neither forgiven nor forgotten. His punishment is merely deferred.' Pausing while he looked around him, he noted a rather nervous-looking Rajesh dressed in Moghul green, with a patch of the same colour over his empty eye socket. His monocular gaze was fixed on the silver plate in front of him and he was abstractedly twisting at one of his buttons.

'But this isn't the time to dwell on past events and their consequences. What matters is the future of the empire.' As he spoke, Jahangir noticed Shahriyar shifting a little on his stool, but despite Mehrunissa's urgings before they left the imperial tent he had decided not to reiterate that Shahriyar was his heir. There was no need to speak about such things tonight – not when his cough seemed to have improved and he was feeling so much more vigorous. Despite Mehrunissa's constant and lavish praise of him, Shahriyar's performance of those duties Jahangir had assigned to him had sometimes failed to convince his father that he had sufficient intellect or ability to command to flourish if he succeeded to the imperial throne. His concerns had been strengthened by reports of Shahriyar's indecision and inactivity during his captivity in Kashmir, mentioned to him discreetly by some of his newly arrived officials.

Also, though he'd said nothing to Mehrunissa, he had begun to wonder whether one day he and Khurram might not be reconciled as he had been with his own father after his years of rebellion. Dara Shukoh's words had caused him to reflect . . . to perceive that there might have been faults on both sides. The love he had once borne Khurram had begun to rekindle, reminding him how auspicious his birth had been . . . what a brave warrior and leader he was . . . how much more worthy a head of the great line founded by Babur he might prove than the submissive but less charismatic Shahriyar. He might be fooling himself, but time would tell . . .

A meaningful cough from one of his officers recalled

Jahangir to the present and to what he had been about to say when carried into his reverie. 'I believe that we are entering a golden time. Our internal enemies have been vanquished and our external foes fear to probe our borders. Peace and prosperity await the citizens of our great empire. That is what I wanted to tell you tonight. But something else as well . . . Before you all I wish to pay tribute to my empress Mehrunissa who has done so much to help me bring our fortunes to this position. It is not often women fill such important roles outside domestic life but she has helped me in every sphere and I thank her.'

Then, raising his arms, Jahangir cried, '*Zinderbad* the Moghuls! *Zinderbad* the Moghul empire!' Long live the Moghul empire! The crowd immediately responded, '*Zinderbad Padishah Jahangir!*' Long live the Emperor Jahangir! A wild cheering broke out as Jahangir took his place on his throne. It reminded him of his first appearance as emperor on the *jharoka* balcony of the Agra fort all those years ago. How far he had travelled. How much of both the best and the worst he had experienced. How much more he wanted to achieve to fulfil fully the vow he had then made to prove worthy of his father Akbar's legacy. Just then the aroma of roasted meat caught his attention. An attendant had placed a dish of venison garnished with ruby-red pomegranate seeds before him. His appetite for food felt stronger than for many months. He began to eat with unaccustomed relish.

• ◆ •

Three hours later Mehrunissa rose from the bed where slowly and patiently, to allow for the frailty of Jahangir's body, and for the first time in some weeks she and Jahangir had made love while the noise of revelry continued outside at the feast. Afterwards she had, as she usually did at night, mixed his opium and rosewater and he had drunk it slowly before drifting into sleep, a contented smile on his face as she had lain down beside him again. Now, pulling her silk robe around her, Mehrunissa looked down on her husband. His tribute – unrehearsed with her, unlike most of his speeches – had deeply touched her. More years would remain for them and with her help they would be his greatest. After that . . . well, with Shahriyar on the throne – as she would make sure he would be – she would still be the most powerful person in the empire. Shahriyar's wits were not of the sharpest and with Ladli's help she would mould him to her will. As for Khurram and sweet Arjumand, she would decide their fate and that of their sons, two of whom were sleeping over there in another part of the tent. Mind full of pleasant reflections, she turned and made her way to her own curtained-off sleeping area.

• ◆ •

'Fetch the *hakims*!'

Mehrunissa sat up as the shout rang out. As she did so, one of her attendants pulled apart the curtains round her bed and cried, 'Majesty, come quickly. It is the emperor. He is ill.'

Mehrunissa rose and pulled on her green silk robe over her sleeping shift, then rushed to Jahangir's quarters. He was lying on the bed, a trickle of vomit leaking from his lips. The *hakim* was already there and Jahangir's servant, who slept nearby, was saying, 'I heard him coughing a little while ago but then there was silence. When I looked in at him as I do every hour I saw him like this.'

374

The *hakim* glanced up and seeing Mehrunissa said without ceremony, 'The emperor is dead, Majesty. He must have coughed and vomited and then choked. There is nothing I can do.'

A violent chill ran through Mehrunissa. Jahangir was dead . . . The man who had never failed her, always wanted her, would never have deserted her and had always been attentive to her thoughts and wishes was gone. As she dropped to her knees and touched his cooling face with the back of her fingers tears began to run down her cheeks – tears of shock, of loss and of love. For some moments she abandoned herself to weeping and to grief, then slowly another thought formed in her splintered consciousness. What of the future? Jahangir had abandoned her, albeit not of his own volition. She must once more look to herself and her position. She brushed aside her tears with the back of her hand, stood, composed herself a little and then said quietly, 'Fetch Shahriyar and Ladli.'

A minute or two later the young couple were led in, sleep, confusion and alarm mingling in their dazed eyes. Mehrunissa spoke. 'As you see, the emperor is dead. Shahriyar, if you wish to rule in his stead you must both now do exactly as I say.'

Chapter 24

The Funeral Cortège

'Shah Shuja, keep your sword up or you'll never make a great swordsman. Stop me attacking you.' In one of the large rooms of the fortress-palace of Burhanpur Khurram smiled as his eleven-year-old son tried valiantly to knock away his own blunted practice weapon. Suddenly Khurram was aware that someone else had entered the room behind him. Turning, he saw one of his *qorchis*.

'Highness, forgive me,' the flustered young man stammered, 'but a group of five riders has just galloped unannounced into the courtyard. They claim they have ridden night and day for the past twenty days from the emperor's camp, pausing only briefly to eat, sleep and change horses in their haste to get here. They say they bring a letter of the utmost importance from Asaf Khan that may only be handed to you personally.'

Khurram immediately put down his sword and, mind racing with the possibilities of what the letter might contain, left the room and descended the flight of steps leading down to the courtyard two at a time. Had something happened to Dara Shukoh or Aurangzeb? Had Mehrunissa persuaded Jahangir to despatch them to some dungeon? Surely not . . . but if so how would he tell Arjumand? But perhaps the letter had more to reveal about the strange story of Mahabat Khan's appointing himself as Jahangir's chief adviser. Only Mahabat Khan's odd but conciliatory letters and Asaf Khan's repeated advice to stay away and stay calm had prevented Khurram from attempting to raise a force to intervene, although he had moved with his family from Balaghat westward to Burhanpur to be closer to the main routes to the north. The latest reports had said that Mehrunissa had seized back control and that Mahabat Khan had fled into the hills. At the time Khurram had thought it strange that such a stalwart fighter as Mahabat Khan should have put up no fight. Perhaps he had returned as part of some great plan.

Emerging into the courtyard and squinting into the harsh sun, Khurram immediately saw the five dusty riders, each still holding the reins of not one but two horses. They must have each taken a lead horse as a spare to speed their journey by changing mounts whenever necessary. As his eyes adjusted Khurram recognised the tall youth standing a little in front of the other four as Hanif, the eldest son of one of Asaf Khan's best commanders and strongest supporters. For Hanif to have come the news must be serious.

Wasting no time on preliminaries Khurram strode across to the youth. 'You have a message for me, Hanif?' Immediately Hanif extracted a letter with Asaf Khan's seal from the leather pouch slung across his chest and handed it to Khurram, who opened it, without a word.

The emperor, your father, is dead. The words burned into Khurram more hotly than the midday sun as he stood bare headed in the courtyard. Beyond the stark news of his father's death Asaf Khan confirmed that Dara Shukoh and Aurangzeb were well, but urged, *Now is the time to act. Come soon before others seize their opportunity and take what should be yours.*

Stunned by the letter's contents, Khurram briefly thanked the five men for the speed with which they had brought the message and dismissed them. Waving away his own attendants he stood alone in the sunny courtyard with the letter dangling from his hand, trying to make sense of what it said and what it left unsaid. His father whom he had not seen for some years was dead. That much was clear. But how and why? Had Mehrunissa poisoned him? After all, she'd openly boasted to her brother Asaf Khan of getting rid of Thomas Roe by constantly lacing his food with rotten meat. But what would she have to gain from his father's death? Perhaps if she had had a hand in it it was accidental, through steadily increasing the strength of the opium and alcohol concoction she fed Jahangir to bind him to her.

As he pondered the nature of his father's death images of Jahangir's life came into Khurram's mind – not of the years of their estrangement but of his youth, of his father standing to one side, stiff and awkward, as Akbar instructed him in the intricacies of camel riding and of chess; of Jahangir's stumbling attempts to rebuild his bonds with him after his rebellion against Akbar; of Akbar's death and Khusrau's revolts and then the good years when he had first married Arjumand and been his father's leading general and confidant.

With these recollections Khurram realised that his father had loved him and he his father. Tears began to form in his eyes. He brushed them away as his thoughts turned to Mehrunissa. She had been the cause of his alientation from Jahangir. She was still alive and had two of his sons in her power. In the three weeks since the emperor's death she had no doubt been planning the next moves for herself and her two creatures, Shahriyar and Ladli. Manipulative, calculating and cold, she would not have spent much time in grieving and nor could he. As Asaf Khan had wisely written, he must act immediately, but first of all he must break the news to Arjumand.

· ◆ ·

'No. For the first time in many years we must part,' Khurram insisted to the stubborn-faced Arjumand. 'Don't you see, it isn't the same as when we went on campaign together for my father or when we fled from his forces? On the first occasion we knew that if we perished my father and your father would care for the children. When we were fleeing they were safest with us. Now that I am splitting our forces and seeking allies it is best that you remain here with them. If you do and if I fail – God forbid I should – they would have you to protect them rather than being left defenceless orphans at the mercy of Mehrunissa.'

Arjumand's expression lost a little of its stubbornness. 'I understand your logic and must accept it, but are your other plans as logical? Why split your few resources, and why travel north with so few men yourself?'

'I thought I'd explained – because I do not know who else may claim the throne and hence where the greatest threats may lie. I need to undertake several tasks simultan-eously. I have to assemble as many men as I can as quickly as I can. The best way of doing that is to send out detachments of troops under trusted officers to raise them from among my friends and supporters. You know that I've already sent Mohun Singh to try to locate Mahabat Khan. The Persian general is a sensible and pragmatic man. He will know that allying himself with me will offer his best chance of restoring his battered fortunes. I also need to send out strong bodies of scouts as well as spies. I cannot allow your father – good man though he is – to be our only eyes and ears. Finally, to take speedy advantage of developments I need to make the quickest and most inconspicuous progress I can towards Agra, leaving my main forces to follow when sufficient men are assembled.'

'Yes, but how are you going to make yourself inconspicuous?'

'That I haven't decided. It's difficult to conceal even a small force and I'm sure Mehrunissa will have spies out.'

'Then why not disguise it rather than conceal it?'

'How?'

'As a merchant's caravan, perhaps?'

'No. In these troubled times any enemy will investigate a caravan, ransack it and even steal from it. But you're right. Disguise is a good idea. I'll think of something.'

• ◆ •

'Whose coffin is this?' Khurram heard a male voice say as he lay in the stifling midday heat in a velvet-lined silver coffin on a black-brocade-draped bier pulled by sixteen white oxen. He longed to scratch a clutch of day-old mosquito bites on his left knuckle and move his right leg, which was beginning to grow numb, but he knew he mustn't do anything that might shake the coffin and betray that the occupant lived. Despite the sandalwood essence with which the cloth wound round his face and mouth had been impregnated, the smell of the ten–day–old piece of meat placed in the coffin with him to give an authentic stench of decay was overpowering. He had climbed into the coffin at the first sight of the approach, amid a cloud of billowing red dust, of a group of horsemen from the great crenellated fortress of Rotgarh. The fort stood atop a craggy promontory that dominated the arid landscape and the road northwest to Agra, and was the stronghold of Wasim Gul, one of Mehrunissa's most stalwart supporters.

It had in fact been Arjumand, not he, who had come up with the idea of a funeral cortège supposedly bearing the body of an officer who had died in the Deccan homeward for burial as a disguise for his force, suggesting that it was the least likely column to be subjected to close scrutiny. It was she, too, who had proposed the refinement of the decaying meat. He, however, had devised another deception: just as his great-grandmother Hamida had prevented news of her husband Humayun's death from leaking out while she gathered support for Akbar by having a man similar in height and build impersonate him, Khurram had designated a trusted officer to dress in his clothes and be seen entering and leaving the private areas of the Burhanpur fortress to give the illusion that he had not yet departed for the north.

All had gone to plan with the ruse of the cortège up to this point. He had only had to use the coffin twice, and on both occasions those approaching had veered off as soon as they saw the sombre nature of the procession. This officer of Wasim Gul's seemed to be different, though, Khurram

381

thought as he struggled to suppress a sudden desire to sneeze. He had already heard him give orders to his men to check some of the baggage carts. It was a good job his extra muskets and powder were either concealed deep beneath animal fodder or in the false bottoms of some of the wagons. Even so a diligent inspection might find them, he thought, as his heart began to beat yet faster.

'It is the body of Hassan Khan – an officer in Prince Khurram's army and a cousin of the ruler of Multan – which we his loyal followers are transporting back to Peshawar for burial in his homeland,' Khurram heard one of his own men reply to the newcomer. 'We are fulfilling his final request, made in the last coherent words he spoke as he lay in his tent sweat soaked and dying of the spotted fever.' Khurram could almost hear the inquisitive officer's intake of breath. It was an inspired idea to mention spotted fever. It was so deadly and spread so quickly that no one ever wanted to stay close to a sufferer or a corpse. After a few moments he heard the voice of Wasim Gul's officer, already a little further off, say, 'Although he supported a traitor, nevertheless may he rest in Paradise. You may proceed.'

· ◆ ·

Khurram smiled with satisfaction as two weeks later he looked around his growing council of advisers in his scarlet command tent fifty miles southeast of Agra. Soon after he had left the territory of Wasim Gul he had abandoned the pretence that his small column was a funeral cortège. Three days ago he had been joined by another large detachment of his troops, including a number of war elephants, who had travelled from Burhanpur under the command of Kamran

Iqbal by a more circuitous route to confuse any lurking spies or scouts. Additionally, many commanders of imperial forces in the areas he had passed through, as well as some of the local vassal rulers, had pledged allegiance to him and joined him with their men. His army now numbered almost fifteen thousand and was well equipped and supplied.

'What do we know of the latest movements of Shahriyar, Ladli and Mehrunissa?' he asked.

'According to our spies, since Shahriyar had himself declared emperor in Lahore a month ago he has remained there with his wife and mother-in-law simply sending out emissaries to seek allies,' Kamran Iqbal responded.

'And Mahabat Khan?'

'The latest message from Mohun Singh says that he is riding with Mahabat Khan and his men to meet your father-in-law Asaf Khan and his troops. He insists there is scarcely any more reason to doubt Mahabat Khan's pledge of allegiance to you than there is that of Asaf Khan himself.'

'Good. Let's hope Mohun Singh is right and that Mahabat Khan has learned not to meddle in politics. He should be wise enough to know that if he wishes to recover a position within the Moghul empire I am his best hope. He can have little expectation of reconciliation with Mehrunissa.'

'Mohun Singh is certain Mahabat Khan is loyal by nature and only his treatment by Mehrunissa drove him to rebellion.'

'We will still keep an eye on him when he joins us with Asaf Khan. When can we expect that to be?'

'Perhaps in three or four weeks, allowing them time to recruit more men as they ride. Mahabat Khan in particular has sent messengers to Rajasthan to recall some of his old comrades as well as to recruit new men from that crucible of warriors.'

'Well, that leaves us only Khusrau, doesn't it? Does he still seem intent on making a bid for the throne?'

'Yes. Even though our reports say that his *hakims*' attempts to unstitch his eyelids and restore his sight have been only partially successful, clearly he has not lost his ability to persuade others to his side. He has won over the Governor of Gwalior, where he was confined for so long, and many of the local commanders, and has had himself proclaimed emperor for the third time.'

'And he will be unsuccessful for a third time,' said Khurram. Why did Khusrau persist in such an impossible ambition? Why couldn't he be content to enjoy what renewed sight he had and the love of his faithful wife Jani who had shared his long years of imprisonment? Why must he set out to oppose me, Khurram thought to himself, biting his lip before asking, 'How many men has he succeeded in recruiting?'

'Perhaps ten thousand – some of them the sons and brothers of those who died in his previous rebellions against your father. They have raided the treasuries and armouries of Gwalior and so are well supplied and armed.'

'Are they still heading for Agra?'

'Yes. Our scouts tell us they are about twenty-five miles west of us and about forty miles from Agra.'

'Given that Shahriyar has made no move from Lahore and we would be wise to await Mahabat Khan and Asaf Khan and the reinforcements they bring before tackling him there, I suggest that first we put paid to Khusrau's ambitions once and for all. If we leave most of the baggage train here, can we overtake him and bring him to battle before he reaches Agra?'

'Yes. According to the scouts he's making no more than eight miles a day, probably hoping to rally more support before he approaches Agra. The terrain separating us from his army is mostly flat with no major rivers, so we could catch him in forty-eight hours, even if we take war elephants as well as horsemen and mounted musketeers and archers.'

'Well then, let's do it. Make sure you leave sufficient forces here to defend the baggage train and heavy cannon, and give the necessary orders immediately.'

• ◆ •

Eager to begin the action that would determine his future, Khurram had ridden ahead of the main body of his troops with a few of his bodyguard when just before midday two days later one of his scouts galloped up to him on a sweating grey horse.

'Khusrau's men are drawing themselves up around that village over there. There are more of them than we thought – perhaps twelve thousand or so. When they became aware of our approach they clearly decided to take advantage of what protection the low mud walls round the villagers' cattle enclosures and even their simple palm-thatched huts provided. They're busy trying to drag cannon into position and they've deployed a small screen of musketeers and archers a couple of hundred yards in front of the village.'

Following the scout's outstretched arm Khurram saw through the heat haze that the village was a small one set on flat ground along the far bank of a stream which in the present dry season looked to be mostly mud. Khusrau had a slight numerical advantage because of the number of his own men he had left behind to guard the baggage train.

385

Nevertheless, though his men were tired by their ride to overtake Khusrau and the day was furnace hot, without waiting for his senior commanders to catch up with him for a council of war Khurram decided to attack and overwhelm Khusrau's forces before they could finish drawing up their defensive positions.

'Take an order to Kamran Iqbal to form up half of our cavalrymen ready for an immediate assault. While he attacks the village head on I will lead the remainder across the stream to get behind the village and take the defenders in the rear. Order the war elephants with the small cannon in their howdahs to follow the cavalry into action as closely as they can.'

A quarter of an hour or so later, Khurram watched as his horsemen, led by the burly figure of Kamran Iqbal on his tall black stallion with four banner-carriers immediately behind him, gathered speed in their charge towards the village. Dust began to obscure Khurram's vision as he in turn, mounted on a favourite chestnut horse, led two thousand of his best riders sweeping left to begin the encirclement of the village. Soon the boom of small cannon and the crackle of musketry showed that Khusrau had got his forces into action against Kamran Iqbal. Through gaps in the swirling dust and smoke Khurram could see that the aim of his half-brother's artillerymen had been good. Several of Kamran Iqbal's men's horses were down. Others were galloping riderless away from the action, reins dangling. Suddenly Khurram saw one of the banner-bearers appear to turn back; the impetus of the attack seemed to be faltering. Then the billowing smoke obscured his view entirely.

Khurram was suddenly stricken with doubt. Had he been

over-eager, rash even, in ordering an immediate attack against stronger forces when he would have been wiser to wait and rest his tired men? Had he been wrong to split his resources twice, once by leaving a strong force to protect the baggage and then again by ordering this two-pronged assault? It was too late for such thoughts. The worst thing he could do now would be to attempt to fall back or to disengage. That would expose his men to a counter-attack by Khusrau. He was committed to the offensive. He must stake his future on the success of the encirclement. Though Khusrau's men were fighting hard and causing casualties among the frontal attackers, they might crumble beneath his own assault on their rear, fearing their route of retreat would be cut off. Besides, Kamran Iqbal and the troops with him were brave and experienced fighters. Even if they suffered an initial setback they would not give in but attack with renewed vigour.

By now Khurram was approaching the margins of the stream. Pockmarked by the feet of many animals, it was indeed more sticky brown mud than water, he thought, as with a wave of his hand he gestured his men to cross and pushed his own chestnut forward. He was soon riding down the opposite bank followed by his bodyguards and the rest of his men. However, twisting his head he saw that a couple of horses were down, presumably having caught their hooves in the deep, clinging mud while being whipped on too hard by their careless riders.

Turning his head to the front again he realised that the first low walls of the villagers' cattle enclosure were only two hundred yards away. Suddenly he saw flashes as musketeers rose from behind the mud walls and fired. Musket balls hissed past him. Another of his horsemen, an extravagantly bearded orange-turbaned Rajput, hit square in the forehead by one, pitched from the saddle and rolled over several times in the dust before being trampled beneath the hooves of the following horses. There were fifty or so musketeers from the number of flashes, thought Khurram. Still, most of them wouldn't be able to reload before he and his men were on them if they rode hard. But then to his dismay archers also appeared from behind the wall and fired quickly before ducking back down beneath the wall's protection. An arrow seemed to be coming directly towards him and time stood still. Before he could even pull on the chestnut's reins it struck the small burnished steel plate which protected the horse's head and glanced off.

The chestnut's momentum was disturbed both by the impact and the shock of the blow and it skittered sideways. Khurram fought frantically to regain control, and by pulling hard on the reins and leaning forward on the horse's neck he succeeded in jumping the crumbling mud wall, which at this point was less than three feet high. So too did most of his men, but at least two of their mounts landed on small dung middens piled behind the wall and their front legs shot from under them, causing their hindquarters to catch the wall and their riders to be catapulted over their heads, smashing into the ground.

Khurram aimed a swinging sword blow at an archer wearing a dark tunic who was preparing to draw back the string of his large double bow to fire again. Before he could do so the sharp sword caught him across the chest and he collapsed backwards, dropping his bow. Around Khurram several more of his men fell from the saddle, dead or wounded.

With the blood of battle pounding in his ears, Khurram pushed onwards into the village itself with two of his bodyguards and swerved around the side of a low shack. A small goat ran out from it under the front legs of one of the bodyguards' horses. The horse stumbled over the goat and the rider fell sideways on to the palm branches from which the roof of the shack was constructed. They collapsed under his weight and he disappeared from view.

Both Khurram's and the other bodyguards' horses were impeded and so once more lost momentum. Soon, however, Khurram had his chestnut moving again and within a few moments was in the single narrow main street of the village. Here his gaze was caught for a moment by a small white-painted shrine housing a red-daubed image of the many-armed Hindu goddess Kali, round whose neck hung a necklace of orange flowers. But then at the end of the street – partly camouflaged by the dappled shade thrown by the branches and leaves of a spreading banyan tree – Khurram saw a cannon with a man about to set light to the powder in the firing hole. Pulling as hard as he could on the reins, Khurram twisted his chestnut off the street into a gap between two small houses, disturbing some scrawny hens scratching and pecking at the dirt, which fluttered off squawking.

Almost immediately he heard the cannon fire and saw white smoke billow above the houses, followed by a thud and a scream. One of his riders had been hit. It wasn't the bodyguard immediately behind him – he too had managed to turn between the houses. Now, determined to surprise and attack the men manning the cannon before they could load and fire again, Khurram and the guard pushed their mounts quickly on through some pieces of spiny bush being used to pen livestock and picked their way round string charpoys and clay cooking pots behind houses from which the inhabitants had long since fled,

Coming to the back corner of the last house and edging his horse round it, Khurram saw the cannon under the banyan tree only a few yards away. Gunners stripped to the waist and sweating in the intense midday heat were struggling valiantly to ram bags of powder and shot down the barrel while three or four musketeers were firing from behind the protection of the tree's broad trunk up the main street towards his men to keep them back while the gunners reloaded. Without pausing to think and urging his chestnut on with hands and heels, Khurram charged towards the cannon, followed by his single bodyguard. On seeing them two of the three gunners turned and started to run, only to be skewered one after the other by the tip of the bodyguard's lance. The third bravely stood his ground and tried to knock Khurram from his saddle with the long ramrod. His unwieldy blow missed, and Khurram drew his sword and struck the man across his naked shoulder. The weapon sliced deep into flesh and sinew and the man collapsed over the cannon barrel, blood gushing from the wound.

Meanwhile, a musketeer had swung his weapon round to aim at Khurram but the musket barrel was long – nearly six feet – and the man nervous. It shook in his grip as he fired so the ball missed both Khurram and his mount, whistling harmlessly past his head. Khurram struck the musketeer's skull so hard with his sword that the impact almost jolted it from his hand and the man's skull split like a ripe watermelon, spewing blood and brain into the dust.

Suddenly Khurram was aware that some of Khusrau's

troops were fleeing, closely pursued by those of his own men who had followed him into the village. As he caught his breath he could still hear the sounds of heavy fighting coming from where Kamran Iqbal's men had attacked head-on. His eyes were stinging with the acrid smoke swirling everywhere. Sparks from either a cannon or muskets must have set the palm roofs of one or two of the houses alight. Now the strong breeze was blowing burning embers from one roof to another. Soon the whole village would be ablaze.

'Let's attack Khusrau's troops from the rear—' shouted Khurram to his men who were gathering around him, but he got no further as suddenly from the direction of the fight a group of horsemen burst from the entrance of a small lane halfway along the main street. Seeing Khurram's mounted men the leaders charged directly towards them, swords extended. As they did so Khurram noticed amid the smoke that in the centre of the group was a rider whose horse had a second set of reins which were being held by the horseman in front. It could only be his partially sighted half-brother.

Khurram kicked his chestnut towards the rider holding the leading reins. The man raised his sword in his free hand and parried Khurram's first sword stroke but could not evade the second, which almost severed his forearm just above the wrist. With blood spurting from the wound he turned away from the fight, dropping the leading reins as he went. Reacting quickly and instinctively Khurram bent and grabbed at the reins, just catching hold of them as they fell.

Jerking Khusrau's horse – a grey mare – away from the fight, Khurram shouted, 'It is I, Khurram. Khusrau, you must surrender. I have you in my custody.' His half-brother said nothing. 'Haven't enough men died on your behalf, not only now but in your other rebellions? Say something,' Khurram shouted again, even louder, just in case his first words had been drowned by the noise of battle and the crackling of the burning roofs. Khusrau's face remained almost impassive. Only one of his eyes seemed at all focused. The other stared blankly, apparently sightless. As a blazing frond from a palm roof was blown down close beside him, causing his mare to jerk up her head, Khusrau spoke.

'I yield.'

• ◆ •

'I've lived by the ancient code of our ancestors from the steppes: "throne or coffin". This is the third time I've bid for the throne and failed. Twice I've evaded the coffin while my brave followers did not. On the second occasion I gave up my sight. If it were not for the love of Jani my wife, I would have abandoned myself to despair. Now I am ready to die. Just allow me to dictate one final letter to her.'

Khusrau's delivery was a monotone as, only twenty minutes later, he stood arms lightly held by two guards before Khurram. His soldiers had obeyed his summons to surrender and were even now being searched and their weapons stacked up. As Khurram — his face streaked with smoke and his clothes and body still wet with the sweat of battle — looked at his half-brother it seemed to him that Khusrau had by a supreme act of will divorced himself from everything going on around him, resigned to whatever fate lay in store for him.

At the moment, unlike Khusrau, he could not be so detached. Elation at his victory and all that it meant for

392

realising his ambitions for the throne mingled with sorrow at the loss of so many of his men. Among the wounded was Kamran Iqbal. His left arm had been so badly smashed by a musket ball while he was rallying Khurram's men in the face of their first setbacks in their frontal assault on the village that the *hakims* had told Khurram that only immediate amputation of the limb at the elbow could save him. They had already begun sharpening their knives and placing the cauterising irons in the fire. Still worse was the condition of one of his young *qorchis*. Nearly the whole of a burning palm-thatched roof had been blown on to him as he lay on the ground already wounded by a sword thrust in the side. His screams of pain had been more animal than human when Khurram had visited him, forcing himself to look at the blackened face from which the skin hung in strips. The *hakims* had said that the only thing they could do was drip opium water into his blistered mouth to smooth his passage to Paradise. Pray God it was quick, Khurram thought.

Anger welled up in him as he looked at his impassive half-brother, the cause of all this suffering, and he drew back his hand to slap him. But then he stopped. What good would that do? He should not act in anger. 'You will be taken to the dungeons of Burhanpur. There you will await my decision. I will not decide your punishment or those of your officers in anger as our father once did.'

'I cannot promise not to be a threat to you. I know myself. While life remains within me so will ambition . . . I am ready to die,' Khusrau replied, still impassive, but after a few moments he asked in a more supplicatory tone, 'May Jani accompany me to Burhanpur?'

393

Khurram was about to deny the request when he remembered Arjumand and his feelings for her. His love for his own wife meant he could not deny his half-brother. 'Yes. However little you deserve her, I grant your request for her sake, not for yours.'

Chapter 25

The Sins of the Father

Lahore, January 1628

Mehrunissa was sitting deep in thought on a low velvet-covered divan in her apartments on the second floor of the palace overlooking the banks of the Ravi river. Beside her were the latest reports from the vassals converging on Lahore with their forces in answer to her summons. The summonses had of course been issued in the name of Shahriyar, who had been proclaimed emperor in Lahore's Friday mosque four months previously, and the replies were similarly addressed to him, but he took even less interest in them than his father would have done. At the recollection of Jahangir Mehrunissa felt the sorrow and grief which since his death had never entirely left her rise again. The depth and persistence of this emotion had surprised her until she came to realise how much his love had meant to her. Despite her pride in her independence she had depended on him just as he had depended on her. She had loved him as well as his power because of it.

Shahriyar was proving even weaker as a ruler than she had anticipated, surrendering himself completely to vanity and outward show. He spent most of his days either choosing ornaments and garments to adorn his admittedly handsome figure or hunting and indulging in frivolous entertainments with companions as empty headed as himself. He did not trouble at all with affairs of state. This should have been pleasing to Mehrunissa but was in fact less than satisfactory. When he sat in council with his advisers his ignorance of both government and military matters was so starkly and woefully obvious that it damaged adherents' trust and confidence in him. Either he did not pay sufficient attention to the briefings and suggestions that Mehrunissa provided to him, repeating them to him in the simplest way possible with Ladli's help, or what intellect he had deserted him under the nervous stress of being before his council.

Mehrunissa once more deeply regretted the restrictions her female sex placed upon her. If only she could attend the council meetings . . . but she knew she should not, must not, waste time in futile regrets or despair. Despite Khurram's defeat of Khusrau and his seemingly remorseless advance on Lahore, many of the leading nobles and rulers of vassal states were refusing to commit themselves to his side until they could be more certain of the outcome of the succession struggle. Indeed, if the letters from her supporters were to be believed, many more contingents would soon be joining her army here in Lahore. She had deployed the contents of the extensive treasuries of Lahore to provide substantial and immediate payments to those who had already joined her, with the promise of much more when Khurram was defeated. Although Lahore had no encircling walls, under her guidance Shahriyar's officers had done excellent work in fortifying the palace by the river, building palisades of mud and wood all round it and constructing emplacements for the large number of cannon of all sizes available to them. Food supplies were high, as were those of powder and other equipment necessary to withstand a siege. Provided she could restrain Shahriyar and his generals from sallying out to face Khurram on open ground they would stand a good chance of repulsing his forces when he first chose to make an assault and subsequently wearing them down before launching a decisive attack of their own. Her prime task would be to instil in Shahriyar, and through him his officers, sufficient confidence and determination to withstand a siege in the belief that they would triumph in the end. Fortunately, she possessed enough confidence and martial spirit for an army.

She realised also that her possession of Dara Shukoh and Aurangzeb gave her a further advantage. In one of his many rebellions against his half-brother the Emperor Humayun, Kamran had exposed Humayun's young son, the future Emperor Akbar, on the walls of Kabul during a battle to force Humayun to desist from his attack on the city, which had been about to succeed. She would not necessarily go that far – at least not until a time of direst emergency – but she knew the thought that she might would play on Khurram's mind, knowing as he did the story of Akbar even better than she. However, the children had already served another purpose – that of binding Shahriyar closer and destroying any chance of his attempting to conclude a separate peace deal. Using Ladli – who fortunately showed no sign of deviating from her absolute loyalty to her mother – as an intermediary, she had convinced Shahriyar that the two young princes were so charismatic and attractive that their presence around the court might detract from his own position, arousing memories among his courtiers of their father whom both closely resembled. She had also suggested that they might either try to escape or be subject to a rescue attempt. Consequently Shahriyar had been only too eager to order them to be closely confined in two small rooms in a distant part of the palace under guard twenty-four hours a day.

Bolstered by the knowledge of the strengths of her position, Mehrunissa began to ponder again some diplomatic initiatives she had in mind. Should she – or formally Shahriyar – send emissaries to bordering states offering territorial concessions if they would intervene on Shahriyar's behalf against Khurram? The Shah of Persia might be only too pleased to do so for the concession of Kandahar and surrounding lands. The sultans of the Deccan might well respond to an offer to restore some of their forfeited territories – they could soon be reconquered when her position was stronger – and their general Malik Ambar, still vigorous in his old age, might lead an army on their behalf. He and Khurram had unfinished business. Perhaps the Portuguese or even the English would send some of their sailors equipped with the deadly modern cannon from their ships in return for trading concessions. There were so many possibilities. Despite Shahriyar's shortcomings she would keep him on the throne. After all, she had ruled for Jahangir for years.

· ◆ ·

Khurram sat with Asaf Khan and Mahabat Khan around a low table in his scarlet command tent. Through the tent flaps, tied back with gold cords, he could see the Ravi river glinting in the evening sun and beyond it the Lahore palace, now snug within encircling palisades and fortifications. He looked across at Mahabat Khan sitting relaxed and sipping a concoction of herbs infused in water he had said was popular as a restorative in his native Persia. The first meetings between the two men had been stiff and formal, not to say mutually suspicious, as might have been expected between commanders who had led opposing forces for many years. Mahabat Khan had shown himself duly respectful and kept in the background until, helped by the emollient presence of Asaf Khan who had joined up with Mahabat Khan some time before the rendezvous with Khurram, the atmosphere had relaxed. Now the two were able to discuss professional matters without inhibitions, even quoting examples from their time as adversaries when advocating particular strategies. That was just as well, thought Khurram. He had been rash in his assault on Khusrau's forces and only his men's courage had prevented his defeat. The forces deployed by Mehrunissa and Shahriyar in Lahore were much stronger and their skilfully constructed defences far superior to those thrown up in haste by Khusrau. He must restrain his eagerness and plan carefully, leaving as little as possible to chance.

'Mahabat Khan, we've previously agreed that a frontal attack would be too costly, involving as it would a river crossing under fire, but where do you advise that we go over the Ravi?'

'I suggest we make two crossings, one upstream and one downstream of Lahore so that we can attack the city from both sides at once. We've already assembled sufficient boats and wood planking to be able to construct two bridges.'

'Your idea is a good one, Mahabat Khan, but how quickly can we put it into action?'

'Overnight.'

'You mean if I gave the order now we could attack in the morning?'

'Yes. Our men are well drilled and the supplies and equipment we need are already being unloaded from the baggage wagons.'

'Well then, let tomorrow be the day. If I command the downstream crossing, will you command the upstream?'

'Of course.'

'But Khurram, should you hazard yourself by leading one of the assault forces? Wouldn't you be better here taking overall command and supervising our artillery?' Asaf Khan interrupted.

'In normal circumstances you might be right, but these aren't normal times. I'm a father as well as emperor. Mehrunissa and Shahriyar hold two of my sons. I want to reach them as soon as possible myself. I trust you completely to command the artillerymen, making sure that they concentrate their fire on the palisades and gun emplacements and avoid anywhere that Shahriyar might be holding my sons – your grandsons.'

• ◆ •

Early the following morning Khurram stood on the banks of the Ravi river two and a half miles downstream of Lahore as parties of his men began to clamber into some of a small flotilla of boats they had commandeered from local fishermen with promises of large rewards. Quietly the soldiers began to lower the oars into the water and to raise the single patched and darned cotton sail with which most of the vessels were equipped. The mission he had given the men was first to cross the river and secure a landing site against any resistance from Shahriyar's forces and then to tow a section of the partly constructed bridge across and anchor it securely to the far bank ready to be joined up to the portion already extending from the bank beneath him. His men had encountered no opposition during the night as they had moved down the river and begun work on the initial construction of the boat bridge. Nor as the sun had risen – an orange ball in the misty morning sky – had there been any sign of Shahriyar's men on the far bank among the low mud hills dipping down to the shore. However, this did not mean they might not be lurking undercover waiting to ambush the landing party. The monsoon had been a poor one, so at least the level of the river was low for the time of year and it was no more than two hundred feet or so wide.

As Khurram watched, the first of the boats began to push off from the bank, the rowers bending their backs to the oars. Each had two or three musketeers lying in the bow, their long-barrelled weapons loaded and levelled at the opposite shore. Despite the effects of the current, which was still quite strong, after a couple of minutes the first boat – one of the larger vessels with a red-painted hull – was nosing ashore still having not met any opposition. Some of the soldiers were balancing on the side, ready to jump into the shallows to wade ashore, when Khurram heard several musket shots. One of the men crouched on the side of the boat fell forward with a splash into the water, to be followed by three others from the boats behind.

Just as Khurram had suspected, the shots came from behind one of the mud hills about a hundred feet from the shoreline. They were followed by a volley of arrows but, his mind working quickly, Khurram was relieved to see that there were no more than about thirty of them. Clearly no large enemy force lurked on the opposite bank. His own men were now running as fast as they could, swords in hand and legs pumping, up the exposed shore towards the mud hills. When they had covered nearly three quarters of the distance more musket shots crackled out in a ragged volley from behind the protection of the hillocks and several of Khurram's soldiers collapsed including the foremost – a green-clad giant of a man brandishing a curved scimitar. However, he was soon back on his feet resuming his charge, but before he or anyone else could reach the top of the mud hills Khurram saw a group of horsemen – perhaps forty strong – emerge from behind the hills and ride hard for Lahore. They had obviously been an outlying picket and had not received reinforcements even if they had requested them.

One of the hindmost riders fell, throwing up his arms and pitching from the saddle, presumably hit by a musket ball. Another horse – a chestnut – crumpled, throwing its rider, but the rest disappeared unscathed behind a clump of scrubby trees. Khurram knew that even if she were not already aware of it Mehrunissa would soon be alerted that his men had crossed the river. 'Hurry,' he shouted to one of his officers. 'Begin towing the sections of boat bridge across to the far shore. Ready our troops to cross. There is no time to lose.'

• ◆ •

Two hours later, Khurram was on the far side of the river. His men had quickly completed the bridge. Although parts of it had had to be kept steady by oarsmen rowing against the current in small boats attached to it by strong taut hemp ropes, it had served its purpose. Even if the bridge snapped now most of his cavalry, many of his war elephants and even some of his small cannon were already across – enough to begin the assault on the fortifications around the Lahore palace.

Drawing around him his officers, all like him accoutred for battle, Khurram briefly addressed them. 'Know this. Today is the most crucial day in my life. By its close with your help I will have secured the imperial throne and rescued my beloved sons or I will have perished in the attempt. But I know that with your support I will triumph. When I do, I will present all of you with magnificent rewards from the treasuries of Lahore and the forfeited lands of my usurping half-brothers' supporters.

'Remember, our plan is simple. As soon as we hear the cannon commanded by Asaf Khan open fire across the Ravi river on the palisades, we and Mahabat Khan's men who messengers tell us have also crossed the river safely upstream will simultaneously storm the palisades from opposite directions.'

Only a few minutes later, Khurram heard the crash and boom of Asaf Khan's cannon. Preceded by four of his body-guard all carrying large dark green banners and four trumpeters sounding their long brass instruments, he pushed his black horse forward at the head of his men. Soon he was trotting quickly along the exposed cracked mud of the riverbank. His heart was beating even faster than it usually did when he headed into battle and he was finding it more difficult to focus entirely on the fighting ahead. His mind was constantly turning to where he might find his sons in the palace if he succeeded in gaining entry to it.

Knowing that he must concentrate on the present and not get ahead of himself if he was to safeguard himself and his men and achieve his objective of saving his sons, he reined in a little. Then he peered through the smoke billowing from the cannonading and counter-cannonading between Asaf Khan's gunners and those of Shahriyar. The palace within its palisades was by now no more than half a mile ahead. However, Shahriyar's men seemed to have demolished most of the houses and other buildings between his present position and the palisades to give themselves a clearer field of fire. The piles of rubble from the destroyed buildings which had not been removed would slow down his horsemen and many of them would be lost before they even reached the fortifications, he thought with dismay. But if they dismounted and went forward on foot for the last eight hundred yards the heaps of rubble would provide cover.

Wheeling his horse, he gave the order to dismount to the leading squadrons of his men. Leaving one man in every six to tether the horses, he led the remainder forward, scuttling bent double from the cover of one pile of bricks and rubble to the next. Before they had covered even a tenth of the distance Shahriyar's men saw them and began to direct cannon and musket fire towards them. Khurram flung himself down behind the remains of a wall. As he did so he saw one of the men sheltering behind some rubble near him suddenly slump, presumably hit by a ricochet since he seemed to be protected fully from the front. Then, waving his gauntleted hand for his men to follow him, which they did bravely, Khurram was up and running forward again, dodging from one rubble heap to another and zigzagging a little as he did so to put his opponents off their aim.

By the time he paused again two minutes later, sweating and gasping for breath behind the stump of a neem tree which had been felled by cannon fire, he had covered another six hundred yards or so, arrows as well as musket balls hissing past him. Feeling what he thought was a trickle of sweat running down his left cheek he dabbed at it with his cream face cloth only to discover the cloth stained with blood. Removing his gauntlet he explored his face to find a wound beside his left ear, but it seemed little more than a graze, perhaps caused by a flying chip of masonry dislodged by either a cannon or a musket ball. Peering round the tree stump he saw that there was very little cover over the remaining distance to the palisades, which were about four feet high but looked in places to have been quite badly damaged by Asaf Khan's cannon fire from across the Ravi river.

After waiting no more than a few minutes to allow his men to gather in strength around him, Khurram shouted orders to the trumpeters to send the prearranged signal to Asaf Khan that they were about to attack the palisades and so to keep his cannon fire away from the area. Next he commanded the banner-bearers to raise their large green standards. Then he stood and surrounded by his bodyguard charged once more head down towards the palisades. Musket balls again whistled past him and an arrow struck his breast-plate and bounced off. Then, a moment later, he tripped over a single mud brick lying almost invisible on the bank and nearly went sprawling. Quickly recovering himself, he was almost immediately up to the palisade. Levering himself up by his muscular arms he'd soon straddled it and was jumping down on the other side.

Landing lightly on his feet he was immediately confronted by a tall musketeer. Having fired his weapon he reversed it and swung it by its barrel at Khurram, who swayed back on his heels out of the way before thrusting his sword deep into the man's ample stomach. As he wrenched his bloodied weapon free from the body there was an audible release of gas. Then Khurram saw another man raising his scimitar above his head to attack him. Attempting to sway back again Khurram slipped, twisting his ankle, and fell sideways. As he did so his opponent loomed over him, preparing to strike, so as soon as he hit the ground he rolled aside. The man's sword thudded into the earth beside his head. Khurram cut at his opponent's legs with his own sword and the man too fell. Struggling quickly to his knees, Khurram brought the sword down with all the force of which he was capable into his opponent's throat as he lay on the ground. Blood gushed for a moment, then the man lay still for ever.

Scrambling to his feet and glancing about him, Khurram saw that the palisades were now in his men's hands and that everywhere their opponents were breaking off the fight and rushing back towards the protection of the palace itself. Then he saw green Moghul banners emerging through the smoke in front of him. Mahabat Khan's Rajputs had breached the palisades from the other direction. 'Charge for the main gate of the palace,' Khurram shouted, his voice hoarse with excitement as well as smoke, and together with his men he ran forward as fast as his painful twisted ankle would allow, all the time expecting to come under attack from musketeers and archers. To his surprise, however, no arrows or musket balls came. Shahriyar's forces seemed to be melting away. Had they lost heart, or were they retreating as part of some pre-arranged plan to an inner stronghold or ambush position?

Running on, Khurram found the ground littered with discarded swords and muskets. He passed overturned wagons and other defensive positions, some equipped with cannon from which gunners as well as musketeers could have wrought deadly havoc, but which had all been abandoned without a shot. Shahriyar's men really were fleeing. Khurram was soon approaching the high, metal-studded wooden gates of the palace, by now open and seemingly undefended. Victory was his, he thought elatedly. Now to find his sons. But suddenly the bodyguard running beside him swerved in front of him to avoid a rock and a moment later sprawled forward on the ground. Looking down as he in turn swerved to avoid the man's body, Khurram saw he had been hit by a musket ball in the forehead. But he had no time to think further about it before he was inside the gatehouse.

◆

Mehrunissa stood back from the casement of her apartment on the second floor of the palace and put down her musket, the one with the mother of pearl-inlaid butt with which she had killed so many tigers. Her aim even at that distance had been good. Why had the bodyguard crossed in front of Khurram? He couldn't have seen her and been protecting the prince. Then her mind, active as ever, began to race through her options now that the palace had fallen, as it clearly had. Soon Khurram and his men would be ransacking the rooms searching for his sons, for herself and for Shahriyar.

Where was Shahriyar? He hadn't led the troops in person, nor was he with Ladli who she knew was in the next room with her child. She could rely on none of them but must depend as before on her own resources alone. She had known that her musket shot had been a long shot in more than one sense. Even if she had succeeded in killing Khurram, it was unlikely that his men would have surrendered. Rather – at the behest of her brother and Arjumand – they would have proclaimed Dara Shukoh as emperor. So should she die fighting, reloading her musket and killing the first of her opponents as they came through the door of her apartments? No. She had survived desperate times since her birth. She was not ready to die yet. A clear, calm and subtle mind could manipulate and ameliorate even the worst circumstances. For once her status as a 'mere woman' would help her. She knew what she must do . . .

• ◆ •

Followed by some of his bodyguards, Khurram quickly ascended the two flights of white marble stairs leading to the second floor of the palace where, after some moments' thought amid the chaos of the gatehouse, he had remembered the imperial quarters were. He began to fling open the ivory-inlaid doors, lining a corridor only dimly lit by a single casement at one end, searching for his sons. Where were they? Had Mehrunissa and Shahriyar spirited them away to act as hostages for their own safe passage? Even worse, had they killed them in sour revenge for his success? He wouldn't put it past Mehrunissa, he thought, involuntarily clenching his hand tighter around his sword hilt.

The first room he went into was entirely empty and the

only movement was that of the muslin curtains blowing in the breeze through the casement. The second was empty too and so was the third, although an overturned silver goblet and a small pool of spilled sherbet suggested that an occupant had recently left in a hurry. As he emerged from that room sword in hand another door opened further along the corridor and a straight-backed dark-clad female figure emerged, a cream shawl shrouding her face. She began to walk steadily towards him, head held high. Almost instantly Khurram realised from the posture and self-possession the form displayed that it was Mehrunissa. Before he could give the order to seize her she pulled back her shawl and flung herself on to the floor twelve feet from him.

'I yield, Khurram. The prize of the throne is yours. Do with me as you will,' she said, but then added, 'but first you will want to know where Dara Shukoh and Aurangzeb are, won't you?'

Khurram started. Was Mehrunissa going to surrender his sons, the only possible bargaining counter she had, without seeking some concessions in return?

'Yes, yes. Where are they?'

'Confined by Shahriyar to two small rooms in the basement of the circular sandstone tower in the east wing of the palace. They were under twenty-four-hour guard, although judging by the courage shown by Shahriyar and his men alike the guards will by now have taken to their heels to save themselves. Don't worry. Your sons are well, even if a little thin and pale from the lack of light and exercise.'

'You're not lying, are you?' Khurram shouted, caught between hope and fear. This all seemed too easy. Was it one of Mehrunissa's tricks – some kind of trap?

'Why should I lie? The game is over. You are the victor. What possible benefit could I gain from rousing your anger? Go to them now.'

'Confine this woman to the *haram* quarters. I will deal with her later,' Khurram ordered as he ran to retrace his steps down the stairs, back through the gatehouse and into the sunlit courtyard. There he saw some of Shahriyar's soldiers squatting arms tied behind their backs against one of the walls while his own men were searching others and stacking up captured weapons.

Yes, there was the circular tower in the east wing and, yes, there seemed to be stairs leading down below ground level to a basement. Khurram ran over to it and descended the stairs two at a time, but his foot slipped on one of the moss-covered bottom steps and he turned his ankle once more. Just saving himself from falling, he looked round to see a low archway leading into a dark, damp, musty-smelling passage. Followed by some of his bodyguards he half ran, half limped into it. It was a dead end, but on either side was a single door. Each door had a small iron grille cut into the top and each was secured by an iron chain.

'Dara and Aurangzeb,' Khurram shouted, 'are you in there?'

There was no reply. Fearing the worst, he forced himself to look through the grille in the right-hand door. Aurangzeb was lying on a string charpoy of the type found in the houses of poor villagers, gagged with a piece of dirty brown cloth and his hands manacled to the wall. Beneath the charpoy was a brass bowl brimming with urine and faeces next to a clay plate on which was a piece of half-eaten chapatti. Relief that his sons were alive mingled with anger that anyone should have treated them in this way as Khurram turned to the other grille and saw Dara Shukoh similarly manacled and gagged.

'Force these doors open,' he shouted to the bodyguards who had followed him. One – a burly Rajput – began to throw himself from one door to the other but to no great effect. Then another produced a large metal rod and inserted it into the chain securing Dara Shukoh's cell and with an immense grunt of effort wrenched one of the links free. As the door creaked open Khurram pushed past the man into the fetid room. Quickly he began with fumbling fingers to untie the gag while his guards got to work on the manacles. 'Dara Shukoh, you're safe,' he said, trying to hold back the welling tears as he finally succeeded in unknotting the cloth. At the same time, his hands freed, Dara Shukoh – his whole body quivering with emotion – threw his arms round his father's neck. Moments later Aurangzeb, released by more of the guards, rushed into his brother's cell and embraced them both. Khurram could not hold back the tears of joy and relief any longer. But despite their distorting effect he could still see that his sons were hollow eyed and much thinner than they should have been.

After a few minutes during which none of the three could speak Khurram asked, 'How long have you been kept like this?'

'Fourteen days, Father,' said Dara Shukoh, his voice still husky and dry from the gag.

'That is since we've been in these cells with just one hand manacled to the wall. It's only been in the last few hours that both our hands have been manacled and we've been gagged,' put in Aurangzeb.

'Who gave the order for you to be imprisoned?'

'When we were first brought here one of the guards told me it was Shahriyar,' said Dara Shukoh. 'The guard was gentle with me and put soft cloth round my wrist before he put the manacle on. Please be merciful to him.'

'I'll make sure he isn't punished too severely. Did he say why Shahriyar was imprisoning you?'

'To prevent us from escaping or being rescued so he could use us as hostages,' said Dara Shukoh, and then added after a moment, 'Father, I think Shahriyar came down here to get us a little while ago. The door rattled as if someone was trying to release the chain and I heard a voice I think was his shouting for the guards. But they didn't come and he could find no way of opening the doors.'

'That was probably fortunate. There's no knowing what panic and fear might have induced him to do,' said Khurram, his anger increasingly turning towards Shahriyar rather than Mehrunissa. She at least had had the courage to confront him and the good sense both to know when she had lost and to reveal his sons' whereabouts. Disengaging himself from his boys' embrace, he said, 'Let's get you into the courtyard, into the sun. Afterwards the two of you can wash and eat while I search for Shahriyar.'

Quickly they left the damp basement rooms and climbed the stairs into the light, both the boys shading their eyes against the glare of the sun they had not seen for a fortnight.

Only a minute or two after they emerged, Khurram saw a female figure being pushed roughly into the courtyard from the direction of the *haram*. His first reaction was to wonder what further outrage Mehrunissa had committed despite her seeming acquiescence in her defeat when she had surrendered herself to him. However, he soon realised that this woman was taller even than Mehrunissa, and broader shouldered. She was using all her strength to resist the guards dragging her towards Khurram, refusing to move her feet and struggling vigorously. When she came closer Khurram saw that her chin was covered with a stubble unknown to even the most hirsute of women. It was a man in woman's clothing – Shahriyar, his handsome features marred by a purple swelling around his right eye, which looked almost closed. Clearly he had not been captured without a struggle.

'Where did you find him?' Khurram asked one of the guards holding on to Shahriyar, who by now had dropped to his knees, hands clasped in supplication.

'We searched the *haram* after confining the Empress Mehrunissa, her daughter Ladli and Ladli's child. We found no one who did not have the right to be there until we came to one of the last and smallest rooms in the complex. I entered it. It was where the soiled linen and dirty garments were collected prior to washing. All seemed to be in order, but when I turned to leave, a small movement in a large pile of white washing near the door caught my eye, small enough even to have been a mouse, but I decided to investigate. I'm glad I did. When I kicked the pile, my foot thudded into flesh and a woman leapt up and tried to escape, scratching at my face as she went. I grabbed her by the shoulder and threw her on her back on to the pile of washing and dropped to my knees, straddling her so she could not escape. "Who are you? Why are you trying to escape?" I shouted. "I fear you're going to rape me. I'm a virgin and don't want to be the victim of a rough warrior like you,"

413

she said in a high voice. Even though it sounded unlike any woman I'd ever heard, I started to get up but as I did so she kneed me in the groin. When I doubled up in pain she tried to push me aside but I held on to her. Next she bit my arm. That was when her veil flapped loose and I saw she was a man and I punched her hard. She didn't struggle any more.'

'You did well,' said Khurram. Turning to Shahriyar, he demanded, 'And you, Shahriyar, what have you to say for yourself?'

'Spare me,' his half-brother pleaded, his eyes fixed imploringly on Khurram.

'Why should I after what you did to my sons? How dare you treat innocent imperial princes like common criminals?'

'It wasn't me. I was only—'

'Only what?'

'Following Mehrunissa's wishes.'

'Let's see what she has to say about that. Bring the empress here,' Khurram ordered one of the guards. Minutes later she stood before him, still looking calm and composed. 'This creature says he was only obeying your orders.'

'Well, let him produce them. What kind of man can so forget himself as to hide behind the skirts of a woman? Did I attend the council meetings? Did I order your sons to be manacled? Ask their guards — if you can find them.'

A good point, thought Khurram, remembering what his sons had told him. 'Well, Shahriyar, answer this charge.'

'But I knew it was what she wanted . . . that my actions would please her and Ladli. Mehrunissa rejoiced in your downfall and disgrace. She was behind it, everyone knows that.'

'Mehrunissa, is this true?'

'I was no friend to you for many years. Of course I admit it. But I did not act out of petty spite or personal animosity. We all look to ourselves first. I acted in my own interest . . . that in doing so I damaged yours and Arjumand's was a side-effect not the object. Yes, I may be responsible for much of your suffering and yes I am ready to die for it . . . but some of the petty, vicious refinements in the treatment of your sons were not mine, you should know that.'

That certainly was true, thought Khurram. Dara Shukoh had told him in the courtyard that the friendly guard had said that Shahriyar had personally instructed him that the food for their cells should be not from the imperial kitchens but water and old chapattis and that their divans should be exchanged for the charpoys. Anger welled within him again as he demanded, 'Is what Mehrunissa said true?' Shahriyar said nothing. 'You deserve to die,' Khurram told him, and then turning to Mehrunissa asked, 'Have you anything to say as to why he should not?'

Mehrunissa steeled herself as she had when she had stood before Jahangir all those years ago beside her bleeding, tortured conspirator of a brother. She could do nothing for Shahriyar. To give herself and Ladli and her granddaughter a chance he was a necessary sacrifice.

'For what the advice of a woman is worth, his deeds merit death. To keep him alive would only be to preserve a threat to your throne. Remember the perils of the leniency shown by your ancestors. Think of Kamran and Humayun, Khusrau and your father. Once rebels taste power they want it again. You, your beloved Arjumand and your children will sleep safer with Shahriyar gone. You know that deep within you. You want Shahriyar dead, and Khusrau too. I see that . . . have you the courage to recognise it? Do what the necessity of

415

survival demands. Use my words to salve your conscience if you are so weak as to need to do so. Let a woman share the blame. Why not?'

Mehrunissa's words resonated in Khurram's head. Yes, even if in his heart he knew he would have acted little differently to his half-brothers in bidding for their father's vacant throne, he would be glad if they were dead and their threat gone for ever. And yes, he was weak enough to wish the decision could be taken out of his hands so that he need not face up to the depths of his selfishness . . . But if he were to be an emperor he must accept the burden of responsibility. After some time during which no one spoke, he said, 'Shahriyar, you will die now — not just because your crimes merit it but for the sake of the dynasty and myself and my sons. Guards, take him away. Execute him by sword stroke. Do it cleanly and quickly.'

Shahriyar seemed to faint and the guards reached down and began to drag him away. Halfway across the courtyard he began to scream, bucking and kicking in their grip. For some reason, perhaps to demonstrate his resolve and responsibility for what was happening, Khurram forced himself to watch until the guards and his struggling half-brother disappeared from sight. Then he turned to Mehrunissa. She was still looking steadily and defiantly at him, eyes focused and lips firmly closed. But as he scrutinised her, Khurram began to realise she was an old woman. There were bags under her eyes and her dark irises were fading round their edges. Fine hairs covered her upper lip and lines radiated around her mouth. Her jawline was sagging. She was an old widow from whom power was ebbing as completely as her looks, however much she might still wish to dominate events. Unlike Shahriyar she seemed unafraid to die. Perhaps a greater punishment would be to ignore her. Let her see how little she would count for any more.

'As for you, Mehrunissa, you will live in the seclusion your grief as an imperial widow demands. I will find some distant place in which you may meditate on your loss and your sins and prayerfully await divine judgement untroubled by the affairs of a world that will soon forget you.'

Mehrunissa said nothing as she was led away. Once again she had what she wanted. She would live. However, as the reality of her fate began to sink in she started to wonder would she have been better to die now rather than to fade into obscurity. Death was inevitable. Why had she not brought it on now as she knew she could have done? Had her courage failed her for once? It was a question that would continue to haunt her.

· ◆ ·

That night, sitting in the imperial quarters listening to the sounds of his men's exuberant feasting, Khurram penned two letters by candlelight. The first was to Arjumand, long and full of love and the news of the safety of their sons and how he had secured the throne. It summoned her to meet him outside Agra with their remaining children as soon as she could in preparation for his coronation in his capital. The second was much shorter and more sombre and addressed to the Governor of Burhanpur.

· ◆ ·

At the sound of a fanfare of trumpets Khurram, quickly followed by Dara Shukoh and Aurangzeb, ducked out of the scarlet tent in his camp at the village of Sikandra, five miles outside Agra. Close to the tomb of his beloved grandfather Akbar – the soaring sandstone gateway was visible through the neem trees – Sikandra had seemed to Khurram a fitting place to halt before his triumphal entry into Agra. This was no campaign camp, with austere lines of soldiers' tents and run with military discipline, but a vast tented city where the celebrations of his triumph had already begun. Banners of Moghul green fluttered from the roofs of the tents of his nobles and commanders, grouped around his own tent and spreading in all directions. Every night since his arrival here from Lahore two weeks ago had seen lavish feasting and entertainments, paid for from the coffers of the Agra treasuries to which he now had the keys. Every day the numbers in his camp had been swelling as vassal rulers arrived in answer to the summons of the Moghul emperor-in-waiting.

And at last the person whose arrival he had been anticipating above all others was approaching. He could see, glinting in the midday sun, Arjumand's silver, emerald-encrusted howdah swaying atop the richly caparisoned elephant he had sent to carry her the final miles of her journey. Ahead of her rode some of Mahabat Khan's Rajput horsemen and behind he could make out the elephant on which his four other children would be travelling, including the new son, Murad Bakhsh, he hadn't yet seen. At the thought that at last his family would be together again, Khurram felt a surge of happiness greater even than when he contemplated the moment he would mount the Moghul throne. He smiled at Dara Shukoh and Aurangzeb, dressed in coats and turbans of silver cloth in readiness for this moment. 'It's your mother. She's coming,' he said softly.

He led the boys to a tall tent nearly twenty feet high at its apex that had been erected in front of the *haram* tents in readiness for the arrival of Arjumand's elephant. Khurram had to force himself to stay still, standing between his sons with a hand on each of their shoulders, as her elephant approached, the two *mahouts* perched behind its gold-painted ears guiding it skilfully with their metal rods towards the great tent. As soon as the elephant had entered, followed by Khurram and his sons, attendants pulled the curtains back in place. Khurram waited while the *mahouts* brought the great beast to its knees and sliding from its neck swiftly positioned the dismounting block of gilded wood that had been placed ready. Then, touching their hands to their breasts, they quickly left the tent.

Heart beating fast, Khurram mounted the steps of the block and slowly drew back the pearl-sewn, green silk curtains. Words were impossible as he looked into Arjumand's eyes. Leaning into the howdah, he took her in his arms and kissed her warm lips. 'I've been waiting for this moment for so long . . . sometimes it seemed impossible that it would ever come. But there are two here who have been waiting even longer than me,' he whispered as at last he released her. He opened the howdah's silver door and held her henna-tipped hand as together they stepped down. Tears were already running down Arjumand's cheeks as she looked about her for her sons. Then, in the soft light of the many oil lamps with which the tent was lit, she saw Dara Shukoh and Aurangzeb, looking hesitant, shy even . . . Smiling through her tears, she held out her arms to them, and they ran to her.

◆

Three nights later, as they lay side by side after making love, Arjumand sat up. Pushing back a lock of his dark hair she looked for a moment into Khurram's eyes. 'May I ask you a question?'

'Of course.'

'As we were travelling towards Sikandra, one of my attendants told me something I found difficult to believe – a story she had got from a messenger just arrived from Burhanpur. I tried to put it from my mind but could not.'

'What was it?' Something in Arjumand's tone made Khurram sit up as well.

'That one morning his attendants found Khusrau dead on his bed in the apartments where you had imprisoned him.'

Khurram said nothing for a moment. Then: 'It is true. My half-brother is dead,' he said quietly.

'But the story is that he was smothered on your orders.'

Khurram was again silent. The second letter – the one he had despatched to the Governor of Burhanpur – had been an order to kill Khusrau as painlessly as possible. He had written with a heavy heart but convinced he was acting out of expediency and in the best interests of his family. But later, as he waited for news that his wishes had been carried out, he had begun to wonder how it would feel to be Khusrau hearing the door to his chamber unexpectedly open . . . turning his partially sighted gaze towards it . . . wondering who his visitors were . . . perhaps hoping that it was his wife Jani. At what stage would his half-brother realise that the opening doors brought not the comfort of a loving wife but assassins? How would Khusrau die? His only orders had been that it should be painless. Would it be a quick dagger thrust to the heart or the clean sweep of a sword blade? A cup of poison forced through resisting lips or suffocation with a pillow?

420

However, he had realised that he could not afford to allow sentiment to master necessity and to think like this. He must think of Khusrau as a past and potential rebel – not as a living, feeling human being. But later, when the news of Khusrau's smothering had reached him, a new concern had grown in his mind. How much had he been influenced by Mehrunissa's words as she stood before him with Shahriyar? Had she played his emotions when they were heightened by his victory and his reunion with his sons and manipulated him into doing something he might regret for ever, just as she had manipulated his father? No, he had again convinced himself. He and he alone had made the fateful decision and it had been justified.

'I cannot lie to you. It is true. But I acted to protect ourselves and our children.' Khurram paused before forcing himself to continue. 'And there is more . . . news that reached me only yesterday. After completing the funeral arrangements for Khusrau, Jani went to her rooms and killed herself – it is said by swallowing a burning coal from the brazier heating her room against the winter chill.'

Tears appeared in Arjumand's eyes and she began to shake. 'How could you, Khurram? What a horrible way to die. I can almost feel the coal burning and scorching my throat, eating my lungs. What terrible, terrible pain she must have endured in those last moments.'

Jani's death – in particular the manner of it – had appalled him too when he had first heard of it, but all he said was, 'I did not order her death.'

'But it was a consequence of your order to execute Khusrau . . . Jani loved him as much as I love you. To take one's life is a sin, I know, and I pray to God that if you died

I would have the courage to live on for our children's sake, but I can understand how grief overcame her.'

Khurram looked at Arjumand's troubled face. What she had said was true. His actions had caused Jani's death. But whatever doubts he might feel – whatever guilt – he must put them behind him and be strong. 'I did it for our children. They are our future – the future of the dynasty,' he said, dismissing from his mind the thought that he had done it to make his own life and rule easier. But perhaps those motives in reality had coalesced. Few men – not even an emperor – had the cool courage to peer unflinching into their minds and motives, preferring to deceive themselves with specious justifications for their actions.

'I pray Khusrau and especially Jani will rest in Paradise,' said Arjumand, 'and I pray too God will forgive you and exact no punishment on you or our children.'

'I pray so too,' said Khurram. He had never meant anything more, nor since his marriage felt so alone. This was what his father and grandfather had told him about the loneliness of power. It would never leave him.

Chapter 26

The Peacock Throne

Agra, 14 February 1628

The great sandstone gateway of the Agra fort – his fort – rose in front of Khurram as his elephant made its stately progress up the flower-strewn ramp at the head of the ceremonial procession. He had chosen the date of his entry into Agra with care – according to the solar calendar it was the 72nd anniversary of the proclamation of his grandfather Akbar's reign. Rising before dawn he had walked through the drifting early morning mist to Akbar's tomb where, as the peacocks fluttered down from their night-time roosts in the surrounding gardens, he had pressed his lips to the cold stone of his sarcophagus. 'I will be a worthy emperor,' he had whispered.

But today was also the 145th anniversary of the birth of Babur whose ambition and daring had first won Hindustan for the Moghuls. Babur's eagled-hilted sword Alamgir now hung from his waist. How many battles Alamgir must have

423

seen on its long journey from beyond the Oxus river into Hindustan . . . The eagle's ruby eyes glittered in the sun. Glancing at his right hand, Khurram smiled with satisfaction at the sight of something that had belonged to an even earlier ancestor – the heavy gold ring engraved with the image of a spitting tiger that had once been Timur's. He, Khurram, was the tenth ruler in direct descent from that great warrior whose empire had once stretched from the Mediterranean in the west to the borders of China in the east, and the conjunction of the planets at his own birth had been the same as at Timur's, much to Akbar's delight. At this moment Khurram felt as if not only his subjects but the spectral figures of his ancestors were there watching him, the thirty-six-year-old Moghul emperor, take upon his broad shoulders the hopes and ambitions of their dynasty.

As Khurram's elephant passed into the purple shadows beneath the main gatehouse kettledrums boomed in salute. For a moment Khurram closed his eyes, savouring the moment, the culmination of his wishes and ambitions. But then a darkness all of his own passed over him, driving out the euphoria. Despite the heat of the day and the weight of his diamond-encrusted green brocade tunic, he shivered as he thought of the anonymous note pinned by a steel dagger to the ground close to his command tent that he had found on his return from his grandfather's tomb. Its content had been brief: *Surely a throne seized in so much blood will be ill omened?*

How had the note got there beneath the noses of his guards? Had it been written by someone he thought of as a friend but who was not – someone whose presence close to his tent wouldn't have attracted attention? Or had it been left by a stranger who had infiltrated the heart of his camp? With the preparations for the triumphal march into Agra under way since well before dawn and with the wispy white mist to shroud them perhaps it wouldn't have been so difficult.

As he had flung the note into a brazier of burning charcoals and watched it consumed in a clear orange flame, Mehrunissa's high-cheekboned face, lips curved in an ironic smile, had floated for a moment before him. He could imagine her writing such a note. Had she really found it possible from the seclusion of her quarters in Lahore to attempt to disturb his peace of mind on what should have been the greatest day of his life? If so she had succeeded. Whoever was responsible, the note had shaken him, but he had tried to push the message from his mind. He hadn't even mentioned it to Arjumand whose parting kiss in the *haram* tents that morning had sent the same erotic shiver through him that it had in all the years of their marriage. It never failed to arouse him and had for a while banished any bleak thoughts.

But now as his elephant emerged back into the sunlight, bearing him onwards towards the throne he had desired for so long, they had returned. Why? Because he felt guilty? No. The deaths of Shahriyar and Khusrau had been necessary, hadn't they? Wasn't a little blood shed at the beginning of the reign better than a lot shed later because he had not had the courage to act? Wouldn't the benefits from the deaths outweigh any sin in them? Yes, he reiterated to himself. With these deaths he had eliminated the potential rivals to the throne and protected himself and his family.

Enough, Khurram told himself. He had done what he

had to do and the past was just that – the past. All that mattered was the present and the future and he had secured both by his actions. Trying to pull himself together, he glanced round at the vast procession following him. The elephant bearing his four sons, the imperial princes, beneath a green silk canopy and the smaller one carrying Arjumand and their two daughters in a howdah enclosed by draperies of cloth of silver into which gold mesh grilles had been inset so that they could see out were following immediately behind. Next, mounted on a white stallion, rode Arjumand's father Asaf Khan and seated on a black stallion with a jewelled saddle-cloth and graciously acknowledging the crowds was Mahabat Khan, now his *khan-i-khanan*, commander-in-chief. Then came the imperial bodyguards followed by cavalrymen riding four abreast – many of them scarlet-turbaned Rajputs – and finally musketmen and archers, all of them magnificently dressed in Moghul green, representatives of the great army that was now his to command.

The sight restored Khurram's confidence. Attendants were running along the battlements of the fort above, showering spectators with gold and silver coins – new minted to mark the start of his reign – and semi-precious stones – amethysts, cat's eyes, topazes. Other servants were flinging stars and moons fashioned from thin-beaten silver and gold. It was as if the heavens were raining riches upon the earth – Moghul riches. He was master of it all and should be glorying in his power and wealth. He would not allow a few malicious words to unsettle him.

Passing through a second great gate Khurram saw before him the wide flower-filled courtyard with its bubbling fountains constructed by Akbar and beyond it the many-pillared

Hall of Public Audience where the golden throne on its marble dais awaited. His chief courtiers were already grouped beneath it in order of precedence. In just a few moments he would take his place on that throne and address his court for the first time. If he had sinned by spilling blood he would more than atone for it to his people. He would show them he deserved the throne and their love and make them rejoice that he was their emperor.

Some words of his grandfather Akbar flashed into his mind. 'The people love show and want to be impressed by their rulers and feel awe for them. A great ruler must be like the sun – too dazzling to look upon but the source of all light and hope and warmth without whom existence would seem impossible.' Akbar had been truly magnificent. But he, Khurram, would strive to follow him, emulate his achievements, even surpass them if he could. He would reign under the title his father had once conferred on him, Shah Jahan, Lord of the World. That golden throne on which he was about to sit would not be splendid enough for the Lord of the World. He had already visited his treasure vaults with their piles of luminous gems too numerous to count which his treasurers instead assessed by weight so that they could tell him, 'See, Majesty, here you have half a ton of diamonds and here a ton of pearls . . .' He would summon the best jewellers in the empire to fashion a throne in which the most glorious of his gems would be displayed. He would sit beneath a jewelled canopy supported by columns studded with rubies. On top of the canopy would be a tree symbolising the tree of life, its trunk set with diamonds and pearls and on either side of it a glittering peacock, tail outspread. Seated on his peacock throne he would indeed be too dazzling to look upon.

If it would be challenging to exceed Akbar as a great and just emperor beloved by all his people, whatever their race or religion or status, he was determined to surpass him as head of an imperial family. Akbar's relations with his sons had been fractured and distant, just as his own had been with Jahangir. In both generations – and before that in Humayun's time – half-brothers had contended against each other for the throne. Unlike Akbar he had the good fortune to have a united, loving family and he would make sure it stayed so. His sons and daughters, born of the same mother and brought yet closer together by all they had endured, would help him transform the dynasty. How could Dara Shukoh and Aurangzeb, having suffered imprisonment together, ever fight each other? The vicious family rivalry – the old code of *taktya takhta*, throne or coffin, that had tainted previous generations and weakened the empire with threats of civil war – would be gone for ever.

What was more, he would guard himself and his family against other weaknesses of his dynasty – the over-fondness for wine and opium that had weakened his father's mind and that of his great-grandfather Humayun and destroyed so many members of his family – his half-brother Parvez and his uncles Daniyal and Murad. One of his first acts would be to renounce alcohol for himself and his family, even though like Akbar and Babur before him he felt strong enough to be the master of those drugs and not their servant.

A roll of drums signalled that it was time for Khurram's elephant to halt and drop to its knees. In a moment, he would descend and advance towards the throne followed by his sons while Arjumand's elephant would bear her and their daughters through into the *haram*. From the women's gallery Arjumand, his love and his comfort throughout all his misfortunes, would watch through the *jali* screen as for the first time he addressed his court. His reign was about to begin. Though it had begun in blood, together with Arjumand he would make sure it ended in glory . . .

Historical Note

Like his great-grandfather Babur, Jahangir wrote his own memoirs − *Tuzuk-i-Jahangiri* − which he began in 1605, the year he became emperor. Although he describes a very different world from Babur's, Jahangir's memoirs are also detailed and lively and often very frank. They reveal a man riven with contradiction − one moment writing lyrically of the intricate beauty of the champa flower or the exquisite taste of the flesh of a mango and at another admitting he had his father Akbar's friend and adviser Abul Fazl assassinated because 'he was not my friend'. In another lengthy and bitter passage he describes his alienation from his once beloved son Khurram, deriding him as 'that one of dark fortune' and *bi-daulat*, 'the wretch'. His adoration of Mehrunissa is clear. In one passage he describes how, firing from a litter, she killed a tiger with a single shot which is, he writes, 'a very difficult matter'. In 1622 the increasingly frail Jahangir handed the task of writing his memoirs to Mutamid Khan, one of his scribes, who was present during

Mahabat Khan's coup. He faithfully continued the journal until 1624 and then wrote his own account – *Iqbal-nama* – of the last three years of Jahangir's life. There are also several other chronicles such as Ferishta's *Gulshan-i-Ibrahami* which deal with Jahangir's life or parts of it. Chronicles such as the *Shahjahannama* tell the story of Khurram.

Quite a few of the foreign visitors to Hindustan in Jahangir's reign wrote vividly of what they witnessed. The book written by Sir Thomas Roe, England's first official envoy to the Moghul court, bursts with detail and, despite its sometimes patronising tone, betrays the amazement felt by Europeans at the Moghul court's magnificence. Other foreign sources include the writings of William Hawkins, sent to Hindustan by the East India Company, who was at Jahangir's court at Agra from 1609 until 1611; William Finch, Hawkins's assistant, who is the source for the story of Akbar's concubine Anarkali, 'Pomegranate Blossom'; Edward Terry, a clergymen who became Roe's chaplain for a while and sailed back to England with him; and the famous English pedestrian Thomas Coryat who travelled overland to Hindustan and in 1615 arrived at Jahangir's court. He described the fabulous ornaments of Jahangir's elephants which included 'furniture for their buttocks of pure gold'.

As with the three earlier novels in the Empire of the Moghul quintet, *Raiders from the North, Brothers at War* and *Ruler of the World*, the main characters in this novel – the imperial Moghul family, the Persian Ghiyas Beg and all his family including Mehrunissa and Arjumand, the opportunistic Mahabat Khan, the Abyssinian commander and former slave Malik Ambar and many others like Sir Thomas Roe – existed. Some of the subsidiary characters like Suleiman Beg, Nicholas Ballantyne and Kamran Iqbal are composites but in turn based on real people.

The main events – Khusrau's revolt, Khurram's campaigns against Malik Ambar and his estrangement from his father, Mahabat Khan's coup – are also true although I've omitted or changed some details and in a few cases compressed or altered timescales. Jahangir was indeed obsessed with Mehrunissa, later known as Nur Jahan, who used her influence to gain personal power and became de facto ruler of Hindustan – a remarkable achievement for a woman of that period. It's striking that in an age when royal women were seldom depicted in paintings several of Mehrunissa have survived including the portrait described in the book. It's clear from the sources that Mehrunissa at first promoted the marriage of her niece Arjumand to Khurram but then turned against them. The dynamics of the story needed little embroidering. Sir Thomas Roe provided a nice snapshot of a reign with all the elements of a Shakespearean tragedy: 'a noble prince, an excellent wife, a faithful councillor, a crafty stepmother, an ambitious son, a cunning favourite . . .' And as so often in great tragedies one overriding message comes through – that the central players will become the authors of their own destruction.

Again one of the great pleasures of writing the book was time spent travelling through India while researching. Like Khurram I went south towards the Deccan, crossing the Narmada river and travelling on through a landscape of golden eroded hills past the sandstone fortress of Asirgarh. My destination was the palace-fortress of Burhanpur on the Tapti river – once the Moghuls' forward command centre in their wars against the Deccan sultanates and a place where many sinister and tragic events were played out. Wandering through the crumbling remains where water once ran through marble channels to feed the exquisitely frescoed *hammam* and Khurram's war elephants once trumpeted in the *hati mahal* I sensed something of the Moghuls' existence in that place.

Near Jodhpur I drank bitter opium water from the palm of a village elder as Rajput warriors must have done before battle. In Agra I renewed my knowledge of many places – the Red Fort where Jahangir's five-foot-high bath hewn from a single lump of stone that always accompanied him on the march sits in a courtyard; Ghiyas Beg's marble-inlaid tomb built by Mehrunissa, known as 'Itimad-ud-Daulah's tomb'; nearby Sikandra, site of Akbar's great sandstone tomb which was completed during Jahangir's reign; the Chambal river with its flourishing colonies of ghariyals (fish-eating crocodiles), dolphins and Sarus cranes. It was also a good opportunity to taste some of the food described in the sources like the luscious mangos Jahangir relished and fiery Rajasthani *lal mas* – lamb cooked with chillies which by this period like pineapples and potatoes were just beginning to appear in India from the New World.

As I travelled I could still picture the Moghul armies moving slowly but deliberately across the vast landscape raising great clouds of dust. I saw them pitching their tents at night in camps the size of small towns and servants lighting the giant bowl filled with cotton seed and oil fixed on a pole twenty feet high – the *Akash-Diya*, Light of the Sky – that sent flames shooting into the night sky. I could smell the bitterish aroma of a thousand dung cooking fires and hear the voices and drums and pipes of the musicians who always accompanied a Moghul force on the move. Though Jahangir and Khurram lived nearly four hundred years ago, at times they and their world didn't seem so far away at all.

Additional Notes

Chapter 1

Akbar was born on 15 October 1542 and died on 15 October 1605.

Jahangir was born on 30 August 1569 and came to the throne on Akbar's death.

Khusrau was born in August 1587 and his first rebellion against Jahangir began in April 1606.

Parvez was born in 1589.

Khurram was born on 5 January 1592.

The date of birth of Shahriyar, the child of a concubine, is not known precisely but was around the time of Akbar's death.

Timur, a chieftain of the nomadic Barlas Turks, is better known in the west as Tamburlaine, a corruption of 'Timur the Lame'. Christopher Marlowe's play portrays him as 'the scourge of God'.

Jahangir would have used the Muslim lunar calendar, but I

have converted dates into the conventional solar, Christian, calendar we use in the west.

Khusrau's two closest commanders were indeed paraded through Lahore in skins in the way described and many others were impaled on stakes.

Chapter 2

Jahangir is said to have had Mehrunissa's husband Sher Afghan murdered, though not by a European.

Chapter 3

Mehrunissa's abandonment as a baby by her family is referred to in some of the chronicles, as is her dropping of her veil before Jahangir.

Chapter 4

Punishments for sexual transgression in the *haram* were severe. For example, a woman was buried up to her neck in sand and left to die in the hot sun.

Chapter 5

Khurram did indeed first meet Arjumand at the Royal Meena Bazaar. She was born in 1593.

Chapter 6

Khusrau's second rebellion and blinding occurred in late summer 1607. Ghiyas Beg was interrogated and released and his son Mir Khan executed for complicity.

Chapter 8

Mehrunissa and Jahangir married in 1611 and Khurram and Arjumand in 1612.

Chapter 9

Khurram's first campaign against Malik Ambar was in 1616. Jahanara, who was in fact Khurram and Arjumand's second child – an elder sister Hur-al-Nisa died in infancy – was born in April 1614.

Chapter 11

Roe arrived in India in 1615 bearing gifts including the carriage, Mercator's maps and paintings.

Chapter 12

Roe's letters do indeed comment on Jahangir's pride, his agnosticism, his religious tolerance, his cruelty and Mehrunissa's influence. On the latter Roe described how she 'governs him and winds him up at her pleasure'.

The portrait of Jahangir with King James at his feet is in the British Library in London.

Chapter 13

Khurram's second campaign against Malik Ambar was in 1620.

Chapter 15

Khurram's estrangement from his father began in 1622 though in fact Roe left India in 1619.

Chapter 21

Mahabat Khan's coup was in 1626 – the same year that Parvez died. Jahangir died on 28 October 1627.

Chapter 24

Several writers including some European authors of the time recount the story of Khurram joining a funeral cortège to conceal his progress, some even claiming he faked a scene of his own death.

In history, Khusrau had died when in Khurram's custody in Burhanpur in 1621. Both modern historians and contemporary observers believe Khurram was responsible. Khusrau's wife did indeed commit suicide. It was Dawar Bakhsh, Khusrau's eldest son, who bid for the throne on Jahangir's death and was defeated and subsequently killed on Khurram's orders together with Shahriyar and some others of his male relations.

Chapter 26

Khurram's (Shah Jahan's) formal accession to the throne was on 14 February 1628 – the 72nd anniversary of Akbar's accession and the 145th anniversary of Babur's birth. Among the lofty titles to which Shah Jahan laid claim were 'King of the World', 'Meteor of the Faith' and 'Second Lord of the Auspicious Conjunctions' – a direct appropriation of the title once proudly used by Timur.

By the time of his accession, Arjumand had borne Khurram ten children of whom six – Jahanara, Dara Shukoh, Shah Shuja, Roshanara, Aurangzeb and Murad Bakhsh – had survived.